Praise for *A Fata*

'*Fatal Inheritance* is GLORIOUS!
I enjoyed it ENORMOUSLY.'
MARIAN KEYES

n exquisite and shimmering read. I completely lost myself in Rhys's lovingly evoked 1940s French Riviera and was ripped by the slow-burn mystery. An essential summer read!'
LISA JEWELL

'Rachel Rhys should be on everyone's summer reading list.'
CLARE MACKINTOSH

'The kind of book that makes you want to kill anyone who stops you reading it.'
VERONICA HENRY

'Atmospheric, totally absorbing and joyfully original.'
JANE FALLON

'I absolutely loved this book. All the intrigue of Agatha Christie with the intelligence of Barbara Vine, in the most glamorous of settings. Rhys writes like an exotic dream!'
LIZ NUGENT

'Utterly enthralling . . . brilliantly evokes the shabby glamour and bruised hearts of the post-war Riviera, where everyone has a secret to hide.'
JANE CASEY

'With a dash of Agatha Christie and a nod to Zelda Fitzgerald . . . simply gorgeous . . . will have you yearning to sip a gin fizz while watching the sun sink into the Mediterranean.'
KATE RIORDAN

'I am racing through this delicious story set on the French Riviera in 1948. Rachel Rhys really is a natural successor to Patricia Highsmith.'
S

'Hidden secrets, dazzling sunshine – utterly seductive. This book is a total joy.'
LUCY DAWSON

'Public service announcement: this book deserves to be massive. A stunningly beautiful, page-turning feast of a novel.'
COLETTE MCBETH

'This atmospheric page-turner is filled with intrigue.'
Sunday Express

'A transporting golden-age infused mystery caper.'
Sunday Times

'This is a fantastic book – glamorous and beautifully written.'
Daily Mail

'[A] high-octane, heart-pounding read.'
Good Housekeeping

'Amid the sun and glamour, there's skulduggery afoot in this perfect poolside book.'
Red Magazine

'Rachel Rhys really knows how to keep you guessing. As the mystery plays out she throws in a dash of romance to go along with the perfect evocation of the decadent time and place.'
Sunday People

'Filled with excitement and danger.'
Stylist

'*Fatal Inheritance* bears all the hallmarks of a golden age mystery.'
The Herald

'With dreamlike descriptions of the Cote d'Azur and the dark underworld of those who live there, it is an addictive page-turner. The perfect summer holiday read.'
The Lady

'This atmospheric and intriguing novel will transport you to a glamorous – and deadly – sun-baked world.'
Irish Times

'Combines glitz and glamour, compelling characters, atmospheric settings and a dark, dramatic secret at its heart.'
jillsbookcafe.wordpress.com

'Rachel Rhys delivers an exquisite fusion of mystery, drama, atmosphere and tension.'
@Ronnie__Turner

'The perfect book to read in the hot sunshine . . . wonderfully atmospheric and rich in detail.'
portobellobookblog.com

'I can't recommend it enough . . . Go get it!'
myreadingcorner.co.uk

'I literally could not put this book down.'
@bookaddictionuk

'[Rachel Rhys] has a fantastic way of taking the reader to another time and place . . . I loved the vivid descriptions of life in the French Riviera.'
overtherainbowbookblog.wordpress.com

'I soon forgot my real surroundings and was transported to the Riviera . . . If you are looking for an escapist and hugely evocative summer reading experience then look no further.'
ontheshelfbookblog.wordpress.com

'I was captivated by this beautiful story from the first page to the last! Five stars from me!'
raereads1.blogspot.com

'The story gallops along, with sublime characters, exquisite descriptions of the glitzy location and the occasional glamorous party.'
beadyjansbooks.blogspot.com

'Oh what a sumptuous piece of historical fiction this is! Atmospheric and bewitching.'
mychestnutreadingtree.wordpress.com

Also by Rachel Rhys

Dangerous Crossing

and published by Black Swan

A Fatal Inheritance

Rachel Rhys

BLACK SWAN

TRANSWORLD PUBLISHERS
61–63 Uxbridge Road, London W5 5SA
www.penguin.co.uk

Transworld is part of the Penguin Random House group of companies
whose addresses can be found at global.penguinrandomhouse.com

First published in Great Britain in 2018 as *Fatal Inheritance* by Doubleday
an imprint of Transworld Publishers
Black Swan edition published as *A Fatal Inheritance* in 2019

A CIP catalogue record for this book
is available from the British Library.

ISBN
9781784162603 (B format)
9781784165086 (A format)

Typeset in 11.52/14.41pt Adobe Garamond by Jouve (UK), Milton Keynes.
Printed and bound in Great Britain by Clays Ltd, Elcograf S.p.A.

Penguin Random House is committed to a sustainable
future for our business, our readers and our planet. This book
is made from Forest Stewardship Council® certified paper.

1 3 5 7 9 10 8 6 4 2

In memory of Fraser Macnaught

I have lived twice as fully, loved a hundred times too much. Gulped the beauty from the world like an oyster. Just to prove I am worth more than the worst thing I ever did. But at night, in the relentless dark, when I am completely alone, that worst thing is still the only thing.

Guy Lester

1

20 May 1948

IF VERA ARRIVES before Harry her whole life will change. Eve watches and waits. Really she ought to be outside, whipping sheets off the line before they are completely sodden, but her limbs remain pinioned to the sofa. Her eyes follow the progress of the two raindrops down the pane of glass until they pool together at the bottom, Vera merging into Harry, having not, after all, triumphed. A fleeting tug of disappointment.

But hadn't she intended it to be the best of three? Most assuredly she had.

Eve scans the top of the window until she locates two more likely looking drops whom she names Bert and Louisa. But before they reach the bottom, she is disturbed by the shrill ringing of the bell.

Mr Ward, the postman, has a florid round face which is forever glazed with some form of precipitation, whether perspiration from the summer heat or, as now, a steady drizzle of rain. He is friendly and nosy and always seems to be expecting something more from his interactions with Eve than she is able to give.

'One for you in there,' he says, handing over a stack of envelopes.

Eve's heart sinks. The only person who writes to her is her mother and she does not think she has the fortitude today to withstand the force of her mother's disappointment.

Mr Ward is lingering on the step as if he expects her to open her letter right there and share the contents with him. But Eve is in no hurry.

'Thank you, Mr Ward,' she says, closing the door so he is caught out mid-mop with his white handkerchief aloft.

Eve flings herself back down on to the lumpy sofa, but she cannot recapture the pleasant indolence of a few minutes before. Even though the letters are safely hidden from view on the table in the hall, the knowledge of them is like a persistent insect buzzing in her ear.

She glances up at the ugly grandfather clock on the opposite wall. All the furniture is Clifford's. Dark, heavy pieces that originated from his grandparents' house and that his grim-faced father reluctantly passed on after she and Clifford married, observing that as Eve most likely didn't know the first thing about caring for furniture of such quality, they would no doubt fall into wrack and ruin.

Chance would be a fine thing.

It is 12.15. Apart from the fifteen minutes from four o'clock when she can lose herself in *Mrs Dale's Diary* on the wireless, the remaining hours of the day stretch ahead long and empty, the silence punctuated only by the tick-ticking of the hideous clock.

At 5.40 Clifford will come home. There will be the usual flurry of anticipation – *company, conversation* – followed by the inevitable downward readjustment when Clifford settles into his armchair, right leg crossed over left, newspaper hiding his face, the only hint of animation provided by the occasional twitch of his right shoe, shined every Sunday evening.

When they were first married she used to fling herself on to the floor by his chair and question him about his day, about what was in the news. But he had soon curtailed that. 'My dear, I am a company director. My entire day is taken up by people asking things of me. When I come home, I should so appreciate a little bit of quiet. I'm sure you can understand.'

So now she waits until dinner time.

The rain seems to have drained away, leaving behind a grey soupy day. Through the bay window she can see the opposite bay window of Number Thirty-Nine. A mirror image of this house. Semi-detached with a garage to the side and a neat front path leading up to the leaded glass-panelled front door. Two elderly sisters live there whom, even nearly two years on, Eve still knows only as the Misses Judd. Sometimes she will see one or other of the Misses Judd standing at one of the upstairs windows, gazing out on to the street. *I will go over there*, she tells herself on these occasions. *Who knows what stories they will have to tell. We might become friends.* But she never does.

Awareness of her mother's letter waiting on the hall table weighs heavily on her. Eventually she can stand it no longer. She gets to her feet and makes her way across the sitting room with its thick wine-coloured carpet and once more out into the hall, where she snatches up the pile of envelopes and searches impatiently through all the letters addressed to Mr C. Forrester until she comes to one with her own name.

But – *oh*.

In place of her mother's cramped, precise handwriting in

blue ink on the usual thin, pale blue envelope, there is a typed address on thick yellowy paper. *Mrs Eve Forrester.*

Eve feels a faint tingling in her nerve endings. She replaces the rest of the envelopes and wanders back into the sitting room. The drawing room, as Clifford insists on calling it. As always when she crosses the threshold, there is a sense of the air being displaced, as if she is walking into a solid mass and pushing it out of shape.

She resumes her place on the sofa, only this time her back is straight, and she perches on the very edge of the cushion with her feet firmly on the floor.

Silly, she scolds herself. *To get excited about a letter.*

She slits open the envelope to find a satisfyingly thick sheet of manila folded in three. She takes her time about opening it up and notes first the letterhead printed in bold at the very top of the page.

Pearson & Wilkes
Solicitors
Commissioners for Oaths

The print is slightly embossed and she runs her fingertip over the raised letters.

She takes a deep breath, and reads on.

'Are you certain there has been no mistake?'

Clifford is looking at her in a way that clearly suggests a mistake has indeed been made and that it will turn out to be hers.

'The letter is definitely addressed to me. And there can be no confusion about what it says. I am requested to present myself at the firm's offices in London next Tuesday to hear something to my advantage. Isn't that deliciously mysterious?'

'It's deuced inconvenient, is what it is. I have an important meeting next Tuesday.'

'So you intend to come?'

Clifford blinks at her as if she has begun, for reasons quite her own, to talk in Swahili.

'Of course I must come. This whole business sounds fishy. We have no idea who these Pearson and Wilkes are or whom they represent. For all we know this could turn out to be some sort of racket and I'm afraid you, my dear, are a sitting duck. Don't forget, Eve, that you moved here straight from your mother's house. You have very little experience of looking out for yourself.'

Clifford is in the middle of eating and a white crumb of potato is lodged in his moustache. Eve watches the crumb move up and down as he speaks. Already she feels the excitement of earlier trickling away.

In the end, then, it is to turn out to be a mistake. A racket, as Clifford says. They will come back from London and everything will be just the same as it ever was.

'But they are offering to cover all travel costs,' she remembers now. 'Would they do such a thing if there was something underhand about the whole affair?'

Clifford, who has paused with his fork halfway to his lips, now resumes his original intention, delivering a brown lump of liver into his mouth. It seems to take for ever to chew. Mrs Jenkins, who comes in two mornings a week to cook and clean, does not believe in lightness of touch when it comes to preparing meat dishes. 'Who knows what germs they could be harbouring,' she said the one time Eve dared ask if they might have their precious chops, still rationed even three years after the war, just a little less well done. Clifford swallows and Eve follows the progress of the lump down her husband's throat. Finally he speaks.

'The first rule of business is that you never trust anyone until they have proved themselves deserving of your trust, and that is a good rule to apply in life, Eve. Otherwise you will be taken advantage of. I will do my best to rearrange my meeting so that I may accompany you.'

He dabs the corners of his mouth with his napkin, dislodging the crumb. As usual, his blue eyes, so close together that at times they almost seem to cross over, remain fixed on a point just past Eve's shoulder, so she feels she is always ceding attention to someone just behind her.

'Thank you,' she says.

2

25 May 1948

'I EXPECT YOU must be quite bemused by all this.' Mr Wilkes gestures expansively around his office with one of his pudgy hands. 'I expect you must be thinking, "Just what in the blazes is all this about?" '

His brown eyes, peeping out between cushions of flesh like the glass-eyed teddy bear Eve had as a child, are focused exclusively on her. So unused is she to the experience of being looked at, she feels her cheeks burning and has to fight the impulse to raise her hand to determine how hot they are.

'We are curious, as you can imagine,' says Clifford.

All the way from Sutton in the train he was cold and unresponsive, leaving Eve in no doubt about the sacrifice he was making to accompany her on this fool's errand. When she tried to engage him in conversation about the terrible murder of poor little June Anne Devaney, which all the newspapers were full of, he shut her down by refusing to indulge in 'ghoulish gossip'. However, since they arrived at the grand corner building in a smart road off Chancery Lane and were shown up in the gilt-edged lift to the offices of Pearson & Wilkes, he has mellowed markedly.

Now he seems almost eager. Leaning forward in his seat when they first arrived, he remarked upon the solid oak desk and the modernity of the telephone system. 'I shall have to invest in one of those myself,' he said. 'For my own company,' he added. He was marking himself out as a man of means, Eve understood, and had surprised herself by feeling embarrassed on his behalf.

'I shall put you out of your misery immediately,' says Mr Wilkes, beaming as if they are all in on the most enormous joke. 'The fact is that I had a client – a very esteemed client – by the name of Guy Lester. Does that name seem familiar to you at all?'

Brown eyes on hers, that uncomfortable sensation of being *seen*.

'I see that it does not. Which is a pity. I did form the opinion the last time I spoke to Mr Lester on the telephone that he intended to contact you in person, Mrs Forrester, to explain matters.'

'Who is he? This Guy Lester?' Clifford wanting to regain control of the situation, to be factored in.

'*Was.* I'm afraid Mr Lester passed away ten days ago, quite suddenly. We'd known he wasn't well but there was no indication he would be taken from us quite so quickly. He lived permanently in the South of France, so he came into the office here only once or twice. But he made himself very popular nonetheless.'

Eve is conscious of Clifford sitting up a little straighter in the leather-cushioned seat next to her, can almost hear his brain whirring.

'The truth is, Mrs Forrester, that Mr Lester made a provision for you in his will.'

'For me?'

Surprise wipes Eve's mind clear.

'But why?' asks Clifford. 'Who was this Mr Lester to *my wife*?'

He emphasizes the last two words as if establishing ownership. Eve feels a pinprick of irritation, though why that should be so she does not know. When they were first married, nearly two years before, she used to invent excuses to drop the phrase 'my husband' into conversation, and thrill at hearing Clifford describe her as his wife. It occurs to her now that she hasn't heard him say it in quite a long time.

Mr Wilkes is sitting behind his desk on a chair that looks altogether too insubstantial for his considerable girth. His greying hair is neatly parted above his ear with the longer strands combed over his bald pate. His dark waistcoat strains across his belly.

Clifford, by contrast, is trim and handsome. Or so Eve had once thought. His hair, about which he is quite vain, is thick and fair, his moustache luxuriant, his nails perfectly kept. Eve has been surprised by how much attention Clifford pays to his personal grooming, how particular he is about his clothes and who is allowed to cut his hair.

Yet Mr Wilkes seems so kind. Even when he frowns, as he is doing now, it appears to be in a spirit of empathy rather than reproach.

'I'm afraid I am as much in the dark as you are about the nature of Mr Lester's connection to Mrs Forrester, if indeed any such connection existed.'

'Nonsense,' says Clifford. 'There must be a connection.

People don't go around leaving things to people they don't know. You must get in touch with your mother straight away, Eve. We can send a telegram. She must know something.'

'If I might make a suggestion.' For someone of his size, Mr Wilkes has a dainty way of talking. Eve is grateful for his interjection. She does not want her mother introduced here, to this office, doesn't want to give her the chance to snuff out the spark of excitement she has felt ever since the letter arrived.

Mr Wilkes goes on: 'We have found in our experience that recipients of potentially valuable bequests often prefer to wait until after they ascertain the full facts before deciding whether or not to let other people know.'

'So you think this inheritance could be valuable?' Clifford is sitting on the edge of his seat, his head so far inclined towards the rotund solicitor that he appears at risk of toppling over.

'There again, Mr Forrester, I must disappoint you. The fact is I do not know the nature of the bequest.'

'I don't understand.'

Eve hears the giveaway twang of impatience in Clifford's voice. 'If you don't know, Mr Wilkes, who does?'

'The exact details of Mrs Forrester's legacy are contained in a codicil to Mr Lester's will, which she can have read to her just as soon as she presents herself at the offices of Mr Lester's notary, Monsieur Bernard Gaillard, in Cannes.'

'I beg your pardon!' Clifford's exclamation explodes from him like a cough. 'You can't seriously be expecting us to drop everything and travel down to the South of France at vast expense just to find out what my wife may or may not have been left by a man neither of us has even heard of?'

Mr Wilkes looks pained. His mouth turns down at the corners, making dimples appear in his chin.

'I understand this must come as quite a surprise, Mr Forrester. But Monsieur Gaillard instructed us to cover all travel expenses – first class, of course – and the cost of staying at the wonderful Appleton hotel. Though you are welcome to choose a different hotel if you prefer.'

'I'm afraid it is still out of the question. I am a businessman, Mr Wilkes. I run a very busy haulage contractors. I cannot just up and leave on a moment's notice.'

Clifford always talks about the company he established three years before as if it is a large, thriving concern, and yet the one time Eve visited his offices on the outskirts of town, she found them cramped and rather depressing; a dusty yard, two or three idle trucks. And she sometimes wonders why, if he is doing so well, they cannot afford some furniture of their own, or why Mrs Jenkins can't come five mornings a week instead of two. Of course, in these post-war times, everyone in business has suffered, but it is the incongruity between the way Clifford talks and the way they live their lives that Eve finds so odd.

'I completely understand, Mr Forrester.' The portly solicitor gazes at Clifford with a look that seems to say, *How put upon we are, we men of substance.* 'But with all due respect, it is only Mrs Forrester who is required to be present when the will is read.'

'Impossible. Eve is not the adventurous sort, I'm afraid, Mr Wilkes. She has led a sheltered life. Why, she rarely ventures into the centre of Sutton, let alone crosses the Channel and travels through a country where she cannot even speak the language.'

'Well, that's not exactly true.' Eve is surprised to find herself contradicting Clifford in public.

'What I mean is, I do speak French. I learned it at school. Not well, admittedly, but certainly enough to get by.'

Mr Wilkes beams as if she has single-handedly brought about world peace.

'Excellent. And all the arrangements would be made by ourselves, or by Monsieur Gaillard at the office in France. So really all you would have to do is pack a small bag and *voilà*!'

'But this is ridiculous,' says Clifford. 'Surely there must be a way to just find out what it is that she has been left without having to travel to the ends of the earth. It could turn out to be anything. A painting. Or a *book*.'

Clifford says the word 'book' as if it is the lowest life form he can conceive of.

'It is true that I have no idea what it is that Mrs Forrester has been left. And, of course, it is for the two of you to decide whether you are prepared to undertake such a journey. But I do think you ought to know that Mr Lester was a very wealthy man. His grandfather made a fortune out in India and Hong Kong at the end of the last century when there were such fortunes to be made, and Mr Lester inherited a very considerable trust.'

That night, Eve lies in bed watching Clifford hang up his trousers, aligning them perfectly along the crease before putting them away in the huge mahogany wardrobe that dominates their bedroom.

'I don't like it,' he says, as he has been saying periodically ever since they left the offices of Pearson & Wilkes earlier that afternoon. 'I don't like it at all.'

Dressed in his stiff blue pyjamas, Clifford sits on the side of the bed to wind his watch before placing it on his bedside table with the strap folded so that the face will be visible when he is lying down. He has done the same thing in the same way every single night of their marriage, but suddenly Eve feels as if she will shrivel and die if she has to watch it happen just one more time.

When Clifford pulls back the sheet and eiderdown to climb into bed, there is a waft of cold air, and Eve instinctively moves towards him in search of warmth. She puts her feet on his. Though they are freezing, they are the only part of him not covered in cotton twill. She feels him stiffen next to her, though he doesn't pull away as he sometimes does.

Emboldened, she rests her hand on his chest and then, when this encounters no resistance, she allows it to stray down his body. He reaches up suddenly and switches off the light so that they are plunged into darkness. There follows the usual silent manoeuvring of pyjama bottoms and then he is inside her so abruptly she exclaims 'Oh,' and then just as abruptly he is finished and out again, with only a trickle on her thigh to show he was ever there.

'Am I doing something wrong?' she asks, as he pulls up his pyjama trousers and shifts away from her. 'Is there something you would like to do differently?'

'Why must you always ask these infernal questions? I've told you before, there is no different way. This is simply how it is.'

Eve, being worldlier than Clifford gives her credit for, knows that this is not simply how it is. There were enough fumbled encounters with Archie in cramped cloakrooms and on deserted park benches to teach her that sex is not always something wordless and dry and over within seconds.

They lie side by side in the dark.

Clifford clears his throat.

'I've been thinking. Perhaps it would do you good to take a trip down to France. Build up your confidence.'

And though Eve wonders if he just wants to be free from this for a few days, free from *her*, hope shoots white-hot through her veins.

Long after Clifford turns away from her and starts to snore, she lies awake, feeling the trickle trace its delicate course along her thigh, and imagines it is a fingertip.

3

31 May 1948

LE TRAIN BLEU.

From the moment Mr Wilkes described how she would be travelling to the French Riviera on the overnight Blue Train from Paris, Eve has been rolling the words around on her tongue, imagining how it will be. But nothing has prepared her for the sheer luxury of it. The thrill as the train pulls away from the splendid Gare de Lyon, with its high vaulted glass ceiling and bustling little cafes, taking her along with it.

Already she feels Clifford receding into the distance. She pictures him as he was that morning, standing stiffly on the platform at Victoria Station. Having given her a long list of types to watch out for and avoid, he was now adding to it furiously, conscious of the fast-approaching departure. 'Beware of gypsies,' he told her. 'The women will try to entice you by telling you how pretty you are or offering you a flower, and then, bang!' He clapped his hands together, startling her. 'They've sold you into the white slave trade.'

'I really don't think—' Mr Wilkes had started.

But Clifford had cut him off. 'We are men of the world,' he said, 'but I'm afraid my wife will make easy pickings for the wrong sort of person.'

It didn't matter how many times Mr Wilkes explained that someone would be there to meet her when she arrived in Cannes to take her to her hotel. Clifford remained convinced that she would be set upon by thieves and opportunists the instant she set foot off the train.

The parting had been awkward. Mr Wilkes – having pressed upon her a packet of Polo mints, which he insisted were the latest thing, though Clifford had viewed them with the utmost suspicion – had already left to return to his office. Eve suspected he was, in his usual delicate way, giving them privacy to say their goodbyes. Not that they'd needed it. They had run dry of conversation long before the train was due to depart and eventually Clifford had said, 'Best be getting on before it leaves without you,' and they'd stepped towards each other and she had gone to kiss him on the lips at the exact moment he had turned his face to peck her on the cheek, so she had ended up with a mouthful of whiskers.

'Do take care of yourself,' he'd mumbled at the last minute as he handed her on to the train steps. She'd had her back to him and so it had taken a few moments for her brain to catch up with her ears, and by the time she realized what he'd said, she was already on the train and someone else was coming up the steps behind her. From her seat she'd watched him frowning down at his watch, and then looking up at the station roof. Anywhere but into the carriage where she sat smiling fixedly and wishing the train would hurry up and leave.

How uncomfortable he is in his own skin, she'd said to herself. And instantly she'd felt a softening towards him. *I should go back out. Say a proper goodbye*, she'd thought. Yet she hadn't moved. And eventually the train driver had sounded the whistle and then the train was pulling out, with Clifford still standing there stiffly, one arm raised in farewell.

Now, ensconced in the dining car, sucking on the remnants of one of Mr Wilkes's sweets – how very odd to find a hole right there in the middle of it – she tries to hold on to her self-reproach, having been conditioned since childhood against letting herself too easily off the hook. But already Clifford is dissolving into the air like a heat haze.

In his place there is wood panelling and white starched tablecloths and brass hooks on the walls for bags and coats. There are waiters in white jackets and slender vases of flowers on each table, and gold and blue plates with napkins folded into the shape of scallop shells. There is the anticipatory hum of people who are already starting to think about their first al fresco cocktail, that first ray of sun.

Earlier, she had unpacked her overnight bag in her sleeper compartment, astonished to find she had it all to herself. A padded bench seat that converts to a bed, engraved panelling on the walls, a narrow shelf for her things, the repetitive, comforting movement of the train wheels underfoot. There she had changed out of her travelling clothes: the heavy wool tailored jacket and skirt, the matching navy blue hat. Now she has on a brown crepe dress with a slight V at the front that comes in at the waist and then flares out over her hips. It's not a new dress, but it is 'quality', as her mother was keen to impress upon her when they bought it together just before the war. *So clever of you to find a dress the exact same colour of your eyes*, Archie had said that first time she wore it. Now there is a darn in the hem where she fell running to an air-raid shelter.

When clothes rationing ends she will burn that wretched pink ration book and buy a wardrobe full of dresses in rainbow colours. *'Make do and mend' be blowed,* she thinks now, comparing her own drab appearance with that of the French mama with her two teenaged daughters on the table behind, all three of them so effortlessly chic in pastel-coloured sweaters and fitted woollen skirts. But hot on the heels of that thought comes the inevitable question of where she would wear them. And for whom?

On the whole, though, the other diners seem to be mostly English. On the table to her right, a man who looks to be around her own age is telling a long, convoluted story to the man and woman opposite him involving a missed train and a subsequent wild night in Paris. The woman has thick blonde hair that waves around her shoulders and a pretty if sulky face. She is in a blue silk dress with long billowing sleeves that come in tightly at the cuffs and she smokes an endless stream of cigarettes through a long silver cigarette holder.

'Really, Duncan,' she says languidly, as if the mere act of opening her crimson-painted mouth to speak had quite worn her out, 'ought you really to have to work quite so hard at being dissolute? Ought it not to come quite naturally?'

The man next to her is slightly older. Early thirties, Eve guesses. In contrast to the first man, who has soft, undefined features and hair that is already receding but nevertheless kept defiantly long, this man is broader, more solid, with a cleft in his square chin and dark eyebrows underneath which his eyes look startlingly green. He is drinking whisky and looking around the carriage as if trying to disassociate himself from his companions. At one stage his eyes alight briefly on Eve, but they slide off her almost instantly, as if she is of no more interest than the table itself, or the chair on which she sits.

There is a middle-aged couple at the table directly in front of Eve, picking at their poached salmon starters in companionable silence.

'Won't you join us?' the woman says, looking up and catching Eve's eye. 'We have a bottle of wine, as you see, that we shall need help drinking.'

Eve feels her cheeks grow flushed. She has always harboured a dread of being the object of other people's pity. But the woman's smile is kind and genuine, and besides, she cannot now think of a reasonable excuse. So she gets awkwardly to her feet and makes her way to their table. The man with the green eyes flicks his gaze over her once more as she passes.

The couple whose table she has just gate-crashed are called Rupert and Ruth Collett.

'Thank God you've saved us from having to spend yet another meal entirely in each other's company,' says Ruth.

'Poor Ruth has heard all my jokes a hundred times or more,' says her husband. 'She drafts in complete strangers off the street to avoid being subjected to them again.'

Rupert is big and wide-shouldered, with a kind face and hangdog eyes. By contrast, his wife is slight and nervous-looking, her face all angles and shadows, through which her smile breaks like a crack in the clouds.

They quiz Eve about her journey and pronounce themselves fascinated by the mystery of it all.

'My husband thinks I will be a target for conmen and tricksters,' says Eve, already adopting the Colletts' gently amused way of speaking, and only belatedly realizing that she has already gone against Clifford's advice by telling them the truth in the first place.

'This is a possibility,' says Rupert solemnly. 'Or, on the other hand, you could be about to discover you are Princess Galina Nikolaevna, secret daughter of the Grand Duchess Anastasia Nikolaevna, last surviving heir to the Romanov fortune.'

Eve pretends to weigh up the two options. 'On the whole, I prefer the second,' she decides.

It is a jolly meal. The Colletts turn out to be far more knowledgeable about their destination than Eve is. Ruth pretends to be scandalized that she has not even heard of the biggest news event of the season – the wedding the following week of Laurent Martin, heir to the Martin shipping fortune, and film star Gloria Hayes. 'Everyone who is anyone will be descending on the Riviera,' Ruth tells her. 'We won't be able to move without crashing into a matinée idol or a visiting royal.'

'Well, I shall be long gone by then.' Eve smiles. 'You will have to crash into Marlene and Greta and Wallis without me.'

Only when Eve questions her new friends about their reasons for being on this train hurtling towards the French Riviera does the levity slip.

'We're here for our oldest boy, Leo,' says Ruth, a strange look on her face.

'Well, that's lov—'

'He was killed during Operation Dragoon in 1944.'

'Oh! I'm so sorry.'

Eve, who is in the middle of eating her dessert, puts her hand to her mouth. Like everyone else, she has had too many conversations like this. Death and loss abutting the pleasantries of everyday discourse. Yet she has never grown used to it. Has never mastered the art of negotiating other people's tragedies over afternoon tea or in the queue for the post office.

'His 'chute didn't open, you see,' Rupert says, helpfully filling her in. 'Just rotten luck. The rest of that operation was a glorious success, as you probably know.'

The Allied victory in driving the Germans out of southern France following the surprise invasion on the beaches of the Riviera was often cited as one of the turning points in the war.

'So he's buried in France?' Eve tries to match the Colletts' almost matter-of-fact tone, but her voice wavers.

Rupert shakes his head.

'He didn't die immediately. He was in hospital in Marseille for a few days and then they brought him home, only he didn't make the journey,' he says. 'We're just here to get a sense of how he spent his last days. We're going to Marseille for a night and then we'll head east to see where he came down, and then tour around Saint-Raphaël and the beaches where the other fellows landed. Make a bit of a holiday of it.'

'Leo would never forgive us if we came to the South of France and moped about wearing black and wringing our hands,' says Ruth, as if she feels the need to justify herself. 'Our lives are very quiet without him. Luckily we have our Jack, Leo's younger brother. He is coming to join us, in fact, in a day or two. We've just left him in Paris finishing up some research for his art history degree.'

Later, when Ruth excuses herself to go to the bathroom, Rupert says, 'She took it very badly. Leo's death. The two of them were so close. We wanted to make the journey before, but the railways in France were so damaged, and to be frank I'm not sure Ruth was up to it.'

When Ruth returns, her eyes are red, but she is smiling determinedly.

'We have shamefully monopolized the conversation, Rupert and I,' she tells Eve. 'Now I insist on knowing all about you.'

And so Eve finds herself talking, to her surprise, about Archie.

'We got engaged on my eighteenth birthday. I wanted to get married straight away. My home life was not the happiest. My father died when I was fifteen, and my mother and I were not close. But Archie said we should wait until he finished college. Then war broke out at the end of his second year and of course he enlisted. He was killed in 1940. Dunkirk.'

Now it is the Colletts' turn to be dismayed. But Eve feels like a fraud accepting their sympathies. The fact is that eight years have passed since then. And she is a different person now to the young woman who'd held Archie Saunders' hand in the back row of the Picturehouse and kissed him around the corner from her mother's home in Banbury. These days she struggles even to remember Archie's face. When she thinks of him he comes back to her in a jigsaw puzzle of various separate features: the thrillingly dark thick hair on his arms, his square hands that felt so rough against her own, his surprisingly high-pitched laugh.

'I'm so very glad you managed to find happiness again,' Ruth says, glancing at her wedding ring.

Eve hopes her cheeks are not flaming.

'Oh yes. I met Clifford at a lecture just after the war. Well, to be accurate, I met his mother at the lecture and Clifford came to fetch her in his car and we got talking and, well, you know.'

She does not mention how desperate she was to make a life for herself outside her mother's house. Or how she told herself that she would grow to love Clifford. So many men – like Leo Collett – hadn't made it through the war; she was fortunate, she reminded herself, to have found anyone willing to marry her. 'You're not exactly at your peak any more,' her mother had said when she'd dared voice her doubts. And, 'You young women need to understand that real life isn't like the pictures. It's not all handsome men and violins playing.'

Clifford, already over thirty when fighting broke out and an only child with a history of respiratory weakness, had escaped being sent overseas, serving out the war doing something in transport administration for the Royal Army Service Corps. Eve hopes the Colletts won't ask her about it as she is embarrassingly hazy on the details. *You'd find it very dull, my dear*, Clifford says whenever she broaches the subject.

Luckily Ruth asks her instead about her own work during the war and Eve cheers up enormously talking about her days with the Women's Voluntary Service, helping to distribute donated second-hand furniture to people whose houses had been bombed out.

'It was so nice to feel useful for a change,' she says, glad of the chance to reminisce; Clifford declared all talk about the war to be 'morbid'. Eve is too ashamed to admit now that those war years, working alongside other women, spending long hours and even days away from home, were the happiest of her life.

While they've been talking, the two young men and the

sulky-looking woman at the table behind have been engaged in an increasingly heated debate. Now there comes an eruption of noise. Eve turns around to see the younger man on his feet, his face stained red to match the large glass of wine he is waving around in his right hand.

'Who made you the bloody paragon of all moral virtues?' he says to the man with the green eyes, and Eve notices how unsteady he is on his feet. 'You can't tell me how to behave. You're not him. No matter how much you might want to imagine you are.'

'Oh, sit down, Duncan, you're being too tiresome for words,' says the young blonde woman, although her voice sounds brighter, as if in gleeful anticipation of a scene.

'That's right. Side with him. You always do. I don't know why you aren't marrying him instead of me. Oh, I forgot, he didn't ask you. He asked someone else. Only we're not allowed to talk about that, are we?'

Now the bigger man is getting to his feet, throwing his napkin down on the table. He also looks none too steady. He has his back to Eve, so she cannot see his expression, but she notes the way his shoulders are tensed, and his hand is clenched into a fist by his side.

'Just fuck off, why don't you?' he says.

A gasp goes around the carriage.

'Now, look here—' begins a diner at the far end, half rising from his seat.

But the man is turning and lurching his way back through the dining car, carrying his Scotch with him. As he passes Eve, their eyes meet briefly and he seems to hesitate, and Eve has the strangest notion that he is about to apologize to her.

But then the moment passes, and he has gone through the door at the end that leads to the sleeping compartments.

'*Well!*' Ruth's blue eyes are bright with amusement. 'I have to say, this is exactly the sort of thing I was hoping for from the French Riviera. Theatrics. Bad behaviour. All we need now is an actual fight. Or better yet, a duel.'

'I will attempt to oblige,' says her husband. 'Although I can't promise to win. My reflexes are not what they were.'

Eve laughs along with them. But later, when she is alone in her compartment, the doubts start to creep in. Clifford had been right when he'd told Mr Wilkes that she had led a sheltered life. Though war broadened her outlook, she is still unsure how to respond to people like that group on the next table. Should she have been appalled by their rudeness, as she is sure Clifford would have been? Or laughed it off, like Ruth? Or just taken it in her stride so that the words ran off her like water off oilskin?

She closes her eyes and the rhythm of the train becomes her mother's voice in her head. *You can't do that*, it tells her. And again: *You can't do that. You can't do that.*

4

1 June 1948

SHE REGISTERS THE change even before she opens her eyes. A shift in the quality of the light creeping around the blind of the tiny window, a fresh feel to the air.

Raising herself on to her elbow, she opens the blind and – *oh.* Sunrise is bursting like a firework across the sky, painting the world in stripes of orange and purple and pink. Eve feels her spirits rise again, last night's doubts all but forgotten in the thrill of this exotic new dawn. Though she cannot see the sea, still she fancies she can sense it, wide and open, the surface rippled with breezes blown in from Africa.

'*Presque Marseille, Madame,*' says the steward, coming in with tea and toast and jam.

She had said goodbye to the Colletts the night before, but nevertheless Eve feels bereft when the train stops to disgorge its passengers. She had so warmed to the couple that she feels a peculiar sense of loss for herself and sadness for them, that their mission is such an unhappy one.

Eve never visited Archie's grave. By the time the war was over he had already been dead five years and the Eve who'd held his hand and dreamed of a happier future was also gone. The two of them belonged to a different world from the one in which Eve found herself once the bombings had stopped and that sense of living a speeded-up life died away, and the job of clearing up and sobering up began, and it gradually dawned on her that this might perhaps be all that there was, that her life might start folding in on itself until it was small enough to fit once again into her little back bedroom in her mother's house.

Her spirits begin to rise when the train passes through the sleepy village of Cassis, the early morning sun setting the bougainvillea around the station ablaze. She gasps out loud at the sight of the Mediterranean sea, its glass-like surface broken by the occasional languid wave.

By mid-morning, when the train passes over the breath-taking Viaduc d'Anthéor, the world falling away steeply on both sides until it seems as if the carriage in which she is sitting has taken wing and is flying through the Riviera sky, her heart is soaring. How could it not be when the sun is so bright, the colours so clear, the sea sequinned with gold, as if the world has been repainted overnight.

The steward knocks. '*Cannes, le prochain.*' He has olive skin and a scar on his forehead in the shape of a smile. Eve doesn't wonder too much about the scar. They are most of them scarred now in one way or another.

Now that the moment has come to get off the train, she finds herself seized by nerves. What does she know, after all, about the situation she is walking into?

Standing on the platform, her misgivings only increase as she looks first one way, then another, in search of the promised welcome party. But though there is plenty of activity with passengers stepping down from the train, hands already raised in greeting, there is no sign reading 'Madame Forrester', no po-faced French clerk dispatched to meet her.

Anxiety builds, and she clutches tight to the handbag that contains her emergency money.

To her horror, she feels tears burning at the back of her eyes. Pressing her lips together, she tries not to cry, turning her gaze inside the train to spare herself the sight of the fast-emptying platform.

And finds herself staring into a pair of startlingly green eyes. The man from the dining car, the one who had gone thundering past her the night before, is sitting on the other side of the window nearest to her, and she is at first mortified then furious to see a small smile playing around his mouth.

So he finds her distress amusing? He thinks it funny to see her standing lost on a now-deserted platform, her suitcase, having been brought to her by a beaming steward, abandoned by her feet?

All the doors are closed and the train jolts back into life with a short blast on the guard's whistle. The man in the carriage raises his hand and makes a discreet pointing gesture at something behind her. Eve looks away. When she glances back again, he repeats the gesture, one black eyebrow raised.

Next to him, the blonde woman from the dining car stares through Eve as if she isn't even there.

The train is now pulling away. And not a moment too soon, for her eyes are starting to blur. Only when she can barely see the back of the last carriage growing smaller in the distance does she finally look behind her where the man had been pointing. And there, hurrying towards her, holding a piece of paper on which is written 'Mme Forrester' in careful curly writing, is a woman with the reddest face Eve has ever seen.

'Oh, Madame. I am so sorry. *Désolée, désolée.*' The woman is breathing so heavily that Eve struggles to understand her heavily accented English. 'The car— The road—' There is a complicated story about a lorry blocking traffic that Eve gives up trying to follow.

'I am Marie Gaillard,' the woman says at last, summoning a porter as if from thin air to carry Eve's luggage. 'I will take you to your hotel for you to rest and later I will take you to see my husband. Please do not tell him how I leave you standing here. Bernard, he will not be happy with me. He will say to me, Marie, didn't I tell you that you are always late so you must leave the house every time half an hour *early* so that you might have a chance of arriving on time.'

She pronounces it *eh-rly*.

'It is perfectly all right,' Eve says. 'You are hardly late at all.'

She is taken aback when they arrive at the car, a small orange vehicle that to Eve resembles nothing so much as a tin can on wheels, to discover that Marie is to drive her to the hotel herself. She glances covertly at her from the passenger seat.

Now that the redness has faded, Eve can see that her chauffeur is in her late forties with a broad, flat face brought to life by lively grey eyes, and a mass of hair of an indeterminate hue that is haphazardly piled on top of her head. She is wearing ill-fitting trousers, which surprises Eve, who had the impression that French women wafted around always in a cloud of perfume and silk.

The little car shoots out into traffic, narrowly missing a motorbike being driven by a man in uniform, who raises a fist and says something into the air as they pass.

'You must be careful here in Cannes. Most of the people have no idea how to drive.'

Eve darts a look to see if Marie is having a joke at her own expense, but her expression is one of sorrow at her countrymen's failings on the road.

Ahead there is a queue of cars. Marie makes a noise in the back of her mouth and suddenly wrenches the wheel to the right so they swing across the oncoming traffic and into a side road.

'Ha!' She smiles in triumph when she finds the road semi-deserted. The tin-can car makes a series of zigs and zags and Eve clutches her seat to steady herself. They pass a butcher's shop with a line of people stretching down the street.

'Everyone is hungry still,' says Marie. 'Never enough meat. Never enough bread. All the time they make the daily ration smaller. See?' She points to a man with cheeks so sunken they must surely meet inside his mouth, sitting on a newspaper in a doorway and staring blankly ahead.

Finally, they pull on to the coastal road, fringed on the right by sparsely planted palm trees swaying in the breeze, and beyond them a drop down to the wide sandy beach scattered with deckchairs even at this time of year, and beyond that, the vastness of the sea itself.

They screech to a halt in front of a grand white building with black-topped turrets at each end. It is at least seven storeys high, with row upon row of large windows, each framed by its own little balcony, and its gleaming facade dazzles against the blue of the sky.

A little bubble of happiness bursts inside Eve, obliterating Clifford's voice in her head warning, *Where's the catch? What will they expect from you in exchange for this?*

'It's so beautiful,' she says to Marie Gaillard.

The Frenchwoman shrugs, for once unsmiling. Eve wonders if she has said the wrong thing.

Inside the grand lobby with its polished black and white floor, Marie has a brief exchange with the receptionist. Though Eve had boasted of her knowledge of French to Clifford and Mr Wilkes, she now discovers to her chagrin she has forgotten almost everything she learned at school and finds the conversation difficult to follow. Instead she focuses on the receptionist's neat grey beard, and the purple mark his spectacles have made in the skin on the bridge of his nose.

Over the previous week, Clifford had been seeking to give her an intensive course in current affairs, and in particular the affairs of this region, reminding her that while northern France had been under German occupation, the south was nominally self-governing, the Riviera itself maintaining an uneasy co-existence with first the Italian fascists and later the Nazis. 'Just a few years ago, these people were our enemies,' he told her. 'Every time you meet someone you must ask yourself what they were doing during the war, who they were greasing up to.'

Eve looks at the man's fleshy fingers, closed now around the nib of the pen with which he is writing her name in the hotel register, and wonders whose hands they have shaken in the past.

While a bellboy is gathering up Eve's solitary suitcase, Marie turns to her. Her smile is back but there is a sudden wariness, and she looks as if she can't wait to get away.

'I will leave you here to rest, but will return at four o'clock if that suits you.'

On her way up in the lift, Eve tries to work out whether she said something that could account for the Frenchwoman's sudden change of mood. But her misgivings are forgotten when they arrive on the fifth floor and the bellboy unlocks the door of a room halfway along the corridor, strides over to the full-length windows to throw open the shutters, and *whoosh!* Eve's senses are flooded by the light that falls hot and white across the room, the harsh call of the seagulls competing with the roar of the traffic below, the strip of brilliant sky, the glimpse of something glittering beneath it, the smell of salt and freshness and that intangible thing she can't put her finger on, only knows is as far away from the smell of her suburban English street as it is possible to get.

I am here, she thinks. *I am really here.*

Only after the bellboy has left, pocketing the coin that Clifford set aside early the previous morning for just this purpose – *Goodness knows how much you'd hand over left to your own devices* – does Eve take a proper look around the room. The bed with its pale blue and pink striped counterpane and tall, carved wooden headboard, the walnut side table and chest of drawers. The height of it. The light.

She walks to the windows and steps out on to the balcony, where only the daintiest of wrought-iron railings stand between her and a steep drop down into the street below. Directly ahead of her, the Mediterranean sea sparkles as if lit by thousands of tiny lights. There is a pier to her left, stretching a long wooden finger out into the water.

She ought to rest after the long journey, but she knows she could not sleep. Instead she unpacks her case, withdrawing items of clothing that already smell of a different life. In the full glare of the sun, her best skirt, a bottle-green linen affair which just yesterday seemed so sophisticated, now appears drab and uninspiring; the swimming costume she had crammed in at the last minute hopelessly middle-aged.

She flops backwards on to the bed, crushing her yellow silk blouse underneath her. The sun throws a slanting shaft of light through the open windows over the bed, warming her face. She closes her eyes so that her lids glow orange and feels her muscles unclenching, her skin expanding.

Suddenly it no longer seems so important to know why she is here. It is sufficient that she *is* here. Alone.

At five minutes to four she heads back down to the lobby. She has had a bath in the small but sumptuous en-suite bathroom and is now dressed in the best skirt, with the crumpled silk blouse. She has on stockings and the clumpy leather shoes Clifford told her would be 'a good investment' but always make her feel, as she puts them on, like a shire horse being shod.

Marie is standing by the lobby exit. Her eyes light up when she sees Eve approaching.

'You see,' she tells her, 'I have left the house half an hour early, like Bernard tells me. *Et voilà!*'

She puts a hand under Eve's elbow and steers her so rapidly through the door that Eve does not even have time to give her room key to the receptionist.

The little orange car is outside, parked so far from the kerb that the cars coming up behind have to swing out to avoid it.

'Now we will see Bernard,' says Marie, beaming, all trace of her earlier prickliness so thoroughly eradicated that Eve wonders if it was ever there at all.

'Did you know Guy Lester, Marie?' she asks her guide as they negotiate a series of narrow back streets.

'Oh yes. Of course. Everybody knew Mr Lester.'

'And was he a *nice* man?'

How prissy she sounds. How much like her mother. As if people must be either nice or not nice. As if it is not possible to be nice on one day and on the next to walk down the street wishing ill on random strangers.

'Mr Lester? He was very charming. And so handsome.'

Marie turns to Eve, her eyes wide, and Eve regrets having asked the question as the car begins to veer to the left.

Finally they arrive outside an old building that must once have been grand, although now the paint is peeling and there are pits and holes in the bisque-coloured facade, which might be from age or disrepair or from mortar and bullets. Eve would really rather not know which.

Inside the high-ceilinged hallway, they squeeze into a small lift with a wrought-iron cage around it. Marie presses the brass button for the fifth floor. Nothing. She mutters something in French that Eve doesn't understand, but can quite easily guess, and presses again. Still nothing.

'I am sorry,' she says, shrugging. 'This happens from time to time. We walk.'

By the fourth floor, Eve's calf muscles are protesting and she is uncomfortably aware of her blouse sticking to her back. She is breathing so heavily that she doesn't register the click-clacking noise of approaching heels on the narrow stone steps until a woman rounds the bend in the stairs and they all but collide.

'Oh, excuse me!' Despite their recent acquaintance, Eve can tell that Marie is flustered by the encounter, the skin on her neck staining pink.

'Madame Lester. Please allow me to—'

'Not now, Marie. I am in a hurry.'

The woman pushes past with as much haste as her four-inch heels and tight-fitting black skirt will allow. Her hair is the honey colour of oak boards, and even in the dim light of the stairwell it shines as if polished. She smells of flowers indecently in bloom. But her amber eyes, alighting briefly on Eve as she passes, are watery and pink-rimmed.

Eve turns around to study the woman more carefully, freezing when she finds herself being intently studied in return. Eve smiles out of politeness, but the woman merely carries on staring, before abruptly turning on her heel.

Eve and Marie exchange a glance as the click-clacking grows fainter. Then they begin climbing again. Eve dares not speak for fear that the sound will carry down the stairway.

Only when they arrive on the fifth floor and stop outside a door that bears a brass plaque reading 'B. Gaillard, Notary' does she risk whispering, 'Was that Guy Lester's wife?'

Marie nods.

'But why—?'

Marie puts a hand on her arm. 'You will find out all,' she says, turning the handle of the door to cut short the conversation.

They enter a small room with high, tobacco-discoloured ceilings and a tall window overlooking the street. There are four empty chairs lined up along one wall and a large desk, behind which sits an elderly woman with tortoiseshell glasses on a stick that she holds up to her eyes as they come in.

'*Bonjour, Madame Galvin*,' calls out Marie.

Madame Galvin starts and puts her hand to her chest as if their sudden arrival has brought about some alarming irregularity of her heart. She and Marie have a brief exchange that involves much gesticulating in the direction of the closed, half-glazed door behind Madame Galvin's desk.

Finally Marie turns to Eve. 'We go in now,' she says,

leading the way past Madame Galvin. Eve shoots an apologetic look at the old woman, whose glare communicates a most profound disapproval.

The room they now enter is cramped and dimly lit, the blind on the single window having been lowered. So at first Eve struggles to make out the features of the man who jumps up from his desk to shake her hand. Gradually her eyes adjust to the darkness and she sees first a thatch of springy hair that starts high up his forehead as if driven back like the tide, and second a pair of deep vertical scores running down his face on either side of his mouth, from midway down his nose almost to his chin. And finally a pair of soft brown eyes.

'Mrs Forrester,' he says in barely accented English. 'How happy I am to see you.'

He presses her hand between both of his and suddenly she finds herself absurdly close to tears agin, thinking back to that moment standing on the platform at Cannes, when she had felt so utterly alone and so foolish, believing that Clifford was to be proved right after all, that she had been taken advantage of, that this would all turn out to be some elaborate ruse.

'I will wait for you outside,' Marie tells her.

Eve watches as Marie kisses her husband full on the lips before leaving. She tries to imagine herself doing the same at Clifford's office and her chest feels tight at the impossibility of it.

When they are alone, Bernard goes back to his seat behind his desk, urging her to sit down in the cushioned chair opposite. Eve is just about to do so when the cushion reveals itself to be alarmingly alive.

Instantly Bernard is on his feet and shouting.

'*Horace! Qu'est-ce que tu fais?*'

The cat jumps lazily to the floor and slinks towards the door, whereupon Bernard swoops upon it and throws it out, slamming the door behind it.

'I apologize, Mrs Forrester. My wife found the animal in the street when he was a baby and took pity on him but he is really beyond control.'

'Don't worry at all,' says Eve, brushing orange hairs off the chair before sitting down.

This is not what she had been expecting. She had imagined somewhere smart and intimidating, with silent clerks bent low over desks and a black-suited solicitor with an officious demeanour and a full diary who would want to do what needs to be done and get back to his work with the minimum of disruption. Not Bernard with his kind eyes and his large ginger cat.

'I am sure you must be wondering, Mrs Forrester, what brings you here. The truth is Mr Lester left very particular instructions.'

'And Mr Lester was someone used to getting his own way?'

She means to convey her disapproval of all this apparent secrecy. Or, rather, Clifford's disapproval. But Bernard merely smiles.

'Oh yes. Everyone wanted to make him happy. Some people have that gift, don't you think?'

'And was he? Happy, I mean?'

The question is out before she realizes how odd it sounds. What business is it of hers whether this man she has never met was content, or whether he died miserable and alone?

'Mr Lester lived a very good life. He enjoyed life. You know what I mean? He dived right into it and splashed around.' Here Bernard makes flapping gestures with his arms in illustration. 'But there was something sad inside him. You know, during the war, the Jewish refugees escaping from the Nazis would arrive here with nothing. They had to leave behind their possessions, their homes. But often they would bring some little thing of value – their mother's wedding ring, a gold coin, even just a photograph – sewn into the inside of their coat.' He opens his own jacket to indicate the brown silk lining. 'With Mr Lester it was like he had a little piece of sadness sewn into his coat. Do you see?'

Eve nods. 'And he had a family?'

She is aware on some level that she is asking questions to stave off the moment when Bernard will reveal the disappointingly mundane reason for her visit and this whole strange, glorious dream will be over. And Clifford will meet her on Saturday morning at Victoria with that face he wears sometimes when they play bridge with his cousin Vernon and his whey-faced wife, and Eve makes a play and he says tightly, 'Are you sure you want to do that, my dear?' and she says yes, just to spite him, and of course it's wrong. That face that says, *You thought you knew better and I let you make your own mistakes, and now look where we are.*

'Oh yes. He had two families, in fact. He married when he was young, and they already had two sons – Noel and Duncan – when they moved here in 1920. The first Mrs Lester, Madeleine, was a very sympathetic lady. Kind. You know. Unfortunately she died in the late twenties. Influenza. Mr Lester married a second time in 1930. Another English lady. Diana.'

'Yes, I think we passed her on the stairs. She seemed in a hurry.'

Bernard casts his eyes downwards and nods before continuing.

'Diana and Guy had a daughter, Libby, who is sixteen now, I believe. She's here now because of her father's death, but usually she is at school in England and Mrs Lester herself spends a lot of time in London and Paris. She finds us rather boring, I think.'

While he is talking, Bernard slides open the bottom drawer in his desk and rummages through. He produces a cardboard box file. The label on the front – 'M. Guy Lester' – is neatly typed, and Eve pictures the elderly secretary clacking at the keys of a typewriter, her mouth set tightly.

He opens the file and produces a leather-bound document from the top.

'This is the last will and testament of Guy Lester,' says Bernard, and Eve sees that his bearing is quite changed, solemn and charged with a formality that was absent a moment ago.

Bernard opens the document. The paper inside is thick and stiff and the colour of clotted cream, the writing in untidy black ink.

'Mr Lester's family was here earlier to hear the will, and Mrs Lester remained after the others left. There were some, ah, surprises. Alas, Mrs Forrester, the final instructions of the people we love are not always what we might wish to hear.'

Bernard pauses, his hand resting on the clotted-cream paper.

'I should tell you, Mrs Forrester, that Mr Lester changed his will only recently. Just weeks ago, in fact. Which is why it has come as a surprise to his family. He had not long before discovered that he was ill. Cancer of the throat.' Here Bernard rests his fingers on his own neck in demonstration. 'But he did not know how advanced it was; certainly he had no idea the end would come so quickly. He went once to England to find you and was intending to go a second time on the very day he died. He wanted to see you in person, he told me. To explain.'

'Explain what?'

'Why he made a provision for you in this new will.'

Eve feels a swell of excitement.

'Do *you* know why, Mr Gaillard? Do you have any idea what his connection was to me?'

Bernard shakes his head.

'I am afraid all I know is what is written in this document. Oh, really, it is most unfortunate that his death was so quick. He was not prepared, do you see?'

The notary's expression is one of such sincere concern, Eve finds herself nodding, which seems to reassure him.

'Are you ready, Mrs Forrester?'

She swallows hard. Now there is a lump in her own throat, with rough, raw edges like freshly sawn wood.

Bernard's eyes soften. '*Courage*,' he says.

He unfolds a pair of tortoiseshell glasses from a box on the desk, blinks to refocus his eyes, then reads: 'I, Guy Lester, being of sound mind, do hereby bequeath to Mrs Eve Forrester (née Shipley) of Newbolt Avenue, Sutton, a quarter share in Villa La Perle in Cap d'Antibes, in atonement for past wrongs.'

Bernard looks up over the top of his glasses, his eyebrows raised in question at Eve's stupefied lack of reaction.

'Villa La Perle, Mrs Forrester. His house.'

*

In the car she is silent, even when Marie overtakes a bus just as they approach a bend and Bernard, who is in the passenger seat, yells out something in French that Eve is glad not to understand.

A share in a house. Here. In the South of France.

The instructions in Guy Lester's will are clear. Ownership of the house is to pass in joint tenancy to Eve, and to Guy's three children, Noel, Duncan and the sixteen-year-old Libby, whose share is to be held in trust by her mother. The four of them can dispose of the house as they see fit, once the legal formalities have been followed, but Guy hopes Eve might spend some time there before it is sold, if that's what they all agree.

'But what about Mrs Lester?' Eve said, when she had recovered sufficiently to speak.

'She is well taken care of. She never liked the villa, finding it small and old-fashioned. When the Lesters returned to the Riviera after the war, when property was cheap, she persuaded Mr Lester to buy a newer house in the hills behind Nice where it is more chic. The family moved there permanently a few months ago. Mrs Lester wanted to sell La Perle to pay for modernizations but Mr Lester always refused.'

'And his sons?'

'They each inherited a small trust when they came of age. They have separate apartments in the same block in the centre of Nice, and incomes of their own. The older son imports motor cars from England, I believe, and the younger works as a translator for various international finance companies – when he is not frequenting the gambling tables. Do not worry, Mrs Forrester. They will not starve. I should also tell you that there is already an interested buyer for the house. Of course, nothing can happen until the legal formalities are dealt with, but he is keen to move in as soon as possible and is prepared to pay six months' rent in advance until the sale can proceed.'

They have left Cannes now, the road following the curve of the coastline with the pine-covered hillside rising up to their left, and to the right, past the train tracks, the sea, calm in the late afternoon sun.

'Do *you* like to gamble, Mrs Forrester?' asks Marie. 'In the next town, Juan-les-Pins, we have a very famous casino where you can lose all your money in beautiful surroundings.'

Sure enough, the pine trees give way to square blocks of flats and some largish houses and soon they are in a small town, full of cars and shops and bars. It is cocktail hour and the streets teem with the most glamorous women Eve has ever seen, some already dressed for the evening in backless gowns that show off their smooth brown spines, others clearly fresh off the beach, in tight high-waisted shorts that leave little to the imagination and halterneck tops cut off at the midriff. Eve sees a young woman walk along in just a two-piece swimsuit, as if it is the most normal thing in the world. She has seen such things in magazines but it is quite another matter in the flesh.

'You are lucky with the weather,' says Bernard. 'It is unpredictable this time of year but for two weeks we have had only sunshine. Next week I think comes the storm, but by then you will be safely back home.'

The road takes them alongside the boulevard that overhangs the sandy beach, where the hardiest sunbathers still lie soaking up the last rays of the early summer sun, even while all around them umbrellas are being folded up and towels shaken out, shirts slipped on to tender, sand-crusted skin.

Ahead is the casino, an impressive long building that flanks the beach, and past that a white building rises above the trees, stamped with the word 'Provençal'.

Nothing feels real. Not the little car now shuddering as the road climbs out of the town, nor the pale golden wash in the sky behind them, nor the palm tree by the side of the road, its fringed branches fluttering in the breeze.

They seem to be leaving the coast now. The road is wide and winding and on both sides there are gates behind which grand villas hide themselves within lush gardens. Eve had thought they were heading inland, but then they crest a hill and there once again ahead of them is, unmistakeably, the sea.

'This is Cap d'Antibes,' says Bernard, as if reading her thoughts. 'It is a small area of land that sticks out from the rest so you are surrounded by sea on three sides.'

'It is a pity it is late in the day,' says Marie. 'The light here is so beautiful in the morning.'

But it is already the most beautiful place Eve has ever been. She cannot imagine how it could possibly be improved upon.

The car passes a white painted wall overhung with foliage and swings suddenly left through a set of wrought-iron gates into a small gravel courtyard, oddly shaped to accommodate the irregular strip of coastline into which it is wedged. They are at the side of a house that is completely screened from view by a row of tall cypresses standing guard like sentries.

'We will not enter the house tonight,' says Bernard. 'It is better to see it in the daylight when you can appreciate it properly. And we ought to give the family time to digest the news of the will.'

'They are upset?' Eve remembers Diana Lester's pink eyes.

'Surprised,' says Bernard tactfully. 'Your existence has come as a shock to them, much as theirs has to you. However, I could show you the outside if you would like.'

Eve nods, but her throat feels tight. After the beauty of the journey, the talk of the Lester family comes as an unwelcome reminder of reality. Very well. She will wander around the outside of the house, to satisfy her curiosity and gorge herself on the light and the colours and the smell of the sea. Then she will explain to these nice Gaillards that she cannot possibly accept a share in a property from a man she does not know. And she will return to England and this will be a dream, a funny anecdote she can wheel out at dinner parties.

Except that she and Clifford don't go to dinner parties.

Marie says she will wait in the car, but Bernard has already shuffled off, his feet crunching on the gravel, and Eve has little choice but to follow.

What harm can it do? she thinks to herself.

But the word *harm* sticks in her throat like a fishbone.

Eve follows Bernard through a gap in the cypress trees and finds herself in an overgrown garden, still vibrant with colour even in the fast-fading light. Vividly green-leafed branches sag with the weight of pink and white blossoms; a dense honeysuckle colonizes the walls, releasing a fragrance that mingles with the smell from the bursting lavender bush, worlds away from the scent of the Yardley lavender water Eve has on her dressing table at home.

The villa itself is curious, silhouetted against the fast-darkening sky. A low-slung, pale pink building, the paint peeling in places, overrun with creepers and with no discernible entrance, just a row of green-shuttered windows gazing blankly at her. Her first reaction is disappointment.

She imagines they will stop and survey the house and then return the following day to go inside, through the door that Eve still cannot locate, but instead Bernard carries on along the gravel path that leads around the side of the house.

And – *oh my.*

She is at the top of a flight of stone steps. Straight ahead is the Mediterranean, lit up gold by the setting sun to their far right. They descend towards it, past a kidney-shaped swimming pool with green tiles set into a wooden terrace, surrounded by assorted deckchairs and umbrellas.

By now the inky sky is streaked with pink and the water is at first orange, then rose. And by the time they arrive at the bottom, the sea is ablaze with colour. A small terrace, shaded by different types of trees, including a low-hanging eucalyptus, drops down on to a wooden jetty.

Bernard leans against the railings and for a moment the two of them stand in silence, drinking in the sight of the molten water. A dove is calling from somewhere above them, a soft coo that mixes with the low hum of the cicadas and a rasping noise that Eve thinks must be a toad.

'And now you must see the house,' says the lawyer finally.

Eve can hardly bear to look away, but she forces herself to turn around.

'My God!'

Her hand flies to her mouth as she takes in the building. Though not overly wide, on this side it rises up two storeys high, complete with gleaming rows of tall windows. But while the front of the house had seemed a dull pink colour, this side blazes orange in the reflection of the setting sun and the glass window panes appear lit by fire. To the side of the entrance, two umbrella pines stretch their fingers skywards like upturned hands. The whole thing seems staged just for her, the house a flaming torch guiding her home.

This is not hers.

And yet.

Guy, 16 April 1948

'HOW LONG?'

'It is so difficult to quantify these things, Mr Lester.'

'Weeks? Months?'

'Oh, months, certainly. No fears on that score. Nine months or a year. Perhaps two – as long as you bear in mind your blood pressure is very high and avoid becoming too exercised. Plenty of time to get your affairs ship-shape.'

Afterwards it's that 'ship-shape' that sticks in my mind.

For a few weeks after the diagnosis I go about my business as if nothing is different. Do I drink more than usual? Probably, but then my usual is quite a prodigious amount. Am I more than ordinarily quick-tempered? Without a doubt. But conversely, I am also given to moments of unbridled sentimentality.

One morning I come across Diana sitting by the pool, huddled in a blanket without a lick of make-up, and she looks so much like the young girl I fell in love with all those years ago that I throw my arms around her and bury my face in her neck as if I could burrow back to the person I was then and do it all differently. I feel her stiffen in my arms, and really who can blame her? How many times have I come home straight from another woman's bed, guilt making me overcompensate wildly with gifts and grand gestures of affection? Too many to count. And always promising myself that this will be the last time, that the itch has been well and truly scratched.

It never is, of course. Always looking for validation. For the proof that I am worth something despite what I've done.

Predictably, after the weeks of denial comes the reckoning. The thought of dying wakes me in the middle of the night, damp with sweat and fear. Throughout my life I have surrounded myself with people – my wives, my children, the parties, the women – so it is a shock to find that, when it comes down to it, I am quite alone.

I start to tell people, breaking the news lightly: 'You know that ugly old lump in my throat?' Noel is furious both at the disease and at me for catching it. He looks like he wants to hit me, then crushes me to him instead and I don't tell him he's hurting my neck. Then we both get very drunk. Duncan cries. So does Libby, though I don't think she really understands.

I'm hoping the diagnosis might make Diana abandon her plans to move to Nice but it only galvanizes her further. 'I don't want to be left here in this crumbling house,' she says. She tries to be sympathetic but ours is a relationship where there are limits on everything. I think I broke Diana's heart so many times early on, she now keeps it buried in a tin box. Impossible to delve too deeply into Diana's emotions without coming up against the clang of metal.

Inevitably during these long wide-awake hours the guilt comes to find me, setting hard in my veins and arteries, until my liver, lungs, heart become leaden inside me.

If I close my eyes, I relive it again as if no time has passed. The stillness of that early morning, the sun casting long shadows of the trees on dewy grass. The birds just waking up. Us jumping the park railings, young and drunk and invincible. The last blissful moments of 'before'.

Lying in bed, my body wracked by spasms of coughing, I put myself on trial. First come the excuses. The money I've given away, the people I've helped. The guests I've welcomed and fed without thought of repayment. I've tried to make amends. I've done what I could.

Now the prosecution. *You ran away. You escaped unpunished. You never probed below the surface because it suited you not to.*

You're a bloody coward.

I close my eyes again and now I see her face. Young and lovely and spattered with blood and lumps of something else, raw and ghastly and gristly, caught on her cheeks and in the long strands of her hair.

I know what I must do.

To get my affairs ship-shape.

5

2 June 1948

'WHAT DO YOU mean, a house?'

Clifford's voice on the long-distance line sounds strange. Tinny. As though he is talking from inside an empty can rather than from his office.

'It's a pink house right on the sea with green shutters, a little shabby, it's true, but—'

'*Pink?*'

Eve stifles a shudder of irritation.

'It's a very nice pink.'

Already she feels deflated. This momentous event, and her husband has reduced it straight away to a question of paint colour. Already she is on the defensive.

'And how much is it worth?'

Eve is silent. She has heard his question but she does not want to recognize that she has heard it. Wants for it to have been a different question entirely. One about the view of the sunset or the scent of the lavender.

'The house. How much will we get for it?'

'I don't know. I have not asked. It doesn't belong to me, don't forget. And I haven't yet set foot inside.'

'But a quarter of it is ours. It will be worth quite a sum. Right by the sea, you say? A devil to keep up, I should think. We will sell at the first opportunity.'

'But don't you think it strange?' she presses him. 'That this man I have never heard of should have left me such a gift? If only he hadn't died before he could meet me to explain, as he planned. I shouldn't accept, should I? Not when we have no idea what these wrongs the will refers to might turn out to be.'

Clifford, however, seems not to share her concerns.

'No doubt there is a close connection somewhere down the line that we will discover when we finally share the news with your mother. Perhaps he was a disgraced uncle whom your parents disowned. Every family has a black sheep hidden away. We can discuss all this when you return on Saturday, though you'll be needing a rest, I'm sure, after travelling all night. And then as soon as I am able I will travel down to France myself to discuss the sale. Rest assured, my dear, you won't have to bother yourself with all this once you're back.'

By the time she puts down the phone in the hotel's reception, the buoyancy of the last fifteen hours has completely drained away. Whatever happens from now with Villa La Perle, it will not alter the facts of her life with Clifford. The house in Sutton. Her daily routine. True, there might be more money for holidays. Perhaps an upgrade to a more luxurious hotel for this summer's annual trip to Bournemouth. Or maybe they'll venture further afield. Clifford has often mentioned Jersey.

In her room, she stands at the open window gazing at the sea. Slightly overcast today. The sun is hidden behind a bank of high white cloud, filtering out weakly through the occasional gap.

All the previous night Eve lay in bed picturing the house blazing gloriously in the reflection of the setting sun, but now she reminds herself that this is nothing more than an amusing interlude in the more serious business of real life.

In the car she is mostly silent. While Marie drives, Bernard explains that they will have some time on their own to look around the house before Mrs Lester arrives to go over the terms of the will. Eve fights her building dread at the thought of seeing Guy Lester's cool, immaculate widow again. What must she think of her? What must they all think of her?

This time they approach the house from a different direction, taking the coastal road after Juan-les-Pins, past rocky inlets and a tiny beach, then cutting across the tip of the tiny peninsula. 'That's the Hôtel du Cap-Eden-Roc, of course,' says Bernard, as if she must already know of it. Eve does not put him right. Further along the road they pass a series of gates, each offering a suggestion of the house it conceals. As the sea comes back into view, another set of gates appears off to the right, higher and grander than any of the others.

'The Duke and Duchess,' Bernard murmurs, and Eve just has time to register the presence of two blond, black-uniformed guards, before they turn left and head back along the coast.

'I will wait for you here,' Marie says once they are parked in the little gravel courtyard of Villa La Perle. She is leaning against the car, lighting a cigarette.

Bernard nods. Smiles. Face creasing with love. Eve looks away.

There is a peculiar weight to the day now, as if the overhanging clouds are dragging down the sky itself so it presses in closer. Yet still, Eve feels it: the quickening of her heart when she glimpses the pink cladding of the villa's walls between the dense green branches of the cypresses.

Stepping through the gap in the trees into the front garden, they pass a jasmine bush so ripe with fragrance Eve feels momentarily light-headed. A monstrous wisteria, sagging with buds, conceals a doorway that had been disguised by shutters the day before. The wooden frame is painted the same green as the shutters, though there are chips and cracks in the paintwork, and the glass panes in the heavy door are opaque so they cannot see in.

As Bernard raises his hand to knock, Eve takes a deep breath to steady her nerves, and he shoots her a look of sympathy.

'*Courage*,' he murmurs again.

Eve is steeling herself for an encounter with Diana Lester, but instead the door is opened by a middle-aged woman wearing a dress printed all over with outsized yellow flowers, and a smile that somehow blooms from her face. She introduces herself as Mrs Finch, the housekeeper.

Oh. Eve has not entertained the possibility of staff. At home there is Mrs Jenkins, but Eve inherited her along with the heavy dark wood furniture and has always looked upon her as something to be borne in the same way as the wardrobe is to be borne, or the hideous grandfather clock.

Where Mrs Jenkins is thin and wiry, Mrs Finch is round and full-bodied, although her face escapes being plump thanks to a set of fine cheekbones. When she smiles, as now, one can see a noticeable gap between her front teeth, but such is the warmth of her smile and the liveliness of her hazel eyes that the flaws in her features seem only to add character to her face. She is one of those ageless women who could as easily be fifty-five as thirty-five.

Bernard begins to explain who Eve is, but Mrs Finch interrupts.

'I'm afraid the jungle drums have already been beating, Monsieur Gaillard.' When Bernard looks confused, she breaks into a peal of laughter. 'What I mean is that I've already been told all about Mrs Forrester.'

As she steps back to let them in, Eve searches for something to say to cover the confusion she feels at finding herself already the subject of local gossip.

'Have you been here long, Mrs Finch? In France, I mean?'

'It was Mrs Lester who hired me. The first Mrs Lester, that is. Just a couple of years before she died, sadly. I've been here ever since, more or less. Well, apart from the war, of course. Everything stopped for *that*.'

They enter a large bright hallway with a black and white tiled floor. There is a miniature palm tree in a blue and white pot and an ivory-coloured chaise longue, but Eve can't help noticing that some of the floor tiles are chipped and cracked, and the cushion of the chaise longue is worn and lumpy. Straight ahead a tall window spills light on to a curving white stairwell leading down to the lower floor. Through the window the grey sky conjoins with a cloudy sea.

'As you know, the house is built into the small hillside, unusual for this section of the coastline, which tends to be quite flat, so you might find it seems upside down compared to what you are used to,' says Bernard. 'We have entered on street level, but this is directly into the upper floor of the house.'

'That's right. We're completely topsy-turvy here,' says Mrs Finch. When she beams, a dimple appears at the top of her right cheek. 'Don't know if we're coming or going most of the time. The two doors you see on the right lead to guest rooms. We call them the floral room and the green room because we're woefully lacking in imagination.' She ushers them into the room at the front, which is painted a pale green with darker green curtains and a large bed with a mint green cover. The floor is waxed parquet and if it wasn't for the extravagant window leading out on to a balcony overlooking the sea, one could almost imagine oneself to be back in England. There is also a small bathroom, which Mrs Finch refers to coyly as 'the facilities'.

'You must excuse the furniture in the house,' she continues. 'Mrs Lester moved all the best pieces to the house in Nice, leaving a mish-mash of the things she didn't like, and other things that had been stored in the cellar – so they might smell a bit mildewy – plus a job lot of old furniture that Mr Lester acquired sight unseen from a chap down the road who was moving abroad. Mrs Lester was furious. She'd been trying to empty the place out ready to sell it.'

Eve thinks she detects a note of satisfaction in the housekeeper's voice as she relates Diana Lester's thwarted plans.

The room at the back also has a small balcony, this time overlooking a thickly planted terrace at the side of the house and the row of cypresses that screen the courtyard where Marie waits in the car. In contrast to the rest of the house, which is immaculate, Eve is surprised to find this room in disarray. There is a messy desk pushed up against the window, on which sits a typewriter and several wine glasses in various states of fullness. A man's mustard-coloured scratchy woollen jumper dangles off the back of the chair that is pulled up underneath the desk, while a canvas shoe lies on its side in the middle of a sand-speckled rug. By the side of the bed, laid with a rumpled chintz counterpane – thus explaining the 'floral' epithet – there are three teetering piles of books, on the tallest of which rests a large, shallow ashtray piled with cigarette ends.

'Mr Sullivan believes orderliness is detrimental to creativity,' says Mrs Finch from the doorway. The dent in her cheek winks like an eye.

'Mr Sullivan?' queries Eve. She notices that Bernard is looking shifty.

'Perhaps I forgot to mention,' he says, not meeting her eyes. 'Mr Lester was a great patron of the arts. He often had painters and writers staying in the house for extended periods of time. Mr Picasso himself spent a couple of days here a few years ago while he was working at Château Grimaldi in Antibes. For the last few months, Mr Sullivan – perhaps you have heard of him, Stanley Sullivan, the American writer?' He looks at Eve hopefully, but she shakes her head. 'Ah, well. Mr Sullivan has been staying here to work on his next book. Of course, if the house is to be sold he will need to make alternative arrangements.'

Eve feels an irrational twinge of guilt.

They cross the hall to the room opposite, which is lighter, with a full-length window overlooking the swimming pool terrace. This room has pale pink tones; the curtains and bed pane are decorated with sprigs of pink flowers and there's an armchair covered in the same fabric. A large wooden dolls' house pushed against the wall in the corner gives off an air of neglect. Arranged on the mantelpiece above the fireplace is a selection of stuffed toys that have seen better days.

'Libby's room,' Mrs Finch remarks unnecessarily. 'At least, it *was* Libby's room.'

She picks up a moth-eaten teddy bear and gazes absently into the bear's glass eyes, lost in some distant memory or other. Momentarily her smile deserts her, making her appear instantly a decade older. Then she replaces the toy with a small, sad sigh.

'Shall we?' she says, leading the way back out to the one remaining door on this level. 'The master bedroom,' she announces.

Eve holds her breath. The room is spectacular. Even on this overcast day, light floods in from the two full-height double doors to the front and the side. A terrace houses a collection of exotic-looking plants in rustic pots, though not all of them appear in the best of health. Aside from the caramel-coloured parquet floor, everything in this room is white or cream, from the thick rugs to the billowing curtains and the velvet sofa behind a low table from where one might sit and watch the painted fishing boats weaving among the gleaming oak prows of the yachts.

There is a dressing room at the back with banks of wardrobes lining each wall. And a huge bathroom with a large window giving out on to the side of the house. A free-standing bath is positioned so one might lie with one's head resting on the rim and gaze at the tops of the trees blowing in the breeze, following the progress of the clouds across the sky.

The bed is vast, with a curved headboard made of shiny walnut and a white counterpane and pillows. Eve looks quickly away, trying not to think about Diana Lester and the mysterious Guy Lester and the things this room might have seen.

She thinks of the bed she shares with Clifford in the front

bedroom at home, crowded with Clifford's parents' ungainly mahogany furniture, remembering how, when she props herself up on her pillows in the mornings after he has left for work, she is looking straight at a wardrobe with brass handles that reminds her of a coffin. That bed is half as wide as this one and sometimes her muscles ache from the effort of keeping herself from rolling down into the dip in the middle where a careless knee or elbow making contact with bare skin might cause her husband to flinch.

Eve imagines lying here in this light, bright room, with the windows thrown open on to the terrace and a breeze coming in and the only thing in sight the vastness of the sky and the sea.

'Ready to go downstairs?'

Mrs Finch is appraising her with those bright, intelligent eyes and Eve feels herself growing hot, wondering if her thoughts are written on her face.

They make their way down the curving staircase. The balustrades are white, and missing in places, but the wooden treads have been lovingly polished. When Eve peers over the edge, she sees the handrail spiralling downwards alarmingly. The window halfway down the staircase has cracks running the length of the frame, but Eve is glad to look through it and see the sun now breaking through the cloud.

This house is partly mine, she tells herself. Testing how it sounds. Then she dismisses the thought, but not in time to halt a treacherous flare of excitement.

The ground floor is wider than the top, reaching out further towards the sea, following the slope of the hill into which the house is set. Downstairs the hallway has high ceilings and towering glazed doors on to the lower terrace where the nascent sunlight filters in through the two umbrella pines, and beyond them the Mediterranean sea roils. Two large square rooms open out on either side of the hallway – one scattered with sofas and rugs and potted plants, and the other bisected by a formal dining table surrounded by tall-backed chairs.

The kitchen is surprisingly modest, and situated at the rear where the house leans into the hillside; it smells slightly of damp. However, to Eve's unprofessional eye, it seems well stocked and equipped with the requisite number of ovens and sinks and cupboards and places for chopping things, and boards for chopping on.

The door on the opposite side of the hall is closed.

'That is my room,' says Mrs Finch. 'I can show you, if you'd like—'

'Oh, no need,' says Eve quickly. The housekeeper is kind and jolly, but there is a certain absence of boundaries in the way she speaks and acts that Eve is finding hard to get used to.

On the way back through the house, she notices a plain doorway in the darkness behind the staircase. 'Cellar,' calls Mrs Finch, following her gaze, and Eve feels a rush of embarrassment, as if she has been caught making an inventory of the house.

They enter the sitting room, which opens out on to the terrace at the front and also on to the side, where the cool green swimming pool shimmers where the ripples catch the light. In the daylight, Eve can see how the far end of the pool appears to be built into the rocks themselves.

'The pool was horribly damaged during the war,' says Mrs Finch. 'Great cracks as big as your arm. Mrs Lester wanted to re-tile it in bright blue, but Mr Lester would not hear of it.'

'I think it is quite lovely as it is,' says Eve.

'Quite right,' says Mrs Finch, beaming. 'Now, tea, I think.'

Before Eve can protest that it's not necessary, Bernard steps in.

'That would be delightful,' he says.

Once Mrs Finch is out of the room, he turns to her.

'This must all seem very strange to you, Mrs Forrester. Like a dream, perhaps?'

Trying to compose herself, Eve wanders to the back of the room, where a photograph in a silver frame sits on a low table. On closer examination, she sees it is a formal posed black and white wedding photograph of a startlingly young Diana, looking like a film star in a long white lace dress, her throat looped with a slender string of pearls and her hand tucked into the arm of a handsome, broad-shouldered man with hair already starting to go grey around the temples. He has a strong nose, and the expansive smile of someone used to getting what he wants, but his eyes, crinkled around the edges with a fan of laughter lines, seem kind.

Guy Lester. Eve peers closely at his face, looking for something, anything, familiar. Waiting for it to jump out from the picture to say, 'Here. Here is your mystery solved.'

Now there comes a noise from the top of the house. A door closing. Footsteps on the stairs. Voices. A woman's, then a man's. Now another man's. 'Completely insupportable,' this last voice says.

Nerves drive Eve up from the armchair in which she has been sitting. Dry-mouthed, she positions herself with her back to the room, looking out of the side doors towards the pool, trying to absorb some of its cool serenity.

'Monsieur Gaillard. It's as well you have such a nice face, or I should be growing quite fed up of seeing it so often.'

Eve turns slowly when she hears that cut-glass voice, unable to put off the confrontation any longer. Diana Lester is framed in the doorway, wearing a pair of dark blue wide-legged trousers and a blue and white striped top with blue wedge shoes. Her silky hair is held back from her face by a pair of large-lensed black sunglasses resting on the top of her head.

'I have brought company, as you see. When Duncan and Noel heard about the contents of their father's will, they were keen to come here and meet Mrs Forrester for themselves, as you can imagine.'

And now Eve sees coming behind her the tall figures of two men. Two familiar men.

'Mrs Forrester, allow me to introduce you.' Bernard is courteous as always, but there is a new formality about him. 'You met Mrs Lester yesterday, I believe. And these two gentlemen are Noel and Duncan Lester, Guy Lester's sons from his first marriage.'

Duncan Lester nods at her without a smile or a trace of recognition.

Noel Lester fixes her with eyes that seem greener even than the swimming pool outside. But there is no hint of the amusement that so vexed her the last time she saw them, through the train window.

'To think I was worried about you stranded on the platform at Cannes all alone,' he says from behind his stepmother's narrow shoulders. 'Such a relief to see you are quite capable of looking out for yourself.'

6

COULD EVER THE swallowing of tea have sounded quite so loud?

Eve is sure her cheeks must be flaming. Still the silence stretches on, broken only by the clinking of a china cup on a saucer. Finally Diana Lester speaks.

'Perhaps you could enlighten us, Mrs Forrester, as to your *relationship* with my husband.'

Shock closes up Eve's throat.

'There was no relationship,' she splutters.

Bernard intervenes.

'Mrs Forrester never met Mr Lester,' he says. 'Before her visit to my English colleague Mr Wilkes last week, she had never even heard his name.'

'Do you think we are idiots?'

Duncan leans forward in his chair with his hands on his knees. Next to his brother's emphatic features, his soft, pallid face appears curiously weak, as if its development was arrested before it could be fully realized, so that when he is angry, as now, he resembles a child unable to master his own feelings.

'Are we expected to believe Guy left you a share of this

house on some charitable whim? Let me tell you something, Mrs Forrester. It is a fact of life that men do not leave houses to younger women they don't know. So please cut out the innocent act.'

Bernard gets to his feet.

'Mr Lester, I understand you are grieving, but I must ask you not to be so—'

'Don't pretend you are taken in for one minute by this ruse, *Monsieur Le Notaire*. All right, this sort of thing happens in France and no one turns a hair, but Englishmen take a different view.'

Eve's face burns. They all assume there was some liaison between her and Guy Lester. And that his bequest to her is payment for it. Frustration at the unfairness of it prickles in her chest, the early warning sign of an old childhood rage she had thought long-since conquered. She takes a deep breath. She cannot lose her temper here in this beautiful house, with all these strangers. She cannot.

'There was no relationship,' she repeats. 'I am a happily married woman. I never met Mr Lester. I have no idea why he included me in his will. I can only guess there is some family connection and when I get home to England you can be sure I will be making enquiries.'

She stops, flustered. She has on the silk blouse from yesterday and is conscious of how it sticks to her skin.

Everything about her is wrong. Next to Diana Lester's louche elegance, her own clothes seem frumpy. *The Lester sons are probably outraged at their father's lapse in taste*, she thinks, painfully aware of the gulf between her slight, flat-chested frame and their stepmother's imposing figure.

'I suppose it's not a bad pay-off,' says Duncan. 'For

whatever this *connection* will turn out to be. Sign a few papers, pick up a nice fat wodge of cash and scuttle back to your nice suburban English life. Let me guess. Pinner? St Albans?'

'Sutton, actually.'

He lets out a bark of laughter and sits back with a smile, as if vindicated.

'What if we don't accept the will?' Diana asks Bernard. 'I presume we could contest it?'

The notary looks uncomfortable.

'Of course that option is available to you, Mrs Lester. In order for there to be a delivery of legacy, all the beneficiaries must sign the notarial act, and if they refuse the matter will have to go before a judge. But I should tell you, such a procedure could take years, during which time you will not be able to sell the house, nor receive money from it. I should also point out, respectfully, that Mr Lester was in perfectly sound mind when he made the will, so any challenge is unlikely to succeed.'

Duncan, who has been sitting to attention since the suggestion of a legal challenge was mooted, now flings himself back in his seat in disgust.

'Bravo, Mrs Forrester. Looks like you have us over a barrel.'

Bernard clears his throat.

'But you have not seen the outside in daylight,' he says, turning to Eve. 'Perhaps you would like to have a look at the terrace while I discuss some business matters with the family?'

She gets to her feet, grateful for his delicacy.

'Do take care,' says Diana as Eve prepares to open the French doors. 'It can get very blowy out there, and you're such a little scrap of a thing. We wouldn't want a gust of wind to take you away.'

Outside Eve leans against the wrought-iron balustrade and takes in great gulps of sea air.

They hate her. Of course they do.

She will cut short her stay and leave. That is the sensible thing. Then she remembers Mr Wilkes had told them Friday was the earliest he could reserve a ticket.

So she won't leave right away, but she will go back to her hotel and remain there for the rest of her stay. She will tell the Lesters they can keep their blasted house and that will be the end of it.

The decision calms her enough for her to begin to take notice of her surroundings. She is standing on the narrow terrace that runs between the house and the sea. Directly below her is the jetty, from which a ladder leads down into the water. A small red and blue painted rowing boat, roped to a post, bobs gently alongside.

Did Diana and Guy sit out here, Eve wonders, on this beautifully weathered terrace with all its exotic plants? Did they linger on summer evenings, sitting at the table under the spreading eucalyptus tree, with the lanterns hanging from the branches overhead forming their own mini galaxy?

A gull screeches somewhere out at sea, and Eve turns to watch it soaring. The cloud is breaking up and sunlight pools on the surface of the water.

'Not a bad view, is it?'

Noel is leaning against the balustrade a few feet away, lighting a cigarette.

Even from that distance, she is conscious of his physical presence, the broad shoulders, the V-shape of his back.

Her mind goes blank. She cannot think how to reply to

his question. If she agrees, might she not be walking into some sort of trap whereby she will be somehow thought to be already totting up the value of her inheritance? But how impossible to shrug and pretend it is all the same to her.

'That bit of land out there is the tip of the cap.' He is pointing ahead and to the right where, in the distance, rocks and pines are met by the sea. 'And in that direction' – he gestures vaguely behind his left shoulder – 'is the old town of Antibes and then Nice, and way over there across the bay is Cap Ferrat.'

Eve nods, guarded.

'Look, I apologize for my brother. He isn't normally so rude. Our father's death has hit him very hard.'

Noel's voice is gruff and uneven, as if the apology is being dragged from him against his will.

Really, Eve thinks hotly. Why bother?

But some response is called for.

'I really am sorry for your loss. However, you must believe I never knew your father. This whole business with the house has been as much of a shock to me as to you.'

She risks a glance at Noel and meets with the eyes that throw her quite off balance, so she instantly looks away again.

'In which case I apologize again. Although it is a natural assumption. Guy, my father, had a weakness for women.'

Her cheeks are aflame once again, and Eve turns away from him, positioning her back to the sea. The house rises up in front of her and she sees now that the paint on the shutters is faded and peeling in places and one of the terrace railings is broken.

'A house directly on the seafront needs a lot of looking

after,' says Noel, following the direction of her gaze. 'All that wind and salt takes its toll. Diana wouldn't let Guy spend anything on this place. Diverted it all into the new house, which is altogether a grander affair.'

Eve assesses the house, trying to see it critically, as the second Mrs Lester must have done, but where there should be objectivity she finds only feeling. There is something about Villa La Perle that causes a quickening in her blood, a warm press against her heart.

'I imagine you will be returning to England now. Sending your husband back to make the arrangements for the sale.'

This is the time to tell him that she has no intention of accepting this absurd gift. Yet Eve remains silent, that word 'husband' like a toothpick against her skin. She thinks of the master bedroom upstairs. The vast empty bed and the windows thrown open so the only view is the sky and the sea stretching away towards Africa. Then she thinks of her room at home, of Clifford. What if this is her one chance to be somewhere as beautiful as this, her one chance to find out why she is here?

They go back into the house. Duncan and Diana are sitting close together, talking in low voices that stop abruptly when they spot Eve in the doorway. Now that Eve has had a chance to see Duncan in the context of his brother, the family resemblance is clear, but it is as if Duncan is the preliminary sketch, and Noel the complete painting. There is a moment's awkward silence, which is broken when Bernard comes back into the room.

'Ah, here you are. I am sure you are ready to go back to your hotel now, Mrs Forrester. It is a lot to take in.'

Eve nods.

'But then I should like to come back,' she says, surprising everyone, none more so than herself.

'I still have two days remaining before my train leaves on Friday evening. In his will, Mr Lester said he hoped I would get to know the house. So, if it's all the same to you, I should like to spend the rest of my stay here.'

7

Eve has always been wilful, according to her mother. Pliant to a point, happy to please as long as it doesn't put her out, but stubborn thereafter, determined that her way is the only way. Liable to be impetuous, to act without thinking things through.

'Eve pleases herself,' her mother is wont to say. As if pleasing oneself is something shameful.

Sitting alone on the edge of the bed in the green guest room on the top floor of the villa, gazing through the window towards an unsettled sea, Eve regrets where her impetuousness has brought her.

It had seemed so easy to be brave this morning, spurred on by a combination of Noel Lester's arrogance and the intoxicating pull of the house itself. And for a few wild moments, it had been worth it. To see how Noel Lester set his jaw so tight a muscle pulsed in the side of his cheek, and how Diana looked at her more closely, as if seeing her for the first time.

But now she is not so sure.

When she arrived back here less than an hour ago, she resisted any suggestion that she stay in the master bedroom, so recently used by Guy and Diana Lester that the vast white bed might still bear the imprint of their bodies.

'The green room, I think, in that case,' Mrs Finch decided. 'What fun it will be to have female company in the house again.'

Eve was touched by the housekeeper's childish pleasure, though she couldn't help feel a twinge of discomfort at how much effort Mrs Finch was making to be agreeable. She wished the woman might just relax a little. But then she was probably just trying to make up for the Lester family's lack of agreeability.

Eve cannot believe the speed at which events have unfolded. It was only this morning that she stepped through the front door of Villa La Perle for the first time. And now here she sits, having already unpacked her paltry things. Afraid to explore the house for fear of encountering Mrs Finch or the mysterious Stanley Sullivan. Worrying that she has overstepped the mark by coming here in such indecent haste, appearing every bit the avaricious gold-digger they all assume her to be.

She opens her door and stands tentatively at the top of the staircase, listening for sounds. If she peers over the middle, she can see the smooth rail curving down to the hallway below.

The house is silent, so she creeps down the stairs, throwing an apprehensive look at the closed door to Sullivan's room. Only now does it occur to her there might be something inappropriate about staying here in this house with this strange man.

At the bottom of the stairs, she hesitates on the threshold of the living room, trying to picture herself going inside and making herself comfortable on one of the plush sofas. Earlier, she had noticed a bookcase up in the master bedroom.

She could bring a book down from there and kick off her shoes and curl up to read. Yet something stops her. Fear of making herself too much at home.

Instead she makes her way out on to the terrace. The day has brightened since the morning, but there is a fresh breeze that ripples the surface of the sea. Her hair is whipped around her face, the dark strands already stiff with salt, like iron bars blocking her vision. She strolls around to the swimming pool deck, which is shielded from the wind. As soon as she rounds the corner, the breeze drops and when she emerges from the shadow of the house the temperature rises. She raises her face to the sun, feeling her skin slowly waking up as if from a long sleep.

The powerful scent of jasmine wafts from a bush at the far end of the terrace. Eve wanders towards it, removing her cardigan and flinging it on to one of the wooden steamers that face the pool.

'I appear to have something on my head.'

It is possibly the deepest voice Eve has ever heard, and its unusual timbre and the fact that it appears to be coming from nowhere cause her to exclaim loudly.

She turn around, and then immediately turns away again when she sees a man on the lounging chair. Naked save for her dusky pink cardigan over his head.

'It's OK, you can look now. I've made myself decent.'

She turns cautiously. He has taken the cardigan off his head and laid it across his lap, and is scrutinizing her with unabashed curiosity.

The blood is pounding around so violently inside her that she sees him only in snatches, like a series of snapshots. A barrel chest and belly covered in whorls of dark hair. A smooth, gleaming brown head, either bald or the hair cut so short as to be hardly there at all. A pair of intense blue eyes set into a face the colour and texture of old tan leather shoes. A close-cut beard, half black, half silver.

'Stan Sullivan,' he says in a drawling American accent. 'But everyone calls me Sully. I would stand up to shake your hand, but—' He looks down at the cardigan covering his lap.

'Oh no, please don't get up,' she says hurriedly.

There is a pause while she tries to gather her thoughts. A seagull shouts angrily from the top of the house. The smell of jasmine stoppers up her nostrils.

'Do you have a name?' he asks at last. 'Or have you perhaps been washed up from a shipwreck in which all your companions perished, with no idea who you are or where you've come from and—'

'Eve Forrester,' she says.

To her surprise he smiles, showing a flash of white teeth, the outer ones longer than the others, creating a distinctly wolfish impression.

'Excellent. I was quite dreading that you'd be one of those stout, moustachioed women who spent the war roaring around the place on motorbikes and are furious with all men for coming back and ruining their fun.'

Eve does not know where to start with this. *Stout and moustachioed.* The cheek of it. When he is both those things. And what does he mean, he was *dreading*?

'You've been expecting me then?' she says.

'Oh yeah. Guy told me weeks ago he'd left you a share in the house. It was all very mysterious, but he said he'd explain all once he'd been over to talk to you in person. Only he never made it.'

'He told you, but he didn't tell his wife?'

'I take it you're not married, sweetheart. Don't you know your spouse is the very last person you tell things to?'

'I *am* married, actually.'

'Never mind.' Before she can wonder what he means, he continues: 'He said it would most likely be sold. The house, I mean. Which would be a shame as it's quite charming. And Guy did love it so.'

'Did he tell you why he included me in his will?'

Stan Sullivan looks surprised.

'I didn't ask. I just assumed you and he—'

'No! Absolutely not.'

He smiles at her vehemence.

'How very mysterious. And how has darling Diana taken the news?'

His teeth are so very white, and, being such uneven lengths, obviously all his own. Which is uncommon in Eve's experience.

'Mrs Lester has been gracious. All things considered.'

'Don't you be taken in by that superficial politeness. There's a nest of poisonous vipers writhing under that lovely exterior. If you look closely you can see her skin undulating. Be wary, little Eve. She complained about this house non-stop but she won't like you having a claim to it. Diana doesn't like to share.'

Eve is silent.

'So will you vote to sell it?'

Eve shrugs, reluctant to disclose to a stranger her many reservations about accepting her surprise inheritance.

'I imagine so. I won't know until I discuss it with my husband.'

Sully smiles again, as if she has said something funny.

'Where will *you* go, if the house is sold? Will you be able to find someone else to stay with? I should not like to think of you destitute.'

The American gives her a long, hard look.

'Tell me, Eve Forrester. Have you never heard of me?'

Eve, taken aback, shakes her head.

'Stanley Sullivan?' he prompts her, as if repeating his name might dislodge some blockage in her memory.

She shakes her head again. 'But then the head librarian at our local library is rather biased against American writers,' she apologizes, when she sees how crestfallen he looks. 'Agatha Christie, on the other hand. P. G. Wodehouse, even—'

'Will you pass me that robe?'

Now Eve notices for the first time a silk robe tossed on to one of the other chairs. She takes a step towards the American's steamer but stops well short and tosses the garment the rest of the way before turning her back discreetly.

She wanders over to the jasmine bush and inhales deeply.

Here I am, she thinks, *by a swimming pool in the South of France, chatting to a naked American writer.*

'You can turn around now.'

Sully is belting up his robe over his rounded belly. He is shorter than she'd imagined, but powerfully built, like a boxer. His bald head glints in the sun. He ought to be ugly, with those muscular shoulders, that flat nose, little discernible neck. And yet there is something about him that makes you look and want to keep looking.

'Mrs Finch tells me you're staying here the next two nights. So how would you like to come to a party with me tonight?'

'Tonight? But it's a Wednesday.'

'Is it?'

Amusement in those discomfiting blue eyes.

'You'll find that days of the week don't mean much here on the Riviera. We have different ways of counting down our lives. Will you come? It's not even a party, more of a reception, and by reception I really mean small, miserable gathering, and it's not far. The next house along. You can't have missed it.'

Eve remembers the black gates. The black-uniformed guards outside with the white-blond hair.

'You can't mean . . . the Duke and Duchess?'

'Exactly.'

Eve stares at him, sure he must be toying with her. But he returns her gaze quite levelly.

'The Duke and Madame Duke, or Fräulein Duke as I like to call her, are throwing a reception to welcome Gloria Hayes to the Riviera. I trust you know *her*, at least. Or does the head projectionist at your local cinema have something against American actresses?'

Eve smiles.

'Oh, please come. Don't worry about anything you may have heard about the parties around here. There will be nothing debauched. The Duke and his wife are notoriously mean and anyway, they are appalled at the idea of a vulgar Yank like Gloria Hayes lowering the tone of the area. Nazis are one thing. But Americans . . . ?' Sully clutches a string of imaginary pearls at his throat in mock horror.

'But you're American,' Eve points out.

'Yeah, but I've been in Europe long enough for them to be willing to overlook it. Besides, they figure that if they surround themselves with people who write books it'll exempt them from actually having to read any.'

'But film stars . . . ?'

'Utterly beyond the pale, I'm afraid. If the Duke and Duchess hadn't been on the receiving end of the Martin family's largesse so many times, you can bet they wouldn't be giving Gloria Hayes the time of day. So their hospitality will be rationed, you can be sure. We will probably be back here and tucked up in bed by ten o'clock. What do you say?'

Gloria Hayes. The Duke and Duchess. Words plucked from a dream. Still Eve hesitates, wary of imposing. Then she thinks of the evening stretching ahead of her, sitting alone on her bed in that green room, not venturing downstairs for fear of disturbing Mrs Finch.

'Why not?' she says.

Isn't this whole thing like a dream anyway? The journey, the house, the night spent completely alone without Clifford's soft snuffling snores making the air over the bed feel damp and spongy. So now she will add royalty and Hollywood stars to the unreality of it all.

Why not?

8

SHE REMEMBERS WHY not on her way back to her room a few moments later, when it occurs to her that she has nothing remotely suitable to wear. She had thought about packing her oyster-coloured evening dress with the embroidered bodice, which rests daringly off the shoulders, but when Clifford had seen it laid out on the bed, he'd laughed. *You won't be needing that, my dear. Just smart, sensible clothes to show them you're someone to be taken seriously.*

So she has the bottle green linen skirt. And the silk blouse she has been wearing all day that now looks like something Mrs Finch might use to mop a floor. And the brown crepe dress and blue travelling suit. But nothing partyish. Nothing to wear to meet Gloria Hayes.

Walking into her bedroom, she stops short, struck by an unsettling conviction that something has changed. She casts her eyes around the room. As she approaches the desk on which she had laid her suitcase, the skin on Eve's arms prickles and she shivers, despite the heat.

Eve hasn't completely unpacked, not wanting to appear to be taking ownership of her room. Though her skirts are draped over the back of the chair, the rest of her clothes are still in her case. Hadn't she left the lid open with her clothes exposed to the air, hoping that might somehow freshen them up?

Has someone been in her room?

But almost immediately she starts to doubt herself. She had been in such a state of tension before venturing out; can she really be sure she didn't close the suitcase herself? Perhaps she did it without thinking. Isn't it exactly the kind of little gesture one could make automatically, without even registering one was doing it?

Mollified, she turns her attention back to the matter of her clothes. Or rather the lack of them. In the end she decides on the skirt suit with a white blouse that is the only clean thing she has. She puts a narrow belt around the skirt's waistband. But when she sees herself in the mirror she reminds herself of the very librarian she was discussing earlier. Her hair, naturally wavy – so she doesn't need to sleep with a head full of uncomfortable knots – has formed tight curls around her face and neck after exposure to the sun and sea air.

Just as she is picturing Diana Lester's immaculate elegance, and deciding she cannot possibly go to the party, there comes a knock on her door.

'You'll do fine,' says Sully when she tries to tell him she has changed her mind. 'Anyway, all eyes will be on Gloria Hayes, so no one will be looking at you.'

'But—'

'You have two more nights here. That's right, isn't it? Before you go back to whatever dreary town you live in. Wouldn't you like to have an adventure? Something to tell your friends over tea and whatever that ridiculous card game you all play is?'

'I only play bridge on Wednesdays. And my town isn't dreary.'

She doesn't tell him that she has no friends.

Still, he is right. In two nights' time she will be on her way home and this will be over. And that future version of her will rage against the wasted opportunities. *Royalty. Film stars. And you stayed home because you had nothing to wear?*

They stroll to the party. The air outside is fresh, the breeze salty against her lips, and Eve regrets her last-minute decision not to bring her pink cardigan on account of the small moth hole she had only just noticed in the sleeve. With every step she is conscious of the man by her side, of the energy that pulses under his tanned skin. He is the kind of American her mother always warned her against during the war. Loud, brash, dominating the space around him so that everything has to be referenced in relation to him; nothing stands entirely on its own.

When they approach the house Eve noticed the day before, the gates are standing open and there is a line of cars waiting to go inside. Two black-clad men stand by the gates checking the cars.

'Is it a prerequisite that the staff must have blond hair?' she asks, meaning to be witty. But Sully is offhand.

'Oh, yes. Only Aryans will do.'

The house is enormous. The combination of bright lights and crowds of people and Eve's own heart beating so loudly makes it hard to take it in dispassionately. Instead it comes to her in fragments – a vast chandelier overhanging an entrance lobby bigger than her whole house in Sutton, corridors with gleaming marble floors stretching endlessly behind double glass doors, a seven-piece orchestra, the violinist fulcruming backwards and forwards at the waist, waiters sliding past with silver trays, champagne flutes made of crystal that cuts the light into tiny sharp shards. And the dresses! Silk and taffeta that rustle and whisper, necklines that plunge into acres of cleavage, straps of magenta and rose and pale ice blue that mould themselves over shoulders and bosoms, waists no bigger than a side plate and hips that shimmer and sashay and sway.

Eve's senses, dulled after the grey war years, feel bludgeoned by the colours, the music, the textures. She has come from an England that is still patching itself up, still rebuilding. Meat is still rationed, and clothing too – that loathsome little pink ration book – and anyway, extravagance feels wrong when so many are still grieving, so much has been lost.

But here there is no moderation. Here there are slices of smoked fish and grouse and dainty hors-d'oeuvres that Eve does not recognize.

'You wouldn't think there was still bread rationing here in France,' says Sully, eyeing up a stack of soft buttery rolls. 'Good to know the war was fought so that the black market can thrive.'

A waitress comes past, dressed in black with a white frilly apron. She is twentyish and pretty with high pink cheeks and Eve feels Sully's energy shift in the young woman's direction.

She is conscious of her own winter-grey skin, her unkempt hair, the matronly clothes.

'Can one really get *anything* here?' Eve asks.

'Sure, as long as you've got the cash to pay for it. Plenty of people did very well out of this war. Are still doing well. Profiteering. Black market. Not to mention the stolen jewellery and artwork the Nazis left behind when they fled that has magically managed to end up in private hands.'

They make their way towards the orchestra and Eve sips at her champagne. Every few steps someone comes forward to greet Sully, or to place a gloved hand on his arm. Others pause as they pass, then lean together to whisper with sideways glances.

He really is famous. The realization makes her hot with embarrassment. She tries to remember what she'd said out there on the swimming pool terrace. Had she really used the word 'destitute'?

She turns to him, but before she can blurt out her apology, he points to a tall, silver-haired man with a thin moustache and pointed beard who seems to be holding court in a corner of the grand room.

'Recognize him?'

Eve shakes her head.

Sully's eyebrows rise up his nut-brown forehead.

'Alberto Alvarez. The world's greatest living painter, or a talentless fraud who has bamboozled the entire art world. Depending on which newspaper you read.'

'That's Alvarez?' Eve stares, rapt, remembering a rare childhood trip to London with her parents, a birthday treat. In an art gallery being trailed around painting after painting that seemed to her young eyes to show just old people in silly clothes standing stiffly or bowls of fruit or dull landscapes of the kind she could see any day from the window of a train – then suddenly coming across this extraordinary image. Colours, shapes, contorted faces that appeared in places where faces should not be. A cat with a tail that turned into a snake, two children sitting behind desks with apples instead of heads. A glimpse of a different world, before her mother steered her firmly away. 'Can you imagine anyone wanting to hang this rubbish on their wall?' she'd asked Eve's father, shaking her head.

Sully takes two more glasses of champagne from a passing waiter.

'Best drink up. The Duke and Duchess are notoriously tight, so who knows how long stocks will last. They always use rationing as an excuse, but everyone knows they have a plane parked just a few miles from here with a pilot ready to fly off at a moment's notice to fetch whatever they want. There's nothing you can't get on the Riviera, sweetheart. For a price. You ought to learn that fast if you're going to be sticking around.'

'Oh but I'm not—'

But Sully's attention has again wandered.

'Here's a question for you. What's the collective noun for a bunch of Lesters? A clutch of Lesters? A murder of Lesters?'

Eve follows his line of sight and her heart sinks as she spots Diana Lester, her shoulders bare, her hair swept back from her face. She is wearing a strapless midnight-blue velvet dress that falls in a column down to the ground. Something sparkles at her throat.

Standing close by with their backs to Eve are Duncan and Noel Lester, the black jackets they both wear emphasizing the difference in their physiques. Duncan is almost a head shorter than his older brother, with sloping shoulders thrown into relief by his brother's broad frame.

'Who is that woman?' asks Eve, recognizing the blonde from the train carriage by the sulky expression she still wears, her rosebud mouth, with the kind of lipstick Eve's mother would describe as 'trashy', set into a pout.

'Oh, that's Clemmie Atwood. Lady Clementine Atwood, don't you know.'

There is a flint in Sully's voice that makes Eve look closely.

'Are you married, Mr Sullivan?' she asks suddenly, wondering why it has not occurred to her to ask before.

'Usually.'

'What do you mean, *usually*?'

He shrugs. 'I mean the state of being married is fairly constant. Though the specifics fluctuate.'

Still Eve must look blank because at length he elaborates.

'I seem to be a serial wedder. The fourth Mrs Sullivan is currently back home in New York buying more furniture we don't need and telling anyone who'll listen what a monster I am. Anyway, back to the lovely Clemmie. She's the youngest daughter of one of those penniless aristocrats you excel at in England. The Riviera used to be awash with British gentry before the war. You couldn't move on the beach without tripping over a duke or an earl languishing on the sand behaving badly. But everyone drifted away once Mussolini's lot arrived and very few of them have come back. Clemmie's cousin Margaret is one of the last stalwarts and Clemmie came over a few years back, ostensibly to look after Margaret's children, but really to snag herself an Italian prince or a French playboy. Instead she fell in love with Noel Lester, only somehow she's ended up engaged to his brother. No wonder she always looks as if she's sucking on a lemon.'

Diana Lester glances up and catches Eve's eye. She says something and now both the Lester sons are turning to look. Eve feels their gaze travel over her, her fuddy-duddy clothes and wayward hair. Noel Lester nods in her direction. Then

Clementine Atwood, who has been staring openly at Eve, leans in to say something and the whole group laughs.

'You've gone awfully red,' Sully says, studying her with interest.

Eve looks away sharply, and finds herself gazing into a pair of amused blue eyes. The eyes are set in a narrow face with a long, aquiline nose under which a fair moustache brushes the top of a surprisingly full mouth. The man is tall and graceful and his elegant clothes seem like an extension of his body, so naturally does he inhabit them.

He raises one eyebrow as if asking her a silent question, the corner of his mouth twitching in a smile.

Eve has no idea why he is looking at her like that, as if they are both in on a joke that no one else shares. But he has a kind face and, surrounded by strangers and feeling so out of her depth, she appreciates that.

But now there is a hush and everyone is looking around as the orchestra suddenly launches into a melody that Eve recognizes as the soundtrack to a movie she and Clifford saw on one of their first dates. A murmur starts among the crowd by the door and spreads outward like dye in water.

And now Eve sees her. Flame-red hair that falls in thick waves to her shoulders and curves constrained in a dress of coral that clings and shimmers. Creamy white skin – so much of it on show – and a full, wide mouth outlined in red. A glow surrounds her, though whether it emanates from her person or her celebrity, Eve couldn't have said.

Beside her, with one hand on the small of her back so that he steers her around as if he is operating her from behind like a ventriloquist with his dummy, is a small man in his late forties or early fifties, with thick black hair and the sly smile of a fisherman who has just landed the catch of the day.

'Laurent is looking particularly pleased with himself,' observes Sully.

'She is so beautiful though,' Eve says.

'Beautiful and high as a kite. Look at those eyes.'

Eve peers more closely. It is true that Gloria Hayes's famous green eyes, reportedly insured for two hundred and fifty thousand dollars each, seem strangely glassy and unblinking.

'I've heard she can't get up in the morning without a pep pill. And I'll bet she needs an elephant's dose of barbiturates to go to bed with him.'

Eve feels herself blushing and turns away, hoping to see the tall fair-haired man with the moustache, but he has disappeared.

'I think he looks distinguished,' she tells Sully. 'And anyway, why would she be with him if she didn't love him? It's not as if she needs the money.'

'No, but her last two pictures have flopped and she needs to keep the studio happy. And what will make the studio happy is a fairytale wedding to a European playboy in front of the whole world's media. Publicity for them, publicity for her. Box office bonanza. Besides, everyone knows she's on the rebound from her marriage to Greg Dalladay. She would probably have married this glass of champagne if it had asked her.'

'You don't have a very high opinion of women, do you, Mr Sullivan?'

'On the contrary, Mrs Forrester. I love women. Though if I could only get into the habit of loving them one at a time, my life would be a lot simpler.'

An elderly woman materializes from the crowd. She has the physique of a squat pillar box, with her shoulders exactly the same width as her middle and her hips, and dyed hair through which her scalp shows pink.

'Sully, you bad man. We waited all night for you at the casino on Saturday and I lost all my money and my jewellery and my firstborn and we had to slink out through the back way in disgrace, and it is all of it your fault and now I am kidnapping you until you have entertained us sufficiently to repay your debt.'

The woman places a heavily ringed hand on Sully's arm and steers him in the direction of a group of similarly aged people, who visibly straighten as they see him approach and step back to leave a space for him to pass through. Sully shoots Eve an apologetic look before the ranks close around him, blocking him from view. An excited buzz travels around the company and the pink-scalped woman smiles, triumphant, the hunter bringing home the prey. Eve has the unpleasant impression that the group has eaten Sully alive.

Suddenly alone and feeling conspicuous in her plain clothes, Eve makes her way to the end of the room, where the doors are thrown open on to a large formal terrace laid out in a grid of paths bordered by bushes. Steps lead down from either side to a further terrace below, where a large floodlit swimming pool seems to fall away into the sea itself.

As soon as she is outside, she laments the cardigan left behind on her bed. The breeze whips up from the sea, coating everything in a cold damp spray. Too late she remembers her hair, already tightening into ringlets from the atmospheric moisture. She shivers but resists going back inside. At least out here it is dark and the few other guests who have braved the wind are huddled on the benches nearest the house, so that if she stands near the railings looking out across the pool to the sea, she feels unobserved.

Raised voices travel towards her from the direction of the house, and looking around she is surprised to see Duncan Lester and Laurent Martin framed in the doorway, deep in conversation. She resumes her scrutiny of the sea before she can be caught staring, and the next time she risks a glance, the two have disappeared.

'Here you are. I was so afraid you might have left early. Like Cinderella.'

The voice is soft with only the slightest hint of a French accent, and even before she turns around, Eve knows it will belong to the tall fair man who had smiled at her across the room earlier, as if they knew each other from somewhere.

Up close he is older than he'd first appeared. Late thirties, she'd guess, with a fan of slender lines that opens up around his eyes when he smiles, as he does now. He leans on a black cane with a silver handle, and she tries to pretend she has not seen it in case it embarrasses him.

'No. Still here,' she says.

He introduces himself as Victor Meunier and interrupts her before she can finish giving him her name.

'I already know who you are, Mrs Forrester. Don't forget, we are a small community, starved of fresh air. Rumours and scandal are our oxygen.'

Eve feels torn between wanting to return his smile, to prolong the feeling that they are both colluding in something amusing, but also resenting that this extraordinary, private thing that has happened to her should have become the local entertainment.

'Well, that puts you at an advantage,' she says stiffly.

Victor's smile falters.

'Please forgive me if I have said something stupid. My English needs improvement.'

His English is faultless. His eyes in the semi-darkness are dark pools of concern. Eve swallows, suddenly acutely conscious of everything – the fat clouds overhead, the wind biting through her blouse and making the fine hairs on her arms stand up, the vibrato of the violin coming from the open doors. Being here, in this place, with this stranger who looks at her as if they share a secret.

'Are you from around here, Monsieur Meunier?'

His face, which is mostly long lines and hollow planes, seems to lose some of its angularity as he smiles.

'No, from Paris. But I have a small art gallery here, in Nice. This is where the artists I love came to paint. Matisse, Chagall, Picabia. Picasso, of course. So this is where I live.'

'Have you lived here for long?'

He shrugs.

'The war has made questions of time so hard to answer. I was living in Paris, but then during the war I spent two years as a prisoner in Germany.' Here he makes a gesture towards the cane, as if explanations are unnecessary. 'I returned to Paris after I was released, but it was too hard to see the Nazis marching down the Champs-Élysées so I came south. And *voilà*. Here I am.'

He smiles, his teeth long and white in the gloom.

'Oh,' says Eve. 'I am sorry to hear that. About the war, I mean, not about you being here.'

How ridiculous she sounds, prattling on. She becomes conscious of a presence behind her, someone momentarily blocking the wind so that her back feels pleasantly warm once more. She looks behind her and is surprised to find Noel Lester there, scowling into the night air.

'You're cold, Mrs Forrester.'

It is a statement rather than a question. Eve feels herself prickling with irritation, both with the presumption of his statement and the way he has interrupted her conversation. She can see by the hardening of Victor Meunier's face that he does not welcome the other man's uninvited arrival. She doesn't turn around, so that her back remains rudely presented to Guy Lester's older son.

'On the contrary. It's at least ten degrees warmer here than in England. Practically balmy.'

Victor's mouth twitches.

'I will take my leave of you,' he says. 'It has been a great pleasure.'

His eyes, for a moment, are fixed on hers and there is the most curious feeling that she is falling headlong into them. Then he glances behind her at Noel Lester and nods politely before moving off, leaning on his cane.

'I see you've been busy making friends,' says Noel stiffly. Then he straightens up, adopting a lighter tone. 'I imagine this isn't the sort of thing you would be doing on a Wednesday evening in Sutton.'

Really. The affront of him. He has taken one look at her and pigeon-holed her as dull and provincial without knowing the first thing about her. The idea that he is imagining her as some bored housewife, stuck in her stuffy front room listening to the wireless, is insupportable.

'I play bridge on Wednesdays,' she says.

She is not looking at him, but she senses his amusement.

'Of course you do.'

Now Eve is angry.

'Look,' she says, turning to face him to prove that she is not intimidated. 'I know you have come out here thinking you can press me into telling you why your father might have included me in his will, but the truth is I don't know any more about it than you, so you might as well save your breath and go back and enjoy the party.'

Her heart is thumping in her chest through her cotton blouse and Noel looks at her in surprise.

'You're right, I did come to talk about the house. The thing is,' he says, recovering quickly, 'there are various taxes that will become due. Inheritance matters. I suppose Bernard warned you that you'll be facing an almighty inheritance tax bill?'

Eve nods, not wanting to appear at a disadvantage, but she can't help feeling foolish. Of course there would be money to pay.

'Plus there are certain other familial financial commitments that make a quick sale imperative,' Noel continues. 'Now, apparently someone wants to buy it, money pit though it is, and the mad bugger is willing to pay six months' rent and commit to a purchase agreement in principle until it is ready to be sold. So, frankly, we don't need any complications. And you, Mrs Forrester, are a complication.'

Now is the time to say it. *You can put your mind at rest. I will not be accepting Mr Lester's bequest.* The words dry up on her tongue. Instead she answers: 'But Bernard – Monsieur Gaillard – assured me you and the rest of your family were well provided for in Mr Lester's will.'

'How kind of *Monsieur Gaillard* to make our financial affairs a matter of public record.'

'That's not how it was. He was—'

But the rest of her sentence is broken off when Noel, in one slight movement, slips off his jacket and drops it over her shoulders.

'You were shivering,' he says matter-of-factly.

The unsolicited jacket burns her shoulders and yet she is so glad to be warm she cannot bring herself to shrug it off.

'Thank you.'

'You're not the first Brit to misjudge the climate of the Riviera.'

His condescension takes her breath away. But before she can think how to reply, he changes the subject.

'What did you think of Gloria Hayes? You're sticking around for the wedding party, I hope. Shame to come all this way and miss out on the social event of the decade.'

'Don't be ridiculous. Why would I be invited to the wedding? I don't know either of them.'

Noel blows out air through his lips in a *pfff* sound.

'That puts you at an advantage around here. Fresh meat in the Riviera is a sought-after commodity. We're all so sick of the sight of ourselves. Everyone outdoing each other with new themes and venues and clothes and cocktails to disguise the fact that it's just the same old faces underneath all the fancy dress and the hats and the baubles. Anyway, Sully will bring you along. He's a sucker for a pretty woman.'

'I wasn't aware Mr Sullivan had been invited.'

'Mr Sullivan needs no invitation.'

Eve is reminded of how she asked the American if he might end up destitute, and something shrivels inside her. She and Noel stare at the sea in silence. Behind them the orchestra is playing 'Night and Day', the music buffeted by the breeze so that the notes waft up into the night sky.

She tries not to think about what he just said, but the word 'pretty' lodges stubbornly in her mind.

Archie had told her she was pretty. He wasn't overly tall so he liked the fact that she was so petite. And he loved looking at her. 'Every bit of you just fits together so perfectly,' he'd tell her. But Clifford has made little mention of her appearance beyond congratulating her on not being *obvious*. Obviousness in a woman was one of the cardinal sins, in Clifford's book. Once, in a moment of weakness, she had tried to push harder. She knows looks aren't important in the scheme of things, but surely it's natural to want to be sure that the person who wakes up with you in the mornings likes what they see. 'You aren't one of those women who expect to get by on their looks,' Clifford eventually ceded. 'You don't thrust your face or your figure forward demanding to be noticed. Men prefer to feel as if they have discovered a hidden prize.'

At first she had felt proud to be a hidden prize. Only later had she grieved for the lack of any one part of her that he could single out and say, *There. That. That's why I fell in love with you.*

'What are those?' Eve points far out to sea where a cluster of small lights are bobbing around in the darkness.

'Fishing boats. Poor bastards. There never used to be so many, but since rationing anyone who can get hold of a boat is out there every night trying to catch tomorrow's supper.'

Eve remembers the queue outside the butcher's that she'd seen from Marie's car and then thinks of the tables she has just walked past, groaning with food.

'Here you are.'

Clemmie Atwood is wearing a strapless white dress that seems to be held up by willpower alone and her long arms are wrapped around her chest for warmth. She looks surprised when Eve turns around but recovers herself quickly, her mouth curling up in imitation of a smile.

'The famous Mrs Forrester, I presume.'

Noel makes the introductions with minimal enthusiasm. Lady Atwood declares herself to be quite agog with curiosity over the mystery of Guy Lester's surprise bequest.

'A love child,' she says. 'There is no other explanation. Which would make the two of you brother and sister, though I have to say I don't see the resemblance.'

Eve feels the blood rush to her face and is glad of the darkness.

'Shut up, Clemmie.'

Even Eve can sense the edge in Noel's voice. But Clemmie's smile grows wider and she sways, and Eve realizes that she is quite drunk.

'Aw, that's so sweet. You don't believe your father would have slept around on your sainted mother?'

'I said shut up.'

Now there is no disguising the note of danger in Noel's voice and Clemmie presses her lips together.

'Oops,' she says. 'Have I gone too far again?'

To Eve's surprise, she sounds quite proud of herself.

'I must go,' says Eve, feeling out of her depth. 'It's getting very late.'

'Late?' Clemmie throws back her head and laughs, her slender throat pale as a bone in the half light. 'How completely charming. My dear, this is the Riviera. The night hasn't even started.'

'No, really. I've had a very long day. Here. Your jacket.'

She holds it out to Noel, but before he can take it, Clemmie has snatched it out of Eve's hands and is shrugging her arms into it. The jacket dwarfs her, emphasizing her fragile blonde beauty.

'I don't care if I look a fright. I simply must get warm. Do I look a fright, darling?'

She turns to Noel, holding her arms stiffly out, the jacket sleeves hanging over her hands, her mouth turned out in a theatrical pout.

'Right. Well. Goodbye then,' says Eve. 'I don't suppose I shall see you both again as I am leaving on Friday.'

'Only a day to make a note of all the things in the house and tot up what they're all worth.'

For a moment Eve doesn't think she has heard Clemmie correctly. But before she can protest, the other woman giggles.

'There I go again, thinking out loud. Ignore me. That's how I am, I'm afraid. I speak as I find.'

Eve glances at Noel, wondering if he will say something in her defence, but he takes a cigarette from a case in his pocket and puts it in his mouth.

'Adieu,' he says, the cigarette moving up and down on his bottom lip. The fingers of his right hand flutter, whether in dismissal or farewell Eve cannot say.

Walking away, she hears Clementine Atwood let out a loud peal of laughter behind her. The sound is carried by the breeze so it seems to Eve to be following her out.

Guy, 18 April 1948

'AND YOU ARE completely sure?'

Bernard has a way of looking at you that conveys all the doubt that he is too polite to express out loud. Many is the time that look has caused me to stop in my tracks.

Today, however, sitting across the desk from him in his small, chaotic office, I hold firm.

'Absolutely.'

'You do not worry about putting the young lady in a delicate position? *Vis-à-vis* your wife and your children, I mean?'

'I already told you, I'm going to England to meet Eve and explain everything. And on my return, I'll talk to my family. There are certain matters that have been too long hidden. It's time to drag them into the light.'

Now that I have made my decision I am impatient to make it happen. Though I have let three decades pass without action, I feel suddenly as if I cannot wait another day.

I can see from Bernard's face that he longs to ask me what these certain matters are, who this Eve Forrester is to me. But he would never pry and I am not ready to tell him. After

I've found Eve, and spoken to her: that will be the time for discussion.

'Guy?'

Even after all these years, Bernard struggles with the pronunciation of my name, so it comes out sometimes as 'gooey', at other times 'goy'.

'Guy, I am concerned about you. You look tired, and I can hear from your voice that your throat is not so good. All of this emotion will put pressure on your heart. Just when your doctor has told you to take it easy. Can you really take the risk of opening this particular box?'

Bernard mimes the action of removing the lid from something, dislodging the big ginger cat who has been lying on his lap all the while. The cat stalks off in disgust, its tail high.

All of a sudden, I feel exhausted, drained of energy. The thought of walking downstairs is daunting enough, let alone travelling back to England. A wave of hopelessness engulfs me.

I have left it too late.

Still, I summon all my strength to reply: 'If the lid remains closed, I'm afraid the whole box will explode, taking my family with it.'

9

3 June 1948

'NO HARD FEELINGS.'

'Of course.'

'You can't blame a guy for trying.'

'It's forgotten.'

'I just—'

'I said it's forgotten.'

Eve, who is lying on her back on a steamer feeling the cells of her skin expanding in the sun, wishes Sully would stop talking. She knows perfectly well that his drunken, half-hearted attempt at a pass while they were walking home from the reception the previous evening came more out of a sense of misplaced duty than an outpouring of passion.

She closes her eyes, allows the jasmine-scented air to settle around her, listens to an insect buzzing somewhere in the vegetation and tries not to remember that this is her last full day in France. The face of Victor Meunier appears in her mind, the blue irises ringed by a darker navy, the angles that dissolve and re-form as his expression changes.

'What do you know about Victor Meunier?' she asks.

'Our local hero? Wounded in the war. Spent some time as a POW in Germany, then returned to Paris, but couldn't stomach life under occupation so managed to talk his way down here.'

'So why the hero part?'

'Rumour has it he helped several Jewish families escape before they could be rounded up and sent to the camps. Mind you, the war made heroes out of so many ordinary people. Bernard and Marie Gaillard, for example, were leading lights in the Resistance around here.'

Eve pictures the sad-eyed notary and his excitable wife, and things start to fall into place.

'Then there's our own Noel and all those endless missions he flew in the RAF.'

'Oh?' Eve keeps her eyes closed.

'Set some sort of record, I believe. Do you know they had to more or less bar him from the airfield in the end because he wouldn't stop turning up to fly? They had his photograph on the wall at the security point, like the casinos with their blacklists.'

'Are you exaggerating, Mr Sullivan?' She peers over at him, shielding her eyes from the sun with her hand.

'Well, maybe just a little. But he did fly an awful lot. I guess he was trying to make up for—'

'For what?'

'Tell me, what did you think of our Gloria?' Sully changes the subject and sits up on his recliner, leaning forward so his powerful shoulders are all Eve can see over his bent knees. 'Didn't you think she looked as if she'd been kidnapped and brought there under duress? I kept watching her lips, waiting for her to mouth, "Help me".'

Eve abandons any hope of peaceful meditation and sits up too.

'I think she's terribly beautiful. But I agree she didn't exactly look like a radiant bride. She hasn't long been divorced from Greg Dalladay, has she? And those two always looked to be so much in love.'

'I'm sure they were – until he met Carla Jasmine on the set of *What the Heart Wants*. Poor Gloria. It's hard enough being abandoned by the man you love, let alone being abandoned so publicly, for a girl not even twenty years old.'

'So you think she is trying to fix her broken heart by marrying someone else?'

'Yeah, but not just any old someone else. A someone else with a private plane and multi-millions in the bank and a big yacht with a full-time staff of twelve.'

'You're very cynical, Mr Sullivan.'

'Sully. And I'm not cynical at all. I'm a hopeless romantic, which is why I've been married so many times. Still trying to find that elusive happy-ever-after. And you?'

'Me?'

'Have you found your happy-ever-after?'

'Of course. I'm perfectly content with my husband.'

Eve closes her eyes so she can't see Sully's expression, but even so she can sense him staring at her. *Content*. Such a half-hearted, mealy-mouthed sort of word.

And what is she doing here anyway? Tomorrow she must return to England. She has just one more day in this idyllic place, so why is she wasting the morning exchanging idle gossip with this forward American writer?

She gets to her feet.

'I'm just going to have a look around.'

She has a sudden flashback to the previous evening and Clemmie Atwood's comment about her totting up the house's contents. Will he think that's what she is doing? Oh dear.

She enters the house through the open glass doors of the sitting room, her shoes making a scudding noise on the polished parquet. She hopes she doesn't bump into Mrs Finch. Though she hasn't seen the friendly housekeeper since the previous day, she was taken aback to find breakfast laid out ready for her when she got up, as if Mrs Finch were tracking her movements through the house.

She considers sitting down on the chaise. Perhaps flicking through one of the magazines piled neatly on the low glass-topped table. But something stops her. A sense of trespassing where she has no right.

In the hallway she hesitates. Above her the polished banister curves upwards. Should she go up to her room? Lie on the bed looking out at the sky? But what a waste of her precious last day. How absurd to think it is only two days since she arrived, and no time at all until she must leave again. Bernard is coming this afternoon with more paperwork. She knows she must not sign anything. Clifford has told her. But still she is looking forward to seeing the French lawyer with his sympathetic eyes.

She walks around to the back of the staircase. Straight ahead is the corridor that leads to the kitchen and to Mrs Finch's domain. And to her left the doorway she'd noticed the day before. She glances around to make sure she is alone before turning the handle.

The door opens into darkness and Eve blinks as her eyes adjust. Eventually she realizes that she is standing at the top of a flight of stone steps, which descend into the gloom. She finds a switch to her left but the sickly yellow light that comes out of the single bulb hanging from the ceiling hardly extends beyond a few feet.

She picks her way down the stairs. The skin on her arms rises up into bumps as the damp air creeps into her bones. At the bottom of the staircase she finds herself in a small, cramped vestibule, with two closed wooden doors leading off it and a floor made up of grey stone slabs that appear almost black in the corners.

She should not be down here. The conviction strikes her as she shivers in her thin cotton blouse. Despite what is written in Guy Lester's will, this is not her house.

And yet, now that she is here, should she not take a look? *Too nosy for your own good*, says her mother's voice in her ear. Curiosity was frowned upon in their house. Resignation. That was the key. Not acceptance, even. Resignation.

She remembers Clemmie Atwood's suggestion that she and Noel Lester were brother and sister, that her mother and Guy Lester had . . .

She feels a warm rush of repugnance. *Impossible.*

Outrage strengthens her resolve and she pushes open the first door. A light switch on the near wall illuminates, as Mrs Finch had said, a small wine cellar lined with row upon row of wooden racks, most of which are empty, although there are a few bottles still dotted around.

I'll just pop down and fetch a bottle of wine from my cellar, Eve imagines herself saying to a table of dinner guests. The thought makes her smile.

The handle of the second door is so stiff that Eve imagines at first that it must be locked. She yanks it down and is dismayed when it comes off in her hand. She manages to slot it back in and has one last go, pulling the door towards her and thrusting the handle at the same time, as she has to do with the back door at home, and is rewarded as it grudgingly gives way. The cold hits her instantly and she pauses on the threshold. She fumbles around for a switch, stepping further into the gloom, but all she encounters is the cold damp stone of the wall.

She hears the door creak behind her and swings around.

'Mrs Forrester? Is that you?'

The rounded figure of Mrs Finch is silhouetted against the sickly light coming from the vestibule.

'Yes. Sorry. I opened the wrong door and thought I would see where it led.'

How ridiculous she sounds. Standing here, where she has no business.

'Oh, thank goodness for that. I thought we had company. Sometimes animals get in down here. Rats and squirrels. Even the occasional stray cat. We like to keep the doors closed to keep the damp smell out.'

'So you don't store anything down here?' Eve asks, peering into the gloom.

'Not really. Just odds and ends Mr Lester didn't want to throw out.'

Mrs Finch moves out of the doorway, allowing the thin light to penetrate further into the room. Eve makes out a shelf on the far wall with a few items on it. Tins of paint. An assortment of tools. Candles. Some crockery. And leaning against it, a collection of objects in various states of disrepair – a rusty bike, some ancient pipes, a stained ceramic sink.

'You must remember, Mrs Forrester, that during the war this house was taken over by enemy soldiers. Officers. First the fascists, then the Germans. It was left in a right old mess,

I'm afraid. As most of the houses were. Things broken or stolen. These people had no respect for property, no manners as we would know them. We only had the cracks in the swimming pool repaired earlier this year. This room is full of junk mostly. Things that were ruined. Every home along this coast will have a similar room, I imagine. Do you know, our neighbour even found an unexploded shell in the nursery?'

Eve finds herself nodding in the darkness. The reminder that everyone had their own war. Everyone suffered in their own way.

Back upstairs, Mrs Finch makes her excuses and bustles away into the kitchen.

Meanwhile, Eve, relieved to be warm once again, sits down in one of the armchairs in the sitting room and picks up a magazine with Gloria Hayes's face on the cover, her lips pouting into the camera lens. But she cannot settle. Her excursion to the cellar has disturbed her. She can still smell the sour dampness on her clothes. Her skin prickles at the memory of cold stone under her fingertips, the pallid waxiness of candles in the gloom.

She is glad when the front doorbell sounds. Seconds later Bernard appears in the doorway and she is so happy to see him, she has to hold herself back from throwing her arms around his neck.

Bernard asks her how she spent the previous evening and seems amused by her account of the reception for Gloria Hayes. 'I have lived here all my life but no invitation. But you have been here just one day and . . .'

He makes a gesture with his expressive hands that somehow conveys unfairness, amusement, irony and acceptance all in one.

'It is a pity you have to leave tomorrow,' he continues. 'A few more days and you would have conquered the Riviera.'

The reminder comes like a physical blow and she realizes she has been pushing the unwelcome thought of returning to England to the back of her mind.

'Noel Lester mentioned inheritance tax to me, Mr Gaillard. It's been on my mind ever since. I have not got . . . that is, my husband and I are not wealthy people.'

Bernard looks stricken.

'Please do not worry yourself, Mrs Forrester. I ought to have discussed this with you yesterday. I'm afraid I have let you down.'

'Oh no. Not at all.'

'The truth is, there will be a large inheritance payment due. And I'm very sorry to say that unless it transpires that you are related to Mr Lester, your own payment will be higher than the other three beneficiaries – perhaps even as much as sixty per cent of your share. However, you have a long time to pay it. Several years. During which time the house will be sold, giving you enough money to pay the tax and have a sizeable amount left over.'

Eve nods.

'I have here something for you. Mr Lester left it with me to look after – I think perhaps he worried about Mrs Lester's reaction if she came across it by chance. But I am quite sure he intended it for you. I would have given it to you yesterday but I thought the news of your inheritance was probably enough for you to digest in one day.'

'A gift? Oh, but I really don't think . . .' Eve tails off, transfixed by the small brown paper package in Bernard's hand.

'Not a gift, no,' says Bernard. 'A restoring of property. That is how Mr Lester spoke of it.'

Eve hesitates, imagining what the Lesters would say if they knew Guy had given her something else. But in the end curiosity wins out.

She unwraps the package slowly, trying to suppress her growing feeling of excitement.

Inside there is a smart green leather box, its corners sharp and new, with a French name printed in the centre, embossed in curling gold writing.

'The box is from a famous jeweller's shop in Nice,' says Bernard. 'But I believe it is entirely unconnected to the contents.'

Eve presses her lips together and pushes up the lid with unsteady fingers, revealing a red velvet cushion. Nestling on the cushion is a gold ring with a distinctive star-shaped green stone that Eve recognizes immediately.

That photograph. The only one she has ever seen of herself as a baby. The one that she found in the bottom of her mother's drawer where she shouldn't have been looking. *How dare you go rifling through my private things?* Only afterwards did it occur to her that this was her history too, but when she'd dared ask her mother again about the photograph, she was told it was lost. And though she'd searched and searched over the years, she'd never found it. But she remembered. A photographic studio clearly set up for a formal family portrait. Her mother's face as Eve had never seen it, soft with youth and laughter, a little blurred, as if she were in the act of turning her head towards her child's. Her own baby face unsmiling, her chubby body twisted towards her mother, who clasps her wriggling child with a strong arm around her middle, her fingers splayed out over the white lace-covered tummy. The ring clearly visible. The irregular shape that had drawn her attention.

'Does it mean something to you?' Bernard's voice is soft, hesitant. As if he worries about intruding.

'I recognize this ring,' Eve says. 'My mother was wearing it in a photograph I saw of myself as a baby.'

'Ah.'

Eve knows what that 'ah' means. So there is a connection between her mother and Guy Lester after all. And there is only one obvious connection that could be. Still Eve cannot believe it. Her mother, with her best clothes that she never wears locked away in a dark cupboard stinking of mothballs. With her frown line clogged with talcum powder. With her 'Don't expect and you won't be disappointed.' She can no sooner imagine a connection between her mother and this sun-soaked house with its charismatic owner than she can imagine being able to fly to the moon.

'I imagine you will have some questions for your mother when you arrive home,' says Bernard.

Eve nods. And yet she cannot envisage it. Walking into that house in Banbury. Sitting down on that hard mustard-coloured sofa with the loose covers her mother made from old sheets to keep the upholstery pristine for the visitors who never came. Asking her mother, *Tell me how you knew Guy Lester.* As if they had that kind of relationship, the kind where one could ask personal questions, and expect to be answered.

No. The more Eve thinks about it, the more certain she is she will find the answers here, in this house where the sun is painting golden stripes across the floor, and the only sound comes from the waves slapping against the wooden jetty far below and a lone bee trapped behind one of the glass panes in the sitting room.

She holds the ring in the palm of her hand, admiring how heavy it feels, how solid. When she angles it under the light in a certain way, she notices there is an inscription on the inside of the band. *From F with love eternal.*

F? Her father's name was Harry.

Perhaps there might have been a middle name, or a pet name, but she simply cannot imagine the quietly spoken, reserved man who shrugged in quiet sympathy behind her mother's back, but rarely spoke up for his daughter, feeling moved to have such an inscription made.

The ring slips on easily and as soon as she feels its reassuring weight on her middle finger, Eve is struck by a most surprising conviction.

She is not going home.

10

'WHAT DO YOU mean, you want to stay longer?' Clifford sounds impatient rather than angry. Certain this will turn out to be a misunderstanding.

'I need to find out who Guy Lester was to me. Why he left me a share in this house. If I come home now I may never learn the truth.'

'Don't be silly, Eve. It's all arranged. Three days in France – which is three days too long in my opinion – and then back on the train tomorrow. We'll get to the bottom of things once you're safely home. It seems clear the connection lies with your mother so the obvious thing is to go to Banbury together and ask her.'

'And if she won't tell me?'

'Then you will just have to accept that there are some things you will never understand. This is all past business, Eve. And to be frank, I'm of the opinion some secrets are best left buried. You come from a respectable family and I'm sure you wouldn't want anything to emerge to jeopardize that respectability. Isn't that right?'

When Eve doesn't reply, he takes her silence as acquiescence and his tone softens.

'My dear, I know this has been very unsettling for you. I can't think what this Guy Lester was about, stirring up all this drama in your life. All these questions. Mind you, I have been doing a little bit of digging around and from what I hear he was quite an unpredictable, maverick sort.'

'Digging around? You mean you've been checking up on him?'

'Of course. It would be highly irresponsible not to do so. I made a few calls. Spoke to some chaps I know. He came from a very wealthy family. Grandfather made a fortune out East. Eton, Cambridge. Trust fund on his twenty-first birthday. Good marriage. Acquitted himself well during the Great War. Promoted to Captain. Awarded the Military Cross and three bars for gallantry on the battlefield. Took up his position at the family firm once he was back home. So much, so straightforward. Perfectly good sort, one might think. But then listen to this. A year or so after the end of the war, something happens, though nobody seems to know what, and he suddenly ups sticks and moves his whole family to France. Never comes back. Never plays any further part in the family business. Sits out the last war in America. Florida, by all accounts.' Clifford says 'Florida' as if it is this detail that is the most unfathomable.

'So the picture emerging here is that Guy Lester appears to be quite a shady character. Wouldn't be at all surprised if there was something murky in his past. You don't hide yourself away all your life for no reason. Now, I understand your curiosity has been piqued, Eve. But the best thing is for you to come home and put this little interlude out of your head. Then as soon as the sale documents are prepared, I'll go down to the South of France myself and make all the necessary arrangements. Whatever little game Mr Lester has been playing is not going to work on us, I'm afraid.'

Eve is silent, listening to her breath echoing down the long-distance line. As the telephone at Villa La Perle was disconnected when the Lesters moved to Nice, Bernard has brought her here to this strange-looking hotel, the Belles Rives, teetering above the seafront on the approach to Juan-les-Pins, to place an international call to Clifford. Now she worries that the call will be costing a fortune, even though Bernard assured her, following a protracted conversation with the hotel concierge, that expenses would be covered by Guy's estate. He'd had to rush off for a meeting shortly afterwards but told her he would call round in the evening to find out what she'd decided to do about returning home.

Eve's unease at the notion of being subsidized by the Lesters is counterbalanced by her delight in the hotel, which has large pine-shaded terraces on different levels overlooking a narrow strip of private beach below and a wooden jetty that protrudes into the sea, on which several people are sitting in low-slung chairs, making the most of the early June sunshine. Across the bay a verdant island squats like a toad above the water.

In a corner of the reception area, Eve wedges the receiver of the phone between her chin and shoulder and holds out her right hand. The emerald changes in the light from bottle green to amber where the sun hits it. Each time Eve sees it, she is taken back to that photograph. Her mother laughing. Her strong hand gripping her baby daughter, keeping her safe.

'Eve? Are you still there?' Clifford's impatient voice interrupts her train of thought. 'Damn these infernal phone lines. Now, I won't be able to get to Victoria to meet you when you arrive, so you will have to take a taxi from Victoria to

Paddington. Make sure the driver takes you directly, mind. You don't want him driving around the houses, clocking up the meter. You'll feel a lot better once you're home and away from all this *fuss*.'

Eve glances again at her finger. At home, when Clifford adopts this lecturing tone, she quickly gives in, agreeing to whatever version of truth he is putting forward, just to get the whole thing over with. But now, separated by hundreds of miles, she finds herself curiously resistant.

'Nevertheless,' she tells him quite affably, 'I am not coming.'

The door to the terrace opens and a couple walk into the reception, he with a light-coloured hat, she with her hair pulled back tightly from her narrow, angular face.

Eve's heart gives a lurch of pleasure as recognition dawns.

'Oh!' she exclaims. 'Hello. How marvellous . . .'

'What the devil are you talking about?' Clifford demands. 'Is there someone else with you? What is going on?'

The Colletts, for it is they, are all smiles as they hurry over.

'My dear. We were so hoping we might run into you here.' Ruth's blue eyes sparkle with pleasure.

'Eve!' The telephone receiver has slipped from her ear so that Clifford's voice sounds tinny and small, like the far-off whine of a mosquito.

'I must go,' she tells him, signalling to the Colletts that they should wait for her. 'My friends are here.'

'Friends? You don't have any friends. Look here, Eve, I must insist—'

'I'll call you,' she tells him, 'when I've found out what I need to know. It's just for a few more days. Please don't worry about me, darling.'

She hasn't called him darling since the early days of their

marriage, but she is conscious of the watching Colletts and their possible expectations of how a married couple should behave towards one another.

'I'm sorry, Eve, but I cannot allow this. If it's answers you want I will try to find them for you, but I must insist you come—'

'Goodbye then, darling.' She keeps her tone light and her smile constant.

As she hangs up, she hears him shout out 'Wait!' but the scratchy little noise is cut short by the satisfying click of the receiver being returned to its cradle.

She feels a small flash of panic followed by a far greater surge of . . . what? Not power, certainly that would be too strong a word. Excitement perhaps. For the first time in her life she feels she has some agency. For the first time she is dictating events rather than responding to them.

But by the time she joins the Colletts, she is already regretting her impulsiveness. She ought to have made more of an effort to explain to Clifford how she felt. She ought to have been more conciliatory. He was only looking out for her best interests, wanting to be sure she was safe and not taken advantage of. She will write to him, she resolves. Tell him about the ring and the way it feels on her finger, the rightness of the weight of it, the immediate sense of connection she felt when she saw it. She will make him understand.

The Colletts insist on going back out on to the terrace for a celebratory cocktail in honour of this serendipitous meeting. Over peach Bellinis, which Eve has not tried before but declares immediately she will drink nothing but from this point forth, they tell her about their night in Marseille and then their trip to Fayence to see the spot where their son Leo came down.

'It was very lovely, very peaceful,' Ruth says. 'A field on a hillside surrounded by pines with a golden village in the distance and a lingering smell of lavender. You'll laugh, but I could hear his voice in my ear, clear as I'm hearing yours now, saying, "If it had to be anywhere, here isn't too bad, is it, Ma?"'

Now they want to know all about her mystery inheritance. Eve brings them up to speed, gratified by their reactions of shock and amazement.

'It's just like a novel,' Rupert says when she finishes. 'In fact, if you weren't married already this would be around the time for the handsome foreign prince to arrive and sweep you off your feet.'

An image of Victor Meunier's face comes into Eve's mind and she stifles a smile.

The Colletts are waiting for their younger son Jack to join them, fresh from researching his dissertation in Paris.

'Jack's the reason we booked this particular hotel,' Ruth explains in her nervous chatty way. 'Because the Fitzgeralds stayed here in the twenties and Jack is such an admirer of Fitzgerald. You have read him, I assume? *The Great Gatsby. The Beautiful and the Damned.*'

Eve shakes her head. She has heard of F. Scott Fitzgerald, of course, but most of her interest has been in his life, not his art. The marriage to the wife who went mad, the alcoholism. The early death.

'My dear, you must read him. He's so good about the futility of everything.'

'I'm not sure that sounds terribly uplifting,' says Rupert, smiling.

'Well, maybe not *everything*,' concedes Ruth. 'Just the

things that people think they most want. Money. Fame. Even love.'

'Well. *Love,*' says Rupert, as if that's all that needs to be said.

Eve wonders how it would have been to be brought up by the Colletts instead of her own parents. Who would she now be? What might she have made of her life? She imagines lively conversation around the dinner table. Art. Literature. Politics. There were no books in her own parents' house apart from a dinner-party cook book that her mother had been given but never used, owing to never giving dinner parties, and a set of encyclopaedias that her father had rashly bought from a door-to-door salesman. There were also some leather-bound volumes of Shakespeare's plays and sonnets with her mother's name inscribed on the inside cover in a schoolgirl's careful writing. But there was no sense of reading for pleasure. And if anyone ever tried to touch on politics at the table, her mother soon shut down the conversation. *This is a home, not a bar room, thank you very much.* As if debate were interchangeable with dissent. So mealtimes were largely silent. Some questions about how she was getting on at school that were answered with a simple yes or no. Some observations about the weather, or the difficulty of getting hold of various ingredients now that rationing had been tightened up. No *unpleasantness,* as her mother called anything that might involve a differing opinion from her own.

The Colletts want to know how Eve plans to proceed in her search for answers. Eve, whose earlier bravado on the phone has given way to a kind of low-level unease, feels a flare of panic as she admits she has no idea what happens next. Suddenly she sees how rash she has been, how little she has thought things through.

'Perhaps I ought to go home, after all,' she says. But they will not hear of it.

'Since the war I sometimes feel,' says Ruth, 'as if we who survived are morally bound to live fully because so many did not. Leo will never get to have the adventures he planned, so I must have them for him.'

They are interrupted by a waiter who tells them they have a guest, and before they have a chance to react, someone sweeps in from the hotel lobby in a great whirl of flapping raincoat and cigarette fug, and then Ruth is up on her feet with her arms around a slight, bespectacled young man whose pale skin is already pinkening in the Mediterranean sun.

'You should have told us!' she says. 'We would have—'

'No need,' he says, laughing. 'I hitched from Paris. It was all very straightforward. I said '*S'il vous plaît*' and '*Merci*' and nodded an awful lot, and that seemed to do the trick. Mind you, I nearly boiled alive in this coat. It's hotter than hell down here.'

Introductions aren't necessary, yet they are made anyway. Jack Collett eyes Eve with frank curiosity through his round, wire-framed glasses and then insists on a second tour around the hotel, so that he can recount the legends attached to the various different areas. 'Here's where Josephine Baker walked her pet cheetah.' And, 'Did you know, Zelda kept packed luggage in every room just in case she needed to make a quick getaway?' And, 'I say, do you think this could be the room where Scott locked that group of musicians, and wouldn't let them out until they'd spent the evening playing for him and Zelda?'

Back on the terrace, Jack declares himself delighted with everything – the elderly man in the old-fashioned striped bathing suit who stands in the sea below them up to his knees performing a sequence of slow squats, the fat bee buzzing in and out of the orange blossom, the sleek schooner that glides across the horizon. Eve, used to her mother's philosophy that good favour must be earned, and Clifford's that if you view everything with suspicion you're less likely to be taken advantage of, finds herself charmed by the unabashed joy with which Jack seems to view the world.

Jack is given a potted history of Eve's strange bequest.

'Oh, but this is wonderful,' he says. 'I must say, my parents are forever collecting waifs and strays, but they've outdone themselves with you.'

Eve assumes this to be a compliment, but is not entirely sure.

11

JACK INSISTS ON going to see Villa La Perle right away. 'If there are any clues to be found, that's the obvious place to start,' he says, dismissing Eve's concerns about how Mrs Finch and the Lesters will react to the idea of her bringing guests to the house as if she owns it. ('You do, don't you, in a way?')

The matter is decided when it is discovered that Eve would otherwise be walking home. What could be more natural than for them to give her a lift back to the villa in the borrowed car, arranged for them by an American officer friend of Leo's?

At the villa, Eve brings her guests around the side of the house so as not to disturb Mrs Finch. In her concern for the housekeeper, she has completely forgotten about Sully, and is at first perplexed when Ruth exclaims, 'Oh my!' until she follows her gaze to see the back of Sully's broad naked shoulders hunched over a typewriter at the bistro table on the bottom terrace.

More introductions are undertaken and Eve is relieved to see that Sully has a pair of short trousers on.

'Wait. You're Stanley Sullivan? *The* Stanley Sullivan?' Jack Collett has grown very still.

'Ah, glad to see some English people at least have an appreciation of good literature,' Sully says, glancing at her. He is trying to act mock severe, but Eve can see he is flattered.

'I have read everything you've written,' says Jack.

'In that case, you and I are going to get along very well.'

There follows an animated conversation about various of Sully's works, during which Sully appears almost shy as he references some lesser-known short stories, breaking into a huge smile when he realizes Jack has indeed read them. When Jack makes a comparison to Fitzgerald and mentions they are staying in the house where the Fitzgeralds stayed, Sully grows suddenly morose.

'I knew them, of course, Zelda and Scott,' he says. 'We met here originally and then back in California.'

'Oh!' Jack's hand is over his mouth. 'What were they like?'

'Utterly impossible. They craved attention, both of them, as if they would shrivel up without it. They were too fragile, do you see? They wanted to go around smashing things up, but in the end they were the ones who got broken.'

Jack gazes at Sully, enraptured, and Eve sees suddenly how young he is. Surely not more than twenty-two. The war has forced them all to grow up too quickly.

At their request, Eve takes the Colletts on a tour around the villa. In the dining room, Ruth stops in front of a photograph on the mantelpiece of Guy Lester with Diana and all three of his children.

'But surely those are the two men from the train?'

Eve nods, and explains the coincidence. She doesn't look at the photograph, has no wish to see Noel Lester's fierce green eyes.

'Well. This whole mystery suddenly got a whole lot more mysterious,' declares Rupert.

On the top floor, Eve points out the other bedrooms without opening the doors, still conscious of the strange position she occupies, neither guest nor proprietor.

When they reach her own bedroom she flings open the door with a flourish.

'Oh!' Eve stands in the doorway with her hand over her mouth.

'What is it?' Ruth asks her.

'Well, it's just that I keep getting this queer feeling someone has been in here while I was out. Someone other than me, I mean.'

Eve is trying to sound amused, but unease is snaking through her. She cannot put her finger on what is wrong, just a general sense of things being disturbed. Her eyes alight on the green leather box that the ring came in. Wasn't it in the centre of the dressing table before, not right on the far edge like that?

'I wouldn't worry about that,' Rupert tells her. 'Ruth is constantly informing me people have been in the house moving things around when really she just forgets where she puts everything.'

'You're probably right.' Eve tries to laugh.

At the bottom of the stairs, Eve leads the way around to the kitchen. As they pass the doorway down into the basement, Jack opens the door.

'We don't need to go down there,' Eve says quickly. 'It's just a wine cellar. Practically empty, I'm afraid.'

Mrs Finch materializes from her room behind the kitchen and claps her hands together in delight.

'More company. How lovely! This house has been so quiet recently, like a mausoleum, and now in one morning we've had visits from all sorts. It's been like Piccadilly Circus in here!'

'Visitors?' asks Eve. 'Who has—'

But her question is cut short by Mrs Finch, suggesting she make a big pot of tea. And even though Eve suspects the Colletts would far rather stick to cocktails, they all nod in appreciation.

Afterwards Sully suggests a trip to Garoupe beach. On the way there, he explains that the small strip of sand on the eastern side of Cap d'Antibes was the scene of many of the flamboyant gatherings organized by Sara and Gerald Murphy, an American couple who'd adopted the young Sully on his first trip to the Riviera as a penniless student.

'I went first to Paris, expecting to spend my days debating philosophy and drinking absinthe, but instead I stayed in a squalid little apartment which was always freezing, with a landlord who beat his wife, and I made no friends and was miserable, so I decided to head to Italy. But on the way I stopped off here in Antibes, just for a couple of nights, and ended up staying for five years. Sara and Gerald were like my surrogate parents. Their life was a constant party with so many famous guests. Not just Scott and Zelda but Hemingway, Dos Passos, Picasso too. You know Scott wrote *Tender is the Night* about them?'

He is addressing himself to Jack now, who nods fervently.

'Did they come back here after the war – the Murphys?' Ruth wants to know, but Sully shakes his bullish head.

'They lost two of their children to illness. After that I think the long days of sunshine and beach parties were over.'

Eve sees how Rupert puts his hand out to touch his wife's arm. Parents who have lost children. It is the saddest club of all.

'I went back to the States not long after they did. By that stage I'd written my first novel and wanted to find a publisher. I always knew I'd come back here, though. There is something about the light that pulls you in. And all the women in bikinis don't hurt either.'

Garoupe, being out of the way of both Antibes and Juan-les-Pins, is quieter than the other beaches Eve has so far glimpsed, the sand strewn with seaweed. At first she is disappointed in the meagreness of this mythical beach, having expected vast white sands, perhaps a smattering of palm trees, but then she follows the path climbing up the low cliff at the far end, and looks down through the crystal-clear water to the fish swimming in and out of the rocks at the bottom, and her nostrils fill up with the heady scent of a white-budded bush she has never seen before. She looks to the left, past the next rocky promontory where Villa La Perle sits hidden by trees, and sees strung across the bay the city of Nice, dazzling white in the afternoon sun, and beyond it the Maritime Alps, almost purple in the haze, while to the right, further along this winding path, the Aleppo pines tumble down over the red rocks towards the sea, and she feels a shifting inside herself, a sense of something slotting into place.

Suddenly she has an overwhelming desire to go into the sea, to feel the cool, clear water on her skin, to wash away her worries about Clifford and home and just be here in this moment in this beautiful place. What would they do, she wonders, if she launched herself off this rock into the water? What would they say? Does she dare?

She returns to the sand and, whipping off her shoes and

stockings, wades into the water, gasping at the freshness of it. Though the sun is deceptively hot, it is only the beginning of June, too early for the sea to be properly warmed through. She senses the hem of the old cotton dress she stuffed into her bag at the last minute – which she has been known to wear as a nightgown back home – growing sodden, even though she is holding it bunched in her left hand, but she does not care. It is glorious to be here, in this cold crisp water.

She turns her back to the sea, waving to the others, who are gathered in a little knot on the sand. Ruth stands and gestures to something behind her, but Eve cannot understand what she is saying until – *slap* – as if from nowhere a large wave breaks across her shoulders, dragging her completely under the surface of the water. She emerges spluttering, but laughing. And now she is so wet, she might as well stay here. She swims for a few moments out to sea, but the water is too cold, and she feels herself beginning to shiver.

'I am defeated!' she cries to the others, turning around to wade back to the shore. But, *oh*, now the small group has become larger, with four extra figures standing over the seated ones on the sand, as if forming some sort of tableau.

As Eve emerges, ungainly, from the sea, she is conscious of her soaking cotton dress clinging to her breasts and thighs, and plucks at the flimsy fabric to peel it off her skin.

'My goodness, I knew English fashions were lagging a little behind since the war, but is that really what passes for swimwear over there these days?'

Clemmie Atwood is wearing a white sundress with a pattern of yellow daisies. It has a tight-fitting bodice that shows off her bronzed shoulders and her neat waist.

Her fiancé leans into his brother, who is standing to his left, and whispers something in his ear. Noel nods and they both turn their faces towards Eve, watching with impassive expressions as she approaches. Only the fourth member of the group, a teenaged girl with freckles and strawberry blonde hair that has curled into damp ringlets around her face, is smiling.

'What a jolly good idea,' she says, bending down impatiently to unlace her tennis shoes. 'I was just thinking I wish I'd brought my cossie, and now I see I don't even need it!'

'Mrs Forrester. This is my sister, Libby,' says Noel Lester. 'She is very impressionable, as you can see.'

'If impressionable means I like going for swims in the sea with my clothes on, then I jolly well am.'

Libby, who appears a lot younger than her sixteen years, smiles at her older brother and Eve watches his face soften, making him look instantly younger and less sure of himself.

'Good idea, Lib, I'll race you in,' says Clemmie, suddenly changing her stance. She kicks off her sandals and makes a big production of running after Libby, hitching up her skirt to show her legs and throwing a glance behind as if to make sure her gay spontaneity is being observed.

She has no sense of herself, Eve sees suddenly, and the realization causes a slight mellowing towards the young woman. She of all people knows how it is to be constantly seeking an approval that never comes.

'Hold up, I'll come with you.' Jack Collett already has his shoes and socks off and is busy rolling his trousers up to the knee.

Clemmie doesn't seem enraptured to have an extra companion, but still she and Libby wait until Jack is ready before heading into the water.

'What a pleasant coincidence, us all ending up on the same beach,' Eve says, regretting her impromptu dip now that her wet dress feels so clammy and cold against her skin.

'Oh, it's no coincidence,' says Duncan Lester, watching his fiancée's retreating back with a thoughtful expression. He is wearing a white singlet and a huge straw hat that shades his face. He has sat down beside Sully, who now appears to be fast asleep.

'We made arrangements earlier on to meet up with this idle chap.' He prods the sleeping American with one of his pale toes. 'I have to say I didn't realize he'd be bringing half of Blighty with him.'

Eve drops to the sand, cradling her knees in her arms and feeling put out, not just by Duncan's scarcely disguised insult but also by the unsettling realization that plans have been made, meetings had, entirely without her involvement. Though, of course, there is no reason why this should not be so, the certainty that she herself would have formed the main topic of conversation on such occasions gives Eve a jittery feeling.

'So, Mrs Forrester. Eve. I hope you've enjoyed your stay here in paradise,' Duncan continues. He seems more relaxed today, less hostile. 'You'll know, I'm sure, that Somerset Maugham, that cantankerous old git, called the Riviera a sunny place for shady people, but that's exactly why we like it. When will your husband be coming over to make the arrangements for the sale?'

Eve resents being put on the spot. Whenever she thinks back to that conversation with Clifford, a feeling akin to nausea rises up inside her.

'Actually, we've persuaded Eve to stay on here a few days and keep us company,' says Ruth.

'Some might say persuaded,' says Rupert. 'Others might prefer the word "forced".'

Eve feels a rush of gratitude to the Colletts for saving her from having to break the news about her change of plans herself.

Duncan doesn't look thrilled.

'The thing is,' he says, 'the sooner we get on with the business of selling Villa La Perle, the better. There are matters that need to be settled. Death duties. Taxes. That sort of thing.'

'But there's time for all that,' Eve says. 'Bernard told me. And he said your father left an account to cover immediate expenses.'

'That won't be enough.' Duncan scowls and Eve is struck by how quickly and easily his face swings from pleasant to downright ugly according to his moods. 'See, I just don't think this is right,' he continues, turning to his brother, who is squatting down on his haunches next to Rupert, his face resting on his hands, his loose white shirt rolled up to the elbows revealing tanned arms with a fuzz of golden hair. 'Why does *she*' – a nod in Eve's direction – 'get to know everything about our private family affairs?'

'Because, for whatever reason, our father wanted it that way.'

The conversation is taking place right in front of Eve and yet she might as well not be there at all. Their rudeness makes her rash.

'And that's another reason I'm not going back to England straight away.' She hugs her arms tighter around her knees so they won't see her shivering and avoids looking at Noel, remembering the weight of his jacket around her shoulders. 'Your father had a reason for doing all this. For inviting me here. For leaving me a share in the house. This morning

I received a ring he'd intended me to have. This ring.' She holds out a mottled blue-ish hand.

Duncan peers at it through narrowed eyes.

'If that's something that used to belong to my mother, Guy had no right—'

'Not your mother, but mine,' Eve says quickly. 'I remember her wearing it in a photograph from when I was a baby but I haven't seen it since. I need to know what it all means.'

'So go home and ask your mummy,' says Duncan, still squinting suspiciously at the ring. 'That's the most obvious thing. Though whether she'll tell you the truth kind of depends upon how compromising it is, wouldn't you think?'

Ruth hands Eve the blanket they have brought to sit on, and she wraps it gratefully around her shoulders. How can she explain to all these people she hardly knows the relationship she has with her mother? Could they understand how it is possible to live with someone for more than a quarter of a century and for them to remain an entirely closed book? How personal information – memories, favourite songs, likes, dislikes, hopes, dreams – can become something shameful, to be hidden away out of sight. No, the impossibility of asking such questions is something she cannot begin to convey to those who did not grow up in a house like hers.

'On the contrary, I think the answers will lie here. Where Guy Lester lived. I'm sure of it.'

There is a spray of cold water as Clemmie wades out from the sea, kicking a shapely leg as she does. The hem of her dress is dripping. Libby skips behind her, clothes and hair soaked.

'You should come in!' cries Clemmie, spraying them all again. 'It's wonderfully refreshing. How about it, Noel? Or are you too chicken?'

Noel wipes the water off his face irritably and stands up, stretching out his legs one at a time.

'Come on, Libs, we should get you home. You're drenched.'

'I am as wet as the wettest thing,' agrees Libby, and Eve sees suddenly that she is not like other teenagers. There is something childlike about her, something not quite finished. As if she became stuck somewhere in the act of growing up.

They get themselves ready to go, and for a moment Eve thinks Noel will leave without ever having properly acknowledged her existence. Then at the last minute he turns to her.

'My father had a friend who lives in Cap Ferrat. Robin Whelan. Well, not really a friend. A contemporary from university. He knew him for decades, both back in England and out here. They weren't close, but if you wanted to talk to someone who might know if there are any skeletons in his past, Whelan might be a good place to start.'

Eve is taken aback, though whether by the information being offered or the person doing the offering, she couldn't have said.

'How will I find him?'

Noel glances away and then back again. And finally he is looking at her properly.

'I'll take you. Tomorrow.'

It isn't a question. There is no space for her to tell him it isn't convenient or that she has other plans.

'Well,' Ruth says as they watch the Lesters walking away, with Clemmie between them in her daisy-print dress like an exotic bloom between two dark stems, Libby dancing ahead. 'They might have money, but their manners leave much to be desired.'

12

4 June 1948

NOEL PICKS HER up in a gleaming black convertible sports car with a chrome grille on the front that makes it look like it is baring its teeth.

'Triumph Roadster,' he tells her proudly, running a hand over its bonnet. 'Hardly any of these around. I brought it down here to sell but couldn't bear to part with it.'

'It's lovely,' says Eve politely, but she can't help adding, 'Don't you think it's ironic, though, that Britain makes all these beautiful cars to sell abroad, while at home we'd have to wait years to get our hands on something like this?'

It is something her mother might have said, and Eve is instantly ashamed. Why can't she be more like Jack Collett, taking unconditional delight in beautiful things?

Noel's face closes like a fist.

'I'm sorry you don't approve.'

In the car, Eve settles miserably into her seat. She has hardly slept. First she'd lain awake worrying about that strange feeling she has had twice now, that someone has been in her room, disturbing her things. At one stage she'd resolved to ask Sully if Mrs Finch ever went into his room while he wasn't there, before it occurred to her that it might just as well be Sully himself. What did she really know about him, after all?

After that she had moved on to fretting about Clifford, wondering whether he might also be lying awake worrying about *her*, or conversely seething with anger. Abandoning all hope of sleep, she'd lain there fiddling with the ring on her finger, feeling the unfamiliar shape of it, those two words, *love eternal*, burning through the metal into her skin.

Could her mother have had a passionate relationship with Guy Lester that explained him coming into possession of her ring? Might the initial 'F' be some sort of code between them, an abbreviation of a name no one else would understand? One of the girls she had worked with in the WVS had been seeing an American soldier who always called her Rose, short for English Rose, while she had called him Jimmy because he reminded her of Jimmy Stewart – as if these made-up identities sealed them into a fantasy bubble, separate from the real world in which her husband languished in a POW camp in Burma, while Jimmy's wife and four children waited for him at home in Missouri.

Yet no matter how Eve tried to convince herself that this was the obvious explanation, she came up against the brick wall of her own certainty that it could not be right.

As a consequence of her wakeful night she now feels out of sorts and unable to think straight, watching the road in front of them with dulled eyes.

'Don't feel obliged to make conversation on my account,' says Noel after they have driven for five minutes in complete silence.

'I'm sorry if you don't find my company sufficiently entertaining,' she says.

He glances over, then turns his attention back to the road. They are driving along the seafront at Nice, with the sea to their right and to their left a series of grand white buildings with ornate balconies.

'The Promenade des Anglais. Surely you have heard of it?' says Noel, seeing her blank look.

Eve shrugs. She has not heard of it.

'What's that?' She is pointing out to sea where rows of dark metal pylons rise up from the water.

'That used to be the Palais de la Jetée. A casino built on a pier. So beautiful. You've never seen anything like it. The Germans dismantled it for the metal. Copper. Brass. Bronze. Steel. Left it like that.'

There is something shameful about the bare, desecrated stumps reaching up from the waves to clutch at nothing but thin air, and Eve looks away. The way Noel emphasizes the word 'Germans' seems to speak of some deep personal bitterness beyond the general attitude of resigned enmity. She recalls what Sully said about Noel flying all those missions during the war. Who knows how many friends he might have lost? There is no set pattern for grief.

Noel heads out of Nice along the coastal Corniche, which he tersely explains is the lower of the three winding roads that cling to this part of the coastline. Glancing up to the left, where a sheer cliff rises up into the cloudless sky, she sees the tell-tale gap where the middle road must be, and way above that, almost in the heavens, the faint scar of the highest Corniche. A stone village rises up from the topmost peak as if it is growing out of the rocky cliff itself.

If it wasn't for her companion's ill temper and her own nervousness, she would be relishing the dramatic scenery – on one side the vertiginous hillside, part forested, part sheer rock, and on the other the Mediterranean, turquoise and white-flecked as it probes its way into the inlets and tiny coves and beaches and harbours of the meandering coastline.

'How well do you know Victor Meunier?' she asks, before she is even properly aware that the art dealer is on her mind. Immediately she regrets having raised the subject. She had wanted only to make conversation, but now he will wonder about her interest.

Noel turns to her, but she glances away to hide her flaming cheeks as if engrossed in the passing scenery.

'I hardly know the man. Sorry to disappoint you.'

His tone is sharp and Eve thinks it is unsurprising that he and the softly spoken Frenchman should have little in common.

For the next ten minutes neither speaks. The tension between them builds until Eve cannot bear it.

'Tell me more about the man we're going to see.' It is the first thing she can think of to break the oppressive silence.

'Robin Whelan? There's not much to say as I met him only once or twice a long time ago. He and my father shared digs for a short while at university in Cambridge, but I think it was a question of convenience rather than because they were particularly close. After they left, Whelan wrote a scandalous and enormously successful novel about the adventures of a gilded but ultimately rather callow undergraduate, who was widely assumed to be based on my father. I don't know if they ever spoke again, even after Whelan moved here in the mid-thirties.'

'But surely their paths must have crossed? The Riviera is not such a big place, after all.'

'They moved in very different circles. Whelan has a reputation for being antisocial and waspish and I don't think he's endeared himself to the society hostesses along the coast. The few occasions they ran into each other, I think they managed to be civil, but I don't suppose there were many pleasantries exchanged. My father was a very charming man – much more so than either of his sons, I'm afraid – but he didn't suffer fools gladly.'

Eve is surprised to hear the arrogant Noel Lester admit so freely to a character flaw. Every time she thinks she has him neatly boxed up, he says or does something that forces her to revise her assessment.

'So why did Robin Whelan agree to meet us when you telephoned him last night?'

Noel shrugs. 'Curiosity, I presume. He's a writer, isn't he? Aren't they supposed to be fascinated by mysteries and intrigue?'

Whelan lives on Cap Ferrat, a pine-clad peninsula that juts out into the sea between Nice and Monaco further along the coast. More elevated and dramatic than Cap d'Antibes, the ambience here also feels different. Muffled. There is a sense of stillness and calm, the windy roads semi-deserted, the tiled roofs of enormous villas just visible above the gates and walls that preserve their privacy.

'It's spectacular, isn't it?' says Eve.

Noel makes a snorting noise. 'It's deathly. Everyone in their luxury homes behind their high gates. Living here would be like being slowly suffocated with a mink pillow.'

While he stops the car to consult a map he keeps in the glove compartment, Eve gazes out of her window where a gap between two walled villas reveals a view of the navy blue Mediterranean far below them and in the distance a dark green shape rising up out of the water. She wants to ask Noel if this is Cap d'Antibes, but won't risk showing her ignorance if it turns out to be something else entirely.

Finally they pull up outside a pair of sleek black gates set into a sheer white wall. Eve prepares to get out to look for a bell, but before she even has her hand on the chrome handle, the gates swing open as if the house has been waiting for them.

Noel turns to her, his eyebrows raised. When he smiles it's as if he is a different person entirely and Eve finds herself feeling once again wrong-footed by him.

A long drive lined with palm trees takes them through gardens of exotic plants, many of which Eve has never seen before. There are cacti as fat as pillar boxes that rise into the air almost as high as the palms, and others with three prongs like enormous spiked forks.

The house reveals itself initially as a smooth white wall rising steeply up, the white line of its clean flat roof dazzling against the sky. Eve is shocked by the brutality of this one eyeless wall. But as they park the car and walk around the building, she realizes that this is the side of the house and that the front curves in a wave of white stucco and glass, almost like the prow of a ship. Following the shape of the curve is a decked terrace with a swimming pool cut into it. There are no chairs outside, no umbrellas. Nothing to spoil the stark lines of the house.

Eve has never seen a building like this. So much unbroken whiteness and glass. But while she can see it is objectively beautiful, it leaves her feeling strangely cold. This is not a home, like Villa La Perle is a home. Living here would be like living inside a priceless work of art that you could admire but not love.

'You've come to the wrong side.'

The voice is high-pitched and sharp.

Eve turns and sees a small, childlike man dressed entirely in bone-coloured linen standing with his arms folded by the wall around which they have just walked.

'This is clearly the back. The front is the other way.'

'So sorry,' says Eve and starts hurrying back towards him, but he holds up a hand.

'You're here now, so we might as well go in this way.'

Robin Whelan turns and leads them across the terrace and into the house through a metal-framed glass door. Inside, everything is open, with shafts of sunlight slanting across the space from all the high-level windows, cutting across floors made of black waxed stone.

They follow him to a sunken level dominated by a white marble fireplace, where two long black leather sofas face each other across a low glass-topped table.

'Sit.'

Whelan gestures to the nearest sofa before positioning himself in the one facing it. In all this time he has not once shaken their hands or asked for introductions.

Now that she has a chance to examine him properly, Eve can see that he must be getting on for sixty, but with that babyish look some men acquire in later age. He has yellow hair of a shade that cannot be natural and a round, sun-tanned face with flat features. His eyes are strangely colourless and they fix upon Noel with a kind of greedy intensity.

'I can see the resemblance,' he says, unsmiling.

Next to Eve, Noel clears his throat. There are at least two feet of black sofa between them; nevertheless she can sense the tension in his body, the way he is holding himself stiffly upright, rather than sinking down into the leather.

'As I told you on the telephone last night, my father, Guy Lester, recently died and we – that is, Mrs Forrester here and I – were hoping you might be able to answer some questions we have about his early life.'

Whelan sits back and hooks one of his short legs over the knee of the other. He is wearing a cream silk cravat and his tiny feet are shod in what must surely be custom-made shoes of soft white leather.

'As I told you, Mr Lester, your father took *issue* with some things I wrote in my first book. He was a man used to being the centre of attention and he became convinced the book was about him. Nothing I could say would convince him otherwise. So we weren't exactly *intimate* over the last few decades.'

Whelan lingers over the word 'intimate', lifting one of his small, pudgy hands to smooth back his hair. From the corner of her eye, Eve sees Noel dig his own fingers into his leg, the ridge of his knuckles pale and taut.

'We're actually interested in the period before that,' she says, trying to move the conversation on, 'while Guy Lester was still living in England with his young family. There are reports that something happened that caused him to leave the country very suddenly. We were hoping that might be something you could shed some light on.'

Now, finally, Robin Whelan turns his pale, colourless eyes to her. She feels them travel over her. She is wearing her brown skirt with her yellow blouse and she sees them through his eyes. The clothes of a woman who has gone uncomplimented for a long time.

'So this is the cat who has been set amongst the Lester pigeons.' He raises his eyebrows, which are so perfectly arched Eve suspects they must be plucked. His smile does not travel to his eyes, which remain coolly fixed on her. 'I have to hand it to Guy, I had no idea he had such a gift for melodrama. All this cloak-and-dagger mystery. Maybe he is the one who ought to have been writing fiction.'

Eve swallows. They have not been offered even a glass of water since they arrived and she is suddenly conscious of being thirsty.

'You're wondering if the key to the mystery lies in Guy's past. A scandalous affair, perhaps, that might have produced this young lady and had him banished from the land? Is your mother perchance a member of the royal family, my dear? Someone whose compromising would have been of sufficient import to get a wealthy, well-connected young man exiled from his life?'

Eve pictures her mother sitting in silence in her front parlour on the sofa with its cover to protect it from dirt, her dark brown hair curled and set tight by the hard rollers she sleeps in at night. Her clothes are blue or brown or occasionally beige, and always with a high neck constricting her throat. She rarely reads or listens to the radio, and does not keep a journal, or knit, or undertake any of the activities with which other women in her situation keep themselves busy. Instead she looks out of the window at the street, waiting for her daughter to return from school or work, fermenting the day's grievances – a breakfast bowl left unwashed or a ladder discovered in a stocking left drying over the bath. Or something not to do with Eve at all – a perceived slight from the woman who works in the post office, the crying of a neighbour's baby that kept her awake all night so that now her nerves are shredded. All this is channelled while Eve's mother sits unmoving, no outside distraction permitted to dilute it, so that when Eve comes through the door, the power of her mother's discontent comes funnelling to meet her.

'She wasn't always so hard to please,' Eve's father whispered to her once, coming to find her in her bedroom where she'd been banished after some misdemeanour. 'She had a disappointment in her youth that affected her badly. Changed something in the balance of her. You know.'

But Eve didn't know. Couldn't remember a time before. When her mother's balance was different.

'No, my mother is not royalty,' she tells Robin Whelan, enjoying how icy her voice sounds here in this cold house. But then she spoils the effect by adding, 'And besides, she would never . . . That is, she is not the kind of person . . .'

Whelan is watching her with a new alertness and she has the sensation of being absorbed by him, perhaps to be regurgitated in the pages of his next novel.

'Look, can you help us or not?' The well of Noel's politeness has, it seems, run dry.

Whelan reaches into his jacket pocket and brings out a slim, silver cigarette box, from which he extracts a long cigarette and a lighter. He does not offer either to his guests.

'How well did you know your father, Mr Lester?' He leans back against the black leather cushion and inhales deeply from his cigarette.

'What do you mean?'

'I mean what kind of relationship did you have with him? Were you close? Buddies, as our American friends might say? Did you play golf together and share confidences? Or was he one of those forbidding sorts of papas who set impossible standards and criticize your attempts to attain them? I suspect the former. Guy had a decent enough intellect and a certain drive to succeed, but he was held back by his insatiable need to be liked, for people to think he was a good fellow. He could never bear for anyone to have a bad word to say about him. That's a tremendous handicap in life, I think.'

He flicks ash into a silver ashtray on the glass-topped table. His eyes have not left Noel.

'We had our arguments over the years, our ups and downs,' Noel replies eventually. 'But we got on pretty well overall. We respected each other.'

'How very heart-warming. But then I suppose you are the same type, you and he. Heroic war records and all that sort of derring-do. Guy was a very lucky man, though of course I always knew he would be. He had that sort of charmed life. Well, except for . . .'

Whelan breaks off to take another drag of his cigarette and Eve waits, impatient, for him to resume, but instead he stays silent, surveying them both with his dishcloth eyes.

She understands that he is waiting for them to beg and plead. He wishes to orchestrate the conversation, to manipulate their reactions. She resolves not to give him the satisfaction.

But, of course, she cannot stay quiet.

'Except for?' she queries, regretting her interjection even while she is making it. *Where is your self-control, Eve?* asks her mother's voice in her ear.

'Except for whatever catastrophic event happened to cause him to flee the country, never to return.'

He does not know. All of a sudden it seems clear he is only stringing them along for his own gratification.

Evidently Noel has reached the same conclusion.

'Well, if you have nothing to add, we won't waste any more of your time, Mr Whelan.'

He has a way of speaking that can imbue even words that seem perfectly appropriate and polite on the surface with an undercurrent of rudeness.

Noel gets up, causing the sofa cushion to spring up underneath Eve.

Whelan watches him through narrowed eyes, as if weighing up his desire to continue toying with them against whatever concession he will need to make to keep them here. Eve suspects he is enjoying their discomfort and his own power too much to want them to leave.

'I don't know what happened to your father, it's true,' he says at last. 'We were not much in contact after my book came out, as I've said. However, there were certain rumours flying around at the time. Unproven, of course.'

Noel sits back down. Together they stare at Robin Whelan across the table, through the fug of cigarette smoke that swirls around his head.

'We understand that,' says Eve, trying to keep the excitement from her voice. 'Nevertheless we should like to hear them.'

'Well,' says Whelan eventually, his flat features coming into focus once again, eyes fixed on Noel. 'The way I understand it, your father had to leave the country because he'd broken the law. There was a court martial. All very hush-hush. I think he might even have served some time in prison.

Good heavens, one hates to think what might have happened to him in there, a handsome man like that. But if he did, it wasn't for more than a few months. Your grandfather was a very generous donor to Lloyd George's lot, don't forget. After that he had to make himself scarce. You and your brother were very small then. And from what I heard, your poor mother never really got over having to leave everything she knew behind.'

'Broken the law?' says Noel sharply, and Eve knows without needing to ask that he is relieved that this might not, after all, turn out to be about some tawdry love affair. 'What was this crime? Something to do with gambling? It would not surprise me. My younger brother has inherited that particular family gene. Not embezzlement, surely, although he did give up his role in the family business rather suddenly.'

'Cold, cold, cold,' says Whelan in a sing-song voice. His mouth twitches at the corners.

'Well, what then?' Noel has lost his patience. His voice carries the low rumble of anger.

Whelan rests his cigarette on the lip of the ashtray, adjusts the knot of his cravat with dainty fingers. Only when he is quite satisfied does he sit back, his gaze flicking from one to the other, giving Eve the unpleasant sensation of being studied, like a butterfly pinned to a board.

'He murdered someone.'

13

THE JOURNEY BACK to Antibes is undertaken in almost unbroken silence as they each try to digest what they have just heard, so Eve is surprised when Noel parks the car at Villa La Perle instead of merely dropping her off as she'd expected.

They find Sully on the lower terrace. He has brought his typewriter out and is sitting at the table under the eucalyptus tree. As they walk over, he tears a piece of paper from the machine and crumples it in his hand.

'You are a piece of shit,' he tells it.

'I don't suppose it thinks much of you either,' says Noel, startling the American, who had thought himself entirely alone.

'Tell me everything,' he says once he has recovered. He turns his chair around and draws up two more for her and Noel, so close that they are all sitting knee to knee, then lights up a cigarette and leans in. 'So, how was that snake, Whelan? Did you have to pick your way over that black floor of his to avoid stepping on dried-up coils of his shed skin? I expect he said something about me with that forked tongue of his. I hope you mentioned Hitchcock has just bought my last book. It's been so long since Robin Whelan last delivered something worth publishing, he probably gave it to his editor in scroll form.'

They fill Sully in on the strange conversation they had in Whelan's cool mausoleum of a house on Cap Ferrat. For once the American seems lost for words.

'Murder? Guy?' Then: 'Do you believe it? I wouldn't put it past Whelan to make something like that up just to get a reaction from you.'

Noel shrugs. He has been inside to raid the bar and is busy pouring gin into three tall glasses, which he tops with a grudging splash of tonic. A persistent fly buzzes around his hand as he pours and he flicks out his fingers.

'I definitely had the impression Whelan got a thrill out of telling me,' he says, pressing a drink into Eve's hand, ignoring her attempts to decline. 'Which makes me believe there must be some truth in it. But I just can't believe Guy would ever have killed anyone deliberately. Not in peacetime, anyway. And surely a rich daddy wouldn't get him off a murder charge, no matter how much money he'd poured into the coffers of the powers that be? But then again, it has to be something pretty damned bad for Guy to have moved us all out of the country and then stayed away for so long.'

'And do you think this could have something to do with him leaving you a share in the house?' Sully asks Eve.

'I don't know,' Eve says, making a face as the gin burns the back of her throat. 'It has thrown up more questions than it has answered.'

The shrill of the doorbell sounds from the house, setting the long, drooping eucalyptus leaves trembling overhead.

Eve looks at Sully, who shakes his head in a 'no idea' way.

They hear voices coming from inside the house. The sound of heels clicking on the stairs.

Mrs Finch appears in the doorway in a gaudily patterned wrap dress, two spots of colour in her cheeks. 'You have a visitor, Mr Sullivan,' she says, flustered.

She steps aside to reveal Gloria Hayes standing behind her, wearing high-waisted navy blue shorts that cling to her bottom and an off-the-shoulder blouse. She has a spotted bandana holding back her thick, red hair and white sandals with a substantial heel.

'Mr Sullivan, I am sorry to say you are quite the hardest man to track down. I've had to turn into a regular Hercule Poirot.'

In her lilting southern accent, she pronounces it *Hurcle Poro*.

Unlike the first time Eve saw her, the film star does not appear glassy-eyed as if in some kind of narcotic daze. Instead her skin is soft and glowing in shades of pink and peach and her teeth are perfectly white against her glistening lips. The garden is already rich with jasmine and juniper, but Gloria brings her own scent of something ripe and powerful and ready to burst. Noel and Sully cannot take their eyes off her. Mrs Finch too seems reluctant to leave her vicinity, hovering expectantly, drinking up their visitor like an exotic cocktail.

'Shall I fetch you some tea, Miss Hayes?'

'Oh my goodness, honey, I think I shall be needing something a whole lot stronger than tea.'

Noel leaps to his feet and shows her the gin bottle.

'Now that is more like it.'

Gloria has come to invite Sully to the wedding. And now

she has met Noel and Eve, they simply must come too. She seems delighted when she discovers Noel is already invited, along with his family.

'I shall need reinforcements,' she tells them. 'There are precious few people in my corner.'

She sounds genuinely wistful and Eve almost feels sorry for her. Then she remembers that this is a film star who is about to marry a man with his own plane.

'Are y'all friends with him?' Gloria wants to know now. 'Laurent, I mean?'

Noel and Sully admit they hardly know him at all and Gloria frowns.

'Well now, isn't that a shame. I was hoping you might fill in a few gaps for me. I hardly know him myself.'

There's something hypnotic about the way Gloria talks that invests everything she says with the quality of a performance being put on purely for the benefit of the listener. No wonder Noel and Sully are so enraptured. Eve wonders how it would be to have so much power. When she was a teenager, she briefly had a friend, Nina, who was like this, effortlessly holding court, the classroom falling silent when she opened her mouth for fear of missing something. Eve had held out at first when Nina asked to come round to her house, but you couldn't say no to Nina for long. Eve's mother hadn't even tried to disguise her dislike. And the funny thing was that the frostier she was, the more charming Nina tried to be, as if Eve's mum were a challenge she needed to rise to. And the more charming she was, the tighter Eve's mother pressed her lips together and the deeper the groove became down the bridge of her nose. 'People like that,' she said to Eve after Nina had gone. '*Females* like that. They're like siphons draining the light from other people. Covering themselves in it.' After that Nina was never the same with Eve and their friendship faltered.

A chair is brought for Gloria, wicker with a padded canvas seat and a cushion made of a rose-printed fabric. The actress doesn't so much sit in as inhabit the chair, as though it is part of her body, her long legs draped over one arm, a neat brown elbow hooked over the back. She throws back the gin Noel has poured her as if it is a glass of water, and he immediately springs up to refresh it.

'My, but you're so pretty,' Gloria says suddenly.

Eve is horrified to find the American looking straight at her.

'Y'all have that tiny bitty frame and those delicate bones like a little bird, while I am this big ungainly creature.'

She holds up one of her endless legs as if to demonstrate her ungainliness.

'Hardly,' says Eve. She knows herself to be blushing, and looks away furiously towards the sea, calm now like a deep blue mirror.

'Y'all will come though, to the wedding?' Once again Gloria sounds apprehensive. Like a child craving her parents' attendance on the first day of school. 'I don't have much in the way of family. Of course, the studio head will be there and some of the other stars they think will benefit from the extra press attention – talentless though they almost certainly are – but I should so love to have some friends there. I can call y'all friends, can't I, even though we just met? Eve, can I count on you?'

'Oh. Well. You know, I have no idea how long I shall be staying. And of course I have nothing at all to wear.'

'Well, the second part is easy. I have trunks and trunks of clothes. I'm sure you'll find something there. I can have someone alter them to fit your dainty little person or you'll just be *swamped*. You could clear fit five of you into just one of me.'

By now Eve is feeling the effects of the gin she has been sipping. Her muscles feel relaxed in the sun, her mood lightened. *Here I am*, she thinks, *drinking cocktails in France with a Hollywood star.*

Eve is lost in her own thoughts when, somewhere around her third or fourth gin, Gloria mentions Victor Meunier.

'Do y'all know him? He's just about the most debonair man I ever saw. Laurent and he are thick as thieves. They are always disappearing into rooms to talk and drink.'

Eve keeps her face averted as if she is hardly listening, but she can sense Noel's eyes on her as if checking for a reaction to the Frenchman's name.

'While they're gone I just kick around that place on my own,' Gloria continues. 'It can get kind of lonely, you know? I was spending time in the kitchen with the cook, who always says things to make me laugh, but Laurent, he doesn't much care for that. He says it's not how it's done here and anyway he wants me all to himself. So I don't go down there so much any more, which is a shame because that cook kind of reminded me of my mama. You know that's what she was too. A cook.'

Eve finds herself again in the strange position of feeling sorry for Gloria Hayes.

Sully, who has been uncharacteristically quiet since their visitor's unexpected arrival, now leans forward, as if having just this moment made up his mind about something.

'Tell me, do you love him?' he asks.

Gloria, caught with her glass to her lips, freezes.

'Well I'm marrying him, aren't I?'

'What's that got to do with it?'

She pauses, considering. 'That's a fair point, Mr Sullivan. However, I do of course love Laurent. I mean, he swept me off of my feet completely.'

'Plus your studio head thinks it will get you headlines all over the world, which doesn't hurt.'

Now Gloria is preparing to leave, unfolding her legs like a paper doll.

'I just came to invite you to a wedding, Mr Sullivan. I didn't come to listen to—'

'He didn't mean anything.' Noel is on his feet. He doesn't want their guest to leave, Eve realizes.

'It's quite all right, Mr Lester. I know he didn't. But I have delivered my invitation now so it's time to get back. Laurent worries when I'm away too long.'

She is swaying on her feet in her high heels, and Eve hopes there is a driver waiting upstairs in the car with his feet up on the dashboard and the windows open to let in the breeze.

After Gloria has gone, the three of them sit in silence. Without her, the day seems suddenly not quite so bright, the distinctive honey-and-almond smell of the mimosa not quite so sweet.

'Why the hell must you always stir things up, Sullivan?' demands Noel at last. 'God knows I have little time for Laurent Martin, but why on earth would Gloria Hayes be getting married if not for love?'

'Because, despite all their airs and their money and their great booming confidence, women like her ultimately do what they're told.'

Eve has never heard Sully sound so bitter. She looks at him sharply, but he is hunched once again over his type-writer, feeding in a sheet of paper.

The gin Eve has drunk no longer makes her feel light and gay, but as if her brain has been coated in fur. She can't stop thinking about Robin Whelan and what he'd said about Guy being a murderer. Could it be true? And if so, might it really turn out to have something to do with her?

She slides the ring off her finger and holds it up to the light so that she can read the inscription on the inside. *From F with love eternal.* Then she thinks about Gloria marrying a man she hardly knows and already lonely even before the wedding, not realizing perhaps how marriage can be a life-time of loneliness.

She needs a lie-down, and hauls herself to standing. Noel watches her leave without a word. As she climbs the stairs, her feet suddenly feeling as if they have heavy weights attached, there is a prolonged silence from outside and she forms the uncomfortable notion that the two men are waiting for her to be out of earshot before they resume their conversation.

Guy, 26 April 1948

I HATE HOW she looks at me. As if I am a piece of mud that someone trailed through the house on the sole of their shoe.

'If you've come to assuage your conscience, I'm afraid you've come to the wrong place. I'm not in the business of handing out absolution.'

'No, not at all. I just want to see Eve, now that she is an adult, to ask if there's something more I can do to help her.'

Of course, she's right. I *do* want absolution. I want to make this woman see I am worth more than the worst thing I ever did. I turn my head, feeling a coughing fit coming on, and quickly pocket the handkerchief before she can see the blood.

We are in a small room at the front of the house, sitting on furniture that is covered in dust sheets. I get the impression that these covers have been on so long, waiting for guests to appear, that by the time of my arrival, the woman has forgotten what they were there for in the first place. Forgotten there is perfectly good furniture underneath.

Being back in England is so strange. The dreary poverty of it. Everything grey and brown. Meat still rationed.

Restaurant portions so frugal you're hungry again an hour after eating. Everyone wearing shabby clothes that have been darned and mended again and again. I see the way she looks me over, taking in my bespoke suit made from navy blue worsted wool with a silk lining, the trousers with the sharp creases and the deep turn-ups. I had no idea until this morning that turn-ups too were banned here during the war when fabric was in such short supply, and now I worry I might appear to be showing off.

She sits in an armchair facing me, but perched on the very edge of it, angling her body away as if she might catch something. The sight incenses me, though God knows she has reason and right enough to judge me.

'I'm dying.' It is the first time I have spoken the words out loud and for a moment I fear I might be sick. 'I would like to set the record straight.'

'I see. You wish to make your peace – at the expense of ours.' Her eyes are hard as glass marbles. 'The best thing you can do for Eve now is to leave her alone. She is settled. Happily married.'

'But I have come all this way.'

'Then you have had a wasted journey, I'm afraid. Do you wish to destroy Eve's life?'

'Of course not.'

'Well then. The truth would shatter her.'

I have to accept it. This is Eve's mother. Surely she knows what is best for her daughter? But still I press on, desperate.

'There must be *something* I can do. Let me at least visit Holke Hall.'

'Quite impossible. That creature is too far gone now for visitors.'

'Only to put my mind at rest.'

'*Now* you want peace of mind? After all these years. Never mind how it affects other people. Never mind the distress. The last thing any of us needs now is more disruption. I would remind you of your promise. That you would keep well away. From all of us. Haven't you caused enough damage?'

14

5 June 1948

THERE IS TO be a meeting.

Eve finds out from Marie, who has driven over in her little orange car, the noise of the engine ripping through the still air so that even six feet under the water, skimming the bottom of the swimming pool, Eve hears her arrive.

The Lester family is convening to discuss the offer they've had for the house. Though it can't be sold until all the legalities are sorted, the putative buyer would sign a binding agreement in principle and pay six months' rent up front to live in the house while the French legal system does its laborious work. The rental alone would give each of them a decent sum to tide them over, and the buyer seems undeterred by the repairs needed to the villa.

Eve, who is surprised by her own delight at seeing Marie again, nevertheless feels something hollow open up inside her at the news. So it is to end so quickly, all of this? The navy sea sparkling through the pine trees, the red rock, the smell of herbs and summer and people with nothing to do and nowhere to rush to. The preparations for Gloria's wedding, for which

Laurent has claimed he will fill his swimming pool with champagne. All of it gone. And in its place, Clifford. The house in Sutton. The heavy dark wardrobe with the brass handle that looks like a coffin.

The meeting is to take place at Diana Lester's villa in the hills behind Nice and, as a quarter-share-holder, Eve's presence is requested. She is relieved to hear that Bernard is also coming.

'But isn't it Saturday?' Eve remembers suddenly.

Marie smiles tightly.

'There are no weekends where the Lesters are concerned.'

Marie will pick her up at Villa La Perle and drive her to Diana's house and then leave to collect Bernard from Cannes. Funny how quickly Eve has come to think of the French notary as an ally, even though in truth he is working on behalf of the Lesters just as much as, if not more than, for her.

Before she leaves, Marie remembers the telegram she has brought with her. It arrived at Bernard's office that morning, addressed to Eve. Marie hands it over with an apologetic air. Eve knows immediately what the telegram will contain and her heart sinks.

She opens it as soon as she is alone. It is from Clifford, as she knew it would be.

INSIST RETURN IMMEDIATELY STOP
TELEPHONE WITH ARRANGEMENTS
STOP CLIFFORD

Eve winces at the thought of how little Clifford will have enjoyed parting with the money for the telegram. How, with each word costing extra after the first six, he will have pared his message down to the absolute minimum. She feels a sharp stab of guilt at her own selfishness in causing all this worry, followed by an equally vicious feeling of resentment. Can she not have just these few days?

The Colletts drop by on their way into Antibes town to find out if she can be persuaded to join them.

'We are going to see the Picassos,' says Jack eagerly. 'Can you believe we are so close to where he lives and works? He's still around here somewhere up in the hills, but Ma and Pa are such philistines they won't take me there.'

'You don't even know where he is,' laughs Rupert. 'Are we to spend the day touring around the rural villages of southern France on the off-chance we might run into him, flagging down any bald old coot in case it is he? Anyway, I don't see what all the fuss is about. The man doesn't even know the first thing about anatomy – two eyes on the same side of the face, an arm coming out of a head.'

They are compromising by going to visit the Château Grimaldi, a stone building towering over the sea in the oldest part of the town, where Picasso was given an entire floor as a studio just two years before. The Château is holding an exhibition of the paintings and drawings the artist donated to the town as a thank-you for his few months' residency.

'If Leo were here, he wouldn't have let you rest until you'd tracked him down and then he'd have forced you both to camp outside his house and follow him wherever he went.'

If Leo were here. Eve tenses up at the mention of the Colletts' dead son, but they seem unfazed. Ruth's face softens into a smile as if she is glad of the memory. So unlike when Eve's father died, when she was just fifteen. She remembers coming home from school after he'd been in bed for a few days with 'a nasty tummy' to find a long black car parked outside and the curtains drawn and a strange man sitting in the best chair in the front room, drinking tea from the china tea set with the blue swan pattern that had sat unused in the dresser for as long as Eve could remember.

Her mother looked pale but perfectly composed. 'Go upstairs to your room until I fetch you, Eve.'

No introduction. No explanation.

Eve wasn't stupid. She knew what the car meant. Who the man was. Yet somehow she couldn't bring herself to make the connection with her father.

After half an hour, she'd heard the front door close. Then her mother's slow tread on the stairs. A pause outside her bedroom door as if she was reluctant to enter. Then she was standing in the doorway, her eyes red-rimmed but her back straight, as if she had a broom handle jammed against her spine.

'Your father has gone, Eve. I'm very sorry.'

'Gone where?'

She hadn't meant to be cheeky, just said the first thing that came into her head as she was wont to do.

Her mother's face closed up like a flower.

'He's dead. Your father is dead, if that is your preferred word. Kidneys gave out, the doctor thinks. As I say, I'm very sorry.'

So stiff she might have been stuffed. She'd stepped forward then into the room, as if she was coming to comfort her daughter, and Eve, curled up on her bed, flinched so violently that her mother froze, marooned on the brown carpet in an attitude of thwarted motion.

'Well.' She recovered herself, turning back the way she came. 'This will have been a shock, I'm sure. I'll leave you to come to terms with it.'

But at the door she'd hesitated, her hand gripping the wooden doorframe. When her voice came again it was different, rough like bark.

'Not many men would have done what he did, you know. Given you love in spite of everything.'

'What do you mean?'

But her mother was already gone.

They had never spoken of it again. Afterwards what had stuck in Eve's mind was that strange phrase *given you love*. As if love was like bread or eggs or ration coupons. Also stuck in Eve's mind was her mother's inability to use the active verb, to say *he loved you*.

The Colletts express surprise at finding Eve all alone in the house. She explains that Mrs Finch is out running errands while Sully was picked up earlier by Duncan and Clemmie and Noel to go on a boat trip organized by a popular singer of their acquaintance.

'And they didn't ask you?' says Ruth.

'There's no reason at all why they should,' says Eve. 'I'll be seeing them soon enough, up at Diana Lester's place. And besides, I'm far happier here. I've had a lovely morning on my own.'

It's not exactly the truth. While she tells herself she wouldn't have accepted had she been invited, Eve had felt a sharp pang of exclusion watching them all leave, while she sat on the sofa pretending to read a magazine. It was made worse by overhearing Clemmie exclaim, 'Well, it's not as if she's a friend,' from the upstairs hallway. Eve understood that yesterday's revelations about what Guy was supposed to have done might have left the Lesters inclined to close ranks, but after they'd gone the house had felt oppressively silent. It was her first experience of being alone in the villa and she started at every creaking floorboard and groaning pipe. When she went to the kitchen for a glass of water, she'd found herself quickening her step passing the door leading down to the cellar.

As the Colletts say their goodbyes at the front door, there comes the noise of an engine powering up the hill in the wrong gear, followed by a screech of brakes.

Marie appears from the side of the house, wearing baggy shorts such as a man might wear, tied at the waist with thick string, and a man's shirt rolled up at the elbows. Her mass of wild hair has come loose at the back and there is a hairpin between her teeth that falls to the ground when she smiles broadly at seeing Eve.

'*Chère* Eve,' she says. Eve loves the way she pronounces her name, short and fresh and bright.

Introductions are made. Eve sees immediately how Ruth and Marie take to each other and is glad. But when she outlines the Colletts' mission in visiting the area, to bring them closer to Leo, Marie grows strangely quiet, her lively eyes for once stilled.

'Our boy also did not come home. Antoine. He was eighteen years old.'

Oh. Eve feels herself pierced with remorse. All this time she has spent with Bernard and his wife, involving them in her cares and questions, and not once has she asked about their lives or tried to probe the sadness she could sense at the outer edges of their words. Another dead boy. Little wonder they would join the Resistance, continuing their son's struggle where he could not.

Ruth steps forward and takes Marie's hand. For a moment

the two women gaze at each other. Then Ruth asks: 'Do people talk about your "sacrifice" and does it make you want to punch them?' She clenches her fist to mime her meaning.

Marie nods, pressing her lips together. 'How is it my sacrifice when I have had no choice in it?'

In the car on the way to Diana Lester's house, Eve feels wretched.

Eventually Marie speaks.

'Please do not be sad on my account.'

Eve opens her mouth in denial, but Marie speaks over her.

'You have a face where everything is written for the world to read. It is a wonderful thing to be so open, but also a dangerous thing for you because you cannot hide like the rest of us.'

She takes a deep breath.

'My son was killed in the Ardennes in 1940. In Sedan. He did not even need to go. He was so young. But he wanted to fight. He thought it would all be over quickly. He thought – we all thought – Germany would never be able to come here. To France. We would fight and they would go back. We did not think about the possibility of losing. And even once we thought about losing, we did not think – not for a minute – about the possibility of capitulation.'

She spits out the word 'capitulation' and Eve is deterred from asking more.

The car splutters out of Antibes and follows the road heading inland, skirting around the back edges of Nice, the buildings all facing the other way as if they are looking out to sea.

It has developed into a strange kind of day. Warm and muggy. The clouds are not white and not grey but some grubby in-between colour, like cotton wool left out on a shelf.

Eve is glad of the subdued weather. When the sun is out and the scents of the Mediterranean perfume the air with lavender and eucalyptus and all the herbs she does not know the names of, it is hard to hold on to the reality of her business here. So it is good that the air is soupy and the sky looks like it needs a good wash.

They pass a pine forest, in the middle of which she glimpses canvas tents of the kind the soldiers used during the war.

'*Congés payés*,' says Marie. 'Paid vacationers. Now it is the law for workers to have paid time off. So they come here, from all over France. They stay in tent cities like this one. All the rich British and Americans hate it. It is all right for them to live here, speak no French, take their tea at four o'clock with other English people, employ only English staff, buy their food on the black market. But for the poor French to come here to enjoy their own country – no, that is not tolerable.'

They have passed Nice now and are winding up into the hills on the far side of the city. The road is bumpy with potholes and, the car having little in the way of suspension, Eve feels every jolt through her sitting bones and her hips, her head hitting the roof with alarming regularity.

'Can you believe it wasn't good enough for her, Villa La Perle?' Marie asks. 'Mrs Lester wants always something bigger. Something newer and better. She is one of those women who thinks everything is a competition.'

Eve wonders for the first time how Marie really feels about all the British, who used the South of France as a playground in the thirties only to abandon it to the fascists and the

Nazis, and are now returning in dribs and drabs as if everything is the same as before.

'There are some English people,' says Marie, as if she has read her mind, 'who treat us as if we lost the war. Not as if we were allies, but as if we were on opposite sides and we should now be sorry and ashamed.'

Eve remembers how Clifford had warned her to be wary of the French, to ask herself which side they'd been on, what they had been doing while the Nazis paraded in their streets and drank in their bars and used their hotels as prisons and torture chambers. War has made them all suspect one another, now they know the terrible things human beings are capable of, how thin is the veneer that separates the civilized from the savage.

The car is climbing now, reluctantly. The window on Eve's side is jammed and the air inside feels thick, stale with cigarette smoke and with their own sour tempers.

How pointless it all is, she thinks, leaning her head against the window. *To be investing so much time and effort in getting to know this place, these people. And for what?* So that she can go home to Sutton and that half-life where her own heartbeat is made to fall in line with the relentless tick of the grandfather clock? She should just accept she will never find out the truth about Guy Lester and who he is to her and what terrible thing he did. What does it matter now anyway? He is dead. She will never get to know him. And her life is not here. It is back there. With her husband. The villa will be sold. And eventually she will get her share, and it will buy a few bits and pieces for the house. A new car, perhaps. Good clothes that she will save to wear to play bridge or to visit Clifford's parents' house.

She sighs, gazing out at the scenery through the grimy glass.

This far up out of town, the houses have thinned out and those that they pass are hidden behind high trees. They drive through a set of open gates and proceed along a short driveway flanked by palm trees planted with regimental uniformity, before parking in front of a large peach-and-cream villa. There is a pool, of course (could she ever have guessed that she might one day be unmoved by the sight?).

The view from the terrace is of the city of Nice strung out along the curving bay, and of the pale sea and, in the distance, the grey smudge of Cap d'Antibes jutting out into the ocean.

Diana Lester materializes from an open doorway, looking cool all in white, with wide-legged trousers and a sleeveless white top and large-brimmed white hat. She appears surprised to see Marie.

'You two have made friends already. How charming. You're really settling in, aren't you, Eve?'

Diana's smile stretches the smooth planes of her face as if forcing something that should not be forced. But Eve senses the meaning behind her words. *Don't make yourself too comfortable here where you don't belong.* Her already low spirits fall still further and she feels a tightening beneath her rib cage, the warning sign that something is building inside her that she might not be able to stop.

'I must go now,' Marie says, with a sullenness to match Eve's. 'I must bring Bernard.'

'Why doesn't he just drive himself?' Eve asks now, wondering why this question has only just occurred to her.

'Oh, Bernard can't drive,' says Diana, tapping a cigarette out from a silver box. 'Can you imagine? Guy would have sooner sawn off his own leg than be driven around by me. I suppose it's a cultural difference. English men like to be men.'

The implied slight is, as always, dressed up in a practised smile. Marie turns on her heel and stalks off towards the car.

'I hope I haven't offended her,' says Diana. The brim of her hat has dropped so that her eyes are hidden. 'The French are so easily offended.'

Eve rubs the side of her temple, where she can feel a headache coming. This damned weather.

Diana leads her inside the house, walking ahead, hips swaying in the white trousers, ash falling carelessly from the lit cigarette between her fingertips. Eve gets the sense the other woman wants her to be impressed. Not because she cares about her opinion, but because of the power imbalance it will create. Diana Lester is someone who needs to be in control.

Eve affects an expression of polite disinterest while Diana shows her the turreted hallway with the marble spiral staircase, the high-ceilinged sitting room with the painted palazzo ceiling, the way each set of double doors on the ground floor aligns perfectly with those in the next room and the next, so that if they are all open one might almost have the illusion of looking into a mirror.

'Oh, it's you! I'm so glad to see you again.'

Libby Lester is hopping from foot to foot in the doorway of the sitting room, where they have stopped in front of a floor-to-ceiling window to admire the view down to the coast. She has on a pair of shorts and her feet are bare. She looks about ten years old.

'Libby, I told you to get changed.'

Diana's voice is sharp, yet Eve sees how her face changes

when her daughter enters the room, her polished features softening.

What is wrong with Libby? It seems clear that the girl is not right in some way. Instantly Eve berates herself for sounding like her mother. What she means is, Libby is not like other girls her age.

Libby dashes to Eve, still standing awkwardly at the window, and flings her arms around her. Her body is solid and very warm and she smells of apple shampoo and seawater and the damp heat of childhood. Eve closes her eyes, unexpectedly overcome both by the force of the girl's affection and by the unfamiliarity of being in such close physical contact with another person. She feels the hot prick of tears and is grateful when the girl breaks away and runs from the room to do her mother's bidding.

'Diana. You look exquisite as ever. I feel like such an almighty frump in comparison. I mean, just look at me. All that bracing sea air on the boat this morning has left me a complete sight.'

Clemmie Atwood, who has appeared in the doorway through which Libby has just dashed, plucks at her canary yellow halterneck dress as if it is an old rag. Her shiny blonde hair is held back from her face by a yellow ribbon, and it is just as if the sun, so little in evidence today, has arrived in human form.

Duncan and Noel follow behind Clemmie, engrossed in a heated discussion.

'I still don't see why you're paying any heed to what that bitter old queen Whelan has to say,' says Duncan, stopping to lean against the metal doorframe as if it might help keep him upright. There are vivid purple shadows under his eyes.

Eve remembers what Clemmie said that first evening on the train when they had no idea she was listening, about whether it should be necessary to have to work so hard at being dissolute. It couldn't be easy for her, Eve thinks suddenly, if she really had been in love with the older brother and settled for the younger, only to find herself in turn playing second fiddle to gambling or drinking – or worse.

'I mean, this is our father we're talking about. Guy. The man who wouldn't even kill mice when we were infested with the damned things. Remember how we had to get that bloody cat to scare them off? And he's supposed to be a murderer? Pull the other one.'

'I don't know how you're so bloody sure of yourself.' Noel has his hands stuffed into the pockets of his linen trousers. 'The truth is that none of us ever really knows anyone else. Surely the war has taught us that much? Guy always had a temper. Who knows what he was capable of.'

'Diana?' Duncan appeals to his stepmother. 'You'd know, wouldn't you, if you'd been married to a murderer? I mean, I presume you didn't sit up at night afraid to go to sleep in case he butchered you in your bed. Are you sure he never told you anything about why we had to leave Blighty?'

Diana, who has removed the floppy hat and is smoothing out her silky hair, shakes her head.

'Your father told me he just didn't like England. Said it held unpleasant memories. I always knew there had to be more to it than that, but you know what Guy was like. He had to have his little secrets.'

She flashes a look at Eve then, her meaning crystal clear, and something tightens inside Eve's chest. A married man's *little secret*.

'But you agree he couldn't have done it.'

Duncan is like a young child, trying to force the answer he wants, but Diana refuses to oblige.

'The more I learn about your father, the less it seems I knew him.'

They wander out on to the terrace, where a long table under a retractable calico awning has been set with pitchers of lemonade. Duncan makes a face when he is offered a glass.

'Haven't you got anything less wholesome?'

Clemmie makes a clicking sound behind her teeth.

'For God's sake, Duncan. It's still practically morning.'

Duncan makes a great show of looking at his watch.

'Actually, it's well past midday. Diana, I don't think it would be breaking any social or moral laws to offer us a martini.'

While Diana pours the lemonade, Duncan wanders into the house, reappearing some minutes later with a chrome cocktail shaker and a couple of martini glasses. 'Who will join me?' he asks, shrugging when they all shake their heads. Eve notices how Clemmie angles herself away from her fiancé as he takes his first sip and surprises herself by feeling sorry for her. She knows what it is like to be locked into a union with someone who treats what you have to say as an irrelevance.

While they all wait for Bernard to arrive, Eve excuses herself to go to the bathroom. Diana insists on summoning the housekeeper to show her the way, even though Eve protests that she knows exactly where it is after her tour of the house earlier on. *She doesn't trust me.* The realization, which comes to her as she follows the unsmiling housekeeper through the hallway, makes her burn with indignation.

Stepping back out through the double doors on to the

terrace after she has finished, Eve hears an agitated buzz of low-level conversation coming from the group at the table, which dries up instantly when she comes into view.

'We were just discussing the disgusting weather,' says Clemmie as Eve resumes her seat. *Liar*, thinks Eve, pretending not to notice the other woman's smirk.

When Bernard finally appears, Eve can't help but notice the lack of warmth between him and Diana Lester. He's meticulously polite, but there's a distance. And the childish part of her feels a secret flush of pleasure.

She studiously ignores Noel Lester, although she feels his gaze on her. What gives him the right to stare so? As if she were an object of curiosity. Which of course she is. How happy he will be to see the back of her. Stirring up all this bad feeling. Standing in the way of the quick sale they all want. She is childishly pleased to note that his mood seems as black as her own. *Good*, she thinks sourly. *Let everyone be miserable.*

Her bad temper makes everything seem unpleasant and sticky. And matters are not improved when Diana Lester glances at the narrow watch on her wrist and frowns.

'Shall we get on?'

To Eve in her current frame of mind, their impatience to be shot of the house translates directly to an impatience to be shot of her. She has been a hitch, a complication, an embarrassment even. That whiff of wrongdoing that accompanies her. The furtive comparisons between her features and those of the Lester children. *Might they be . . . ? Could he have . . . ?*

People create their own narratives, Eve knows that. And once that narrative is written they cannot abide for it to be questioned.

The meeting begins. Sitting across the table from Eve, Bernard talks in his calm way, reminding them of how Guy Lester had wished his property to be divided up. He mentions what the villa is worth and Eve stifles a gasp when she hears the amount, mentally calculating what her quarter share will come to, even after the inheritance tax is paid. *Well, that should make Clifford happy.*

'As you know, there is someone interested in buying the villa. And renting it until it is ready to be sold.'

'Which is a stroke of bloody luck,' says Duncan. 'Since the war you haven't been able to give property away around here. Everyone so broke. All those empty houses.'

'A great many people died in the war,' says Bernard, and his voice, while measured, has a hardness that is unusual for him. 'Or were driven out of their homes.'

'Exactly my point,' says Duncan, misunderstanding. 'And of course Villa La Perle is in a pretty grim state. Diana saw to that.'

Duncan glances pointedly at Diana, who affects not to have heard. Eve sees Noel try to catch his brother's eye and shake his head almost imperceptibly. She is so used to the brothers arguing that this intimate gesture comes as a shock. For the first time she tries to imagine how it would have been for them. Losing their mother. A father preoccupied with a new wife and child.

No one gets through life unscathed.

'Obviously we're delighted to have a buyer,' says Noel, oddly formal.

Across the table Clemmie arches her back and shakes her hair loose from its ribbon before retying it. They all watch. Such a foreign species they are, thinks Eve, these strikingly attractive people, used to getting a reaction merely by being, nothing more.

'Well, I for one will be delighted to be shot of the place,' says Diana. 'It eats money, you know. I simply cannot afford the upkeep.'

Eve looks around her. At the swimming pool with its black mosaic tiles. At the view of Nice with its grand white buildings curving around the bay. At Diana herself, groomed and perfect and sleek with her skin golden and gleaming as if gilded.

Diana gets to her feet to summon the housekeeper to bring more drinks. 'I'm so glad we're all in agreement,' she says once the chilled wine is poured. 'Here's to new beginnings.'

Eve raises her glass obediently. The wine is delicious, crisp and delicate.

The Lesters begin chatting among themselves. There's a new lightness in their voices, as if all has been decided and a shadow has been lifted.

Eve looks around the table, from face to face, a lump of something hard and heavy building in her stomach. Must she really return home now, leaving all of this behind? Must she never find out why she is here, or what Guy has done? She looks at the Lester sons, and Clemmie Atwood, still invigorated after their morning's sail, and at Diana Lester, drawing languorously on a cigarette. When Eve has gone, the circle will close over the place where she now sits, and none of these people will remember she was ever here.

Her mother's voice comes to her again. *You must learn, Eve, that you're not the most important person in the world.* It used to make her feel selfish, but now for the first time it occurs to her that while she might not be the most important person in the world, oughtn't she at least be the most important person in *her* world? If she doesn't matter to herself, what chance has she of mattering to someone else?

For years, growing up, she dreamed of someone coming to rescue her from her life, but no one came, and she settled for Clifford because he was the best thing available. Looking around at the Lesters now, realizing how little she registers in their lives, she understands finally that whatever she needs she will have to take, instead of waiting around in vain for it to be offered.

She puts down her glass, straightens her back and lifts her head, then clears her throat before speaking. 'I don't want to sell.'

15

'IT JUST CAME out,' Eve says, though her head is in her hands so her words sound muffled. 'I kept telling myself to drink up and stay quiet, but my mouth wouldn't cooperate. And now they all hate me.'

'I'm sure they don't,' says Sully. 'No. Wait a minute. On second thoughts, you're right. They probably do.'

They are down on the jetty in front of Villa La Perle, sitting on the side of the wooden structure with their bare feet dangling in the water. The sun is setting to the side of them and throwing colours at the sea; reds and pinks and oranges cast down in spattered pools on the surface. The muggy clouds of earlier have broken up and are now drifting away, black against the darkening sky.

'They hardly spoke to me as I left. None of them.'

Eve's heart lurches queasily as she remembers the scene on Diana's picture-book terrace after she'd made her surprise announcement. First there had been amused disbelief. Then false jocularity as they tried to change her mind. And finally anger.

'It strikes me,' Diana had said, 'that this is a play for attention. You've realized you have some power, probably for the first time in your drab little life, and you can't bear to give it up.'

'No, that's not it,' she had tried to say, but the phrase 'drab little life' reverberated around her head and she couldn't think of a way to describe the gnawing need to find out why she was here, and how she was becoming increasingly convinced it might explain the feeling she has always had of being a stranger in her own life.

Bernard had been subdued during the car journey back. 'I would not be doing my duty if I did not ask you if you are sure you wish to delay the sale,' he'd said. 'It might not be so easy to find another buyer. And you do not wish to make enemies of the Lester family. Also—' But here he stopped.

'Also?' Eve echoed, like a child.

'It's not important.'

They'd sat in a silence that was punctuated only by Marie's occasional outbursts – at another driver she deemed to have encroached into her space, and once at an old gentleman with a pipe who stepped into the road to cross just as Marie swung suddenly left.

Finally Bernard spoke again. 'What will your husband say?'

'Oh, I'm sure he will understand.'

But Eve knows this to be a lie. And sitting here on the jetty, talking to Sully, with her feet bare and dangling in a way she is sure Clifford would not approve of, she feels her earlier bravado trickling away.

How is she to explain this to Clifford? She dreads telling him, dreads the questions he will ask that she cannot answer. She does not know much about Clifford's business, but she suspects it is not doing as well as he pretends. How shocked he would be to find out how much she has just passed up.

She thinks of the telegram with its sparse money-saving wording and feels suddenly as if she might have to lean over to be sick into the sea.

'Seriously, though' – Sully is still talking – 'you don't want to get on the wrong side of Diana Lester.'

'Bit late for that,' Eve replies, slapping a mosquito from her arm. She has a collection of unattractive pink lumps now, peppering her too-pale skin. 'Anyway, I don't understand why she has to be so horrible all the time. I mean, I know she's grieving and everything—'

'Be assured, widowhood has not changed her one bit.'

'So what is it then? She has a lifestyle most people in the world could only dream of. Yet she seems so unhappy and bitter.'

Sully lies back on the jetty. Such a strange shape he is, with his chest and stomach rising up like the curve of a whale.

'Insecurity?' he ventures.

Eve makes one of those *pfff* noises that are halfway between an exclamation and a laugh. The idea of Diana, so poised and self-contained, being insecure about anything is absurd.

'Would it surprise you to know that Diana's father was a stationmaster? That her mother started life as a lady's maid? Everything about her is an invention. That cut-glass accent. The haughty manner. When Guy first found her she was a paid companion to some ghastly old woman. She'd worked on herself by then, of course – the voice, the clothes – but even so, some of the older crowd refused to acknowledge her. But she wore them all down in the end, becoming more upper-class than any of them, and eventually they all forgot where she'd come from, or pretended to forget, which is almost the same thing. It didn't hurt that she was so beautiful, even at eighteen. Everyone was in love with her.'

Eve is quiet, trying to digest this new information, to reframe Diana Lester in this surprising new light. Having formed a hearty dislike of Guy's widow, she now finds herself reluctant to relinquish it, though already she feels her animosity breaking up into tiny crumbs that slip away like sand.

'And you? Were you in love with her too?'

'Like I said. Everyone. But Diana never made any secret of the fact that she was out for the money. I was a penniless young writer, staying with the Murphys at that time, Sara and Gerald. Dependent on their charity. That wasn't her style at all.'

'But she loved Guy? She must have done. She married him.'

Sully drums his stubby fingers on the wooden jetty.

'Come on, Eve. You're not that naive. The two things have nothing to do with one another. As I suspect you already know.'

There is a sudden burning behind Eve's eyes as the meaning behind Sully's last sentence dawns. How can he know what she has never admitted even to herself?

But she *does* love Clifford. She must. He's her husband.

'I don't know what you mean.'

'Fair enough.'

Soon after, Eve excuses herself and climbs up the rocky steps that lead from the jetty to the house. How dare he, she thinks, presume to know the first thing about her private affairs?

Suddenly it sickens her, all of it. All of *them*. The wealth, the lazy speculation about other people's lives. The insular self-absorption. They live here in their huge houses behind their high gates and drink champagne and swim in their pools, while just outside, in the towns, in Cannes and Nice, people are queuing in the streets to buy bread and vegetables. Going hungry so their children can eat.

Back in her room, she lies on her bed, her head throbbing. What do these people know about real life? About her?

She thinks of Gloria Hayes's glazed eyes at the reception that first night and Sully's assertion that she had to numb herself with drugs just to go through with the wedding.

Eve hadn't had to do that. She had gone into marriage with a clear head and an open heart. There are no similarities whatsoever between her and Gloria or Diana. Sully is just trying to stir up trouble, as always. All marriages are transactions of one kind or another. That doesn't make them any less valid.

For the first time that day, Eve thinks properly about what she has just done. Perhaps the house sale could have been agreed by now, in principle at least, and she would be packing up to go home, back to what is real, instead of being stuck in this fantasy world where the shiny surface is everything and no one wants to scratch too hard for fear of what might be lurking underneath, for fear of how deep the darkness goes.

She thinks of how Noel Lester had glared at her after she'd said she didn't want to sell, and how for a moment Duncan had looked as if he might cry. She wonders about Diana's flash of anger. Of all the family, she had thought Guy's widow would be the least bothered about her share of the money; after all, she has been well provided for. She can afford to wait. But after what Sully just told her, Diana's animosity makes more sense. Being blasé with money is a skill one learns in childhood, and people who come from nothing seldom, if ever, acquire it.

16

6 June 1948

EVE SLEEPS FITFULLY and wakes with a start, sure she can hear a noise outside her door. She lies in bed, every muscle tense, but whatever it was that woke her does not repeat itself.

Opening the curtains, she is greeted by a sunrise to her far left that soaks the world in streaks of mauve and pink. The sea is flat and glossy, reflecting back the slowly brightening sky – a vast lake of calm into which all of her petty concerns dissolve. In the face of so much beauty, what is there to do except give in to it entirely?

If Eve could bottle the feeling she has that early morning, she might be able to take it with her into the day, coating herself in it like invisible armour. But that is not the way things work, and by breakfast time anxiety is once again prickling at the base of her neck. She can hear the keys of Sully's type-writer clacking on the terrace, but is held back from going to see him by some residual resentment at his overstepping of the mark during their last conversation. She can't forget how excluded she'd felt when he'd gone off on the boat trip with the Lester brothers and Clemmie the previous morning, or Clemmie's overheard *It's not as if she's a friend.*

Instead she decides to walk to the Belles Rives to see the Colletts. There is something about that family that makes her feel less of an outsider, less other.

The quickest way is to follow the road that goes up the hill across the middle of the Cap, past the lighthouse, and then drops back down the other side in the direction of Juan-les-Pins. She sets off with purpose, enjoying the unfamiliar feeling of taking control. The road is quiet, only the odd car or motorbike passing. There is no pavement so Eve walks close to the side, where the line of trees and bushes is broken intermittently by driveways leading to palm-shaded villas.

Somewhere near the top, Eve spots a bush she does not recognize studded with pink flowers and bends to take a closer look, pressing her nose to the buds to breathe in the delicate fragrance. She is vaguely aware of a car approaching up the hill from the direction of Juan-les-Pins but she pays it no heed, keeping her back to the road, her face buried in the soft pink petals. It is only when the noise of the engine becomes uncommonly loud that she finally looks over her shoulder, just in time to see a car bonnet hurtling towards her at speed.

Without giving herself time to think, she dives straight into the bush, scratching her face and her arms and legs on its branches, and crouches there, chest heaving, as the car, skimming the bush close enough to set its leaves trembling, thunders on ahead without slowing.

Shaken, she emerges back on to the road and waits on trembling legs for her pulse to stop racing and her breath to get back to normal. She surveys the spot in which she had been standing. Was it possible the driver of the car had simply not seen her? It seems so unlikely, and yet what other explanation is there? She tries to conjure an image of the car, but it all happened so quickly she cannot now even recall the colour of it, save that it seemed to be dark, and she has no picture at all of who was driving it.

By the time she finally reaches the Belles Rives, keeping her eyes firmly fixed on the road all the way, Eve's nerves are calmer.

The Colletts exclaim over her scratches.

'It doesn't surprise me though,' says Rupert. 'The French are bloody awful drivers.'

Jack recounts several anecdotes of having been almost run down in Paris while looking the wrong way crossing the road, and Eve relaxes. It was an accident. That is all.

Over coffee taken at a round table out on the terrace, she tells them about the meeting at Diana's house, and is instantly glad she came when Rupert and Ruth declare themselves to be in complete agreement with her regarding the immediate sale of the house.

'It is just money to them,' says Ruth, pushing a plate of dainty pastries towards Eve. 'And they already have so much of that. But to you it means so much more. To you it is your whole identity. Your whole self. Naturally you would wish to postpone matters until you've got to the bottom of things.'

Once it is put like that, Eve cheers up. Obviously it is so. She isn't being obstructive. She is merely in search of answers.

Jack is thrilled by her subversiveness.

'I should so like to have been there to see their faces,' he says. 'People like that are so unused to being thwarted.'

The morning has ripened into a perfect early summer day. Out on the water, small boats bob lazily and Eve spies the dark dot of a bold swimmer's head, while nearer the shore two elderly women in bathing suits and brightly coloured swimming hats paddle uncertainly in the shallows. A waiter bustles around the terrace on which they sit, serving hot drinks from large metal pots, and the smell of ground coffee mingles with the scent of orange blossom from the potted trees.

'What shall I do?' she says to no one in particular. 'I must tell my husband *something.* He was worried enough to send a *telegram*. My behaviour is very out of character. But I can't admit that I have passed up a small fortune just because I'm curious about something that happened a long time ago and that I may well never get to the bottom of.'

'Why don't you set yourself a deadline?' suggests Ruth, holding up the empty milk jug to the waiter, gesturing for more. 'It's Sunday now. Give yourself until Tuesday to uncover some more information, but if nothing fresh is forthcoming return to England on Wednesday.'

'Wednesday?' Eve is dismayed. 'But I will miss the wedding!'

Ruth smiles. 'Ah yes, I forgot about Gloria Hayes and Laurent Martin. I agree you cannot miss that. Not when half the world would kill for an invitation.'

'And will you be going as the guest of Stanley Sullivan?' Jack sounds almost coy, and his eyes, behind the round spectacles, are bright.

Eve's spirits plunge.

'If we are back on good terms by then,' she says.

Inevitably the Colletts want to know what has happened between them and Eve wishes she hadn't spoken.

'He made presumptions about me and my private life,' she says primly.

'Well then, give yourself another week,' says Ruth. 'Make a holiday of it. You can book your return home for the day after the wedding. By then you must have made more headway, surely?'

But Eve is not so convinced.

Trudging back over the hill towards Villa La Perle, her feet feel heavy in the heat, as if she has boulders attached to them. She glances again at the ring on her finger. *From F with love eternal.* Will she ever discover the truth about who had that ring engraved with those words, and why it came into Guy Lester's possession when she is so convinced it is the same one her mother was wearing in the photograph?

It is now properly hot, and sweat pools behind her knees. She wishes she had thought to bring a pair of sandals so she wouldn't have to wear stockings. But then she hadn't expected to be away for so long.

She thinks about Clifford and tries to imagine him back at home pacing the floor, frantic with worry, unable even to face going into work. The thought is impossible. Still, he will be concerned. She has a flash of the old guilt that used to set in whenever she'd upset her mother. Not that she ever set out to upset her mother; she just didn't seem to know how to act otherwise. How do you avoid distressing someone when it's not what you do that causes them pain, but what and who you are?

The sound of a car engine roaring up the hill behind her causes her heart to pound. Though she has tried to put her earlier close encounter on her way to see the Colletts out of her mind, she hasn't forgotten that breathless dive into the foliage, the sense of having narrowly avoided injury. She steps to the side of the road, waiting for the car to pass, but instead there is a sudden screech of brakes. Whirling around, she sees Noel Lester sitting behind the wheel of his convertible, glowering at her.

'Well? Get in.'

'No, thank you. I'm enjoying the walk.'

'Don't be an ass. You're positively melting. Have you seen the colour of your face – it's halfway between a decent Merlot and a beetroot. Which is not surprising if you're going to jump out of your skin every time a car comes along.'

Eve's stomach muscles clench. She refuses to tell him about her near-miss earlier, for fear of sounding foolish. Instead she focuses her resentment on his comments about her ruddy complexion. Noel probably doesn't know any women who actually walk. She expects all the women of his acquaintance have cars and drivers at their disposal. She wonders that they even bother having legs!

'Besides,' Noel continues, 'I was on my way to see you, so you might as well get in and save me the bother.'

Eve thinks about refusing, but really what's the point? And the thought of walking another ten minutes or more in this heat is not one she relishes.

In the passenger seat, she turns her head as if there is something more interesting happening outside the car and waits for him to speak, but Noel seems to have nothing to say.

Finally she cracks.

'Why exactly were you coming to see me?'

'Diana telephoned me. She says there are three trunks of Guy's correspondence in the attic of the new house from when she cleared out Guy's study. By which, of course, she means from when Mrs Finch cleared out his study. He left instructions that none of it was to be touched when they moved house, insisted only he would know what to keep and what to throw out. But of course he didn't plan on upping and dying quite so suddenly.'

'And what has that got to do with me?'

'She wonders if perhaps there is something in his papers that could help you find out why you're here.'

'And why didn't she say this before?'

Noel turns his head to look at her, a wry smile curling the corners of his mouth.

'Maybe because you weren't standing in the way of what she wants before.'

It makes a dismal kind of sense. Diana wants Eve gone. And she knows the easiest way to get rid of her is to get her the information she needs.

Stupid to take the rejection so personally.

'So, will you come?' Noel is impatient.

'What, right now?'

'Unless you have some other pressing engagement.'

Eve considers inventing something, just for the satisfaction of preventing him getting his own way, but stops herself.

'Fine.'

At the peach-and-cream villa in the hills, Diana herself comes to meet them at the door, wearing a diaphanous tunic over a white bathing suit.

'Bernard says the buyer will give us a week,' Diana says by way of greeting. 'After that he will begin negotiations on a different house down the coast towards Monte Carlo. So if you could hurry your very touching quest for personal identity along, we'd all be most grateful.'

So cool she is, this woman. Eve searches for the traces of the girl Sully described. The one whose mother was a lady's maid, and who earned her living dealing with the personal needs of an elderly woman, not even a relative. But she can see none.

They follow Diana up the grand staircase to a first-floor corridor, which stretches ahead in both directions. Everything is white, modern, sleek. No wonder she had not found Villa La Perle to her taste.

A second, narrower staircase leads up to an attic floor where there is a door on one side, ajar, through which Eve can glimpse a suite of modest rooms she assumes must belong to the staff.

'Will Mrs Finch be coming to join you here when . . . if . . . Villa La Perle is sold?' she asks.

Diana's face freezes.

'Alas not. I already have my own housekeeper in place and simply can't afford to take on anyone else. Caroline Finch was Guy's responsibility. He provided for her in his will and I gave her ample warning that we wouldn't be needing her services in the new house. Besides, it was Guy she was in love with. Not me. I would be a poor consolation prize.'

In love with? Eve's mouth falls open with surprise and she is glad that Diana has turned to lead the way through the door on the opposite side. She glances at Noel, who shrugs, as if it is all the same to him that his childhood housekeeper should have been in love with his father. What is wrong with these people? Why must everything be greeted with such languid indifference, as if none of it really matters? Poor Mrs Finch. If it is true that she harboured some decades-long unrequited passion for Guy, it is no wonder she should now be at pains to appear so relentlessly cheerful and eager to please. The man she devoted her life to was dead, and what was to become of her?

The door Diana has just disappeared through leads into a

large attic room piled high with furniture: bureaux made of dark polished wood, a set of green wicker chairs – some where the weave has come undone and sticks out from the arm or back – a deep red rolled-up rug, eaten away at the edges by some sort of bug, a tarnished mirror in an ornate chipped frame leaning redundantly against the wall.

'Guy would insist on keeping this old junk,' says Diana. 'Said it reminded him of the house he grew up in.'

'Where was that?' Eve sounds too eager, but she can't help herself. 'Where did Guy grow up?'

Diana frowns, as if it is none of her business, but Noel answers.

'My grandparents had an estate in West Sussex and a rather gloomy townhouse in Kensington.'

'So you visited them?'

'Only once. When I was at boarding school. I think I must have been about twelve or thirteen. I knew there had been some rift between Guy and his parents but I was so sure I could be the one to breach it. You know the arrogance of young people. I saved my tuck allowance for a term and used it to buy a train ticket to London. I thought it might be hard to find them, but it wasn't at all. The family had an investment company, you see. It didn't take much effort to find out where the head office was. A tall building in Mayfair. I went in and asked to see my grandfather. I expect I thought he'd be beside himself with joy. Watched too many Hollywood movies.'

'He wasn't pleased to see you?'

'No. In fact, he seemed scared. He took me back home to Kensington because he didn't know what else to do with me. My grandmother was at home, but she refused to come downstairs to meet me. My grandfather said it was because she would find it too painful, on account of them being estranged from my father. I'd never heard the word "estranged" before, and I thought they were using "strange" as a verb. Couldn't make head or tail of it. He was embarrassed, I could tell. He got the cook to make me some tea and called the school and waited with me for the cab to come and take me to the station. Only as I was leaving did he ask me about my father, trying to make it sound casual, although I could tell he'd been waiting to say his name all afternoon. I so wanted to ask him what my father had done that was so dreadful, but instead I found myself waxing lyrical about Guy – how well respected he was in France, how well we lived. Hoping he might say, "Well, in that case, we should let bygones be bygones," but of course he didn't. When I was about to get into the cab, he put a hand out as if he was going to touch me, but I turned away as if I hadn't seen.'

To her consternation, Eve finds a lump in her throat, large and painful.

'That must have been upsetting,' she says, and her voice is thin and strangled.

Noel shrugs and thrusts his hands deep into his pockets. 'Character-building,' he says.

The stacked furniture takes up most of the space in the room, but there is a clearing towards the front where they are standing, and in the middle of that clearing are three battered leather trunks.

'I had the gardener dig them out,' says Diana. 'I started to look through myself, but there's too much in there and I have a luncheon engagement at Rosita's.'

'Rosita Winston,' says Noel once Diana has gone. 'The reigning queen of the Côte d'Azur. Nothing happens in

Riviera society without Rosita's say-so. Diana is quite enamoured. Mind you, Diana is enamoured of anyone in a position to do her favours. They say Rosita's luncheons cost her a hundred and fifty thousand francs a week.'

Eve gasps.

'Anyway,' Noel continues, 'I don't believe she didn't have time to go through the trunks. The fact is, Diana has always hated being reminded of Guy's life before he met her. She wanted him to be born anew the moment he set eyes on her.'

'She must have loved him very much, in that case.'

'That's nothing to do with love, Mrs Forrester. It's to do with possession. Well, that and insecurity.'

Insecurity. That word again. It makes more sense given what Eve now knows about Diana's background.

'I feel sorry for Caroline Finch,' she says, remembering Diana's easy dismissal of the woman. 'Even if she did have a . . . crush . . . on your father. It will be hard for her to start again somewhere else after being with your family so long.'

Noel shrugs. 'I'm sure you think us very heartless, but she has been well provided for in Guy's will. And of course we'll do what we can to help her find another position, if that's what she wants.'

He glances at Eve, perhaps reading some sort of silent accusation in her expression because his tone becomes defensive.

'Anyway, Duncan and I were never that close to Caroline Finch. She arrived when we were already too old to form those kinds of attachments, and besides, we were mostly away at boarding school. And—'

He presses his lips together.

'And?'

'It sounds awful to say it, but she always tried so hard to

get chummy with us, particularly when my father was around. It ended up putting us off.'

Noel opens the first trunk. It is packed full of books and papers, some old trophies presumably from youthful sporting events long since completed. A striped university scarf is crammed in down the side.

Noel groans. 'He always was a messy beggar. This will take us all day. You'd better make a start on one of the other two.'

'But are you sure I should be looking through your father's private things? And what am I looking for?'

'Just anything that chimes with you, anything you recognize from your own life. And as for the other, I think Guy sacrificed his claim to privacy when he involved a complete stranger in our family finances, don't you?'

The 'complete stranger' stings, and Eve unbuckles the lid of the trunk furthest from Noel in silence.

This trunk seems to be full of correspondence. She starts working through it with a tingle of excitement, sure she is about to discover a signature she recognizes or an address that seems familiar. But soon anticipation turns to weariness. It's clear Guy was someone who never threw anything away. There are letters to bank managers, to accountants, to old army chums. There's a protracted correspondence involving a trust fund Guy came into on his twenty-first birthday. The letters fly between the firm of lawyers involved and Guy himself, chomping at the bit to hurry the process along.

In an old cardboard folder she finds a sheaf of letters from Guy's father, starting when Guy was a boy at boarding school. The letters are formal and stilted, and fail to grow any less so when Guy leaves university and joins the family business.

'Overall I am pleased with your performance since you joined the company. That having been said, I would remind you that you are still a junior partner and your holiday accrual is significantly lower than you are requesting,' reads one.

Another speaks of Mr Lester Senior's 'profound regret' that Guy should be coming into his inheritance from his grandfather at an age when, in his opinion, he remains 'woefully lacking in the maturity to manage the responsibility of such a fortune'.

Eve prickles with discomfort. She should not be reading this. Whatever happened between Guy Lester and his father, whatever the ins and outs of the Lester family purse, it is none of her business. But Noel is in no mood to entertain her protests.

'Do you wish to go home, Mrs Forrester? Back to your husband?'

He seems to be waiting for a response, so she says, 'Of course' with a vehemence that surprises them both.

'Then I suggest you give me a hand to go through all this stuff. I can't believe the things he held on to. I mean, look at this.'

Noel holds up a pen-and-ink drawing of a man's face, clearly done by a child. The letters below – painstakingly, if unevenly – spell out 'Daddy'.

'Don't tell me – that's an example of your early work.'

Eve is joking, but Noel shrugs and turns away, putting the drawing face down, and it occurs to her too late that he might have been shyly offering her a glimpse of the child he used to be.

They continue sorting through the trunks in awkward silence. Eve starts thinking about that word 'Daddy'.

'When did you and Duncan start calling your father Guy?'

She has never got used to the Lester brothers' casual use of their father's first name. She knows it is probably very modern and sophisticated, but it seems disrespectful, as if denying Guy his status as parent.

'When he got together with Diana so soon after Mum – our mother – died. It was embarrassing. Diana was only eighteen when they met, twenty when they married. I wasn't far off that age myself. Guy had given us this great speech after my mother's funeral, how it was the three of us together now, how we would be our own tight little unit and he would be both father and mother. And then just a few meagre months later, he was telling us that we were adults now and as all adults together we should be glad that he had found happiness again.'

'Oh. Yes. I can see that would have been difficult.'

She picks up a small leather-bound photograph album. Someone, presumably Diana, has inscribed in the inside cover 'The Family, 1932–39'. Glancing up to make sure Noel is preoccupied, she leafs through the pages. Here are endless pictures of the baby Libby engaged in various infantile activities. 'Libby sleeping, 1932', reads the description underneath one, followed immediately by 'Libby waving' and 'Libby laughing', from 1933 and 1934 respectively. There are images of the other Lesters in their youthful incarnations. Diana being pulled behind a boat on water skis, her hair flying behind her. Guy, handsome and bare-chested, sitting on the sand reading a newspaper, a cigarette hanging from his mouth. A skinnier version of Noel playing a bat and ball game with his father, thigh deep in the water, watched from the shore by a painfully young Duncan sitting under an umbrella.

Towards the back there are various posed family

photographs. The last has an extra person in addition to the usual line-up of Lester children, a striking young woman with sparkling eyes that seem to be asking a question, and a smile that draws Eve's attention as if it is a magnet. 'Libby, Duncan, Noel and Anna, 1938' reads the inscription underneath. Eve tries to ignore the dull thud in her chest when she notices how Noel's left hand seems to be resting lightly on the mystery woman's back.

'What is it? Have you found something?'

Eve looks up to find Noel watching her from the other side of the room.

'No. Just old photographs,' she says. Then, before she can stop herself, she asks, 'Who's Anna?'

In two strides, Noel has crossed the floor and snatched the album from her hand.

'No one,' he says, tossing it into his own trunk.

They continue working in awkward silence for a few minutes, Eve aware of having said the wrong thing. Then he clears his throat.

'She was my fiancée.'

'Oh.'

Suddenly it all makes sense. The particular bitterness when he'd talked about the Germans the other day; flying all those missions, above and beyond what was required of him.

'I also had a fiancé who died,' she blurts out, wanting him to know she understands. 'His name was Archie and he—'

'I am sincerely sorry for your loss.' Noel's head is once again bent over the open trunk so she cannot see his expression. 'But the two things are not at all the same.'

The subject is closed, and Eve finds herself feeling as if she has blundered.

Fine, she thinks. *What should it matter to me that he is unwilling to believe we might have anything in common?*

She returns to the letters in the trunk, and after a while she becomes conscious of a kind of deflating feeling. She realizes now that she has been cherishing a romantic notion of Guy Lester as someone noble, larger than life. An heroic figure. Still no nearer to discovering what the connection is between him and her, she has cultivated a man she could gladly lay claim to, but Noel's earlier words have trimmed Guy down to size. Just a man, after all. Capable of hypocrisy as they all are, of bending his principles to suit his desires.

She opens a large manila envelope. At first she believes it to be empty, but when she holds it out and shakes it, a shower of newspaper cuttings flutter to the floor. The first is a small clipping from the *Daily Herald*, dated 12 July 1920.

MYSTERIOUS DEATH OF A SOLDIER

A former guardsman, Francis Garvey, was shot in St James's Park early yesterday morning. Police investigating the incident have appealed for witnesses. 'We do not have any further information at this point,' said Detective Sergeant Thomas Hawley.

Curious, Eve flicks through the other cuttings. All involve the same case, and all are equally brief and non-committal. The most recent comes from the *Daily Mirror* on 8 September of the same year.

INQUEST CONCLUDES

An inquest into the shooting of former soldier Francis Garvey reached a conclusion of accidental death. Lt Garvey was found dead in July this year. 'It is a very unfortunate case,' said Detective Sergeant Thomas Hawley. No further details were released.

'Do you recognize the name Francis Garvey?' Eve calls out.

Noel, his face sheened with the heat and the effort of extracting the items from the very bottom of his trunk, straightens up and shakes his head.

'No,' he says. 'Should I?'

'I don't know. It's just that your father has an envelope of newspaper clippings about his death, so one would imagine he must have meant something to him.'

Noel comes over to have a look, reading the cuttings over Eve's shoulder. His breath is hot on her neck, his body solid and radiating warmth.

'1920 is the year Guy came over here, according to that snake Whelan,' says Noel.

'So this could be the man he . . . That is, if you were to believe Whelan's accusations, which obviously I don't . . .'

Noel smiles tightly.

'For God's sake, just say it, woman. If my father was a murderer, this could be his victim. This Francis Garvey.'

Eve nods.

Noel reaches his hand over her shoulder to take the clippings, his fingers brushing hers, sending the pieces of paper fluttering to the floor. She drops to her knees, taking longer than necessary over picking them up, giving her time to compose herself. How jittery she is at the moment.

While Noel stands to the side going through the clippings, Eve resumes rifling through the trunk, but there is nothing more that seems relevant.

'I don't know,' says Noel eventually. 'I feel that there has to be some connection here, with this Francis Garvey. But I cannot find it.'

After another hour's fruitless searching, they descend the staircase, their footsteps heavy. *He was hoping for some resolution*, Eve thinks. *Some end to this. To me.*

They find Diana recently returned from lunch and reclining by the swimming pool. When they ask her about the name Francis Garvey, she wrinkles her nose as if in irritation that this is all they have to show for their labours.

'Guy never mentioned him. Or not that I can recall.'

Once again they have come up against a brick wall. And wasted one of Eve's precious remaining days.

In the car on the way back to Antibes, a blanket of silence descends over them. The beauty of the day and the scenery seem to Eve to be mocking her. The vast expanse of sea, the exact same navy as the ribbon on Eve's old school summer hat. She remembers taking the hat off on the bus on the way home and holding her face up to the little open window so that the breeze could blow the smell of freedom through her hair.

What would that younger self say if she could see her now, driving in a convertible along the seafront of Nice with this man at the wheel, all broad shoulders and too-big hands and Heathcliff hair?

Eve smiles to herself. Is there no limit to her subterfuge? Creating false worlds to impress her younger self, hiding the fact that it is only borrowed, all of this. Not hers at all. She used to think, staring out of her childhood bedroom window for hours at a time, that her life was out there somewhere, waiting for her. Yet here she is, very nearly thirty years old, and life is still going on elsewhere, and she can only wait and watch.

'I expect you think us very money-grabbing,' Noel says

suddenly as they exit Nice towards Antibes, skimming the coast. The sea has a turquoise tint here, revealing its rocky bed where dark fish dart in crystal-clear water.

Eve glances across at him in surprise. Where has this come from?

'Not at all,' she lies. 'I haven't given it any consideration.'

'You are a god-awful liar, Mrs Forrester.'

'Oh for heaven's sake, can't you just call me Eve?'

The outburst seems to come from nowhere. She wasn't even aware she was bothered about his almost mocking over-politeness.

'Fine. You're a god-awful liar, *Eve*.'

She knows it to be the case. She has always been too ready to say what is on her mind, not able to hold back, or dissemble. When you grow up in a house where nothing is brought out into the open, where every conversation seems to happen behind a closed door, you either end up retreating further into the darkness, or you try to drag everything out into the light, regardless of whether it can withstand the exposure.

'What you do with your family money is entirely your own affair,' she says, gazing fixedly ahead.

A heavy pause. Then: 'The thing is, *Eve*, you have no idea about us. You think you do. You've drawn your conclusions from what you've seen and heard. But really you haven't the first clue. Duncan, for example. I'm sure you think him weak and spoiled. He has been laid very low by our father's death.'

'They were close, then?'

Eve is surprised. From what she has learned of Guy Lester, she cannot see that he would share much common ground with his errant younger son.

'No. Of course they were not close. But that is the thing, you see. Now they never can be. All his life Duncan wanted to please Guy, to make him proud, but he couldn't seem to find the way. They missed each other; do you know what I mean? Like those two boats over there.'

He gestures to his left where a sleek yacht has just passed within a couple of feet of an old fishing boat, its blue paint chipped and peeling.

'And now he can never make that right. Never make up that distance. I'm sure you come from a normal close family where you're nice to each other all the time, but just try to imagine how that might feel for Duncan. First to lose his mother when so young and now to know he'll never get the chance to have the connection with Guy that he craved.'

'I do have some idea—'

'He's in trouble,' Noel blurts out, just as Eve is about to challenge his impression of her. 'Duncan gambles. Well, you know that. Blackjack mostly, but really anything will do. The South of France is awash with casinos. Duncan and I moved here when we were very young and we were playing cards as soon as we learned to count. But he never grew out of it. He racked up debts. So he borrowed money from the kind of people you really don't want to borrow money from. And if you do borrow money from them you really, really want to pay it back. People like Laurent Martin.'

Eve remembers Laurent and Duncan framed in the doorway at the Duke and Duchess's reception.

'Oh, but that's not so bad then, is it? I mean, Laurent Martin is from a well-known family. He's marrying Gloria Hayes. He seems perfectly civilized.'

Noel is looking at her incredulously. 'Do you really think

that inherited money and an Oxford education and a trophy wife are all it takes to ensure fair play and decency?'

'No, of course not. It's just that—'

'The Martin family made their money from slavery, and even now they have a reputation for ruthlessness in business that's almost unparalleled. Laurent is a chip off the old block.'

'Yet you said nothing to Gloria Hayes the other night.'

'What should I have said, exactly? That there are rumours about the way her fiancé treats people who cross him, but nothing has ever been proven? I can see that going down well. Besides, just because Laurent is unscrupulous in business, it doesn't mean he won't treat his wife like a princess.'

Eve nods, but her throat feels tight. 'So is Duncan in danger?'

'Not yet. But he could be.'

'You take your elder-brother duties quite seriously I think, Mr Lester. Noel.'

Noel shrugs.

They are just turning into the gates of Villa La Perle. In spite of her misgivings over what she has just heard, Eve feels herself relaxing at the glimpse of the pink walls through the cypress trees, a releasing of muscles she hadn't known were tensed.

'The thing is,' says Noel, and then stops. The car is parked now, and he turns the engine off. He and Eve regard each other in the sudden silence.

'The thing is, we argue a lot, my brother and I. We are very different. But I was there when our mother died. I saw what he went through. I know who he is but . . . I know also who he could be. Who he has the potential to be. Oh, forget it. I'm no good at making myself clear.'

'On the contrary.' Now something occurs to Eve. 'That's why you're so keen to sell the house, isn't it? So that you can bail your brother out of the mess he's in?'

Noel nods stiffly. 'I am responsible for him, now that Guy is dead. He has no one else.'

'But your brother is a grown-up. Don't you think perhaps you ought to leave him to take responsibility for himself?'

Noel flings open his car door and steps out on to the gravel, leaving Eve no choice but to follow suit, wishing that she had not spoken. Instead of being grateful that he is finally being open with her, she has slapped him down.

'I'm sorry,' she says, following his broad back along the path, listening to the crunch of the gravel underfoot and the noise of the distant cicadas. 'I didn't mean . . .'

But Noel has disappeared through the gap in the trees. Eve stops. Takes a deep breath. Brings her hands up to her face in a gesture of frustration. The ring catches in the sun, glowing green like a cat's eye in the dark. The inscription comes back to her.

From F with love eternal.

F.

Francis Garvey.

17

THE TERRACE OUTSIDE Le Crystal is crowded, chairs and tables crammed so closely together Eve feels as if she is practically sitting on the lap of the woman behind her. It is a warm, balmy evening of the type that reminds her how far from home she has come.

'Well, if you'd brought that home, I shouldn't allow it in the house,' Rupert is saying. 'I suppose I would grant it space in the garden with a nice geranium planted in it to draw the eye away from the ghastliness of the object itself.'

The Colletts have visited the little village of Vallauris, where Picasso has been tracked down to a studio, where apparently he has been engaged in the prolific production of ceramic pots. Of the artist himself there was no sign, much to Jack's disappointment, but they saw a selection of his work on display in a neighbouring studio and Ruth pretended to toy with the idea of investing in a vase, though Eve suspects her interest was mostly a ruse to tease her husband.

'It was quite the ugliest thing I've ever seen,' Rupert tells her. 'Great big bulbous thing with a face and two handles made to look like arms resting on hips.'

'I thought it was beautiful,' says Ruth. 'Jack insists we'll regret not buying it.'

'Emperor's new clothes,' says Rupert dismissively. 'In ten years' time, when the next shiny new thing comes along, his Picasso will be quite forgotten.'

Jack has stayed behind in the village, still hoping for a sighting. He will hitch back or find a barn to sleep in. 'That's one thing about the war, isn't it?' says his mother. 'We're none of us fussy any more.'

Le Crystal is on the corner at the junction of two roads. On the opposite corner is another bar, and all around them are people – parading up and down in their best going-out clothes, peering at restaurant menus, wheeling babies in huge prams who Eve can't help thinking ought to have been in bed hours ago. The pavements are alive. So different from the centre of Sutton, where nothing is open beyond ten o'clock, and anyway, no one has the money for going out, and there is still no decent food in the restaurants.

The terrace on which they sit is three tables deep and they are in the middle row, square in the centre of things. All around Eve is a cacophony of sounds – the clinking of glasses as the waiter brings the wine for the table behind, the chatter of a hundred people in what seems like a hundred different languages, the growl of the occasional car motor as the traffic goes by.

'*Pardon, Madame!*'

The woman at the next table leans over to unpeel her baby's chubby fingers from the hank of Eve's hair that he has wrapped them around.

'Please don't worry,' Eve smiles. The baby has a round face, with a mouth that opens into a perfect 'O' of outrage when he finds himself disengaged from the object of his attention.

'Can I ask why *you* don't have children?' says Rupert, once the child has been enticed away with the offer of a piece of bread sprinkled with sugar.

'Rupert!' Ruth frowns at her husband. 'You cannot ask questions like that. Such things are private.'

'It's quite all right,' says Eve, although really it isn't. 'There's no problem, the doctor says, it just hasn't happened yet. Still plenty of time, though.'

'Absolutely,' says Ruth.

'Mrs Forrester? Eve. It *is* you. I thought it was so. How very fortunate to see you.'

Victor Meunier's voice is so soft and yet somehow it carries over the contented gurgles of the baby at the next table, and the clinking of glasses at the one behind, over the shrieks of laughter and the buzz of animated conversation.

Eve senses Ruth's curiosity, the way her friend's sharp, appraising eyes travel over the smooth planes of the Frenchman's face and the tall frame from which his clothes hang as if custom made for him.

Introductions are made and after a show of protest – 'I could not disturb you when you are having so happy a moment' – Victor gives in to the Colletts' entreaties to join them.

As they resume talking, Eve is conscious of a warmth spreading from a point right in the centre of her and radiating outwards. She wishes she could stop time. Right here and now, sitting at this table with friends on a warm summer's evening, with the scent of candles and cigarette smoke and pines and petrol coating her nostrils like exotic perfume.

Another bottle of wine is ordered. Eve does not usually

drink much, but here on the Riviera she finds she is a different person, and the person she is now likes the feeling of sitting back in her seat, holding the thin stem of the wine glass between her fingers, enjoying how it loosens her tongue and her mood.

All afternoon she has felt as if there is a cloud over her head, despite the perfection of the day. She has kept going over the events of earlier. Her tactless question about Noel's dead fiancée and the way he'd shut her down when she tried to talk to him about Archie. Then the unsettling conversation about Duncan and her own sense of having blundered in, suggesting he should allow Duncan to stand on his own two feet.

She'd caught up with Noel by the front door of the villa, losing no time telling him about the inscription on the ring and the letter F for Francis, only to feel flattened by his lack of enthusiasm.

'It could turn out to be important,' he'd agreed politely. 'Although there are, of course, many names that begin with F. My father had a favourite cousin called Flora who kept in touch with him secretly against the express wishes of her family. He had a friend called François who died during the war, and a godson called Freddy. It's also quite possible he had a raft of lady friends with names like Felicity or Freida or Fenella.'

'Yes, but none of them has any connection to *me*.'

'And Francis Garvey? What connection does he have?'

To which she had no reply.

After he'd gone, she'd sought out Sully, last night's crossness quite forgotten in her eagerness to tell him what they'd discovered, but the American was not there. Instead she'd found Mrs Finch wrapping crystal glasses in newspaper and packing them into a chest. Mr Sullivan had had a visitor, the housekeeper had imparted with excitement. She couldn't be sure as she'd been occupied downstairs at the time, but it sounded very much like Gloria Hayes. And soon after that he'd gone out and had yet to return.

As ever, Mrs Finch had been warm and welcoming, and Eve had briefly considered staying to talk things over with her, but she was deterred by Diana's strange remark about the housekeeper being in love with Guy. And there was still the issue of where Eve stood in the household, neither guest nor family. She was grateful for Mrs Finch's efforts to make her feel at home, but she still couldn't quite relax around her.

So Eve had had no one with whom to discuss the day's events. Which is why she'd been so happy when the Colletts had called in to invite her for dinner in Juan-les-Pins.

Now that Victor has joined them, she feels happier still. He is so charming, so intent on putting the Colletts at their ease. Their account of the day's pilgrimage to Vallauris leads to a lively discussion of art. Victor is knowledgeable about all the artists of the region – Chagall, Picabia, Matisse. Rupert's prejudices against what he insists on calling, to his wife's evident embarrassment, 'abstract claptrap' melt away in the face of the Frenchman's passionate defence of modern art.

The dinner plates are taken away, and the wine is replaced by cocktails that Victor orders with a deferential 'Please allow me to suggest . . .' Eve finds herself beginning to float above her surroundings in a most pleasant way. The three-piece band that has been playing softly throughout their meal now launches into a Glenn Miller number. These days Eve hardly listens to anything other than classical music, which is Clifford's preference, but she remembers this one from the war years.

'Would you like to dance?' Victor asks.

Eve, taken by surprise, glances at his cane without thinking.

'I admit I am not as quick on my feet as I used to be, but I will try not to embarrass you,' he says, smiling, and she feels a rush of embarrassment, remembering his war history, how he had not let his injury prevent him from helping others.

Victor abandons his cane on a table near the dance floor and Eve finds that his limp is far less pronounced than she had thought. In fact, though he perhaps clutches more tightly to her hand than is normal, leans a fraction more towards her than she is used to, she cannot say she minds. The knot she has been carrying in her chest since Noel Lester dropped her off at the house begins to unravel and she closes her eyes, conscious only of the music and the warmth of Victor's palm on her waist.

'I am so glad you came here, Eve,' Victor says in his soft voice.

She casts her eyes down, suddenly finding something fascinating on the floor.

'I am glad too,' she says. 'It is such a lovely part of the world.'

'That is not what I meant, as I think you know.'

Eve looks up and freezes as she finds his eyes fixed on her. Oh, but this isn't what she intended. She likes Victor very much and is flattered that someone so cultured, with such a reputation, should have singled her out for attention, but surely he cannot think that she . . . ?

They rejoin the others outside and Eve gulps in the fresher air as if she has been suffocating.

With her face turned towards the street, she has the strangest sensation of being watched, but when she peers out into the shadows there is no one there, just the customers outside the bar opposite – a couple who only have eyes for each other, and a large table of US airmen. Eve wonders if their presence here in Europe has anything to do with the deepening crisis in Berlin the papers back home were so full of. She has read that the Soviets are threatening to block the Allies' access to the part of the city under Western control, isolating its citizens. This bloody war. Every time she thinks it is well and truly in the past, something happens to make all her fears rear up again.

She and Ruth go in search of the ladies' cloakroom. Eve is glad to find the facilities quite civilized, having been shocked in one cafe near the beach at Juan-les-Pins at being confronted by what amounted to little more than a hole in the ground.

'He is very charming, your Monsieur Meunier,' says Ruth as they wash their hands side by side.

'He is not *my* anything,' says Eve, noticing how wild her expression looks in her reflection and raising her wet hands to her cheeks in an effort to cool them.

'Do you think, perhaps, just a little too charming?'

Eve is conscious of Ruth's gaze seeking out her own in the mirror, but she resolutely refuses to meet it, or to treat Ruth's question as serious.

'We are in France,' she says. 'I think charm is something taught at infant school, like mathematics or Latin.'

By one in the morning, the Colletts are ready to leave.

'Why don't you come back with us?' Ruth asks Eve. 'There's a sofa in our room that Jack could sleep on if he comes back tonight and you could have his room.'

Eve looks around at the people and the lights, listens to the saxophone playing in the background, breathes in the smell of freedom and youth, and her spirits plummet at the thought of the night ending so soon.

'But it is still early, by Riviera standards,' says Victor. 'Don't worry. I have my car here. I can deliver Eve safely back to her villa when she is ready to leave.'

Ruth looks uncertain. 'Perhaps we ought to stay a little longer,' she appeals to Rupert. But he has had enough.

'My love, Eve is a grown-up,' Rupert says. 'We must pay her the courtesy of allowing her to know her own mind.'

When they wave the Colletts off, Eve is reassured to see the streets are still teeming with people. Victor summons the waiter and orders two Soixante Quinzes.

The cocktail slips down so easily, like lemonade, but with a kick in the tail that suggests something much stronger.

'What does it have in it?'

'Lemon, sugar, champagne. And perhaps a little gin.'

Eve knows she should not drink any more, and yet it is so seductive sitting here listening to the music, feeling that particular breeze that raises the fine hairs on your arms and lets you know you're very close to the sea even when it's nowhere in sight.

Victor is such good company, with his old-fashioned politeness, his slow, shy smile, the sadness that lives in the hollows of his face.

'Will you tell me about your accident?' she asks. And then, almost immediately, she is sorry. 'Forget I spoke. Please. You do not have to relive anything unpleasant on my account.'

'It is perfectly all right, Eve. I am not ashamed of this old leg. There are plenty of others who have uglier injuries. I was shot in the leg during the Battle of Hannut in Belgium, just before I became a prisoner of war.'

'I am sorry.'

'No need to be. I own an art gallery; I am not an athlete or a mountain climber. I can still appreciate fine paintings and enjoy a glass of something special and dance with a beautiful woman.'

Eve feels her cheeks burning and is glad of the breeze and the darkness. The crowds have thinned out considerably now and she is surprised, when she looks around, to see how many tables are empty.

She is aware suddenly of how much she has drunk. Everything on the outer edges of her vision seems to be in constant motion and she has a strong desire to be lying down.

'I think I must go,' she says.

'Is it something I said? Because I called you beautiful?'

'No. Don't be silly.'

Victor summons the waiter and produces some notes from his pocket.

'Here, let me pay,' says Eve, scrabbling in her bag for her purse, too drunk even to worry about the bill they might have run up.

Victor reaches out to stop her, elegant fingers curling around her arm.

'Please, do not offend me.'

They stand up to go and Eve feels herself swaying. Victor cups her elbow with his hand. They take one of the roads that shoot off from the junction where Le Crystal sits, heading towards the seafront. It is dark and Eve stumbles. Immediately Victor's arm is around her. She feels the weight of it, like something inanimate, a heavy fur stole on too hot a day. She has an urge to shrug it off, but she does not want to offend him.

'My car is just this way.'

Only now, too late, does Eve think about what she is doing, alone with a strange man in a strange country on a near-deserted road. A man who, despite his gentleness, is not her husband.

To her relief she sees a couple ahead, taking photographs against the backdrop of the moonlit sea. As they pass, there is the flash of a camera and a giggle from the woman posing.

'Here,' says Victor, opening up the passenger door of a long, low car and sliding her inside.

The car is stuffy and Eve winds the window down so that she can take big lungfuls of fresh air.

When Victor gets behind the wheel, he sits still for a moment, his lips pressed together. Then he turns to her.

'I don't suppose,' he says, 'you would like to come back to my home? I live above my art gallery. You could view the paintings.'

In that confined space, Eve is aware of her heart thumping in her chest, the sound of blood in her ears. She yearns suddenly for her bedroom back in Villa La Perle. For the big bed where she can reach out in all directions and feel nothing but air.

'Thank you, but I'm not feeling terribly well,' she says.

'Then we shall take you home.'

Victor starts the car and Eve sinks back in relief, although already a small, contrary part of her is wondering about the road not taken.

Outside the car window, the moon dances across the still surface of the sea.

Waiting. Always waiting.

18

7 June 1948

THE INSIDE OF Eve's mouth has been coated in felt. Overnight, someone has wrapped her head tight in wet bandages that are slowly constricting as they dry so that her skull feels held in some sort of vice. When she opens her eyes, the light is a white-hot blade coming towards her.

Eve has never been a drinker, though more through lack of opportunity than any kind of inbuilt moderation. Also, she is someone who fears losing control. When you have felt out of place all your life you tend to keep a tight rein on yourself, not trusting your surroundings to protect you if you are unable to protect yourself.

Now the previous night comes back to her. Victor's palm hot against her waist, the weight of his arm around her shoulders.

She thinks of Clifford in a rush of guilt and nostalgia. Remembering his diffident courtship, how he'd asked her if he might hold her hand, and then again if he might kiss her, as if physical desire were something to be negotiated up front, like a dinner invitation that might be turned down with an apology and no hard feelings and never spoken of again.

'I would like to take care of you,' he'd said when he proposed. At the time she'd felt something inside her cave in at the very idea of it. Self-reliant from childhood and then faced with a blank future following the end of the war, the idea that she might hand over responsibility for herself to someone else, even momentarily, was seductive. His flush of pleasure when she said yes was so gratifying.

No one believed in true love any more. Not since the war. Duty was the thing, that's what she told herself. And respect. And honour. A desire to build a solid, peaceful future.

When she and Clifford had stood quietly in the registry office in front of seven members of their families, she had felt optimistic. The registrar had the tremors and had barely been able to sign the register, but Eve had been full of hope. 'You look very nice,' her mother had said. 'He's a good man. You've done well.' And her heart had swelled with pride.

She resolves to phone Clifford later today. When she is feeling better. She will explain that she intends to return at the weekend, as Ruth suggested. She will apologize. She will tie up what needs to be tied up here and go home.

Villa La Perle will be rented out and then sold. The Lesters will get their money.

Eve finds Sully outside at his garden desk, typing away in the dappled shade of the eucalyptus tree.

'Feeling a bit delicate?' he asks without turning round.

Eve is nonplussed. 'How did you—'

'Oh, please. This is a very small town. Kick one, they all limp.'

Eve sinks down heavily into a wicker chair. It is another flawless day but the beauty of her surroundings just seems to emphasize her own shortcomings – her sluggishness, the way her hair feels frizzy and tangled like coir matting, her sallow skin and the sour taste of yesterday's wine in the back of her mouth.

'I apologize for the other day,' Sully says, still without looking at her. 'What I said about your marriage. I tend to make assumptions about people based on nothing more than the fact that I've made so many mistakes myself I want to believe others are just as foolish.'

'It's forgotten.'

Now, finally, he turns towards her. Gives a low whistle.

'Boy, you really look *bad*.'

'Thanks.'

'No, I mean, really *terrible*.'

Eve thinks about going back to bed; at the very same moment she is also thinking about jumping off the jetty into the sea, fully clothed, letting the glorious cool water instantly wake her.

In the end she does neither.

'I'm going in search of breakfast,' she tells Sully. 'Coffee will either cure me or kill me.'

'When it comes to Mrs Finch's coffee, there's a third category,' says Sully. 'A sort of low-level maiming.'

Inside, the cool of the house provides relief for her throbbing head. She goes into the kitchen, but finds no trace of either housekeeper or breakfast. Nor does she dare raid the cupboards herself for fear of appearing to be taking liberties.

She wanders, disconsolate, into the hallway, jumping when she hears the slamming of the front door one storey up. There comes the sound of voices, a man and a woman seemingly mid-argument. 'If you don't like the way I drive, you can bloody well drive yourself,' the man retorts.

Eve groans as she recognizes Duncan Lester's voice and, seconds later, Clemmie Atwood's. Just the people she least wants to see while looking like something the cat dug up. On an impulse, she dives in through the door that leads down to the cellar, pulling it closed behind her. Feeling around for the switch, she flicks on the dim bulb.

For a moment she hovers at the top of the stairs, unsure what to do, jumping when Duncan and Clemmie resume their argument seemingly inches from the door she is leaning against.

Well, she can't go back out there. Nor can she remain where she is without running the risk of appearing very foolish should they come bursting in here.

Instead she decides to go downstairs and investigate Guy's junk room. It is a long shot, she knows, but didn't Mrs Finch say that Guy couldn't bear to throw anything away? Mightn't there be something in that room that kick-starts a memory in her mind or provides a clue? At least it would be a way of justifying her presence down here if Duncan and Clemmie did make an appearance.

Near the bottom of the stairs, the first doubts set in. The walls down here are damp. When Eve puts her hand on the bare brick to her left, it comes away wet. The light bulb is a long way above, over the top of the steps, and the stairwell where she stands is shrouded in shadow.

Eve takes hold of the metal handle of the door. It feels clammy, and she wipes her palm on her dress after she turns it, giving it an extra shove to counterbalance the stiffness.

There's an immediate smell of musty earth, a cold dankness that her skin absorbs like ink on blotting paper. She steps forward, feeling along the brick wall for the light switch she feels sure must be here. She tries not to breathe in as she casts her eyes around, trying to identify the shapes in the dark corners by the yellow light from outside the open door.

Unable to locate a switch, she edges further into the room, conscious now of the goosebumps rising up on her bare arms, the chill on the back of her neck. For a moment she thinks about turning around and going back upstairs, but the thought of bursting out on to Duncan and Clemmie stops her.

There is a movement in the back corner where various cast-off items lean against the shelving. A rustling sound. Just as she begins to realize there is something in here with her – a mouse or, heaven forbid, a rat – there is a loud *bang*, the door slams shut, and everything is pitch black.

For a moment, all is still. Eve is so stunned she cannot formulate a single thought. There is a strange noise echoing around the darkness, a rasping sound, which she only belatedly realizes is the sound of her own breathing, harsh and ragged.

Panic begins to build in the pit of her stomach, a bubbling anxiety that she knows she must keep under control. *Breathe*, she orders herself. *The door has blown shut. That is all.* She thinks of how she will craft this into a story to tell Sully when she gets out. How amusing she will make it. Gradually the panic ebbs away.

She reaches out a hand, pawing at the darkness until her fingers make contact with something cold and damp. She feels rough stone under her skin. The wall, then. With her palm flat against the surface, she slides her hand along, praying it will eventually lead her to the door.

Her foot knocks into something, sending it clattering to

the ground, and she cries out. But it is nothing, she tells herself. A half-empty tin of paint, perhaps.

She continues feeling her way along the wall, braced against whatever other objects she might encounter, but thankfully there is nothing more and soon her hand encounters the smooth wood of the door.

Relief floods through her, so strong she almost laughs from the force of it. How foolish to have allowed herself to become so scared. Her fingers find the handle and twist.

Nothing.

She takes her hand off, wipes her palm once more on the fabric of her dress, and tries again, making sure she has a firm grip.

The door will not budge.

No. No, no, no, no, no. She rattles the handle, first gently, then with increasing ferocity.

'Help! I'm trapped in the cellar. Please help!'

She pictures Sully outside, the keys of his typewriter loudly clattering, and a tight band snaps inside her.

Mrs Finch then. But the housekeeper hasn't been around all day. She remembers the empty kitchen, the lack of breakfast things laid out on the dining table.

'Please!' she shouts again. 'Someone.'

Even Duncan and Clemmie would be welcome now. But of course the chances of them having stayed put all this time in the passageway behind the stairs are minimal. No, they will have gone off in search of Sully or whatever else brought them here in the first place.

The damp chill is overwhelming. Eve remembers her reaction the first time she came to this room, how she'd had a sense of something unpleasant here, had even recoiled. And now here she is, stuck.

Turning around so that her back is to the door, she slides down until she is sitting on the hard, cold stone floor, her hungover exhaustion overcoming her fear of a mouse or rat crawling over her legs.

She peers around. Does darkness have different qualities, different depths? She tries to make out whether the black is denser in the corners, or where she imagines the corners to be.

Even when her eyes finally adjust a little so that she can make out some vague shapes, it merely makes things worse. What's that black thing over there? Did that large looming shadow really move or is it just the darkness playing tricks on her?

She hugs her bent knees close to her chest, feeling her heart hammering against her thighs.

She is wearing the brown crepe dress and the cold seeps in through her clothes, to her very bones. She lowers her head until it is resting on her knees and she no longer has to look into the black void.

She weeps.

19

'I TOLD YOU, she was there one minute and then *pfff*!'

'What the hell does *pfff* mean?'

The voices, male, jolt Eve from her slump. How long has she been sitting here in the dark? She has no clue.

'Help!'

Has she even spoken aloud? She is so discombobulated, here in this endless, depthless black hole, that she no longer seems able to recognize what is real from what exists in her head.

'Help!' she tries again. Louder. She scrambles to her feet, fumbling for the door handle.

For a long, agonizing moment she thinks they have not heard her. She rattles the handle as violently as she can.

'What in hell?'

Now there is a noise on the other side of the door.

'In here!' she shouts.

'How did you—? Hang on, the blasted handle has fallen off.'

There is a low exchange that she cannot make out and then the sound of something clicking into place, and now, without warning, the door bursts open, knocking her backwards.

She tries to open her eyes, but the sudden light is too

strong and she remains on the floor, blinking, until she feels someone's hands on her bare arm, pulling her up.

A few minutes later, she is upstairs in the sitting room lying back on the velvet sofa.

'What were you doing in there?'

Noel Lester is standing in front of her, blocking the sunlight and not looking very happy.

'I told you, I was just poking about. You know. Seeing if anything down there triggered any memories.'

'What I don't get is how you managed to shut yourself in,' says Sully, who is sprawled on the chaise longue on the other side of the room. What is it with this man, that he cannot just sit, that he must be forever in a horizontal position? 'You must have given the door a pretty good slam to make the handle fall off like that.'

'I didn't slam it. I didn't even touch it. Perhaps someone else did.'

Noel smiles in a way that makes Eve want to slap him.

'Who would have done that? Mrs Finch is out, Sully was working. You know, I didn't even know they'd found the key for that room. It was locked for years, after Guy gave up on building a boat from the parts he used to store down there. No wonder bits of it are falling off.'

'Your brother could have closed it. Or Miss Atwood. They were here earlier. Perhaps they didn't know I was in there.'

'Duncan and Clemmie were here? That's news to me.'

Noel looks at Sully, who shrugs.

'I didn't see them either. Probably came to batter some sense into Eve here about selling the house, and slunk off when they couldn't find her.'

Eve is quiet, remembering the raised voices behind the

door, the heart-thumping dread of discovery. She can still feel the creep of the damp on her skin in that cellar, the sense of something lurking in the dark corners of the room. Yet, after they'd pulled her out of there, Noel had brought a torch from the storeroom next door and shone it around just to prove to her she'd been quite alone.

This place is making her into a fool. A fanciful fool.

Noel wants to ask her about her mother. Specifically, whether Eve has been in touch with her to ask her about that name, Francis Garvey. When Eve explains that she's waiting for her mother to reply to the letter she's written to her, she is incensed by the astonishment he doesn't even try to hide. As if everyone in the world has a telephone of their own!

'So send her a telegram, asking her to telephone you at the hotel.'

'It would be too much of a shock for her, seeing a telegram boy arrive.'

He has no answer to that. Everyone who lived through the last decade learned to live in fear of the surprise knock at the door.

She doesn't tell him that she has no language with which to begin this conversation with her mother. That at least a letter presents an extra distance between them, across which the words must travel and hopefully lose some of their impact by the time of landing.

'Am I right in thinking you're not that close to your mother?'

'I don't know where you got that idea, Mr Lester.'

If voices could cut through glass.

Sully, as if sensing the cooling in the atmosphere, changes the subject.

'Have you decided yet, Eve, what you will be wearing to the wedding of the decade?'

He has propped himself up so he is draped across the back of the chaise, leaning towards them as if agog, but Eve thinks she can hear a new tinny note in his voice.

'I heard she has to be drugged just to spend a night with Laurent Martin. How is the poor woman to endure a whole lifetime?' asks Noel.

'Why must everyone here be so cynical?' Eve asks. 'It's practically a sport with you all. Laurent obviously adores her and she him. She's just nervous about the wedding, as anyone would be. Anyway' – Eve's curiosity gets the better of her – 'where did you go with her yesterday, Sully?'

'She wanted some recommendations of local places to go.'

'Beauty parlours?' asks Noel.

'Bookshops, actually,' says Sully, and Eve relishes the expression of surprise on Noel's face.

'Gloria is trying to better herself,' continues Sully. 'She has read the entire works of the Russian masters and last year slogged her way through *Ulysses*, although she gaily admits to not understanding a darn word.'

Sully's imitation of Gloria's accent is unnerving, but still he has this hard edge to his voice.

There is a noise from above. The sound of the front door closing. Rapid footsteps on the stairs.

'Good afternoon all,' says a breathless Mrs Finch, her eyes flicking from one to the other. Hooked over her right arm is a basket of vegetables, as if she is fresh from the market. In her left hand she holds a large stiff brown envelope.

'This was in the hallway. It must have been hand delivered,' she says. 'It's for you, Mrs Forrester.'

Eve stands up to reach for the letter, all of a sudden nervous that it will turn out to be from her mother, somehow redirected by some local sorting office. She wonders what her mother could possibly find to say that would require such capacious stationery. Her mother does not easily tolerate excess in any form.

There is no stamp on the letter to give away where it comes from. Her name is written in blue ink pen in capital letters, very different from her mother's cramped, precise hand. Eve is conscious of Noel and Sully watching her and Mrs Finch lingering in the doorway.

She slips her hand inside the envelope and extracts a piece of card. No, not card: a photograph.

Eve stares at it for a long moment while her mind struggles to register what she is seeing, then she gasps. Lets the photograph drop to the floor where it lies face up. There is a silence.

And then: 'I had not realized you were quite so well acquainted with Victor Meunier,' says Noel.

'You do seem very . . . cosy,' agrees Sully, his head twisted to the side so he can see the picture the right way around.

Eve, who has frozen to the spot, angles her head down so she is seeing the same thing they are seeing. A black and white image, grainy, but clear enough to make out the two figures. His arm protectively around her back, her head resting on his shoulder. His face turned towards her as hers tilts up to him, as if they are at the very point of a kiss.

With a sickening *thunk*, Eve remembers the couple she and Victor had passed on the way to the car, taking pictures of the moon on the water.

'I don't understand,' she says, and her voice is like a stranger's, high-pitched and strained.

'I imagine there'll be a letter in there to go with this,' says Sully. He reaches out a hand and she passes him the envelope as if she has no free will of her own.

He is right. The letter is typed on a single sheet of white paper.

Perhaps your husband would like a copy of this photograph? Go home, Mrs Forrester.

Eve sinks down heavily on to the sofa from which she has just risen, her heart juddering.

'We were not . . . that is, there was nothing . . .' She stops, unsure how to continue. 'Mr Meunier was only helping me to the car as I was feeling unwell.'

'I'm sure *Mr Meunier* was most attentive.' Noel practically spits out the Frenchman's name, and Eve feels grubby, even though she is sure she has nothing to feel grubby about.

In her head she hears Victor's voice asking her back to his house. Calling her beautiful. Sees herself lapping up his words like a cat with milk. She feels sick.

'Oh, but this is quite thrilling,' says Sully. Now that he has recovered from his surprise, he looks to be almost relishing this unexpected drama. 'I've never been blackmailed. I don't suppose I ever had anything worth being blackmailed for. No money and certainly no reputation. I'm almost jealous.'

'But who would do such a thing?' asks Eve. Her voice trembles dangerously and she realizes she is on the verge of tears.

'Shall we make a list of all the people who'd like you to just sign the sales papers for the house and be on your way?' says Sully.

'Hold on a minute.' Noel's eyes seem to grow darker when he's angry so that now they are the green of deep woods where the sun never penetrates, or the reeds on a muddy riverbed. 'Are you implying that someone in my family—'

Sully holds up a hand, and Eve sees that he is indeed enjoying himself.

'I'm not implying anything. Just examining the facts.'

'The *facts* are that Mrs Forrester has placed herself in a very vulnerable, compromising position.'

Now the tears that have been threatening arrive in earnest, pooling in her eyes and spilling down her face. Eve swipes them angrily away, but not before both men have seen them.

'Oh, for heaven's sake, it's a bit late for tears now,' says Noel.

Sully drops down on to the sofa next to her and takes her hand.

'It's not as bad as you think,' he says kindly. 'Whoever sent the letter won't have your home address, will they?'

'My husband is in the phone book,' Eve splutters between sobs. 'He has his own business. Oh, what will he think of me?'

'Perhaps you should have thought of that before carrying on with Victor Meunier in the street,' says Noel.

Carrying on?

'Are you sure you didn't hear a car coming up to the house to drop the envelope off?' Mrs Finch asks from the doorway, startling Eve, who has forgotten the housekeeper is there. She holds her hand to her face to hide her tears.

An image comes into her head of her father's funeral, she and her mother walking stiffly into the church side by side like two black chess pieces. Before they entered, her mother put a warning hand on her daughter's arm and leaned towards her. Eve can still remember the rush of shock, thinking at first that her mother was about to embrace her, or at least to whisper some message of emotional support. Instead she hissed, 'If you feel the tears coming, focus on a point just above the vicar's head and concentrate on that until the feeling passes.'

Hold it in, was her message. *Cover it up, present your best blank face to the world.*

The sound of the doorbell rips through the emotionally charged air, and Mrs Finch retreats to the hallway and up the stairs. There is a murmur of voices.

She reappears in the doorway, looking agitated.

'It's Mr Meunier wanting to speak to Mrs Forrester. He does not wish to come in. He seems a little on edge.'

A flame works its way up from Eve's chest to her neck, then into her cheeks until all the capillaries in her face are on fire. She will not look at Noel. Will not give him that satisfaction. After the shock of that image of her and Victor so close together they might almost have been lovers, the prospect of speaking to him now brings on a rush of shame.

But if she refuses to speak to him, how much worse will that look? As if she has something to hide?

'I'm coming.'

She gets heavily to her feet.

'Eve?' Victor's voice, usually so soft, has an edge of urgency. Standing in a pool of weak sunshine on the doorstep, he looks pale and leans heavily on his cane.

'I don't wish to alarm you, but I felt I had to speak with you. I have received an . . . *unfortunate* letter.'

'You too!' It has not occurred to her that Victor might also be compromised by the photograph. After all, he is not married, so what does he have to lose? The answer comes with Victor's next words.

'I have some clients who are very, shall we say, conservative – and who would not be happy about me being . . . how do I say it . . . involved . . . with a married woman.'

Eve feels the blood rush to her face.

'Involved? But nothing—'

'Of course you and I know the truth, but there is the question of how it appears. How other people will see it. These clients have a lot of influence, and I do a lot of business with them. I cannot afford to lose them. Do you see?'

'Yes. Of course. I'm sorry. I also have received the same letter. With a threat to send the photograph to my husband.'

Victor's eyes soften.

'Please forgive me, I have been so concerned with myself I have not asked about you. What a shock it must be for you. But perhaps your husband will see it for what it was, just two . . . friends, walking home after a lovely night.'

Eve laughs – a particularly mirthless sound. 'I'm afraid I very much doubt it.'

Victor sighs. 'I suppose one cannot blame him. When a man has such a beautiful wife, it would be hard not to become jealous and think the worst. So you will be going home, then, Eve?'

Again the heat in her cheeks, and a chasm opening up under her rib cage. *Home*. Just a four-letter word, but was there ever one more freighted with meaning?

'Yes. I haven't had a chance to make plans, but I expect I shall.'

'That is a great pity.'

After Victor leaves, she stands for a moment in the hallway with her back to the door. The words *going home* echo in her head.

Something of her distress must show in her face because as soon as she walks back into the sitting room, Sully summons her to sit down next to him.

'Listen,' he says, his big, square hand reaching out to squeeze one of hers. 'Someone is just trying to frighten you. Make arrangements to go back to England if you must, but delay them for a few days and stay for the wedding as you originally planned. Whoever sent this will see that you're intending to leave and ease up. Gloria will never forgive me if you leave her in the lurch; she's taken quite a shine to you. In fact she has commanded me to bring you over to her house tomorrow so that she can dress you up in some of her discarded finery. After that you are free to go back to your home and your husband and this will all seem like a preposterous dream. Don't let malice or jealousy scare you away prematurely. You will stay, won't you?'

Eve hesitates, and then nods. She has always been a passenger in her own life. Only this trip to France has been driven by her. And look where it has ended up. Easier to do as she is directed, to hand over the responsibility for her choices to someone else.

'That's settled then,' says Noel. 'And happily Victor Meunier will be at the wedding too. You can renew your acquaintance there.'

Eve focuses on a point just past Noel's head, and stares at it until the backs of her eyes no longer burn from her unshed tears and she feels nothing at all.

Guy, 28 April 1948

HOLKE HALL IS a terrible place. All red brick walls and a tower at one end with an enormous clock that looks like an eye. The sky behind the tower is the same slate grey as the wire fences that surround the whole building.

The screams are like skin ripping.

Endless corridors that smell like shit and bleach mixed together. I hold my breath and fight the urge to turn and run. This is not what I imagined. This is not what my money is for.

The nurse who shows me the way wears shoes that squeak on the polished floors. She looks at me sideways through lowered eyes and I know she is sizing me up. My clothes, my accent. The way my skin hangs so loose after my rapid recent weight loss. Strange to think that just a few months ago I would have been sizing her up too. Her figure, how old she is, whether it is worth the effort of flirtation. Now that I am beyond all of that, preoccupied only with staying alive, it strikes me how very shallow my dealings with women have been. I have not given myself time to do more than skate the surface of them, so hurried have I been to move on to the next and then the next.

My poor Diana.

I am shown into the visitors' room, a comfortless space, with windows set way up in the walls so that all I can see is the sky, the colour of gunmetal. There are tables here and I sit down at one in a hard-backed chair, thinking about all the other people who have sat here before me, so that I don't have to think about her and how she might react when she sees me.

When the door opens I get to my feet, my heart thudding like something wild and out of control.

'There's been a mistake.'

They've brought the wrong woman. This one is old with broken capillaries in her cheeks and eyes that are cloudy and unfocused. She wears a smock-type dress that is soft with age and her hands flutter, moth-like, at her collarbones. A vein stands up on her leg like a worm under her stocking and there's a purple, puckered dent on either side of her forehead, around which her hair falls lank and almost entirely grey.

'No, sir,' says the nurse, frowning. 'This is the lady you requested to see. I did think it queer though. She hasn't had a visitor in the whole time I've worked here.'

I look again and something shatters inside me, tiny needle-sharp shards embedding into my chest as I recognize the distinctive ring she wears on her finger, with the green stone.

I remember a girl with smooth dewy skin spattered with blood and long thick curls in which globules of red matter lodged themselves like beads.

Oh God, what have I done?

'Of course. I remember now,' I say, for the benefit of the nurse. Then I ask the woman, 'Do you remember me?'

The nurse laughs. She doesn't look like she should be a nurse. Doesn't look to be much more than Libby's age.

'Since Dr Cranleigh had a good poke about in her head with his ice pick she doesn't remember her own name most days.'

The woman is staring at me with those unsettling eyes, only now there is something in there, some spark of something.

'I remember,' she says eventually, in a voice that sounds croaky as if not much used. Still she stares. Unblinking.

'I am sorry,' I tell her. 'I didn't know. This place. What has happened to you. I didn't know.'

The truth is I didn't want to know. It is only death that has brought me scurrying here to this dreadful place in search of eleventh-hour forgiveness.

That night I go out and drink whisky until my thoughts drown in the stuff.

20

8 June 1948

'I WOULD JUST about saw off my own legs at the knee if I could be as petite and dainty as you.'

Gloria Hayes is surveying one of her shapely bare legs as if it is the ugliest thing she has ever seen.

Eve can't help laughing, conscious that it is the first time she has done so since the events of yesterday.

Only now, here with Gloria Hayes in this fairytale palace with different tiers each painted a different shade, like frosted icing on a wedding cake, does she feel the dark cloud that has hung over her every breath since the arrival of that photograph finally lift.

'I told Sully I would never speak to him again if he didn't force you to stay. You know, Eve, we don't know each other, do we, but I get the idea we are in the same position, you and I. Both of us outsiders here. I can see I've spooked you. You're thinking I'm like one of the crazies who hang around outside the studio gates for someone to invite me to a picture show or for a Coke or to meet their mother or take a drive somewhere. They think they know me because they've seen me forty feet high and practically naked and they've watched me eat and sleep and cry and fall in love and that bonds us together somehow.'

Eve assures Gloria she does not consider her in the least bit crazy.

'I'm glad to be here,' she says. 'I needed to get away from Villa La Perle.'

Without even knowing she is going to, she starts telling Gloria about the damp cellar, the photograph and the letter and the way the stark black type left an impression in the paper as if someone had bashed the typewriter keys with violent force.

Gloria – who is sipping from a tall gin fizz that she'd tried without success to make Eve join her in – makes sympathetic noises, but Eve is disappointed by how little the American seems to appreciate the full horror of the situation. She tries to explain again, but Gloria flaps one of her manicured hands.

'Oh, blackmail,' she says, as if it is something so run-of-the-mill as to be hardly worth bothering about. 'You can't give in to those kinds of people, honey, or it'll never end.'

'But who would have sent it?' Now that she has dredged the painful subject up, Eve is reluctant to let it go. 'I can't believe someone hates me so much.'

Her voice cracks and she disguises it by coughing, as if she has something stuck in her throat. The truth is that this is what troubles her most. Not the threat to involve Clifford – although she feels nauseous whenever she thinks of a brown envelope like that one arriving at his office or dropping into the hallway of the house in Sutton or, worse, being handed over by Mr Ward the postman, hovering with that expectant expression on his round florid face – but the idea that someone dislikes her enough to go to these lengths.

All Eve's life she has structured her interactions with other people around a desire to be liked, and if not liked then at least not disliked. She supposes now she might have been trying to make up for the lack of affection at home with the knowledge that she was accepted or at least tolerated outside it, whether at school or working alongside the other women volunteers during the war.

And now this. The hatred in those little black letters gouged deep into the page.

'Any of the Lester family could have done it. From what Sully says they all have a reason for wanting money, and you're the one standing in the way of them getting it.'

'Diana doesn't need the money.'

'Diana Lester is a bitch. I could see it the second I saw her. Bitches don't need reasons for trying to screw you over. It's in their blood.'

Eve's mouth hangs open. This isn't the first time she's heard someone talk this way. One of her friends during her WVS days had a filthy tongue, but then she'd come from a family with five older brothers. To hear Gloria Hayes, star of *Rose of Alabama*, being so casually profane is thrillingly shocking.

'Here. This one. You must. It would be too perfect.'

Gloria has produced the most glorious dress Eve has ever seen. Silver that shimmers when she stands in front of the huge windows and holds it up to the light.

They are in the pink middle tier of the house. A grand balustraded terrace runs along the length of the building, including Gloria's dressing room, in which Eve now finds herself installed in a black velvet armchair with ornately carved wooden arms.

Eve had had no intention of coming, had even suspected it

to be some sort of joke on Sully's behalf. She had thought she would remain all day in her room, feeling sorry for herself and trying to reach some sort of decision about what to do next. The Colletts had called round but she had asked Mrs Finch to tell them she was unwell, unable to face telling them about the photograph. What would they think of her? She remembered how uncertain Ruth had been as they left Le Crystal, how she'd entreated Eve to come back to the hotel with them. Oh, why hadn't she just said yes?

Then towards lunchtime when she'd been lying on her bed, wondering whether she could nip down to the kitchen unseen to bring up a snack, she had heard a car pulling on to the gravel to the side of the house.

A few minutes later, Mrs Finch was knocking on her door.

'Miss Hayes is waiting in the car for you, Mrs Forrester. I tried telling her you were under the weather, but she was most insistent. I rather think she is not used to being told *no*.'

So Eve had gone to explain, but had somehow found herself sitting instead in the back of the car, powerless to protest. So here she is. Nestled in this very peculiar chair while a woman who until a few days ago she had seen only on a cinema screen goes through a wardrobe larger than Eve's childhood bedroom, in search of a dress for her to wear to what the newspapers are already billing the most lavish wedding of all time.

Gloria hands her the silver gown, which Eve already knows will trail along the floor, but still she holds it up in front of her, obedient, while Gloria frowns in a way that manages not to cause so much as a wrinkle in her smooth forehead.

'Not that one then,' she says, snatching it away and flinging it on to the floor. 'Oh, but this one. Yes, this is the one.

It's meant to come to the knee, but it won't matter but it's a little longer on you.'

'But blue doesn't suit me.'

Gloria stands stock-still and stares at Eve, her hand on her hip.

'Who in God's name has been filling your head with such cock-eyed nonsense? You were made to wear blue. It will set off your heavenly brown eyes.'

Eve remembers their neighbour Nora sitting at the tiny table in their back parlour drinking tea with her mother and saying, *I'm afraid poor Eve will find that complexion quite restricting when it comes to clothes. Just browns and greys, rather than any of the pretty colours.*

But now, here is Gloria holding the dress up in front of Eve's reflection. Kingfisher blue and made of satin that gathers wide on the shoulders and then stretches over the bones of whatever is holding it in shape, and she sees instantly how it brightens her face. Gloria takes hold of Eve's ungovernable hair and twists it up, securing it off her face with an ivory clip.

'There,' she says. 'Much better. Now try on the dress.'

It won't fit her, though. She is convinced of it. Gloria is a completely different shape to her, broader across the shoulders with long limbs.

Yet somehow it does. It is more off the shoulder than on, and the hem, which she is sure should sit on top of the knee, comes midway down her calf. But the clever construction moulds itself exactly to her body, or rather to a perfected version of her body. It is almost indecent how well it suits her.

Gloria, who has sat herself down on a stool, cocktail beside her, claps her hands in delight.

'You will need shoes, of course. And your dainty li'l feet

would be swimming around in these great ugly boats I have to wear.'

'I shall just have to wear my own shoes.'

Gloria glares down at Eve's feet, leaving no doubt as to her feelings on the subject of her companion's footwear.

'Honey, I don't want to offend you, but . . . oh, just wait a minute!'

Suddenly Gloria is back on her feet and heading to a second wardrobe on the other side of the room. She opens the door and shoes start flying. Eve narrowly escapes being hit by a black slingback with a velvet bow on the toe. Finally Gloria emerges with a pink box tied up with ribbon.

'I think this is them – I never forget a designer box.'

She impatiently tugs the ribbon and casts it aside, tearing the lid off the box.

'Yes! I knew it!'

Reaching in, she delves through layers of tissue paper, emerging with a pair of cream high-heeled peep-toe shoes with a strap around the ankle and a blue platform.

'The studio sent a photographer to capture the blushing bride in the run-up to her wedding and the idiot stylist got the English and American sizes mixed up.'

'Ow, they're too tight.'

The shoes pinch cruelly at the toe, but Gloria insists that Eve strap them up anyway, no mean feat on account of the invisible boning in the dress, which makes bending difficult.

'Perfect,' she says. 'What did I tell you?'

'But they hurt.'

'Of course they hurt. Everything beautiful hurts. The trick is not to let anyone else see that it hurts.'

Eve stands up and attempts a few steps.

'I really don't think I could . . . oh!'

She has hobbled as far as the mirror at the end of the room that reaches from the ceiling right down to the carpeted floor, and now she sees the full effect of the dress and the shoes together. It is not that she looks beautiful, but that she looks like someone else.

She looks like a woman who belongs here on the Riviera, a woman who dresses up to go lunching with other women just like her, to whom marriage is like a fur stole to be shrugged on and off as the fancy takes her, who flaps her hand instead of bothering to reply.

For fifteen minutes Eve practises walking in the tortuous shoes under Gloria's tutelage, adjusting her normal strides according to the restrictions of the boned dress. Now she not only looks like someone else, she also moves like someone else. And before long she begins to feel like someone else.

It is with reluctance that she changes back into her old clothes.

At least you have clothes to put on, she scolds herself, remembering the man she'd seen sitting on the newspaper just after she'd arrived in the country.

'Does it ever make you feel guilty, all of this?' she asks, gesturing at the rows of designer shoes in every different colour on display through the open wardrobe door, the ornate dressing table with its gold-framed mirror and the bottles of scent lined up like empties outside a pub door. 'What I mean is that you – that *we*' – she doesn't want Gloria to feel singled out – 'have so much, while those men sit there in those fishing boats, hour upon hour, trying to catch enough fish that their families might eat tonight.'

Gloria follows the direction of Eve's gaze, out of the double doors, across the balustrades of the terrace to the sea, where the black dots that are the boats bob around under the blazing sun.

'Honey, I grew up with eight brothers and sisters in a three-room shack. I know what it is to have a belly full of nothing but dreams. Two of my brothers are dead now. Let me tell you, the thirties were no time to be poor. Not where we lived anyhow. But I got out. Survival of the fittest. Ain't that what the scientists call it? So no, I don't feel guilty. I won't even tell you some of the things I've had to do to get here – it'd turn your hair clean white. I've earned my right to be in this house, in this room, with this view and as many goddamned pairs of shoes as I like.'

While delivering this speech, Gloria has been rummaging in a large white shiny handbag, from which she now produces a small bottle. She unscrews the lid and shakes two pink pills into her hand.

'Want one?'

Eve shakes her head.

'Suit yourself.'

Gloria pops both pills into her mouth, tipping back her head so that her throat is stretched taut.

'What are those?' Eve's curiosity gets the better of her.

'Oh, I forget the actual name. I just call them my sweeteners 'cause that's what they do, make life a bit sweeter.'

'So they make you feel happier?'

Gloria laughs. She really has the biggest mouth Eve has ever seen.

'Honey, you don't feel *anything* on these pills. That's the joy of them.'

Eve doesn't know what to say. Already she fancies she sees Gloria's beautiful eyes dulling as if a layer of steam has built up over them. Perhaps she should say nothing. Act as if this behaviour is all perfectly normal. Most assuredly that's what she should do. But . . .

'Gloria. Please tell me to mind my own business if you wish, but you do *want* to get married, don't you?'

The words are out before she has time to vet them, and she wishes she could reel them back in.

'I'm sorry,' she says, seeing Gloria's expression. 'I didn't mean to pry. Ignore me.'

Gloria wanders through a door into the connecting bedroom and flings herself face down across a bed so huge that she can lie diagonally with no part of her long-limbed body overhanging the sides.

'Do you ever,' she says, her voice muffled, 'feel like a leaf being blown around by the wind this way and that way' – she waves a long arm from side to side in demonstration – 'without you actually having much say in it?'

On the other side of the doorway, Eve considers. Was that how it was when she married Clifford? But no, she wasn't wafted into that marriage on a gust of wind that she had no control over. She'd weighed up the options open to her and made a choice. She'd chosen to believe she could grow to love Clifford, that love was a plant that would automatically grow, given the right conditions.

'But surely if you have any doubts you can just call a halt to the whole thing?'

Gloria laughs.

'Oh honey, you're sweet, but Laurent Martin is not the kind of man you call a halt to. And all that moolah the studio has spent already. They want their fairytale wedding. Eve darlin', have you read any fairytales? They're really the nastiest things. Swans who make themselves human for love but when they walk it's like razor blades under their feet, children kept in cages and force fed so that they're fat enough to eat. And besides, I had the real fairytale when I married Greg. My, but I loved that man so. And look what happened there. He went off and fucked a woman with teeth bigger than her titties, and I became Poor Heartbroken Gloria, the most pitiful wife in America.'

Gloria has turned over so she is lying on her back on the white sheets, her red hair spread out around her head, one bare leg resting on the knee of the other so her foot with its painted toenails points high into the air.

'So this time I am marrying with this' – Gloria taps her head – 'and not this.' A tap to her chest. 'Laurent is a catch. Did you know, *Vogue* magazine named him the most eligible bachelor in the world, two years running? He's the kind of man folk take notice of, but he also has a cultured side. He and Victor Meunier spend so much time together talking about art. You can always tell a lot about a man by his friends, can't you? With Laurent I get financial security beyond my wildest dreams, but also I get to take back control. If my face is all over the papers it's because of what I've done, what I chose, *who* I chose, not because someone else has made a goddam fool of me.'

When Eve thinks of the reception at the Duke and Duchess's house and how Laurent paraded Gloria around as if she were one of his racehorses, she feels a flutter of unease.

'Even so, if you did have second thoughts I would help you,' she says. 'So would Sully. I suspect he'd do anything for you.'

'Sully is a darling man.'

And with that damning phrase, Eve understands that whatever secret desires her fellow lodger might be harbouring towards Gloria Hayes, they are not reciprocated.

She is ruminating on this later, sitting back in a canvas deckchair on the terrace at the villa, looking at the stars and listening to Sully explain why his most recent marriage didn't work out.

'I was on the rebound from my third wife, Nancy, when I met Geraldine. By that stage I'd spent six years with someone who hated my guts and who tried to pin every terrible, god-awful thing that was happening anywhere in the world on me. The war itself was a direct result of the kind of aggressive prose I was churning out in my novels, apparently. So I was a sitting duck for anyone who came along offering some morsel of affection. And Geraldine adored me. Christ, if it's possible to smother a person to death with adoration, she would have done it. But you know, when you've been starved of love and someone comes along offering it to you on a plate, it's very seductive. By the time I realized we had exactly nothing in common, it was too late.'

'Nothing in common apart from loving you,' says Eve.

'That's harsh, Mrs Forrester.'

'Sorry.'

Eve is in a strange, jittery mood. She tries to calm herself by focusing on the blue satin dress hanging upstairs in her closet, remembering the way she'd felt looking in the mirror, as if she was someone else, free of the constrictions of being herself. But still knowledge of the existence of that grainy photograph is like a stone in her shoe, always there. She tries not to think about how Clifford would feel opening up an envelope and taking that picture out, tries not to imagine the depth of his disappointment.

Above her the black night has been sprayed with stars as if they have been blown there through a straw. From the bushes comes the sound of cicadas, that strange noise that is such a part of life here that you end up noticing it no more than the noise of the blood rushing in your ears or the breath entering and leaving your body, until it stops suddenly and the night rings with silence. The air is scented with eucalyptus and a dim light flickers from a yellow lantern hanging from one of the branches.

A star shoots across the sky in an arc of light that is gone almost before she registers it, and two bats flap in and out of the eaves of the house.

But now there is another sound ripping through the still night. A car roaring up a hill in the wrong gear, the screeching of brakes and the noise of gravel flying from under wheels.

There is the sound of the doorbell, long and unbroken as if someone is leaning on it. And then raised voices from inside the house. A woman laughing or crying, it's impossible to tell.

Eve sits up and exchanges a glance with Sully, who shakes his head and shrugs.

There is the clicking of heels on polished floor and a familiar voice saying, 'Where in hell are they?' followed by a reply from Mrs Finch that they can't make out.

Gloria Hayes bursts through the curtained doors in a blaze of light like the shooting star Eve saw just moments ago. She seems unsteady on red heels, and a thick line of mascara runs down each side of her face.

'Here y'all are. My two very favourite people in all the world.'

Gloria is clutching on to the door frame. She wears a red satin dress that has a dark stain down the front.

She staggers the couple of steps towards them and collapses on to Sully's lap, hooking her arm around his neck.

'Is it a party? Shall we make it a party? Call the maid back and get her to bring us something to drink.'

The maid.

Eve's eyes flick towards the interior of the house, hoping Mrs Finch didn't hear.

'I'll go,' she says, getting to her feet. 'What would you like?'

'I don't know, surprise me. A glass of something wonderful. No, wait, what am I talking about, stupid Gloria.' She holds out her own hand and slaps it. 'Bring a *bottle* of something wonderful. Bring two.'

But when Eve steps inside the house, she finds that Mrs Finch already has the situation in hand. The two of them meet at the foot of the stairs, the housekeeper carrying a tray on which there sits a bottle of whisky, a small bucket of ice and three glasses.

'Might I suggest slightly more ice than liquid for Miss Hayes.' Mrs Finch's smile doesn't quite meet her eyes.

'Thank you, Mrs Finch. I'll take this out, shall I?'

'Of course, if you like.'

Eve cannot meet the older woman's gaze as the tray is handed over. She feels ashamed, although it wasn't her who'd used the word 'maid'. She realizes she has been here in the house for almost a week and she has not had one meaningful conversation with the housekeeper. Has not made an effort to find out what path brought her here, or what she intends to do when the house is sold. How quickly she has fallen in with the Lesters' view of the world, in which people are tiered just like Laurent Martin's fairytale villa, and those in the uppermost tier don't question their right to be there.

Outside, she finds Gloria still seated on Sully's lap, and he seemingly disinclined to have it otherwise.

'Gloria is running away,' announces Sully.

'Yes. After our talk this afternoon I got to thinking about the wedding and Laurent and how he has a man who comes in twice a week to pluck the hairs from his nose and I was feeling kinda glum. Then I said to myself, "Gloria, you don't have to go through with this." And here I am. Aren't you proud of me, Eve?'

She is slurring her words so that they flow one into the other and the strap of her dress has fallen down her shoulder. Five grape-sized purple bruises bloom on the top of her arm.

'Can I stay here with the two of you?' Gloria says, nuzzling Sully's neck. 'I could fix you drinks and snacks while you work, Sully. I wouldn't get in your way. You'd hardly notice I was here.'

'Although perhaps the presence of the world's press camped outside the door might just give you away,' says Sully.

She gives him a playful slap. And then buries her face in his neck and bursts into tears.

Eve and Sully stare at each other over her shaking head.

Now there is more disturbance. Another car arrives.

Footsteps come not through the house but down the

path to the side, past the swimming pool terrace. Two men appear, wearing dark uniforms and expressions that are impossible to read. Tall and broad across the shoulders, they do not speak. At first Eve is too surprised to be frightened. But now here comes Laurent Martin himself, small and slight, but so densely packed, a restless energy emanating from him.

He contemplates the scene before him. His dishevelled bride-to-be sitting on the lap of another man, sobbing into his neck, the straps of her red dress slipping down her arms. Eve feels the first prick of alarm. Laurent stands so still. So silent.

Finally: 'Gloria, my sweet. It's time to go home now.'

His voice is quiet, measured.

Gloria doesn't respond, but her entire body goes rigid.

'Come, Gloria. I am waiting. There is much to do tomorrow. Our guests will begin arriving. You need to rest, my love.'

His voice is low and controlled, but there is something behind it, some tang of metallic sharpness.

Gloria raises her head, the black lines of mascara now thicker and more shocking against her pale skin in the semi-light.

'I think I might stay here with my friends,' she says. But already her voice is wavering, uncertain.

'I'm sure your friends have plans of their own, darling. It is time to come back home now. Remember the medicine that nice doctor prescribed to help you sleep? You wouldn't want to have to face the night without that, would you?'

Gloria shakes her head almost imperceptibly. Her eyes are wide and fixed on her fiancé, even while she clutches Sully's shoulder. Eve's heart buckles at the sight of her.

'You don't have to go,' Sully says gruffly, focusing on Gloria. 'You can stay here. Mrs Finch will make you up a room.'

'That's very kind, Mr Sullivan,' says Laurent. The oil on his slicked-back black hair glints when it catches the light from the lantern suspended overhead. 'But my bride needs to get home to rest. She has a busy few days ahead. The excitement has been too much for her. I'm sure you can understand.'

When he smiles, his teeth shine white in the moonlight.

Sully tries addressing Gloria again directly, as if Laurent isn't right there with his two henchmen.

'Gloria, you don't—'

But already she is getting to her feet. Swaying and blinking as if she has no idea how she has come to be here in this place, with these people.

'Gloria—' Sully tries again.

She turns towards him and smiles politely.

'Thank you. I've had a most lovely time.'

It is as if she is excusing herself from a society tea party. She walks unsteadily over to Laurent. Docile. Her shoulders slumped. He takes her arm.

'Come, my darling.'

Eve's gaze is drawn to the point where Laurent's hand, with its perfect nails, wraps itself around Gloria's wrist, his fingers digging into her skin.

Fear makes her mute.

Gloria and Laurent start climbing the steps back up towards the road, the uneven click of her heels ringing out in the night. Now the black-clad bodyguards turn to leave, their set expressions betraying nothing.

After the others are gone, after the sound of the car engine has faded into the warm night air, Eve and Sully remain out on the terrace, not speaking. Nor do they look each other in the eye, as if they are both afraid of seeing their own cowardice reflected back at them.

21

9 June 1948

EVE IS WOKEN by the sound of raised voices, but when she arrives downstairs there is no one there. She searches in the sitting room and out on the terrace. She hesitates before braving the kitchen in case of bumping into Mrs Finch. But the room is empty.

She heads out to the swimming pool. It is one of those fresh, clear Riviera days when the world seems to be retouched in Technicolor, the sky the rich blue of cornflower petals, the green of the laurel bush leaves as vibrant as the jewel in the ring Bernard gave her, which she now wears on her finger as a constant reminder of the answers she still seeks.

Sitting down on a wooden steamer, she breathes it all in as if she might somehow absorb it, down through her airways and into her lungs, until it is a part of who and what she is.

She looks at the great expanse of sea, studded with the nodding black dots of the yachts and the fishing boats; at the low smudge of Cap Ferrat across the water to her left and beyond it the mauve tips of the Maritime Alps; and straight ahead hundreds of miles of nothing at all, and again she senses a weight being lifted. *I am the merest speck of nothing*, she thinks. But it makes her feel relieved rather than unhappy.

By the time she dives into the pool, every nerve bursting into life at that moment of impact when her body hits the cool water, she is feeling greatly cheered and full of equanimity. She settles into a swim, moving smoothly and steadily from one end to the other, enjoying how her heightened heartbeat thrums in her ears. At first she keeps count of her lengths but finally she gives up.

So engrossed is she in her exertions that she doesn't at first notice the presence of someone else on the terrace. In fact, it is not until she has stopped swimming – and hauled herself inelegantly out on to the side of the pool, blown the water from her nostrils, first one and then the other, and reached out towards the steamer for her towel – that she realizes she is not alone.

'I didn't want to disturb you when you seemed to be having such a fine time.'

Noel holds out the towel that she had left on the cushion upon which he now sits.

'I wouldn't say that exactly.' Eve snatches the towel, aware of her saggy swimming costume and her bare, goosepimply thighs. 'What are you doing here anyway?' she asks, aware of how rude she sounds. This is what the Riviera has done to her, rubbing as if with sandpaper at her polite veneer, revealing the coarseness underneath.

'My stepmother, the Goddess Diana, has invited you for lunch at the Hôtel du Cap. She has sent me to fetch you so that you cannot say no. That is, unless you have other plans?'

By 'other plans' he is referring to Victor. Her certainty of this causes her to answer far too quickly. 'No, of course not.'

And now she is stuck with it.

'Why does Diana want to see me?'

Noel shrugs. 'Perhaps she just likes your company.' Then he seems to relent. 'She'll be wanting to size you up, to find out exactly what you intend to do about the house. Diana likes to be in control, if you hadn't noticed.'

'What was she like?' Eve's curiosity makes her forget momentarily about her dripping hair and her irritation at the ruination of this perfect morning. 'I mean, when you were growing up. It must have been hard losing your mother and then having her replaced by someone so . . . *cold*.'

Noel lies back on the steamer. Looks down at the ground. Looks up in the air.

'She was very young. Not much older than me. And she was afraid of getting things wrong and, more importantly, of being seen to get things wrong. She tried with Duncan and me, in her own way, but we were determined to resist and she did not have the nerve to bulldoze her way through. She had very little sense of who she was, if you know what I mean, so she had to keep trying to prove that Guy loved her more than he did us, which wasn't terribly endearing. Now I understand it more, but at that age you're so wrapped up in yourself.'

He has picked up a leaf from the ground and is turning it over carefully between his thumb and forefinger. Eve has the strangest, strongest wish to be that leaf, held in his hand. She pushes it from her mind. This man could turn out to be her *brother*.

She forces herself to focus on what he has just said, about

Diana not knowing who she was. It ties in with what Sully told her about Guy's widow's background. Yet it doesn't excuse her behaviour. Eve isn't someone who automatically thinks the worst of others, but once she has taken such a view, she is liable to cling stubbornly to it.

'I remember one night coming across her crying,' Noel continues. 'Guy had gone to bed and I'd been out somewhere I wasn't supposed to be and was trying to sneak back in and she was outside on the terrace, sobbing. And when I asked her why, she said a really curious thing. She said, "A word of advice. If you're going to have a dream you'd better make damned sure it's unattainable." '

'What did she mean?'

'At the time I didn't have a clue. The next morning she was back to her usual frosty self and we never referred to it again, to my great relief.'

'And now?'

Noel pauses. Looks down at the leaf in his hand and then crushes it between his thumb and finger.

'Now I don't bother with dreams. They're more trouble than they're worth.'

Eve feels her stomach drop with disappointment and is instantly cross with herself. What exactly had she been hoping? That Noel Lester would share his innermost secrets with her, perhaps open up to her about his dead fiancée? She remembers that day in Diana's attic when she'd tried to talk about Archie, how quickly Noel had cut short the conversation, as if her grief could have nothing to do with his own.

On the way to the hotel, Noel is terse, as if regretting giving too much away. Eve, wearing the brown dress once again, feels the sun burning her arm and the side of her face. These convertible cars are all very well, but they leave one so terribly exposed. She finds herself thinking about Diana and what she'd said to the young Noel. How must it be to dream of a life of luxury and society lunches and charity balls and a handsome, wealthy husband, and then to get it all and more? How great a vacuum must the loss of that dream leave in a life that has been entirely geared up to its attainment?

Unaccountably, Eve finds herself thinking of her mother. The great unfathomable well of her disappointment. How bizarre to imagine a connection between these two polar opposite women.

The Hôtel du Cap-Eden-Roc is approached through a set of gates along a wide, tree-lined drive. The building itself sits on top of a slight hill, all the better for visitors to appreciate the grandeur of its ivory-coloured facade with its rows of windows flanked by blue-grey shutters and its elegant mansard roof.

'Diana thought you might be more comfortable lunching outside on the terrace.'

Noel is not looking at her when he says this, but she is burningly aware of the frumpy provinciality of her dress, and her hair, which, following her swim, has dried in curls that spring out from her scalp. In desperation she had rolled up her silk scarf into a fat ribbon and tied it around her head, hoping to emulate Clemmie Atwood, but the ends hang limply down on either side and she now feels it to have been a mistake.

A man in white uniform hurries down the steps that lead from the main doors of the hotel. At first Eve thinks he has come to greet them and remains seated with a smile, but when Noel springs out of his seat and comes around to hold her door open, she realizes this is a valet come to park the car.

To her relief they walk around the side of the building rather than through it. As they round the corner at the back, she lets out an audible *oh* at the sight of the straight gravel path bordered by pine trees on each side, at the end of which the sea rolls itself out into the distance. Floating on the horizon, there appears to be a series of hazy hills.

'That's the Île Sainte-Marguerite there in the distance,' says Noel, disconcertingly answering the question she hasn't even asked. 'There's a prison fort there. Have you heard of the Man in the Iron Mask? That is where he was kept. In a cell, in a fort on an island in the middle of the sea, and in a metal mask, quite alone. Can you imagine the horror?'

'But that is a myth, surely?' asks Eve, feeling chilled despite the warm sun on her face.

Noel shrugs. 'It used to give me nightmares to think about it, when I was growing up. Perhaps it doesn't appear so terrible now in the warmth of a June day, but when it's winter and the Mistral wind is churning up the sea and everything is the colour of grey cement, it's the bleakest place on earth.'

They pass two people in large hats and beach gear trudging up the path from the sea. Eve recognizes the squat woman with all the rings who'd called Sully a bad man and whisked him away at the reception for Gloria Hayes that first night in Antibes, what seems like a lifetime ago.

'Good morning, Mr Lester,' the woman says, nodding her head so that the brim of her hat wobbles ferociously.

Behind her trails a younger woman, whose correspondingly square shape leads Eve to believe she must be her daughter.

She has plump pink cheeks and large myopic grey eyes through which she blinks at them both.

As they draw level, the younger woman slows as if she is about to speak.

'Come along, Beatrice,' snaps her companion, who has walked some way up the path towards the hotel. 'Why must you always lag?'

The girl's cheeks grow even pinker under her yellow hat and she smiles unhappily and moves on, clutching a basket in which are piled books and magazines and a large jar of cocoa butter such as women use to help their skin tan quicker, although Beatrice doesn't seem to have the type of complexion that takes kindly to the sun.

'Who was that?' Eve asks, watching the girl lumber away.

'Beatrice Ryder. Her father made a fortune from luxury hotels, and at one stage she grew very attached to Duncan, though I don't expect he was very kind to her.'

'That seems to be a family trait,' Eve retorts.

'What's that supposed to—'

'You're here. I'm so glad. Mummy's been so horrid.'

Libby Lester throws her arms around her brother's waist so violently that Noel has to take a big step back to stop them both tumbling to the floor.

'What's been going on, Libs?'

'She's so mean. She won't let me go on the trapeze. She says it's too high. Daddy used to let me. Oh Noel, I do really miss him so much. I feel like I could die from missing him.'

Eve looks away, suddenly acutely reminded of her outsider status.

'What trapeze?' she asks when the two of them finally break apart.

'I'll show you,' says Libby, suddenly cheerful, seizing Eve's arm to lead her down the path. All but hidden from view by the pines to the right, a low white building is spread out along the cliff, descending perilously down the rocks in long restaurant terraces that overhang the sea, their wooden decks shaded by canvas canopies, the horizontal white railings seemingly all that stand between the diners and the deep waters beneath.

But rather than head that way, they turn to the left where there is a narrow concrete sunning platform laid out with deckchairs and umbrellas, and in front of it, several sets of stone steps that lead, to Eve's amazement, to a swimming pool seemingly growing out of the cliff face. Prone sunbathers on towels vie for space in the cramped area around the pool, beyond which there appears to be a sheer drop down to the sea. A row of bathers, their tanned skin drying in the sun, perch on the far side of the swimming pool. Eve at first believes them to be dangling their legs over the cliff and her chest tightens in panic, until she realizes that the side of the pool is raised off the ground and there is a short platform before the edge. A couple of diving boards overhang the drop, making Eve feel dizzy just looking at them. And beyond that, jutting way out over the water, is a beam from which hang a knotted rope, a rope ladder, a trapeze with a wooden bar, and, in the centre, a pair of rings of the type gymnasts use to perform impossible feats of strength and control.

There are two people on the equipment: a couple, both gleaming and, even this early in June, quite golden. The man is in the process of transferring from the rope, which he has clearly just scaled from the sea, to the rings, while the woman is sitting on the trapeze, moving her legs to and fro to make it swing. Then, as Eve watches, she drops backwards so that she is hanging by her knees upside down as the trapeze makes great swooping arcs through the air, suspended far above the surface of the water.

'Oh!'

Eve has exclaimed so loudly that one or two of the bathers around the pool raise their heads off their towels to take a closer look.

Libby giggles. 'It's so much fun, Eve. It's like flying. Mummy used to be the queen of the trapeze, apparently. It's where Daddy first saw her and he fell in love with her at once, like that.' She snaps her fingers in front of Eve's face. 'She was standing up on the bar, bending her legs so it went faster and faster and higher and higher, and she had long hair then, down to her waist, and it was flying out behind her and he said she was like a goddess riding a flying chariot.'

Diana is waiting for them on the upper terrace of the restaurant pavilion at a round table under the shade of the canopy.

'Can't we sit over there?' asks Libby, pointing to the far corner, which is the only spot bathed in sunshine, and is currently occupied by a group of noisy young people who have been there quite some time, judging by the three near-empty bottles of champagne on the table. One of the women is perched on the railing, her back to the sea and her bare legs entwined in the bars, and Eve doesn't know which she finds more shocking: the fact that one lapse in concentration could send her flying backwards into the water below, or that she is wearing nothing more than a bikini.

'The sun coarsens your skin, Libby,' says Diana. 'How many times do I need to remind you?'

Then she relents.

'However, since your brother is now here, I suppose you could go on the trapeze if he's willing to supervise.'

Libby flings her arms around her mother's neck by way of reply.

When the younger Lesters are gone, Diana lights a cigarette and leans back in her chair.

'Thank you for coming. I'm aware you might have had other invitations.'

Eve feels the blood rush to her face. Does the whole of the Riviera know about the compromising photograph?

'Don't worry. I haven't asked you here to discuss Victor Meunier. You're a big girl. I'm sure you know what you're doing. I want only to know how long you intend to stay in Antibes, Mrs Forrester. I think it's always best to be upfront with people, don't you? So we all know where we stand. This has been a very difficult time for the family. My husband dying so suddenly, before we all had a proper chance to say goodbye, and then your arrival stirring up so much bad feeling. I would like to know when we might be allowed to start grieving in peace.'

She is so cool, so completely in control, in a pink sleeveless dress with white stitching around the neck to match the white sunglasses that hold back her glossy hair. No hint of the heartbroken widow, or the insecure new young bride of Noel's description.

'I am sorry,' Eve mumbles. 'I didn't mean . . . That is, my intention was never . . .'

Diana snaps open a cigarette box. Sits back. Disinterested. Imperious.

Eve, having been inclined to give her the benefit of the doubt, now feels her old animosity returning.

'As we're speaking frankly, may I ask a question of my own?'

'Of course.'

If Diana is taken aback by Eve's newfound assertiveness, she does not show it.

'Why is it so important to you? You're well provided for. I've seen your house. Why the rush?'

Diana flicks ash into the ashtray and takes a sip of her drink. She has ordered them both whisky sours, despite Eve's protestations that she rarely drinks at lunchtime.

'I don't know what it is you're imagining, Mrs Forrester, but the truth is Guy did not leave nearly as large an estate as you appear to think. He was disinherited by his family in England, and though he did come into a trust when he was very young, it has largely been spent. Buying the Nice villa practically wiped him out financially. Now there will be inheritance dues to be paid, bills to meet. The coffers are all but bare.'

It has the ring of truth about it, although Eve is quite sure Diana's idea of bare coffers bears little resemblance to her own.

'You think me greedy, Mrs Forrester. You think I have everything I need; why should I push for more?'

Before Eve can protest, Diana gets to her feet.

'Please, come with me a moment.'

She strides to the railing at the edge of the terrace, leaving Eve no option but to follow.

'Look at her.'

Diana is pointing along the cliff to the left, where in the distance they can see Libby trying to get up on to the trapeze, helped by Noel. The girl is not a natural athlete and takes several attempts before she manages to haul herself up out of the water, where she grasps the bar under her armpits and kicks out wildly with her chunky legs.

Below her, Noel pretends to make a grab for her foot and Libby flails even more wildly. Something solid in Eve's chest starts to dissolve.

'You have no children, Mrs Forrester.'

It is a statement of fact rather than a question, but still Eve feels the need to reply. To justify herself.

'No. Not yet.'

Two brief words and yet such a world they contain. Those intermittent furtive fumblings in the dark with Clifford. The monthly creep of excitement and dread. How is it possible to be both dismayed and relieved at the same time? A child would be a validation, and furthermore would provide some shape to the featureless landscape of her future. And yet. What about her? What about that voice she has had inside her the whole of her life asking, *Is this it? Is this all?* Will a baby silence that voice, or amplify it?

'Then you will have no idea what it is like to love someone fiercely and yet be disappointed in them. No, that's not fair. Not disappointed in *them*, because of course they are as they are. But disappointed you will never get to meet the person you thought they'd be. That dream child who is you, only better.'

Eve, struggling to understand what Diana is telling her, is surprised by the intensity of the urge that comes over her to protect Libby and keep her from hurt.

'You think me unfeeling,' says Diana. 'Unmotherly, perhaps. And you may be right. But I know how the world is. I know what it does to young women who fail to conform to the ideal. Libby is not like other girls her age, as I'm sure you've noticed. She has a *simplicity* that means she will be easily taken advantage of. And, let's be frank, she is no beauty. And I'm afraid if there's one thing I've learned it's that if a woman can't be beautiful, she'd damned well better be rich.'

'What hope is there, then, for those of us who are neither?'

Eve means to sound droll, but there is no mistaking the plaintive tang. Diana raises a perfectly shaped eyebrow and turns to lead the way back to the table.

'I meant no reflection on you, Mrs Forrester. I was merely trying to explain why money matters to me. Libby is nearly sixteen years old. I should like for her to have a decent trust settled by the time she reaches eighteen.'

'To make her a more attractive marriage proposition?'

Eve doesn't bother to disguise her disdain, and Diana's face hardens.

'Don't judge me, Mrs Forrester. I have always tried to make the best choice possible given the restrictions of the options open to me. I have never, like so many women, left my life to chance or to the whim of whatever man might happen to come my way and like the look of me.'

'No? Just Guy Lester, who saw you swinging on the trapeze and decided there and then he was going to have you.'

Diana laughs, but there is little mirth in it.

'I see you've been talking to Libby. But ask yourself this, Eve – may I call you Eve, now we're talking so frankly? Thank you. Ask yourself how long I'd been on that trapeze, waiting for him to come past. It had only just turned May. The sea was not warm. Guy always thought he had plucked me like a wildflower he happened upon. He never wondered if I could have deliberately planted myself in his way.'

'But surely you loved him?'

'He was thirty-seven, and I was barely eighteen. He was hardly the romantic hero I'd imagined. I married him because he was rich.'

'But kind also. And decent.'

Now Diana's eyes blaze, as if a light has been switched on inside them.

'Guy had affairs throughout our marriage. He cheated on me, just like he cheated on his first wife. He was kind and decent as long as you didn't ask anything of him. Let me tell you something, Eve. I've earned every penny of the money I'm entitled to. I don't know what it is that you've done to inveigle yourself into Guy's will, into this place, this family – but you are not taking that from me. Or from my daughter.'

Diana has made this whole speech without once raising her voice. No one in the restaurant has looked up; the two elderly women on the next table with their hair set hard like caramelized sugar haven't paused in their gossiping to turn their way. The champagne-drinking young people in the corner haven't glanced over.

What must it cost her, Eve wonders, this iron self-control?

Eve herself is feeling far from controlled. Her thoughts churn from anger at the slur implied in Diana's reference to her, to pity for the woman and for the daughter who will bear the brunt of her mother's sacrifice, to a tugging sense of disappointment in the man who posthumously summoned her here.

'I see I've dented your shiny view of Guy,' says Diana. 'Perhaps you're thinking this is just sour grapes from a widow with an axe to grind. But let me ask you one more thing, Eve. Do you know why Caroline Finch has stuck around?'

Now Eve is genuinely surprised. Why would Diana be suddenly mentioning the housekeeper at this point, when they'd been in the middle of discussing . . . *Oh.*

'I see the penny has dropped. I already told you that Caroline was in love with Guy. But perhaps it would surprise you to know those feelings were not entirely without foundation. She was one of his early conquests when he was still married to Madeleine, Duncan and Noel's mother. I don't know how long it lasted, but Caroline never got over it. You know, I really think she believed all the way through that if she just hung around long enough, made herself useful enough, he would come back to her. Or perhaps by the time she realized he never would, it was all too late and she'd used it all up. Her youth and her *currency*, if you know what I mean.'

Eve is saved from having to reply by the reappearance of Noel and Libby. Both with dripping hair and that flushed exuberance of the recently exercised.

'Do you know, there are people picnicking down there by the pool,' says Libby. 'Duncs and Clemmie are there, although they said they won't come and join us because it would make them die of boredom. Oops.' She claps a hand over her mouth, as if remembering she ought not to have said that, before continuing. 'Can we have a picnic one day, instead of always coming here where it's so stuffy?'

'It's not stuffy enough,' says Diana. 'Some people are wearing nothing more than their bathing suits. Besides, the only reason people are picnicking is to save on paying for lunch. It never happened before the war when everyone here had money to burn, but since then everything is different. Have you seen those fields full of canvas tents? Now all French workers have to have their precious two weeks of holiday, everything here has changed. Clerks and teachers and shopkeepers from Lyon and Lille all sitting out there in the fields playing cards and eating their bread and cheese and hoping some of the magic of the Riviera will rub off on them so they can take it back to their humdrum lives. Most of the old crowd didn't come back after the war, and the ones that did are sitting on blankets eating marinated sardines from greaseproof paper and pretending it's a great wheeze rather than a financial necessity.'

'She only asked for a picnic,' says Noel. 'Not a bloody great lecture.'

To their right, a shriek of laughter goes up from the young woman perched on the railings.

'Libby must learn it's not always possible, or even desirable, to get what one wants.'

Diana is talking about her daughter, but it is Eve whom she fixes with her long, cool, discomfiting stare.

Eve has had enough of the Lesters. Enough of second-guessing and worrying about what she says and who she is. Enough of the confusion that being around Noel induces in her. And, looking around at the restaurant tables piled with poached fish and steaks and soufflés as light as air, at the diners with their perfect skin and their bored expressions and their little wisps of swimming costume that probably cost more than her winter coat, she has had enough of this too.

'Very well, I will agree,' she says out of the blue. 'I will sign the papers. The house can be rented or sold as you wish. It is high time I returned to my life.'

From the corner of her eye she sees Noel's head jerk up.

'I'm pleased to hear it,' says Diana, her shoulders visibly relaxing. 'I should think tomorrow would be an excellent time to complete the formalities. We will anyway all be together for the wedding reception in the afternoon, and afterwards Bernard can meet us at Villa La Perle with the paperwork. And after that you can get home to your husband.'

She is anxious to act before Eve can change her mind.

Well, good, thinks Eve emphatically. Time to draw a line under all this.

When lunch is over and Noel announces in his usual autocratic way that he will take her home now, she surprises them both by refusing.

'Thank you, but I should prefer to walk,' she says.

It is not entirely a lie. She has spotted a gate leading from the hotel out on to a path that looks, from their vantage point on the terrace, to follow the coastline in the direction of Antibes, hopefully as far as Garoupe beach. Suddenly she has a great urge to be alone with her thoughts, and the idea of a stroll with only the sea for company seems irresistible.

'You can't mean you intend to walk on that rocky path? Don't be ridiculous. I don't think it is even passable. No one uses it now. There are places where the sea comes right up over it.'

Noel doesn't even try to hide his impatience – which only increases Eve's resolve.

'If the path is closed or impassable I shall turn back.'

Out on the path, alone, her spirits rise. There is a glorious smell coming from the same type of bush she'd noticed before while climbing around Garoupe, the one with long, waxy green leaves and garlanded all over with pale flowers. She bends to inhale deeply, her nostrils filling with the strong, sweet scent. Further along there is another bush, and again another.

The path skirts around the perimeter of the hotel grounds, keeping in line with the rocks, which in some places are wide and shallow, but in others rise up steeply, falling away abruptly into the sea on one side so that Eve finds herself reaching with her left hand to feel the comforting solidity of the hotel wall. She tries to bring her thoughts back to her predicament, to the damning photograph in its stark brown envelope, the unwelcome prospect of one last meeting with the Lesters en masse at the wedding reception the next day. But such concerns trickle away in the face of the here and now.

She arrives at a point where the path rises steeply, curving around a bend. The surface here is very uneven as if the path has crumbled away, or perhaps been damaged by an explosion during the war. Twice she loses her footing, sending loose stones skating down the almost sheer rock face to her right and splashing into the deep water below. To her left the hotel wall has given way to more rocks and rough plants, which she tries to grasp on to.

Rounding the bend, she stops. She has reached a place where the high rocks peak. Behind her, she knows, is the hotel, with its preening guests and its groaning tables, and off to the right, out of sight, that beautiful prison island where, supposedly, a man was kept in isolation with a metal mask locked to his face. And around the next bend in the other direction lies Garoupe and then Villa La Perle, where Sully is angrily bashing at his typewriter and Mrs Finch is trying to mend her damaged heart. But here, there is only the sea, where directly ahead in the distance a boat with a white sail progresses languidly across the horizon.

Eve steps to the edge of the path so she can look down to where the small rocky cliff on which she stands meets the sea, the water clear near the surface but turning inky blue as it gets deeper. Here in this still place, she becomes aware for the first time of the chorus of cicadas behind her and the gulls overhead, and now she's heard it, the noise seems almost deafening. The lightest of breezes wafts the heady smell from those white flowers her way until the air seems swollen with it. She feels hot suddenly and closes her eyes to feel the sun on her lids, swaying in the heat and the thick scented air.

Slam. The blow is such a shock it seems to come from everywhere at the same time, and now, before she has a chance to work out what has happened, she is falling forward into that awful, empty space in front of her and her heart is flying up through her windpipe and out into the scented sky and this is how it ends.

This.

This.

Like this.

The first thing she notices when she opens her eyes is that she is lying on a rock, with a stream of foaming water running from her mouth. The second thing she notices is the pain from her head, her arm, her legs. And the third thing she notices is Noel Lester.

His shirt is soaked and sticking to him, water dripping from his hair on to her face as he leans over her, inspecting the damage.

'You could have been killed.'

He sounds so cross about it. His mouth set hard, his eyes like green granite. As if she has done it on purpose. As if she had been able to think of nothing better to do than to fling herself off a cliff.

'If I hadn't come after you, convinced you'd set off one of the mines the Germans left behind, if I hadn't heard you scream when you fell—'

'I didn't fall.' Eve raises herself painfully to a sitting position. 'Something hit me. Or someone.'

She feels again that hot slam, the awful realization of having nothing under her feet.

'I didn't see anyone on the path.'

Eve peers through the blood that still streams from her head, mixing with the salt water running off her hair.

'They could have gone the opposite way from the hotel.'

But already it sounds far-fetched. The sort of thing a person might say to cover up their own innate clumsiness.

Noel, still crouched down so that he is on a level with her, puts out a hand and lifts the strands of her hair that are getting caught in the cut in her head with a gentleness that belies the hard lines of his face. Suddenly self-conscious, Eve tries to raise her own left hand to her hair, triggering shooting pains in her wrist.

'I think I've broken it,' she cries.

Noel takes her hand very lightly between his own to get a better view of her wrist, already fat and swollen.

'I saw enough broken limbs during the war to last a lifetime,' he says. 'Luckily I don't think this is one.'

He raises his eyes from her arm to her face. And now there is a most peculiar meeting of gazes, a sense of someone climbing in past her irises, through her pupils until her head is filled with him.

For a moment all of it is forgotten: the blood, which has now slowed to a trickle that snakes down her cheek and into the corner of her mouth, the throbbing in her wrist, the cuts to her legs, which are only now making themselves felt.

Then: *He could be your brother.* That voice in her head.

She scrambles to her feet, ignoring the way her body erupts into shooting sparks of pain. And he stands too, wet and solid and flint-eyed, and follows as she makes her way slowly back to the hotel, trying not to hobble even though it hurts to bend her knee, because the thought of him touching her is not to be borne. But he doesn't even try, doesn't put a hand under her elbow or an arm around her waist. Instead they walk in single file, like strangers who just happen to be going in the same direction.

And then – after the stares of the hotel guests, the mamas with their disapproving eyes and all the bored young things sniffing for something, anything, to take their minds off the relentless pursuit of leisure and pleasure – he drives her home.

She leans back in the passenger seat and squeezes her eyes shut so the tears cannot come out.

22

10 June 1948

'IT LOOKS RIDICULOUS.'

'Not ridiculous, exactly. Interesting. Mysterious.'

'Ugly as sin.'

'Well . . .'

Even Sully cannot deny that the deep red scratches that criss-cross Eve's calves, virulent even under her nylon stockings, are seriously unattractive. And that's not to mention the deep gash in her forehead or the purple bruising around her eye that no amount of make-up can cover.

Eve stands in front of the large mirror in the villa's master bedroom, surveying her reflection with a pain in her heart equal almost to the pain in her sprained wrist. The blue dress is just as it was, sumptuous, stylish, beautifully made to tailor itself to her shape. It is her body that lets it down. Scarred with cuts and scrapes and bruises that bloom like blowsy black flowers on her skin, the flesh around them already taking on a greenish hue.

There is a bandage that winds from the tips of the fingers on her left hand to a point halfway between her wrist and her elbow. She has tried to keep it clean but already the edges are fraying and grubby.

And her face. Her poor, ruined face with that clot of blackened blood scabbing over the point where her forehead hit the rock as she entered the water.

'You know, the French have a neat term, *l'appel du vide* – meaning the impulse that comes over you when you're standing at the top of a building or a cliff, just to fling yourself off. I had it myself once on the Eiffel Tower.'

'I did *not* fling myself off.'

Outrage makes her shrill and Sully holds up his hands in mock appeasement.

'Still, you could have been killed.'

Eve has heard this a lot over the twenty-four hours since Noel first said it as he bent over her on the rocks, and now she fervently wishes never to hear it again.

Ruth Collett arrives to help prepare her hair for the wedding.

'Oh my,' she says, standing in the doorway, transfixed.

'Please don't try to tell me it's not as bad as you thought.'

'No, it's far worse,' admits Ruth. 'But it gives you a back-story. Something to make you stand out amongst all the starlets and society madams. It makes you look mysterious and interesting.'

Eve groans and sinks down on to the bed with her head in her one good hand.

'But I don't want to be mysterious and interesting. I want to be ravishing.'

Ruth does her best with Eve's tangle of hair. Washing it over the sink in the bathroom and combing it out with a little drop of oil before drying it using a square-backed brush so that it feels for once silky and controllable, and then twisting it up and holding it in place with a handful of dark pins.

'Though I don't know why I'm bothering,' she says, standing back to survey her handiwork. 'The forecast is for a storm later. Then everyone will look like drowned rats.'

Eve has to admit her hair looks better than it ever has before, but with her forehead still gouged with a deep claret line and her eye ringed with purple, the effect of the whole thing is of an attractive set of curtains framing a view of a bomb site.

Matters only deteriorate once they arrive at the fairytale house with its icing-coloured tiers and fight their way to the gate through the crowds of people and police, and the unlucky members of the press pack who haven't managed to wangle an invitation to the event itself.

'All the women are so beautiful,' says Eve despairingly as they step on to the terrace, following the sound of the band who have set up on the far side of the enormous swimming pool.

'But none of them have thought to decorate their skin,' says Sully. 'You'll see. You'll set a trend. They'll all be going home to scratch their arms and legs.'

He is smiling, but his voice has that hard edge Eve has come to recognize. She knows he has been drinking since the morning. Bourbon, which he swigs from a small metal flask he keeps in the pocket of his black suit jacket.

'What is that strange smell?'

Eve had first smelled it on the way in through the front door, but out here in the back it is overpowering.

'Laurent has had the swimming pool filled with Gloria's favourite cologne,' says Sully. 'Romantic, isn't it? If you can get past the urge to gag.'

Eve doesn't believe the vast pool can be entirely filled with perfume but she doesn't want to argue with Sully in his current mood. Whatever the ratio of cologne to water, it is clearly far too much.

They mingle uneasily with the other guests, waiting for the wedding party to arrive from the ceremony in Vallauris. Eve had been surprised at first to learn that the glamorous couple planned to marry in a simple town hall, until she remembered Gloria's divorcee status.

'My God, are those tribal markings?'

Clemmie Atwood is standing in front of her, looking immaculate in a floor-length pink gown slashed practically to the navel, her hair piled up high and woven with silk roses the exact shade of her dress. Her skin glows, healthy and rose-cheeked – and entirely unblemished.

Next to her, Duncan looks sallow and ill at ease, for once not bothering with the world-weary facade he usually tries to construct. And indeed, what would be the point of pretending to be anything in this company, where Eve has already spotted Elizabeth Taylor and Marlene Dietrich and the man, whose name she forgets, who is being feted as the fastest runner ever recorded. She has glimpsed the Windsors talking to a trio of singing sisters from America. Rumour has it Picasso is here somewhere, and she keeps an eye out for him, hoping to be able to report back to Jack Collett. The fashion designer Coco Chanel stands in the centre of a little knot of admirers, wearing a plain dark gown looped with strings of pearls.

In such a crowd of the world's highest achievers it would be foolish to attempt to appear bigger or tougher or richer or more successful. Better just to observe and absorb and be dazzled.

There is no sign of Noel. *Good*, thinks Eve.

A hush now. The musicians fall silent. The crowd around the entrance to the house parts and then erupts into a spontaneous *ooh* as the newly married couple make their entrance amid a lightning storm of camera flashes from the press, who are penned up along the sidelines of the partygoers.

Eve can tell right away there is something wrong. Gloria looks as beautiful as it is possible for a human being to look, in a white dress that moulds itself to her like a second skin, her red hair tumbling in thick, perfect curls over her shoulders. But she is leaning on her much shorter new husband as if nursing some injury and the famous smile seems painted on to her face. Eve looks for the bruises she'd seen on the actress's arm, but the long satin sleeves of the dress cover her from shoulder to wrist. Next to Eve, Sully reaches his hand into his suit pocket as if checking that the flask is still in place.

Laurent leads Gloria to stand by the pool, facing the band, who have launched into a gutsy version of the 'Wedding March', to pose for choreographed photographs. Her smile never wavers, and her eyes have that wide, glassy look Eve now recognizes.

'My dear Eve. What has happened to your lovely face?'

The soft, French accent is unmistakeable even before Eve registers that Victor Meunier is standing by her shoulder, appraising her with an expression of such tender solicitude that she feels like crying. For a moment she forgets all about the photograph and the gossip that has been flying around about her and the Frenchman. She sees only the sympathy in his eyes, and the way the smooth planes of his face stretch out in concern.

'I fell,' she says. Already the idea of someone deliberately slamming into her as she peered over the edge of the rocks seems preposterous, a memory her treacherous mind invented to save itself from the shame of having allowed herself to topple forwards.

'You must take better care of yourself, my dear Mrs Forrester.' Victor's words are like a soothing compress.

He leans towards her and reaches out one of his long, elegant fingers to her forehead, the lightest of touches on the hard shell of her cut, and she briefly closes her eyes. When she opens them again, there is Noel Lester, directly in her line of sight, wearing a black suit that brings out the fierce green of his eyes. Staring at her as if she is someone he doesn't know. Someone he doesn't want to know.

Now Duncan breaks away from the group and steps in front of his brother. Eve sees him lay a hand on Noel's arm, murmur something in a low voice that makes Noel nod and, finally, drop his eyes. Eve guesses she is the subject of their discussion and her cheeks burn as Noel turns to disappear back into the crowd as if he was never there.

'The boys are in a celebratory mood, I see,' says Sully, who has been observing the interaction between the brothers. 'You've got to admire Duncan's nerve, showing up here when he's so in hock to the groom. If I were him I'd be keeping my back to the wall.'

Eve notices how Sully's words are slurred together and how he keeps one hand resting on his flask inside his pocket even while holding a newly replenished glass of champagne in the other.

On her left, Victor leans in towards Eve, creating the illusion that they are alone here in the midst of this public circus.

'That photograph,' he says, his face so close to hers she can feel his warm breath on her cheek, sweet from whatever he has just been drinking. 'I hope it has not made things difficult for you. Your husband . . .'

'If my husband receives such a photograph he will see it for what it is,' says Eve, moving slightly away in case Noel Lester should happen to glance over again. 'Somebody attempting to make trouble.'

Her voice comes out more clipped than she intended.

There is a crash from the swimming pool area behind her, followed by a collective cry from the crowd. Eve turns towards the source of the disruption and sees to her horror that Gloria has fallen over and is sprawled inelegantly on the floor, her dress hitched up around her thighs, exposing the legs that the studio uses to great effect to promote every Gloria Hayes picture.

Laurent leans down to help her back to her feet.

Even from this distance Eve can see the vein throbbing in his high forehead, the fingers closed like a vice around Gloria's arm as he tries to drag her upright. Everyone around them is staring in appalled fascination as if this is just another part of the spectacle that has been laid on for their entertainment. Even Laurent's henchmen hold back, unsure whether their intervention would be welcomed.

Are they all just going to stand and stare? Will no one help?

Eve can bear it no longer. She hurries forward on her silly heels, crouching down beside Gloria so that she can put her good arm around her waist and get some leverage to help lift her to her feet.

'Why, bless your heart,' says Gloria, turning her full-watt smile on Eve. The lipstick is smudged towards the corner of her mouth. 'I think I must have tripped on something. Laurent, darlin', you need to make this terrace more level.'

Eve looks down at the perfectly flat tiled surface. She does not dare look at Laurent himself.

'Stand up straight, you drunk whore.'

The words are hissed so they don't carry to the press photographers, snapping from the sidelines, or the guests, still gawping in their finery.

For a moment Eve is too shocked to register what she has heard, then – *whump* – it hits her like a punch to the stomach.

But Gloria herself doesn't seem to notice.

'I'll be right as rain now, honey,' she says to Eve, finally upright and straightening to her full impressive height.

She produces a smile for the assembled crowd as if she has just stepped out of a limousine at a premiere.

Eve looks at her eyes, noticing their lack of focus, and the way Gloria seems unaware of the dirty marks streaking her white gown, or the single mascara-blackened tear sliding down her face. And she realizes that wherever the star is in her head, it is not here, present at her own wedding.

'I'll certainly have someone come to flatten down those tiles just as soon as the wedding is over. Anyone could have fallen over them,' says Laurent, talking at a normal volume for the benefit of the onlookers. 'Thank goodness you weren't hurt, my sweet.'

He makes a gesture with his head, a jerk so slight it might almost have been a stretch. Instantly the two henchmen from the other night are by his side.

'Now why don't you go with Hugo and Marc, my love, to freshen up.'

The way he says it, it's not a question.

Eve becomes aware now of a movement to the side of her. Sully is making his way slowly through the crowd. Though his eyes are fixed on Laurent he still has his hand in his suit pocket. Really, can the man not do without a drink, even now? Her stomach falls away when she sees him withdraw from the pocket not the flask she is expecting, but—

The pistol Sully is holding is compact. Small enough to fit into the palm of a hand. No one else seems to have noticed it.

Propped up between the two expressionless bodyguards, Gloria allows herself to be led away in the direction of the house. The crowd parts to let her through. All the time, she is beaming, a queen on walkabout among her subjects, head hold high as she sails through, steered by her two silent companions.

Eve feels as if a hole has opened up deep down inside her. She keeps her eyes trained on Sully. *Don't,* she says to him wordlessly. *Don't.* Still he approaches, the gun now tucked just out of sight inside his pocket, a curiously detached expression on his face.

With the bodyguards out of the way, Laurent is alone.

Sully reaches the front of the crowd. Stops.

His hand reaches once again for the pistol.

Eve finds her feet and plunges forward, placing herself between Sully and his target.

For a moment, Sully's expression doesn't change, as if he doesn't see her standing in front of him. Then his eyes refocus.

'Are you crazy? What are you doing?'

Sully blinks as she speaks. Sways.

'It's not loaded,' he says finally, letting the gun fall back into his pocket and dropping his hands by his side. 'I don't even know if it's real. I won it from a French soldier in a drunken bet in a bar in Monte Carlo. I just thought I should do something. Act. You know. Rather than stand there watching. Acting is the thing.'

So drunk he hardly makes sense.

'You scared me half to death.'

Weak with relief, Eve takes him firmly by the shoulders and turns him roughly around.

She begins to follow Sully away from the house, but feels a tap on her bare shoulder. Turning, she sees Laurent standing there. He looks her up and down so intently that she feels the throbbing from the wound in her head and the ache of her wrist under her bandage and the sharp pain of those deep scratches on her shins.

'Go home, Mrs Forrester.'

There is a smile playing around his lips as he says it, as though they are sharing a joke or a wry observation. But there is no humour in his glittering black eyes.

Eve wants nothing more than to do as Laurent bids and go. Everything disgusts her. The stench of perfume coming off the pool. The leathery man next to her, tipping back his head to let an oyster slide down his throat. All the people who've eaten Laurent's caviar and drunk the champagne laid on by the studio, who have come because of who Gloria is, yet who didn't try to pick her up or find out why she'd had to stuff herself full of pills in order to get through her own wedding.

The weather has turned oppressive now. The heat is wet and grey.

Eve starts picking her way through the crowd after Sully's retreating back. Laurent's unmistakeable warning takes hold of her throat, making it difficult to breathe, and for a moment she wishes she had not stopped Sully, had just stood back and let events unfold.

'Are you ready to go?' Diana has materialized from the crowd and stands blocking Eve's way, the light catching the gold material of her dress so that she resembles a statue.

'You haven't forgotten that we are all meeting at Villa La Perle to sign Bernard's papers?'

Eve has not forgotten. Rather she has deliberately wiped the information from her mind.

Diana, noting her hesitation, continues. 'I don't need to remind you, Eve, that we could still decide to challenge the will, if you continue to drag your heels.'

Eve knows she can put it off no longer. The wedding party is coming to an end anyway. Hollywood has its fairy-tale. Laurent has his trophy bride. The specially invited photographers have each signed a contract guaranteeing that the studio will have final approval over all pictures used, so the images of Gloria Hayes collapsed on the floor will never appear, though a few will surface years later in private collections.

Tonight the newlyweds will entertain a few dozen dignitaries at home and tomorrow they will leave for their honeymoon on board Laurent's yacht, the recently renamed *Princess Gloria*.

Is this how it is? Eve wants to ask Diana. Are there no happy couples, only people going through the motions out of convenience or habit or because it's easier to say yes than no? But then she thinks of Bernard and the way he loves that orange cat in his office only because Marie too loves it, and the Colletts and how they seem like two trees she saw once whose trunks had twisted around each other as they grew, so it was as if they were one single organism, unbreakable even during the very worst storm.

'We'll take the party home with us,' declares Sully, who has only now turned around to find out where she is. They are all so self-absorbed, Eve realizes now, all these people she has met since she came here. So totally convinced that their story will turn out to be the only story.

She glimpses Noel standing talking to Clemmie, who has her hand on his arm and her face turned up towards his, laughing at something he has said. They look so perfect together. Eve thinks of the photograph she saw among Guy's things of Anna, Noel's dead fiancée, with her enquiring eyes and her wide smile, and is reminded of her own bruised face, the grubby bandage circling her lower arm.

'I can see what you're thinking, Mrs Forrester.' She hadn't even noticed Duncan standing by her side, swaying, gazing at his own fiancée as if trying to commit her to memory. 'But Clemmie loves me, whatever she might have felt for Noel in the past. I know you and she haven't exactly hit it off. Clemmie can scratch like a cat if she feels herself to be up against the wall, but she's fun and she's loyal. As soon as I've paid off the debts, we will be married and then she'll calm down and everyone will stop thinking, *Poor Clemmie, ending up with the wrong brother*.'

Eve is astonished. Duncan has never said so much as a few words to her unprompted.

'Do you have brothers and sisters, Eve?'

Eve shakes her head.

'I envy you. Although, please don't get me wrong, I pity you too. I was a mummy's boy, I'm sure Noel will have told you. After she died I spent my childhood trying to live up to my father and my older brother, and then my adolescence trying to come to terms with the fact that I never would. Do you know, the war was almost a relief? I was stationed in the Far East, you know. Whole continents away from all the other Lesters. No one knew who Guy was, who Noel was. When they looked at me, it was just me they saw. Not whoever it was they were comparing me to. It was quite the novelty.'

This is Duncan's bid then, his clumsy explanation of why she must sign the sale document – so that he can pay off his creditors and make a fresh start. She almost laughs. Does he not know it is all over, and she has given up? He could have saved himself the indignity. But still a part of her is moved by his honesty. Just as Eve will always remain in some small way that child yearning for her mother's approval, so Duncan cannot escape his brother's shadow, his father's expectations, destined not to be met.

'He loves you though, your brother,' she says, aware on some level that a sober Duncan will regret the confidences this lit-up Duncan has shared so freely, and resent her even more for being the one he shared them with.

'I know that. He wants it for me, you know. The money from the house. Wants to ride in like the bloody cavalry and rescue me from the mess I've got myself in, just like he always does.'

'Well, aren't you the lucky one then?' she says. 'Not everyone has the luxury of knowing there are people who care enough to want to help.'

Duncan blinks in surprise, taken aback at her vehemence. For a moment, while the band behind them plays a Glenn Miller number, the notes sliding and gliding in the scented air, they gaze at each other as if seeing one another afresh, and something is exchanged that, if it is not understanding, is not far removed.

Clemmie arrives, looping her hand through her fiancé's arm as if claiming him for her own, and the moment is broken.

'I demand to know what the two of you are talking about.'

Clemmie looks at them both in turn.

'We were only talking about the wedding,' says Eve, turning away.

When Duncan wanders off to get more drinks, Clemmie and Eve are left standing awkwardly together.

Eve casts her eyes over the crowd while she tries to think of something to say, coming to rest without even realizing it on Noel, who is standing a few yards away, talking to a man she does not recognize.

'You are wasting your time there,' Clemmie snaps.

Eve looks puzzled.

'Noel. Oh, don't bother protesting. I've seen you looking. But the fact is that Noel was in love once and something dreadful happened and that was enough. Once bitten, twice shy, as they say.'

'I presume you're talking about Anna.'

Clemmie's mouth opens in surprise.

'He told you about her? My, you two have become quite the bosom buddies.' Clemmie steps back to scrutinize Eve, as if seeing her in a different light, before asking, 'And it hasn't put you off him?'

'There is nothing to put off. I'm not the slightest bit interested in Noel Lester, apart from in what he might be able to tell me about what I am doing here. And besides, I also had a fiancé who was killed in the war, so the idea that it might be something—'

'He told you Anna died during the war?'

'Clemmie!'

Duncan has returned and there is no mistaking the warning note in his voice.

For once Clemmie looks shamefaced.

'Oops,' she says. 'Sorry, Duncs.'

She mimes sewing up her own lips.

Arrangements are made to regroup at the villa for the meeting with Bernard. After the excitement and the champagne, no one has much appetite for it. But it has to be done.

The blue dress is sticking to Eve, and she sees grey clouds building up over the horizon, reminding her of Ruth's prediction of stormy weather. The others have left already, departing en masse so suddenly that Eve didn't even see them go. Gathering up Sully in preparation for leaving herself, Eve notices Laurent over by the swimming pool, deep in conversation with Victor.

After a short wait, a car is summoned to take her and Sully home, the driver a young man in a dark blue suit with a frosting of virulent acne over his chin and neck. She is too relieved to take the weight off her feet to enquire who he is and who is paying for him.

Rounding the final bend before Villa La Perle, she experiences a moment of pure relief to be home, followed almost immediately by a savage jab of pain as she remembers that she will soon be leaving here, that she will have no more right to call it home than this pimply young man, who seems far too young to be behind the wheel of a car.

In the gravelled car park to the side of the house, she sees Noel's black convertible and Marie Gaillard's orange tin can, and Marie herself leaning back in the driver's seat with a newspaper over her face, clearly asleep. And also a third car, which she recognizes with a sinking heart as Victor Meunier's.

'What is Victor doing here?' she asks, but Sully, who has spent the journey in dense, brooding introspection, has already opened the car door and spilled out on to the gravel.

The wall of the house facing them looks almost grey in the heat, rather than its usual warm rose colour.

The back of Eve's neck prickles. It is something about that blank wall. Something about the stillness of this house which she knows to be filled with people. As if the whole of it were watching and waiting.

On the doorstep she turns to Sully.

'I wish—' she says. But whatever she was going to wish for is cut short by the opening of the front door.

Mrs Finch stands there in a flowery blouse that gapes across her breasts as if bought for a much thinner version of herself. She seems flustered as she says, 'You have visitors, Mrs Forrester.'

Sully lets out a bark of laughter.

'Don't let Diana hear you call her a visitor,' he says.

Mrs Finch's expression doesn't change, but Eve sees a pink stain rise up her neck.

'Naturally I'm not talking about the Lesters, Mr Sullivan. I'm referring to the other English lady and gentleman who arrived about an hour ago.'

She will mean the Colletts, thinks Eve. But something is tightening inside her, like a cord being wound and then wound again.

As they descend the staircase, Eve is conscious of the clicking of the heels of her borrowed shoes against the stone, how they announce each and every step. From down below there is no sound at all.

At the bottom, she lets Mrs Finch lead the way into the silent sitting room, hanging back in the hallway trying to quell the panic that seems to be rising up from that low place in her abdomen.

Maybe I should just turn around now. At least go to change out of these clothes.

'Mrs Forrester and Mr Sullivan are back now.'

And now there is no turning, no escaping back up the stairs to the sanctuary of her empty room, where she can put on the fan and lie on the big bed and close her mind to it all.

Instead she follows the housekeeper's flowery back into the sitting room, normally so bright and light but today shadowed by the dark clouds blowing in from the sea.

Perhaps it is because of the uncustomary gloom that she does not at first see them.

Instead her gaze falls on Diana, sitting straight-backed in her gold dress like a party guest who has got the time wrong and arrived an hour too early and must now make the best of it, and next to her, Duncan and Clemmie, pressed close together by the restrictive proportions of the sofa on which they are all squeezed. And now she notices Bernard in the velvet armchair, his hands resting on the briefcase in his lap, his kind eyes sending her a message she cannot decipher. Her gaze sweeps across to a black cane propped up against the foot of the chaise longue, and next to it the unmistakeable figure of Victor Meunier.

In this strange half-light Noel, leaning against the back wall, in between the two sets of double doors that open out on to the swimming pool terrace, appears a sombre figure in his black suit, with only those two pools of green providing some softness. *What on earth did Clemmie mean about her being put off him because of what happened to his fiancée?* But there is no time to follow this train of thought because as she looks at him, he turns his head deliberately and she follows his gaze.

There, sitting on a hard-backed chair that has been pulled out from its usual home against the wall, is Clifford, his lips parted under his moustache as if in astonishment as he takes in the borrowed dress and shoes, the bandaged wrist and blackened eye, the clotted cut on her forehead that even Ruth's best efforts haven't been able to disguise.

But it is not her husband who holds Eve's attention. Her entire focus, every beat of her racing heart, is trained on the woman who sits by his side in a matching chair, wearing a heavy plaid woollen suit far too warm for early June on the Riviera and a black linen hat that Eve recognizes from her father's funeral some fifteen years earlier, and a look that Eve remembers all too well – awkwardness and nerves mixed with rigid disapproval.

Mother.

23

'WHAT ARE YOU doing here?'

It is as if all the various, disparate parts of her life have collided here in this weather-darkened room, and Eve's brain just cannot seem to comprehend how such a thing might be possible.

She has a moment of sheer terror as she suddenly remembers the photograph and the threat to send it to Clifford. Is that what has brought him here? But surely there would not have been sufficient time?

Clifford's expression is hard to read. Well, of course the moustache covering up half of his face doesn't help. Why has she never noticed before how very out of proportion it is against his hollowed-out features? And have his eyes always been so close together, as if they are trying to connect across the bridge of his nose?

'You left me very little alternative, Eve. Your actions were so out of character, for all I knew you could be being kept here against your will. I made the journey to Banbury to talk to your mother, even though it was dashed inconvenient to take the time away from the office, and naturally when I discussed it with her she was most anxious to come here and see for herself what on earth was going on, as any responsible parent would be.'

Eve, dropping into the one remaining free seat, an old Lloyd Loom chair that has been dragged in from the terrace, cannot look at the Lesters. Cannot bear to see what will be written on their faces. She is acutely aware, without needing to look at it again, of her mother's ill-fitting woollen suit, bought well before the war when she was a much larger woman with a weakness for puddings and fruitcake. Nothing tasted the same made with powdered egg, she'd complain. And how were carrots a proper substitute for apricots?

Bernard gets to his feet. His trousers are wrinkled where the briefcase has rested on them and he tries to smooth them with his hand. Even so, Eve senses her mother watching.

'I think, in the circumstances, we should perhaps leave the three of you to talk . . .'

But Diana is having none of it.

'Don't be ridiculous, Bernard. Here we all are. Gathered. If Mrs Forrester is about to be whisked off back home, it's the perfect opportunity to get this business sorted out once and for all. I still don't know what Guy thought he was playing at, but we shall just have to accept that we probably never will know. Unless, that is, Eve's mother has any light to shed on the matter.'

All eyes swing towards the woman in the woollen suit, who responds by sitting up straighter in her chair and pressing her lips together.

Eve feels her cheeks burn. *Could Guy Lester really have had a relationship with this woman? Surely they will all see how completely impossible—*

'I'm sure I haven't the faintest idea,' says Eve's mother. It is the first time she's spoken. 'I'm here only out of concern for my daughter's welfare.'

She glances at Eve, this brittle, proud woman, and Eve feels a caving inside her at all the ways she and her mother have failed each other.

Across the room, Victor clears his throat.

'Shall we get on with things, then?'

Bernard looks over at Eve, awaiting a response. When none is forthcoming, the notary shrugs and opens his briefcase.

'Very well. Let us proceed. I have here two documents. One is the rental agreement – six months, payable in advance, while the legalities of Mr Lester's estate are settled – and the other a sale in principle, drawn up between the four beneficiaries of Villa La Perle – Noel Lester, Duncan Lester, Elizabeth Lester and Eve Forrester – and the interested buyer. Monsieur Meunier, shall we start with you?'

To Eve's considerable surprise, Bernard holds out the papers that he has just withdrawn from his briefcase to Victor.

Finally, she understands. It is Victor who has made such a generous offer for Villa La Perle. How extraordinary. That he would have made no mention of this coincidence to her while they were talking so intimately the other evening seems to her extremely odd. Judging by the look on Noel's face and those of his brother and stepmother, it has come as something of a surprise to them too.

'Why has no one mentioned this before?' Diana wants to know. 'I fail to understand, Bernard, why you didn't tell us that the prospective buyer was someone known to us.'

'Monsieur Meunier requested that his name be kept quiet while he extracts himself from his current lease,' says Bernard, looking ill at ease.

'It is all my fault,' Victor says. 'I requested secrecy from Monsieur Gaillard while I dealt with my landlord. The Riviera is a small place. Word gets passed along quickly. But now everything is arranged, I am happy to say we can proceed.'

Victor takes the document from Bernard and signs it with a flourish, the nib of the pen making a scratching sound across the paper. He looks up and catches Eve's eye and gives an almost imperceptible nod as if thanking her for something, and she remembers the dead weight of his arm around her as he helped her back to the car, the flash of the camera as they passed.

And all that time he said nothing.

Something is nagging at her.

She is conscious of time slipping away, and with it the chance to find the answers she's seeking.

Guy. The ring.

The ring.

'Look!'

She swings round to face her mother, holding up her hand, the glint of green and gold on her finger.

'Do you recognize this? It's your ring.'

Her mother's eyes widen, though whether this is owing to the existence of the ring itself or being questioned like this out of the blue, in front of all these strangers, Eve cannot tell.

'I'm sure I've never seen it before in my life,' she says eventually.

'That's a lie!'

An intake of breath from the assembled onlookers.

Eve is out of her seat. Standing in front of her mother, pulling at the ring, twisting it off her finger.

'You were wearing this in the photograph.'

'What photograph?'

'Of when I was a baby. The one I found years ago. You snatched it away but I remember it perfectly. This is your ring.'

'Don't be ridiculous, Eve.'

How well she recognizes that tone, the one that says *I will brook no argument.*

'I'm not being ridiculous. This is yours. I know it.'

The ring is off now and she thrusts it towards her mother, who makes no attempt to take it, keeping her hands firmly in her lap.

'Look at the size of that ring, Eve. It would never fit me. You know I'm big-boned.'

Eve glances at her mother's fingers resting on the fabric of her skirt and she sees instantly that she is right. Despite her wartime weight loss the ring is far too small. It wouldn't even fit over the knuckle of her little finger.

Eve's mother sees her waver and she sits up straighter. Eve is familiar enough with her mother's body language to recognize what the gesture means. She would never allow herself a smile of triumph – nothing so vulgar – but this lengthening of the spine is her way of claiming victory.

'Shall we get on with it then?'

Duncan is impatient to be gone. Eve sees his foot bouncing up and down as if he has no control over it. Clemmie reaches out two fingers and presses them on his thigh to calm him. It is the most intimate gesture she has witnessed between the couple. Panic wells up within her. The sight of the pen poised over the paper. The sense of time running out, of a door closing on all the questions she has.

Her desperation bursts. She swings back towards her mother. 'Do you know the name Francis Garvey? Lieutenant Francis Garvey?'

Eve doesn't know where this has come from or why she is asking now. But instantly she knows she has struck a chord. Her mother's square, flat face, normally the livid pink of cooked ham, now drains of colour and Eve sees her swallow hard.

'No,' says her mother. 'I can't say that I have.'

'Think again. Maybe you didn't know him as Francis. How about Frank, or Frankie?'

'No,' says her mother. 'I told you, I've never heard of him.'

She is lying. Eve knows it just as surely as she knows that her eyes are brown. She feels her mother's discomfort as if it is her own.

'Frankie?'

The voice has come from across the room and Eve turns her head to see Diana wearing an expression of knitted concentration as if trying to pluck a memory from the furthest reaches of her mind.

'It's ringing a bell. Now why is it ringing a bell?'

A brief flare of hope shoots through Eve that is extinguished almost as soon as it began when Diana shakes her head.

'No. It's gone.'

'Oh for crying out loud, can we just get a bloody move on?'

In the pause that greets Noel Lester's outburst, several things happen:

Eve's mother sucks in her breath, raising herself up in her seat until she is practically levitating.

Clifford puts his hand to his moustache, smoothing it down as if it is a startled pet that needs to be stroked.

There is a loud and prolonged ring of the doorbell, as if

someone is leaning their weight against it, which ends with the sound of voices and the clattering of feet down the stairs.

Jack Collett bursts into the room, closely followed by his breathless parents.

'Have you heard?' His pleasant face is rigid with shock.

'We were passing the house, and one of the cooks told us what had happened,' says Ruth, panting. 'We wanted to make sure you're all right. So upsetting for everyone.'

Ruth stops short when she notices that Eve is far from alone.

'Oh, I'm sorry,' she says. 'I didn't realize you had company. Only the most awful thing has happened. Gloria Hayes just tried to kill herself.'

There is a collective gasp. Sully, who has been leaning against the doorway behind Eve, steps towards Ruth.

'How?' he wants to know. Then, without waiting for an answer, he asks, 'When? Why?'

Across the room, Clemmie leans towards Diana. 'I knew it,' she says. 'I told Dunc at the wedding that there was something very wrong with that woman.'

The Colletts recount what they have heard – that the new bride locked herself in her bedroom and emptied every pill packet she had down her throat.

Sully's usually nut-brown face drains of colour.

'I'll go to the hospital,' he says, suddenly completely sober. 'I'll find out how she is and report back.'

The hubbub that greets his hurried departure is finally pierced by Diana's cool, commanding voice.

'Naturally it's all very upsetting, but as there's not a lot the rest of us can do, I propose we remain here and get these papers signed.'

'I couldn't agree more,' says Clifford.

'Then, if you're all sure, let us proceed,' says Victor, who is still holding the documents.

Eve, whose mind has been churning with thoughts of Gloria and Clifford and her mother, becomes aware of Jack Collett standing next to her, staring at Victor through his wire-framed spectacles with an intensity that borders on the rude.

'I beg your pardon, have we met?' he asks finally.

Victor looks up, startled.

'No. I don't think so.'

'In that case, forgive me. It's just, you look so familiar. Are you sure we haven't come across each other before?'

'Absolutely.' Victor gives him an apologetic smile before returning his attention to the papers in his lap.

'Paris, perhaps?'

'Jack, really.' Ruth frowns at her son. 'I'm dreadfully sorry, Mr Meunier. I can't think where this boy learned to be so rude.'

'Please do not worry yourself, Mrs Collett.' Victor smiles again. 'But, you know, I think after all we must delay.' He hands the papers back to Bernard and gets heavily to his feet, picking up his cane. 'Mr Martin is my dear friend and for something so terrible to happen, on his wedding day . . . Well, I must see if there is some service I can do for him.'

'But this won't take a minute.' Diana is not going to give up without a protest.

'*Désolé, Madame*,' Victor murmurs, already almost at the door. 'But I'm sure you will agree it would not be appropriate to go ahead in the present sad circumstances.'

Eve watches Victor progress purposefully across the hallway, barging clumsily past Mrs Finch as she tries to attract his attention.

'Well, what a drama,' says Clemmie with relish, after the front door closes on the French art dealer. It is as if the afternoon's events have been laid on entirely for her entertainment.

'For Christ's sake, Clemmie, a woman is seriously hurt,' snaps Duncan, to everyone's considerable surprise.

The Lesters take their leave soon after in dribs and drabs. Diana first, followed by her stepsons and Clemmie. The Colletts are next to depart.

'Such a terribly sad business,' says Ruth.

Jack, though, is more concerned about Victor and his inability to place him.

'It's the rummest thing,' he says, removing his spectacles to rub the bridge of his nose. 'I'm so sure I recognize him from somewhere. You don't forget a face like that.'

After the Colletts have left the room, Eve listens to their fading footsteps with rising panic.

Now it will come, she thinks. Now she will be held to account. She turns back into the sitting room to face her mother and her husband. Oh, but she has forgotten about Bernard. The French notary is so unobtrusive she has almost overlooked his presence.

'If there's nothing more I can do for you, Mrs Forrester, Marie is waiting outside to take me back to Cannes.'

Eve's gratitude turns to dismay as Bernard gets to his feet, ready to leave.

'Cannes?' Clifford has perked up suddenly. 'But that is where our hotel is. It seems silly to pay for a taxi when you are going that way.'

Amid all the goings-on of the last few hours, Eve hasn't

even considered where her mother and husband will stay. But now it transpires that they have already booked a hotel in Cannes. Not the Appleton, it turns out, but a small place a few roads back from the beach.

'No point paying silly prices just to catch a chill from that sea breeze,' says her mother, apparently oblivious to the oppressive warmth outside. 'You'll be coming with us, of course, Eve. Your husband has taken a twin room.'

Going with them. The idea had not even occurred to Eve and she is overcome by a flood of panic.

She looks down furiously at her hands, but not before she has seen Clifford's face redden. *He does not want to be alone with me either.*

'I'm afraid that's out of the question,' she says, emboldened by Clifford's unspoken dismay. 'All my things are here. And I need to be around in case there is news of Gloria.'

Her mother's face sets hard.

'You are talking about this woman as if she is your friend, Eve. The truth is you come from such different worlds she has probably forgotten you ever met. It's as well to be realistic. I should not like to see you disappointed.'

'But I have her dress. Her shoes.'

Eve knows how childish she sounds. But really, the thought of being confined with Clifford in some poky backstreet hotel room, watching him smooth down the crease in his trousers before arranging them on the hanger, position his watch just so on the bedside table. Why, it is simply not to be borne.

Luckily Clifford himself comes to her rescue.

'You're right. It is probably for the best if you stay here one last night, to arrange your things. Then tomorrow we can all sign the sales papers and put this vexing business to bed before catching the evening train home. I don't suppose we know yet how much our share is worth?'

She shakes her head and changes the subject, arranging to meet them on Garoupe beach the next morning so that they might have a chance to talk away from the distractions of Villa La Perle and the Lester family. There is a fuss about directions, but Bernard assures Clifford that any taxi driver will know it.

Finally, they are gone, and Eve is alone.

But long after the noise of Marie's car engine has been swallowed up by the evening air, Clifford's voice still sounds in her ear.

We. Our.

Guy, 29 April 1948

THE SECOND TIME I visit, I wonder if she will even agree to see me, but she shuffles into the room holding out a stack of letters written on paper as thin as onion skin.

'You keep these safe,' she says.

I glance at the nurse, who shrugs her shoulders as if it's all the same to her.

'They're just letters to a dead man,' says the nurse. 'She was keeping them under her mattress.'

'Can't do that any more,' says the woman. 'Or Annie will have them.'

The nurse laughs. 'Oh, Annie would have the gold fillings from your teeth if you slept with your mouth open.'

Now the woman slips something off her finger. The gold ring with the green stone.

'So Annie doesn't get it,' she says, holding it out to me.

'Oh no. I couldn't take that,' I tell her.

'Please. Pretty please.'

She sounds so desperate, my protestations dissolve before I can utter them.

'Tell her I can't take it,' I say to the nurse.

She sucks in her breath. 'You may as well. She doesn't have any other visitors to give it to. It's either you or Annie.'

'But why?' I ask her directly. 'Don't you know who I am? What I've done? Why would you want to entrust your ring to me?'

She looks at me with cloudy eyes and then the strangest thing happens. They sharpen like binocular lenses coming into focus. And I almost have to look away because I realize that she knows me – she *knows* me – and it feels as if the shame might drown me. *You owe me this*, her eyes are saying.

'Pretty please,' she repeats, thrusting her paltry possessions at me. Her gums are livid red. I cannot look at her.

'But what would you have me do with it?'

The woman looks at the nurse, as if she does not want to speak in front of her.

'You know,' she says, meaningfully. 'You know what to do. Who to look for.'

I find myself nodding, even though everything in me is telling me not to make promises I might not be able to fulfil.

'What would Annie do with all these things?' I ask the nurse, reluctantly pocketing the ring and the letters.

'Swallow them, probably. Though sometimes she'll bury them. "Annie's little treasures", she calls them. Oh, they're all mad here.'

24

11 June 1948

'IF THIS IS the legendary French Riviera, you can give me Sutton any day.'

Clifford is kicking at the long dark strands of seaweed on the deserted Garoupe beach.

Though the storm predicted by Ruth Collett has yet to materialize, yesterday's grey clouds have lingered, growing blacker and denser so that there is a sense of the sky being swollen to bursting, which is why Eve's mother refused to venture on to the sand, instead taking shelter on a bench set well back from the beach up near the promenade. Yet the air remains hot and clammy. No wonder the holidaymakers are sticking to their hotels, where they sit in the lounges under ceiling fans, playing bad-tempered games of cards.

Eve stops to contemplate the churning mass of the sea, and finds herself thinking of Gloria, wondering if she too had stopped to feast her eyes on this same sea before locking herself in the bathroom, emptying out all the pill bottles in the cabinet and washing the lot down with a bottle of Laurent's Sazerac de Forge cognac.

By the time Sully arrived at the hospital the previous evening, the studio's publicity machine had already swung into action. Yes, Ms Hayes had been admitted suffering from exhaustion after the excitement of the wedding. No, sadly, the new Mrs Martin was not up to receiving visitors at the moment. Complete bed rest, the doctors had ordered. And certainly there was no truth whatsoever in the rumours currently circulating. Some rogue elements of the press, unhappy at not being granted an invitation to cover the wedding party, were seizing on the new bride's hospital stay – the result of a worrying but completely understandable bout of nervous exhaustion – to spread false stories.

Eve, still in her borrowed blue dress, had felt a sheen of shame that she had stood aside at that terrible wedding party and allowed Gloria to be led away, despite what she'd heard Laurent say to her out there by the pool; despite knowing that Gloria was afraid.

Yet what else could she have done?

'Really, Eve, your behaviour has been dashed inconsiderate,' Clifford continues now. 'Because of your failure to come home when arranged, I've had to leave my business at a devilish awkward time and your mother is missing her rotary club social. And you know she doesn't travel well.'

'Nobody asked you to come. Or her, for that matter. And since when does my mother do anything social? To be frank, I still don't understand what she's doing here.'

'She was concerned about you. As soon as she heard that you were down here alone and refusing to return, she insisted on coming. I did try to dissuade her.'

The plaintive note in his voice betrays his sense of grievance and Eve feels a jolt of pity. It can't have been an easy journey.

'I'm sorry,' she says, her shoulders dropping. 'I'm sorry about not coming home. I just needed to know why Guy Lester wanted me to come here. Who he was to me. I've always felt—'

Here she stops short, embarrassed suddenly to be talking to Clifford about her private feelings.

'I've always felt there was a big part of me missing. I don't know how to explain it properly. I've always felt *unfinished.* And I thought . . . that is, I hoped . . . perhaps coming here would fill some of that missing bit in. That's why I couldn't bear to come home without finding the answers.'

Clifford gives her a strange look that she cannot interpret, but his voice when he replies is kinder.

'My dear, sometimes the answers are worse than the not knowing.'

Eve glances over sharply at her husband. This is a side of him she has not seen before. For a moment hope lifts in her chest. Perhaps they can find an understanding, after all.

But then: 'Besides, we are married now. I should have thought you have quite enough to occupy yourself in running our home and you wouldn't have time to feel a lack of anything.'

Just like that, the fragile window of communication that had briefly opened just a crack slams shut again.

'Why did you marry me?'

They have resumed walking along the beach, so Eve can ask her question without having to make direct eye contact.

She senses Clifford's displeasure in the stiffening of his shoulders.

'Must we really go into all this now, when there is so much

else to be done – travel arrangements to be made, papers to be signed, bags to pack?'

'Yes, I'm afraid we must.'

'Really, Eve. What is it you want me to say? I married you because we got along, didn't we? We were each what the other needed.'

'And love?'

'Yes, of course, that as well. But this is not some sappy romantic film. We are realists, you and I. We lived through a war, for heaven's sake. That's what I liked about you. You seemed so level-headed. Not the type of girl to expect life to be all roses and chocolates and then fall to pieces when the nine-to-five routine set in.'

Clifford hesitates, kicking aside a stone with sudden ferocity.

'But, dash it, if roses and chocolates are what will make you happy, I'll do that. Look here, I know I've been preoccupied with work, and perhaps life has seemed a little dull, but I'll make more of an effort. I promise. We could go to the pictures once a week. You'd like that, wouldn't you? Just come home and we will pick up our lives and all this will seem like some absurd dream. We'll have a good laugh about it all one day, once those silly cuts and bruises of yours have faded. You'll see.'

It is this that finally convinces her. Her total failure to picture she and Clifford sharing a good laugh about anything. Indeed, her inability to conjure up a single instance in which such an event has ever taken place.

'Clifford,' she begins, turning to look at him.

But whatever she was about to say is cut short as the rain, which has been threatening all morning, now begins in earnest, prompting a cry from her mother, who is still huddled on the bench some distance behind them.

By the time they have hurried back to her, all three of them are wet through.

'I told you we should not have come out in this weather,' Eve's mother says, wiping the rain from her face. 'And now we must walk back to the house. Really, Eve.'

As if Eve has deliberately laid on the weather to vex her.

They set out along the coast road towards the villa. It is not far, but it seems to Eve as if every waterlogged step lasts a lifetime.

Conditions are far from conducive to meaningful conversation, focused as they all are on reaching shelter as quickly as possible. However, Eve finds she cannot quite let the opportunity slip. She has not yet had a chance to speak properly to her mother. After she and Clifford arrived at the beach earlier from their hotel in Cannes, complaining that the taxi driver had driven them a very long way round, her mother had lost no time in announcing her intention to rest a while on the bench on account of not having slept the night before, leaving Eve and Clifford to take their walk together.

'Now that you've had time to think, are you sure you don't recognize the name Francis Garvey?' she asks her mother now, panting as they hurry along the puddle-pitted road. 'Nor Guy Lester?'

'No. I already told you.'

Her mother stops to brush angrily at her stocking, which has become splattered with mud. Her head is bent, revealing the pink scalp showing through hair that was once dark but is now liberally threaded with grey, and set so tight that it does not yield even in this rain.

But Eve saw her expression before she bent over.

Her mother is lying.

They are soaked to the skin when they arrive back at the villa. Despite the best ministrations of Mrs Finch, who offers to fetch warm tea and to dig out clean clothes from the upstairs wardrobes, Clifford and Eve's mother insist on returning to their hotel to change, ferried there by an agreeable driver Mrs Finch summons from a neighbouring house.

They will return with Bernard later in the afternoon when the Lesters are once again convening to sign the documents, and then Eve and her mother and husband will catch the evening train back to Paris, and onwards to London.

Over. It is over.

Sully arrives not long after the others have left, having once more visited the hospital hoping for word of Gloria. He is disconsolate at having been again refused entry.

'Do you know what the hospital spokesperson had the gall to tell the press?' Sully rages. 'That Gloria Hayes is suffering from "post wedding-fatigue". *Post-wedding fatigue?* Do they think we're all imbeciles? Luckily I managed to corner a friendly nurse. Well. She wasn't friendly to start with, but five hundred francs made her a lot friendlier. She says Gloria is at least alive, although she is very weak. She said something else but I didn't understand it. Her French was very vulgar.'

It does not take long for Eve to pack up her things. There are so few of them, after all. When her case is full, she sits on her bed and looks around the room that has been hers for the last week. Her eye lingers on the green curtains, bleached by the sun, and the peeling paint of the window frames.

Gloria's blue dress is laid out on the bed. Eve glances down at her silk blouse and navy woollen skirt. Sighs.

She is tired out from the effort of trying to escape herself.

It is just as well that she is leaving now. Before she becomes attached. She will always think of Sully and Gloria and Libby with fondness, but really they belong to a different life. Duncan, Diana and Clemmie will just be relieved to have her gone. Such an unnecessary vexation she has been, while they are trying to deal with their own private grief.

About Noel she does not allow herself to think.

Restless, she gets to her feet and flings open the window, staring out at the rain and the surface of the sea, which crawls with tiny white waves.

The air outside is thick and heavy and throbbing, as if waiting for something to happen. Eve notices some cracked tiles on the terrace floor, and the way a section of the balustrade is crumbling. Victor Meunier will have his work cut out.

It is only when she closes the window again that Eve becomes aware of a faint clanging sound. Puzzled, she goes to the door of her room and listens. The clanging is louder here, echoing tinnily up the stone staircase.

Padding down the stairs on her stockinged feet, Eve pauses in the bottom hallway. 'Sully?' she calls, before remembering the American is out at a luncheon he claimed not to be able to get out of. Though he had gone off complaining bitterly, it was still a painful reminder to Eve that the world of the Riviera would continue long after she was no longer here to observe it.

The noise seems to be coming from the direction of the kitchen. Eve follows the hallway around behind the stairs, finding the kitchen empty. 'Mrs Finch?' she calls out. Only when the noise strikes up again does she realize it is actually coming from beneath her. She wonders what Mrs Finch can be doing down in the cellar. Whatever it is, it sounds very physical. Perhaps she could do with a hand.

In the back of Eve's mind, there is also the awareness that this is a chance – her last chance – to poke around in Guy's old junk while someone else is there to keep her company in that ghastly damp place.

At the top of the steps leading down to the cellar she hesitates. Here in this part of the house that never receives any direct light, the temperature is ten degrees cooler than everywhere else, and Eve shivers in her thin blouse. The memory of the last time she went down these stairs is still vivid in her mind. That particular wet-earth dankness. The heart-stopping fear of finding herself trapped, alone, in the dark.

The clanging starts up again, coming from the junk room whose door stands ajar but not wide open enough for Eve to see inside. She turns on the light at the top of the stairs, making sure to leave the door to the hallway open. The bottom half of the stairs is plunged into a gloom that the thin yellow glow from the overhead bulb fails to penetrate, and she descends gingerly. Down here, the noise is much louder, and the clangs have increased in frequency, so that when Eve calls out 'Mrs Finch?' her voice is lost in the clamour.

In the small vestibule, Eve once again pauses. What if Mrs Finch tells Diana and her stepsons that Eve has been nosing around? For a split second she almost turns back. Then she remembers that she is leaving today; what does it matter what the Lesters think of her? She nudges open the door and steps inside and—

Oh.

For a moment she frowns, unable to process what she is

seeing, because standing hunched over, his curved back facing her, wielding a pickaxe that clatters again and again against the brick wall at the far end of the cellar, is Victor Meunier.

It is dark in here, but there is a flashlight on the floor and in its weak beam Eve sees that the shelving that had covered the back wall has been dismantled and all the junk that had been leaning against it moved to the side. Where Victor is swinging the axe, he has created a jagged black hole in the brick, under which loose masonry has piled up on the stone floor.

Before Eve can start to wonder what it might mean, Victor stops and mutters something in French. There follows a sudden, sickening silence in which the air particles themselves seem to stand still. Frozen to the spot, Eve tries not to breathe, but that familiar chill coming from the cellar works its way into her nostrils, infiltrating her bloodstream until her very bones feel damp.

Without being able to identify exactly why, she has a strong feeling that she should not draw attention to herself, at least not until she has worked out what is going on. While she simply cannot imagine the charming Frenchman engaged in anything untoward, she equally cannot come up with one good reason why he should be here in this cellar trying to knock a hole in the wall.

Moving slowly, she pulls herself back into the shadows and is rewarded when he once again hefts the axe above his head and swings it at the wall.

Every instinct tells her to turn and hurry back up the stairs. She could wait for Sully. Tell him what she has seen. Or she could just leave well alone. *Stop minding everyone else's business*, her mother would say. She could just go back up to her room and pick up her case and leave the dramas of the Riviera behind. There is bound to be a straightforward explanation. Perhaps Victor has already somehow taken ownership of Villa La Perle. Perhaps it was all agreed last night after the others left and nobody thought to tell her.

Yet still she remains, unable to shake off the feeling that whatever Victor is up to is somehow tied up with all the strange things that have happened to her since she arrived here.

What if someone really did deliberately remove the handle of the cellar door the last time, trapping her inside? What if someone has been trying to harm her, or at the very least scare her away?

Who hates me so much?

Her racing thoughts are brought up short by the sound of metal on stone as Victor casts the axe to the floor. Breathing heavily, he picks up the flashlight and shines it into the black cavity through the part-demolished wall, where there seems to be a second, much smaller chamber.

'*C'est où? C'est où?*' he mutters, moving the beam around, until, finally, it comes to rest on a bulky shape that looms in the corner.

He gives a grunt of triumph and starts squeezing himself through the hole in the brickwork, sending more loose masonry clattering to the floor.

Inside the hidden chamber, he crouches down as low as his stiff leg will allow and starts fiddling with the bulky shape. Then he says something that sounds to Eve like 'intact'.

Victor reaches out his hands wide and grasps the

mysterious object, which is as high as his waist and almost a yard across. Half lifting, half dragging, he wrestles it through the gap in the wall, while Eve shrinks back until she is all but hidden by the open door.

She wants only to see what is in the package. Eve knows she has always been too curious, too interested in other people's lives, as if by dipping into them she can somehow make up for the deficiencies of her own. But one glimpse is all she needs.

Victor manhandles the package back into the main room, letting it rest against the wall directly in Eve's line of gaze.

Eve cranes forward in her eagerness to see what it is.

The mystery object is wrapped in a blanket, tied around with string again and again. Victor reaches into his pocket and produces a penknife, which he flicks impatiently open. Eve flinches as the knife severs the string. *Slash.* Finally he lifts a corner of the covering and Eve sees from the shiny surface, as it catches the thin light, that it is an oilskin, not a blanket. With this pervading damp it makes sense.

He unwinds the oilskin, which appears to have been wrapped several times around whatever is inside.

There is a sense of breath being held as the thick, greasy material falls to the ground, revealing its contents. A stack of paintings in tarnished gold frames, the uppermost a discordant jumble of colours with intersecting lines that form irregular shapes in which different body parts are painted – a sweep of hair in this one, an eye in that, all seemingly unconnected to those next to them – the overall impression being one of visual cacophony, yet so compelling you cannot look away.

Eve gasps, so softly it might in other circumstances have

sounded like the air shifting and changing. But in this place, every slight noise is amplified. Victor looks up sharply, and before Eve can register what has happened, he is across the room, his limp all but forgotten, and Eve is turning to leave, but he has hold of her blouse.

There is a tearing sound as Eve tries to pull away. Now he grabs her arm and he is so much stronger than she thought.

'Eve, stop,' he says, urgency accenting his English more strongly than ever before. 'I want only to talk to you.'

But his fingers are digging into her arm, and Eve knows in some deep primeval place inside her where fear is generated that she has to get away.

'Go away!' she shouts.

There is a noise. Footsteps on the stairs. Relief engulfs her as the comforting figure of Mrs Finch comes into view.

'Mrs Finch. Thank God!'

Victor, clearly sensing the game is up, drops his hold on her and Eve lunges forward, gripping the housekeeper's hand in gratitude.

'Mr Meunier has gone mad. I don't know what it's all about, but we must go upstairs at once and call the police.'

Mrs Finch does not move. 'What on earth is going on?' she asks.

'I told you,' says Eve, by now desperate to get away. 'He was doing something he shouldn't, knocking holes in walls, and now he has gone mad.'

'I did not know she was there.'

At first Eve cannot understand why Victor should be addressing Mrs Finch like that, as if Eve wasn't present, or why Mrs Finch is still standing there, gripping her hands, instead of hurrying back up the stairs. But when the housekeeper advances into the cellar, yanking Eve along behind her rather than heading back up to safety, the realization dawns.

Whatever Victor is involved with, Mrs Finch is in on it too.

25

VICTOR MEUNIER AND Mrs Finch. What kind of bizarre pairing is this? Eve tries to remember the occasions when she has seen the two together. Were there any clues she missed that hinted at more than a passing acquaintance?

Without letting go of her grip on Eve's hand, this new unsmiling Mrs Finch begins a heated conversation with Victor in French. Eve, her mouth dry as dust, chest tight, struggles to follow it.

'Why couldn't you have waited? She would have been gone by this evening.' Mrs Finch's cheeks are stained pink, and her hazel eyes are wide with reproach.

'That damned boy recognized me. The one with the glasses.'

'Recognized you from where? How is that even possible?'

'It doesn't matter. What matters is what we do with her now.'

Finally the two of them turn their attention to Eve. Mrs Finch is flushed and agitated, Victor dishevelled from his earlier exertions and looking very unlike his usual self. Eve cannot imagine what it was about Victor that she had found so attractive at first. His eyes now seem to her to be lacking in depth, his face too narrow, as if life has pinched the pleasure from it.

Eve's skin prickles under their hostile scrutiny. She swallows, trying to find her voice.

'Whatever is going on here has nothing to do with me. I insist you let me go.'

How squeaky her voice is. She tries to shake her arm free from Mrs Finch, but the housekeeper is deceptively strong, and anyway Victor has now manoeuvred himself so he is blocking the door.

'I only wish we could let you go,' he tells her in English. 'But alas.'

'What do you mean, alas?' Mrs Finch asks him sharply. 'Look here, you told me no one would get hurt. You told me it was risk-free, that no one would ever know. I would *never* have involved myself if—'

'And yet here you are.' Victor smiles.

There's a pressure in Eve's skull as if it is being squeezed by a giant hand. Nothing makes sense. Not Victor, nor Mrs Finch, nor that stack of paintings leaning against the wall, nor the hidden chamber behind the wall in which, she now notices, there are other packages, also wrapped in oilskin.

'Why didn't you just go when you were supposed to? Why did you even have to come?' Mrs Finch is almost crying, her chest and neck blotched purple.

'I don't understand,' Eve says, trying not to cry herself. 'What have I done? Why shouldn't I be here?'

But Victor has heard enough.

'There is no time for this,' he tells Mrs Finch. 'There is a boat arriving any moment now. We must take what we can. The rest of it, the ones in the garden, we will have to leave.'

'And her?'

Victor shrugs.

'I won't tell anyone,' Eve says stupidly. 'I have no idea what's happening, so how could I tell? Just let me go and I'll get on my train back to England and you'll never hear from me again.'

She is talking too fast and too loud, hoping someone might hear her, even though she's well aware no one is expected back to the house until later. Her brain races this way and that, trying to find a solution, or at least an explanation, but none is forthcoming.

'Come,' says Victor finally, grabbing her roughly by the top of her arm and pulling her with him towards the back of the room where the jagged black hole gapes.

Eve struggles, trying to break free.

'Hold her,' Victor calls to Mrs Finch.

'I don't want—'

'Do you want to go to prison? Is that what you want?'

A red vein pulses in Victor's neck and those navy blue eyes she'd once thought so fine are like hard balls of glass.

Mrs Finch moves to stand behind Eve, holding her arms still. Her fingers shake and Eve realizes she is crying in earnest now.

Victor picks up the pickaxe.

'You can't do this!' Eve is shouting at Mrs Finch, trying to swivel her head to look at her. If she can only make eye contact, surely she can get through to her. 'My husband and my mother will be here any minute. This is the first place they'll look if they can't find me.'

'Not if you're well hidden.'

Eve follows Victor's gaze. Through the jagged hole.

'We'll put the shelves back and lean all these things against them to hide the hole,' Victor is telling Mrs Finch, indicating the broken bike, and the old sink he has pushed up against the left-hand wall of the cellar. He holds the wooden handle of the axe in his left hand, with the blade resting on the palm of his right as if he is weighing it up.

Eve, her arms still being held from behind, fights back a wave of nausea. Surely Victor would not seriously harm her? But war, she knows only too well, does strange things to people. When there has been so much death and suffering, human life can lose its value. Her breath is coming out in short shallow bursts, her chest too tight to inhale properly. *Please*, she says inside her head. *Please. Please. Please.*

Victor raises his hands, and Eve closes her eyes, gulping in the sour air. There is a moment when time seems to stand still, the universe holding its breath. And then:

Bang.

Eve drops to the floor, wrapping her arms around her head, so convinced is she of having been struck.

It is some moments before she recovers sufficiently to become aware of several things – that she is not, after all, hurt; that Mrs Finch has let go of her arms; and that they are no longer alone.

26

'I KNEW IT, you see. Just as soon as I saw him. Only it took a while to make the connections.'

Jack Collett, too agitated to sit, paces up and down the sitting room until Eve, curled up in a corner of the sofa, wrapped in a blanket despite the soggy heat, grows dizzy from watching him.

'What connections? Who did you see?' Eve wonders if her brain has simply stopped working, which is why she is finding it so hard to follow what Jack is saying.

'Jack, darling, perhaps it might make more sense to Eve if you start from the beginning,' says Ruth who, having ministered to Eve, helping her up from the cellar, fetching a blanket and a cup of sweet tea, now sits next to her as if on guard duty.

'Him. Victor Meunier,' says Jack, falling over his own words in his haste to get them out. 'I knew I recognized him from somewhere and all night I was racking my brains, trying to remember. Wasn't I?' He appeals to his parents for corroboration. 'I couldn't even eat dinner. Not a crumb.'

'Well, that's not entirely accurate,' says Rupert. 'There was that egg sandwich, and that—'

'So then I tried to think strategically. Where might I have

come across him? I realized it was likely to have been in Paris, so I started running through all the different things I'd done there. And I remembered I was working on my dissertation one day in the library at the Sorbonne. One of my old professors is on sabbatical there as a guest lecturer. And there was this French art magazine filled with articles. All in French, which was a damned nuisance.'

'The nerve of those French,' says Rupert.

Jack makes a face at his father and continues. 'Because I didn't understand the words, I spent a long time studying the photographs. So this morning I dragged my parents off to Nice and we trawled in vain around every shop looking for that blasted magazine until a shopkeeper mentioned a retired professor out towards Vence who has a whole library of such publications that he orders straight from Paris. So we drove off to see him and after Mother sweet-talked him into letting us look through his collection, we found just the one we were looking for. And of course as soon as we made the connection, we came rushing straight over.'

'Yes, but what *is* the connection?'

'Yes, do get to the point, darling,' chivvies Ruth.

'Well, it's about Victor Meunier, as I said. Except his real name is Gustave Borde. As he told you, he has a gallery down here in Nice, but what he didn't tell you is that he is on the list of art experts suspected of being affiliated with the Galerie nationale du Jeu de Paume in Paris during the war. It's where the Nazis brought works of art once owned by French Jews and others who'd been carted off to the camps. The art was assessed and catalogued by experts and then transported to Germany, for the private collections of high-ranking SS officials.'

'And Victor worked for them?' Eve cannot hide her dismay. 'But surely not? He was himself imprisoned in Germany. His leg injury . . . '

Eve realizes how naive she sounds. As if she might be the first woman ever to have been lied to by a man.

'He may well have been a prisoner of war for a time,' suggests Rupert. 'Before being released in exchange for a German POW. Or until the Nazis realized he could be useful to them – and vice versa. And the leg wound could have happened as he said. Or perhaps that too is a convenient story.'

Eve cannot, will not, believe it.

'But he helped the Jews during the war,' she remembers suddenly. 'He was a local hero.'

Rupert shrugs. 'I don't know anything about that. Though it would be useful to know if he helped all Jews, regardless of where they came from, or whether those he rescued happened to be the more prosperous ones, who could pay for their escape in jewellery or property or even art.'

A worm of dread is wriggling at the base of Eve's stomach. Could you really spend time chatting to someone, laughing with them, feeling happy to be in their company, and not suspect that until three years before they were on the side of the people who wanted to kill you and everyone you knew?

'But if this was true he would be in prison,' she says.

'My dear girl, if all the people who behaved badly during the war were imprisoned, there would be more people in jail than out,' says Rupert.

'Nothing was ever proven,' says Jack. 'And the article just said he left Paris shortly before the end of the war, current whereabouts unknown. Look here, Eve, are you sure they can't get out?'

'Well, I certainly couldn't.'

They have trapped Victor and Mrs Finch in the cellar while they wait for the police to arrive. It now seems nothing short of miraculous that, amid the panic and confusion of the Colletts' arrival in the junk room, the memory should have come so clearly to Eve of how she herself had been incarcerated by the removal – accidental or not – of the outside door handle. And miraculous also that, having been rescued by the Colletts, she'd retained enough wits to slam shut the door and yank the handle so it came off in her hand, before bolting, leaving two people imprisoned in that place.

'What would have happened if you hadn't come?' she asks, seemingly for the hundredth time. 'Or had turned away when no one answered the door instead of coming down the side?'

It was Jack, so eager to share what he'd learned, who had insisted on going round the house in case Eve and Sully were outside on the bottom terrace. And that's where they'd heard Eve shouting.

'By heaven, Ruth, it's a damned good thing we've raised a child with no manners whatsoever. Quite happy to barge into someone else's home uninvited,' says Rupert. 'By the way, Eve, there was a boat at the jetty below when we arrived with a few chaps on board, but they pulled off sharpish when they saw us.'

Sully arrives home from his luncheon and they fill him in on the bizarre events of the last hour. Funny how their power decreases in the retelling, the choosing of words and the pausing for dramatic effect already beginning the process of turning the most nightmarish experience of Eve's life into an entertaining story.

Sully, never usually short of conversation, listens in silence.

'I always knew there was something not kosher about Victor Meunier,' he says at last.

Eve gazes at him in disbelief. 'What complete tosh. You were the one who told me he was a local hero.'

Sully looks pained. 'My dear Eve, I'm a writer. What we say is usually diametrically opposed to what we actually think.'

'Well, I wonder that you bother saying anything at all, in that case.'

'The thing is,' continues Sully, as if she hasn't spoken, 'nothing about people surprises me any more. Particularly the sort who end up round here. The Riviera is full of folk who'd prefer you not to question them too closely about what they got up to during the war. Take the grand hotels that the Nazis holed up in after the fascists left. Some of those places were used as holding pens for Jews rounded up after being ratted out by the fine upstanding citizens of Nice and Cannes in return for money or even food. People were tortured there. Yet ask yourself how many of the same staff that cooked for the SS and cleaned and brought them fresh towels and wished them good morning are still there, performing the same tasks for holidaymakers, as if there is no difference at all.'

Eve remembers how Marie refused to acknowledge the concierge at the Appleton hotel.

'But I've seen photographs – of women collaborators being paraded through the streets.'

'Oh, sure. When it comes to poor people, principles are always very strictly applied. Strange thing, but there seems to be a link between the amount of money involved and the corresponding haziness of people's memories.'

'But Marie and Bernard . . .'

'Of course there was heroism as well, people like the

Gaillards risking their lives, often for perfect strangers. But self-interest can usually be relied upon to command greater loyalty than honour. I must say, though, I'm surprised at Caroline Finch.'

Eve moves to put her head in her hands, wincing with pain as she remembers her sprained wrist. What a mess she has made of everything. She remembers how she'd felt that first day in the Appleton hotel, lying on that bed with the sun slanting warm across her face, and feeling light as air, sure that this would turn out to be the start of her proper life.

'But what exactly were they doing?' asks Ruth.

'Isn't it obvious?' says Sully. 'We know this house was occupied during the war. We now know also that Victor Meunier was advising the Nazis on stolen art.'

'Suspected of,' says Eve.

Sully raises an eyebrow.

'All I'm saying is it's not so much of a leap to imagine he helped them stash things here, in the basement, once they realized the war wasn't going their way.'

'But I thought the Germans were meticulous about logging the things they looted,' says Rupert. 'Wasn't it all earmarked for Hitler's museum or the SS high command's private collections?'

'Apart from the degenerate stuff.'

They all stare at Jack, who is suffused in a pink glow of excitement.

'The Nazis had long lists of work they considered degenerate. Anything too modern, or painted by Jews or communists or, heaven forbid, homosexuals, was either sold off or destroyed.'

Sully nods to himself. 'So they could have passed them on to Victor to get rid of, and instead he hid them here in the cellar at some point between the Nazis leaving and the Lesters returning?'

'Yes, but that still doesn't explain Mrs Finch,' says Eve.

Their conversation is interrupted by the ringing of the doorbell. For a moment she and Sully remain in position, before remembering that Mrs Finch is currently confined to the cellar, whereupon the American hurries off to open the door.

He returns with two policemen and Bernard, closely followed by Eve's husband and mother. The latter's pursed lips leave no doubt about what she thinks of arriving on the doorstep at the same time as the local constabulary.

'What in blazes is going on, Eve?' asks Clifford. 'Really, must there always be some drama?'

Before Eve can reply, there is another furore at the door and in troop the Lesters en masse. Libby, in front, is seemingly unfazed by finding the sitting room of her old home filled with strangers.

'Eve! Oh, how lovely that you're here and how lovely you look and now I must, must, must go up to my room to see if I can find my bear. I've had him since I was born and I miss him to distraction.' The girl flings herself at Eve before darting away up the stairs, leaving the air behind her throbbing with motion.

So now Eve must explain what has happened. There is no small amount of 'I knew it' when Victor's wartime history is revealed. Several people announce that they have always suspected the Frenchman to be not what he seemed. Clemmie declares she has a nose for auras and that his always did smell fishy.

Noel, who has been silently leaning against the wall, now straightens up.

'Why didn't you go straight to fetch help rather than spying on Meunier, trying to play the big heroine?' he asks, chin jutting.

'I wasn't doing any such thing.' Eve feels her cheeks burning. 'I was merely *observing*.'

But is that what she was doing? She tries to think back to those fevered moments in that dank passage. She could have slipped back up the stairs, but she had wanted to know what was happening. Hadn't she? Or was she merely trying to insert herself into the drama, unwilling even now to let go of her fantasy that this would turn out to be the time when everything fell into place, her life spluttering into forward motion like a stalled motor car engine?

The older of the two policemen looks alarmed once Bernard has finished translating Eve's version of events. He has a square face, the symmetry of which is thrown out by a nose that bends slightly to the left as if it has been broken and badly set. He goes to the hall, standing in the doorway at the top of the stairs that lead down to the cellar. Opens the door. Waits. Listens.

The younger man, sensing perhaps the scent of glory, urges action.

They confer in urgent whispers before deciding to go down the stairs to confront the imprisoned pair, taking Bernard with them as an independent witness. The others are instructed to wait in the living room.

'I don't understand,' Diana says. 'What is Caroline Finch thinking of, getting mixed up in something like this? Are you completely sure it happened just the way you said?'

She is glaring at Eve as if she might have invented the whole thing just to make herself more interesting in some way. And now Eve is doubting herself. Might there yet turn out to be some perfectly reasonable explanation?

Clifford has listened to the whole story with an expression of shocked concentration. *He must love me*, thinks Eve, seeing how worry has scored vertical lines into his face.

But when her husband speaks, it is of practicalities.

'Does this mean,' he wants to know, 'that there will be no sale?'

Duncan groans. 'I'm as good as a dead man. Or as bad as.'

He is collapsed at one end of the sofa, wearing a white shirt with a stain on the sleeve, and Eve has the strong impression that he has not gone to bed since yesterday. Eve thinks about the various people he owes money to, thinks about Laurent Martin's compressed fury, and, though all his problems are self-inflicted, she feels a pang of pity for him.

There is a noise out in the passageway. The low murmur of voices. Doors being opened and closed.

Bernard reappears in the doorway, followed by the two policemen, each escorting one of the two recently liberated captives.

The older policeman, whose meaty fingers are closed around the sleeve of Victor Meunier's jacket, says something quickly to Bernard in French that Eve does not catch.

'He asks that you all remain here for the next two or three hours. They will need to return to question you.'

Clifford raises his arm and frowns at his watch.

'As long as he bears in mind that my wife and mother-in-law and I will be needing to catch our train later. We were very much hoping to tie up the business side of things before we leave.'

He means the money, Eve realizes. In the end, it is all about the money.

'Obviously there will not now be any question of a sale in principle,' says Bernard slowly.

'*Je suis désolé*,' says Victor, who is pale but composed, as if being under arrest is an eventuality he has prepared for. His eyes fix on Eve and he gives the slightest of nods. 'It has been a pleasure,' he tells her, as if they are saying goodbye after a dance or some other social event.

'No,' says Diana suddenly. 'No, this cannot be supported.'

She gets to her feet from the chaise on which she has been perched and positions herself in front of Mrs Finch. The housekeeper, her eyes pink from weeping, is standing towards the back of the group, her elbow firmly in the grip of the younger policeman.

'I need to know why,' Diana says to the wretched-looking woman. 'Wasn't Guy always good to you? Heaven knows you wouldn't have been my choice, especially once I found out about your *history* together, but Guy insisted on showing you loyalty after all the years you'd been with him. Why would you collaborate with someone like him?' She gestures with her head in the direction of Victor. 'Involving this house and this family in such a sordid business? Think of the sacrifices Noel and Duncan made fighting the Germans. All those missions Noel flew, one after the other, watching his friends getting shot down all around him.'

'We all know what drove *him*,' mutters Mrs Finch.

'Then think of Guy,' continues Diana. 'Is this how you show your appreciation for everything he did for you?'

And now something changes in the housekeeper, as if a

switch is being thrown inside her, causing her to stand upright, looking round, eyes blazing.

'Everything he did for me?' She spits out the words like apple pips. 'I was young when I first came here. Attractive. I see you smirking, but you didn't know me then. I could have had a husband, a family. But instead there was Guy Lester letting me believe he'd leave his wife, just as soon as the children were a little older, or his wife a little stronger. So I waited and I waited. I took care of his boys, spoilt though they were. I looked after his house. And when she died, I thought, now it will come. Now is my time. I'd been so patient. I'd *proved* myself as a wife and a mother. But then you came along. And only then did I realize that, of course, before you there'd been others and I was just too blind to see. "Don't worry," he said. "There'll always be a job for you. I'll always make sure you're all right." He wanted me to absolve him of guilt. You know how he always had to feel himself to be in the right?'

For a moment it is as if she is appealing to Diana, woman to woman, about a mutual friend. Then she remembers where she is.

'Do you know what he left me in his will? Two hundred and fifty pounds. In compensation for everything I gave him. For the life I should have had. I *loved* him.'

They all stare at this new, unfamiliar Mrs Finch in varying degrees of horrified fascination. Her cheeks are flushed pink, her hair is loose and falls wild around her shoulders. Passion has rendered her unrecognizable.

'I found it, you know. The new will. After you all moved to the new house in Nice and I was packing up Guy's things to bring them over. I saw how much he'd left me. And then I saw he'd left a quarter of this house to an Eve Forrester.'

Now her gaze comes to rest on Eve and some of the fire goes from her eyes.

'I assumed you were another one of his affairs. Don't pretend you didn't all think the same thing. That's why I said yes when Monsieur Meunier asked me to help him, after Mrs Forrester here refused to leave. I was owed something, don't you see?'

She is appealing directly to Eve, who doesn't know where to look.

'I suppose Meunier had no intention of buying the bloody house,' says Duncan, whose skin is now paler than his shirt.

Victor, standing nearest to Eve with his policeman minder, shrugs.

'Of course not,' he says. 'I am afraid greed blinded you all to sense. There are houses like this one for sale all the way up and down this coast. I would have signed the agreement and paid a few months' rent.'

'Giving you time and space to excavate the paintings from the cellar before disappearing,' says Sully.

'Exactly,' says Victor politely. Then he turns to Diana. 'And you might like to try digging in the terrace as well. Who knows what you might find.'

Noel, who has been quiet up until now, approaches Mrs Finch.

'What did you do when you found my father's will?' he asks, his voice low and dangerously tight.

The housekeeper swallows loudly enough that they all hear, and just for a moment Eve finds herself feeling sorry for her.

'I confronted him, of course. There was a horrible scene.'

'When?' asks Noel, stepping towards Mrs Finch so that she visibly recoils. 'When did you confront my father?'

The housekeeper looks nervous, her gaze falling to the ground, those purple blotches livid on her chest again. But Noel will not relent.

'When was this confrontation?'

'The morning of the day he died.'

'It was your fault!' Duncan is on his feet. 'You knew he had to avoid stress.'

'I was upset! I had every right to be.'

'No.' Noel is shaking his head, his face just inches from Mrs Finch's so that she cannot look away. 'You do not get to look for sympathy. You do not get to play the victim. You didn't have to stay here, once you knew Guy wasn't interested in you. You weren't a prisoner. The war gave everyone a chance to reinvent themselves. Why didn't you build yourself a new life instead of coming back here?'

'He needed me. You all needed me.'

'You were the *housekeeper*,' says Duncan. 'We could have replaced you a dozen times over.'

The exchange is interrupted by an exclamation from the hallway.

'Mrs Finch. It's you!' cries Libby, barrelling into the room and giving the housekeeper a hug from behind. Then she notices the two policemen and her eyes grow wide.

'Are you under arrest? Did you *kill* someone?'

Mrs Finch seems to shrink as if someone has knocked the air out of her. The high colour fades from her cheeks, and the eyes that just moments before were burning with that conviction unique to those who consider themselves grievously wronged turn suddenly dull.

'*Alors*,' says the older policeman, blinking above his crooked nose.

The two gendarmes turn around, steering their charges in front of them.

As he is led away, Victor reaches out and grasps Eve's hand.

'It was only about the art,' he says, smiling sadly. 'It was never personal.'

27

AFTERWARDS EVE WILL wish she had asked Victor what he meant by *personal.* Is it that it was never about her at all, that she could really have been anyone, and the muttered 'beautiful' that she has been hoarding in her head like secret treasure since the night in Le Crystal was as specific to her as to that vase over there, or that cloud outside the window? Or is it his crimes that she is not to take personally?

The truth is lost in the departing of the gendarmes and their detainees, and the bristling of Clifford next to her at Victor's gesture of familiarity, in the shocked faces of the Lester family and her mother's unexpressed but still evident displeasure at everything she has seen. In saying goodbye to the Colletts, who will need to go back to their hotel to change their plans before heading to the police station to make a statement.

'Goodbye, my dear,' says Ruth, hugging Eve tightly. 'I do hope we shall see each other back in England.'

Eve nods, not trusting herself to speak.

Now what is to be done?

There can be no signing of papers. No transfer of ownership.

No pleasing sums of money changing hands. Duncan's creditors will not be paid. Diana's sacrifice will go unrewarded.

Outside the grey cloud persists.

Diana shakes her head.

'How extraordinary,' she says. 'It's as if she hates us all.'

'Don't be so hard on yourself. Mrs Finch was motivated as much by the desire to line her own pockets as by her undiluted hatred of you all,' says Sully cheerfully.

'She as good as murdered my father,' Duncan says. 'I know the cancer would have got him sooner or later, but it was the shock of being confronted like that which brought on the haemorrhage. I'm sure of it. Did you know he drowned in his own blood?'

'It's so awful,' Clemmie says, her eyes round. 'A spy in our midst. Who knows what danger we might all have been in.'

For the first time Eve realizes just how much of an impediment she must have been to Victor. Content to bide his time while Guy was alive and the heat was settling on the stolen art market, when he made the initial approach to Bernard, following Guy's death, it must have seemed such a straightforward matter to take possession of an empty property that no one really wanted and remove the paintings at leisure. Then along came the mystery beneficiary from England, insisting on moving into the house, refusing to sign the papers. How far might he have gone to scare her off? As far as persuading Mrs Finch to shut her in the cellar? As far as pushing her off the rocks? Blackmail?

She turns to Bernard.

'I don't believe you ever trusted Victor. Is there something else you know about him?'

Bernard shakes his head.

'Not *know*. Not for sure. But the Riviera is a small place. People talk. Make judgements. Marie, for example, will not breathe the same air as him.'

'Judgements about what?'

'That he was too friendly with the Nazis while they were in occupation – he and Laurent Martin.'

'Laurent is involved?' asks Sully, suddenly serious.

Bernard raises his hand.

'This is only rumour. Conjecture.'

'But they'll be wanting to speak to him? The police?'

Bernard shrugs.

'There are some men coming from the *Préfecture* in Paris. Then we will know more.'

'Poppycock,' says Clemmie. 'Someone like Laurent wouldn't need to make money through smuggling. Did you see the photographs of the wedding, Mr Gaillard? Did that look to you like a man who was short of a bob or two?'

Bernard turns his sad eyes to the young girl who chafes with her own conviction of being right.

'Sometimes,' he says, 'it is not a question of money but a question of superiority. Of proving oneself to be outside the law.'

In the silence that follows, Eve tries to process in her mind the strange events of the morning, all the time conscious of Clifford and her mother watching her from the other side of the room.

Her mother had seemed to experience the war almost entirely as a personal inconvenience. It was because of the Germans that she had had to sacrifice the roses in her garden to grow lettuce and potatoes, and spend her mornings queuing up to buy bacon, and risk skin rashes in unmentionable areas by using squares of cut-up newspaper instead of toilet paper. Because of the Germans that Eve was out all the time delivering used furniture to people who'd lost everything, and she had to endure night after night alone in that house with the blackout blinds that made one feel like one was sealed into a tomb, or, worse, crowd into a shelter with the very neighbours she spent her life trying to avoid. And now, here in France, she finds her daughter has been mingling with people who, if not German, are seemingly the next best thing.

But no, Eve is being too harsh. she finds herself remembering a scene in their tiny back kitchen at home in Banbury with their neighbour, Nora, sobbing at the fold-out table, still clutching the telegram informing her that her youngest son wouldn't be coming home. Eve looking at her mother and being shocked at her brimming eyes, her naked empathy. *She understands*, Eve had thought. *She understands this deep, gut-level loss.* And simultaneous with this thought came the conviction that it was not the loss of her steady, timid father that inspired such a groundswell of feeling.

'Oh, I nearly forgot in all the excitement.'

Diana's voice cuts through the tension in the room. She has reached down to open the white handbag at her feet and is feeling around in it, her hair forming a curtain around her face that shimmers as she straightens with an exclamation of satisfaction.

'Yes, here.' She has withdrawn a bundle of papers, tied up with an elastic band, which she holds out towards Eve.

'What is it?' Though there has been some small softening between her and the second Mrs Lester over recent days, Eve remains wary.

'It was something you said yesterday that made me think of it. When you were asking your mother about Francis Garvey. When you said maybe she might know him as Frank or Frankie. It rang a bell in the back of my mind. And so I went home and here they were.'

'Yes, but what are they?' Duncan asks his stepmother as Eve leans across to take the papers being proffered. 'You still haven't said.'

'They're letters. Love letters. To someone called Frankie. They were in a box in Guy's dressing room that he thought I didn't know about.'

'I don't understand,' says Noel, impatient. 'Why would Guy have someone else's love letters?'

'There were a lot of letters in that box.' Diana's face has darkened from its usual honey colour. Normally so composed, she looks, briefly, shaky. 'Letters from other women, going back years. Look, your father was no saint. I know that won't come as news to any of you. He cheated on me and he cheated on Madeleine before me, and there we are. If the other woman was married, they'd come up with pet names for each other, aliases if you like. There was one who called him Huck and another who signed her letters Sugar, if you can believe that. It added to the illicit thrill of it all, I suppose.'

Eve, who has been loosening the rubber band that holds the letters together, looks up at the note of bitterness that has crept into Diana's voice.

She glances at Clifford, who is seemingly rendered mute by the strangeness of his surroundings and the unorthodoxy of events. He is sitting in a straight-backed chair, his eyes darting around the company. *My husband.* She repeats the phrase in her head, as if the repetition itself might make it true. And yet this man with his perfectly groomed moustache and his impeccably creased trousers seems more of a stranger to her than Stanley Sullivan, sitting to his left, of whose existence she had been unaware just ten days ago.

Her eyes slide away to Clifford's other side, alighting on her mother. Eve's heart lurches. Her mother is sitting, rigid, her face completely drained of colour, eyes fixed on the stack of letters in Eve's hand.

Slowly Eve unfolds the top letter and reads.

My most darling Frankie, Do you remember how I used to trace the contours of your face with my tongue? She stops reading, flushed with embarrassment. Her eyes scan to the bottom of the letter, her heart leaping into her throat and swelling there until she cannot breathe. *Your Own Hen x.*

So Diana is right. These are lovers' names. She doesn't look up, but even so she is aware of her mother's chalk-white face. A wave of nausea sweeps through her. Could this woman, who collected china figurines that no one ever saw and turned off the news when it came on the wireless because life was bad enough and what was the point of knowing there are even worse things out there, be another Mrs Finch, swept off her feet by a handsome face and a suitcase full of empty promises? Could her mother really be this 'Hen'?

Then she remembers Francis Garvey. The man Guy is supposed to have killed. If he turns out to be Frankie, it makes scarcely more sense. Why would Guy take possession of another man's intimate letters and keep them all these years?

'What does it say, for Pete's sake?' Clemmie is not used to being kept waiting.

Eve forces herself to scan through the letter.

'I don't think you should be reading other people's private correspondence.'

Her mother's voice.

Eve hesitates.

Her mother is right. It is a gross intrusion. And yet, this might turn out to be her last chance to find answers, to know why she has been brought here.

'I'm just skimming the lines to see if there's anything that leaps out at me,' she says.

But her mother is already on her feet, gathering herself up straight.

'You might be able to clear it with *your* conscience, Evelyn, but I will not be part of it,' she says, and she steps out through the open doors to the terrace where the darkening sky hints of more rain to come.

Eve turns her attention back to the letters in her lap, trying to ignore the stinging behind her eyeballs.

She folds up the first letter, noting the many crease marks that betray how often it has been folded and refolded. Now she opens up the second letter. *The smooth right angle of your jaw as I lie with my cheek on your chest looking up at your face. Your heart beating in my ear through your skin.* She swallows, folds up that letter too.

By the time she starts the third letter, she has lost her appetite for this.

'Do you need to do this in private?' Noel asks, seeing something in her face.

'No, I don't think there is anything here,' she says, her eyes flicking, unseeing, across the page. 'Just someone else's love letters.'

She folds the letter over once and is just about to fold it

again when a word jumps out at her from the line nearest the crease.

'Oh!'

'What is it?' So many different voices chorusing at her.

'It's nothing. It's just a name. *Mary.*' She reads aloud: 'You even loved the birthmark I've always tried to hide. Mother told me it was God's thumbprint, then after she'd gone Mary said it was how He marked out bad children, like putting a stamp on the bad eggs. But you said it was an extra heart that I wore on the outside not the inside, so I could absorb your love like sunlight.'

Clemmie laughs. 'Oh, good grief. It's like the stories you read in magazines for women of a certain age.'

'Shut up, Clemmie,' says Noel. He turns towards Eve, and now she cannot avoid looking at him as he asks steadily, 'Who is Mary?'

Eve swallows, feeling herself pulled towards him like a boat on a rope being tugged into its mooring.

'Mary is my mother's name.'

28

AS SOON AS Eve steps out on to the terrace, she is aware of the black sky pressing down on her, of the damp heat of the unseen sun, the dense mass of moisture in the air. She spots her mother down on the wooden jetty, gazing out to sea, her arms folded under the beige cardigan she wears draped over her shoulders.

'There's something curious in one of the letters,' Eve says, joining her mother. She has brought the paper with her and unfolds it, ready to read, but her mother holds up a hand.

'I don't wish to hear any more.'

'But the writer mentions a Mary and I just thought . . .' Eve looks at her mother's straight back, at her fingernails digging into the skin of her upper arms under the curtain-fall of the draped cardigan, and the resolution that has carried her out of the living room and all the way here deserts her.

'But of course there are a great many Marys,' she tails off.

Her mother turns back to look at the sea, so when she speaks, Eve at first isn't sure she has heard correctly or whether the words have been distorted by the cloud that comes so low it seems almost to be touching the water.

'She was my sister. Is.'

'Who? Who are you talking about? You don't have a sister.'

Far across the sea, a flash of lightning cracks open the black sky.

'Henrietta. *Hen.* She is my sister, though I stopped recognizing her as such many years ago.'

'Why?' Shock thins Eve's voice like acetone.

'She stole something from me. The thing she knew mattered more to me than any other.'

Her next words are drowned out by a clap of thunder that makes Eve jump.

'Him,' her mother says when Eve asks her to repeat them. 'She stole him. Francis. *Frankie.*'

'But who was he?'

'He was the love of my life.' She pauses. 'Our parents died young, Henrietta's and mine. Mother in 1912 of influenza and Father not long after. Pneumonia, they said, but I think it was just a broken heart. I was seventeen and Henrietta was two years younger. We weren't particularly close, but I tried to do the right thing by her. I left school to work as a clerk in the post office to support us both. We had the house in Banbury, but very little in the way of income. The job was so dull I thought I should die from boredom, but then he came to work there. Francis. And everything changed. Not that he knew I was there. Not at first anyway. But I used to watch him across the office – men and women worked separately then, of course. And just knowing he was there was enough.'

Eve is waiting for the things her mother is saying to slot into place, into a shape she can identify, but they refuse to. Instead she finds herself staring at a woman who looks like her mother and wears her mother's clothes, but who Eve no longer recognizes.

'I used to come home and tell Hen about him. How he'd looked that day, if he'd done something different to his hair or smiled at me when we passed on the steps outside. As I say, as sisters we weren't particularly close, but she knew how I felt. Then finally it happened. He invited me to see a concert with him. And then a week later, to have tea. I was so happy. I hadn't believed it was possible to be that happy. I truly thought he was my reward, finally, for everything I'd been through. Losing Mother, then Father. Then having to give up school to earn money.'

Eve's mother is standing there on the jetty and looking at Eve with her eyes wide and a smile on her face, as if she cannot feel the rain that has begun to fall in fat drops.

'So what happened?'

'I invited him home. That's what happened. Stupid, stupid me. And Hen came down the stairs wearing her sky blue dress that showed off her tiny waist, and I saw Francis's face when he looked at her that first time and I knew. I just knew.'

'He fell in love with her?'

'Yes.' The word sours in her mother's mouth. 'And she with him. He came to see me a few weeks later. They had not meant it to happen, he said. You can't help who you fall in love with. Do you know what else he told me? At least we had only been out together twice so feelings hadn't had a chance to develop.'

For the second time that day, rain is running in rivulets down the hard shell of her mother's hair but she seems hardly to notice. Now she has started talking, there is to be no shutting her up.

'Hen pleaded for my forgiveness. "You can't argue with love," she told me. But you know, Eve, love is like any other raw material. You bend it and mould it until it does what you want.'

'And then?'

'And then' – her mother shrugs, almost dislodging the cardigan from her shoulders – 'they married quickly. Well, Hen and I couldn't exactly go on sharing a house. They moved to London. Then came the war. And do you know what? God help me, I hoped that he wouldn't come home. Or if he came home, I hoped he'd be one of those dribbling vegetables you saw back then being wheeled through the streets, moaning and gibbering. But no, he came back whole. Perfectly intact. When all those hundreds of thousands of others didn't.'

'And you?'

'I got on with my life. Married the first man who was nice to me. Your father. I was lucky. Men were in short supply after the Great War. He had an injury. But there were many in a worse state.'

'And did you see her again? Henrietta?'

'Once.' Her mother puts up a hand to wipe the rainwater from her face, and waits impatiently for a new burst of thunder to pass.

'She came to see me. They both did. She was eight months pregnant, plump as a ripe fig. They wanted my blessing, I think. Wanted everything to be perfect. I couldn't bear to look at her. Told her not to come back. Not ever.'

Happiness explodes in Eve like a firework.

'A cousin,' she breathes. 'I have a cousin.'

Now her mother stares at her as if only just seeing her properly for the first time. And suddenly, she laughs.

'Do you really not see?' she asks. 'Are you so wilfully

blind? The injury your father sustained in the war meant we could never have children of our own. *They* were your parents. Hen and Francis.'

In the pause that follows, there comes shouting from up at the house behind her.

Clifford's voice. Querulous. 'Eve? Mary? Come in now. It's filthy weather and we must get ready to go.'

Eve's mother starts, looks up at the sky as if just registering the rain, and Eve panics, convinced that there is something about being here in this elemental weather that has opened the floodgates of her mother's secrets, as if the lightning that splits open the sky has found a corresponding crack in the locked safe of her mother's memories, and that if they go back indoors to sit in those straight-backed chairs and take tea in china cups until it's time to go, it will seal itself up again, with all those answers still inside.

A figure appears on the jetty. At first Eve thinks it is Clifford again and her heart sags in her chest, but no, the shoulders are too broad, the frame too tall. Noel Lester.

'Eve? What the hell is happening here?'

Eve ignores him.

'Where are they?' she asks, stepping in front of Noel so she forms a barrier between him and her mother. 'Where are Henrietta and Francis? Where are my parents?'

She trips over the final word, and behind her she hears Noel exclaim in surprise, but she doesn't turn around.

Her mother shrugs again, and clutches her cardigan tightly at her neck so it doesn't fall off.

'Francis died, after all. And the shock of it sent Henrietta quite mad. She was talking nonsense, apparently, leaving the child – you – alone while she walked the streets searching for her dead husband. Two policemen turned up one day on the doorstep to ask if I would sign the committal papers, and then they took her to Holke Hall asylum. As far as I know she is there still. Then they asked if we would take you in. It was that or the orphanage. Of course, I said yes. I am not a monster.'

Eve feels as if it is all falling away – the jetty, the house, Noel. All of it. She remembers the photograph of her as a baby. So that was Henrietta holding her, not her mother? Everything she thought she knew about herself was a lie.

'But why did Francis die? I don't understand. You said he came home from the war perfectly intact. Those were your words. "Perfectly intact."'

Her mother puts a hand to her head, where the rain has finally penetrated even her tightly set hair.

'I think we should go in,' she says suddenly. Eve closes her eyes, sensing the door closing on the answers she still seeks.

'For pity's sake, answer. Can you not see what you are doing to her?'

Noel has moved forward so he is standing next to Eve. Not touching, but so close she can feel the heat coming off his bare skin where his shirtsleeves are rolled up.

'All these years you've kept this from her. Did you not think she had the right to know?'

'That her real father was dead and her real mother is an imbecile? A madwoman? No, Mr Lester. It was best she didn't know. I did it for her sake.'

'Well, for her sake tell her the whole truth now, if you have any kind of humanity.'

'Don't you dare pass judgement on me. Or tell me what to do.'

'So just tell her. And then we'll all go inside and you can get on your train and go back to your life.'

The rain is falling more or less solidly and now a loud burst of thunder directly overhead causes Eve to cry out. Noel's hand finds hers, fingers closing around her own, squeezing them tightly.

The intimate gesture has an immediate effect on Eve's mother, who narrows her eyes as she asks, 'Tell her what?'

'Tell her how her father died. Women don't get sent mad for no reason. Especially when there are small children to think of.'

Eve's mother comes closer, closing the gap between them, her eyes still fixed on the point where their hands meet. Eve tries to shake her hand free, but Noel's grip is too strong.

'You want to know how he died?' she asks. Close enough now that Eve sees, with embarrassment, how the rain has soaked through the part of her blouse not covered by the cardigan so that her bra shows through. 'I'll tell you how he died, shall I?' Her mother's eyes glitter. 'He was murdered. In front of his wife. In front of his baby.'

And now a cold dread is rising inside Eve, and this has been a mistake. She wants it to be ten minutes ago. Wants not to know what she now knows, not to hear what she is about to hear. But her mother has not finished.

'They were out for an early morning stroll all together, being the perfect family that they were. You were a terrible sleeper, Eve. Always awake by five in the morning, wanting to be up and about. So there they were, walking through St James's Park. This perfect young family. And coming also through the park on their way home from an all-night regimental reunion were two former army officers, drunk on spirits and life and the memory of victory. One of them had brought a pistol to the reunion that he'd taken from a German prisoner during the war. As a memento, he said afterwards in that kangaroo court martial. A drunk man, a loaded gun. You can imagine the rest.'

Noel loosens his hold on Eve's hand.

'Who was it?' he asks. 'This drunk man.'

And she hears it. That catch in his voice that tells her he knows. He knows already, even before Eve's mother closes down her face, so there can be no tell-tale hint of triumph.

'I'm afraid it was your father. Guy Lester. He shot Francis Garvey's face clean off.'

Guy, night of 28 April 1948

THERE HAVE BEEN two Guy Lesters.

One is the Guy Lester who went out that night to the regimental reunion, two weeks before his thirtieth birthday. Struggling to adapt to civilian routine, with a wife and two children and an office job that felt like being slowly strangled, I was determined to make the most of this chance to let off steam, to wring the last drop of youth out of life.

I remember going downstairs and pausing halfway down, remembering the Beholla pistol I'd taken from a German prisoner and smuggled back home as a souvenir. Madeleine insisted it stay hidden away in a box on the top of my wardrobe, so that Noel and Duncan couldn't get hold of it, even though they were barely walking, let alone climbing. This seemed like a chance, finally, to get it out of its box, show it off to the only fellows who'd appreciate it. I turned around and went back upstairs.

It was the worst decision I ever made.

This first Guy Lester went to the club. Drank, sang, laughed, showed off the Beholla. Was young and vigorous and, just for this one night, carefree. Staggered out at 5 a.m. with Owen, who'd been at my side in the trenches, witnessed with me the things we could not talk about with anyone else. The dawn was just breaking, I remember, the sky still ribboned with pink. We climbed over the fence into St James's Park. I think we had some idea we would find deckchairs there, set out in the grass where we could sleep off the worst of it.

We approached a point where our path crossed with another running perpendicular to it. Owen went on ahead, to urinate behind a bush. I could see clearly where he was standing off to the left, his burgundy tie vivid through the foliage.

Wouldn't it be funny, I thought in my drink-heightened state, to fire the pistol into the right-hand side of the bush? I imagined the leaves rustling, how Owen would jump in surprise, pissing all over himself. I didn't even know if the pistol would fire after all this time. I knew there were bullets in there, but it was so long since it had been used.

I took out the pistol as I approached the crossing. I remember I was shaking with suppressed laughter as I raised it up. Pulled the trigger. And as I did so, that's when they appeared. Out of nowhere.

If only there hadn't been a tree on the near corner, screening off that other path.

If only the child hadn't just fallen asleep, finally, so that the parents were deliberately trying not to make a sound as they wheeled her home.

If only they'd been a split second earlier or later.

This is when the second Guy Lester takes over. My shaking hand still raised, holding the gun. My head refusing to believe what my eyes were telling it.

Fragments of memory.

Him, Francis, on the ground, a red, pulpy, pulsing mass where the left side of his face should be. Her, Henrietta, leaning over him, blood everywhere and other stuff in her hair, on her lovely face, on her clothes, on the baby who is wide awake now, screaming.

Owen rushing, ashen-faced, from behind the bush. 'What have you done, man?' Vomiting on to the grass in long yellow strings.

After it happened, I wanted to be punished. Craved it, even, despite Madeleine's anguished refrain: *Think of the boys.* When the court martial, carried out behind closed doors, decided there was no criminal negligence case to be answered I wanted to protest, to tell them they were wrong. And when instead I was found guilty of possessing a gun without a firearm certificate, I welcomed the three-month custodial sentence. Wished only for it to be longer, the fine greater.

Even now, decades later, lying awake in the night after my second visit to Holke Hall, I try to rewind time. To take back the minutes, one by one, to make it not have happened. In the endless early hours I bargain with what I have. With my home in France and my own life, such as it is. In my blackest moments, Lord forgive me, I have even bargained with my own children's lives. Offering everything up in return for it to have turned out differently. For it never to have happened at all.

29

11 June 1948

'I STILL DON'T understand why Guy left it so late to make amends,' Duncan says. 'If he felt so damned guilty.'

The revelations about his father seem to have had a peculiar effect on Duncan, dislodging the affectations and the posturing, leaving him uncertain and vulnerable, his face puffy and floury.

'He didn't,' says Eve's mother, who is sitting on an upright chair in the sitting room, patting at her wet hair with a tea towel, her expression set, as if this too is something that must be endured. 'He insisted on paying monthly support for Eve while she was growing up.'

Eve, leaning against the back wall where she has been since she and Noel and her mother came crashing in from outside, feels as if she has turned suddenly to stone. *What monthly support?* She remembers all those times she asked for a new book or a pair of shoes so that she wouldn't have to wear her hated school shoes all the time and was told no, because money didn't grow on trees. She hadn't gone hungry, not like so many others, but there had never been money left over for fun.

'I don't know why you're looking at me like that,' her mother tells her now. 'I didn't spend it. I didn't touch it. Blood money. I kept it in a separate account. For when I judged you were mature enough to manage your own affairs.'

'And I suppose you're still waiting for that day to arrive?'

Eve cannot keep the bitterness from her voice. To her surprise, her mother's face twists with hurt.

'Don't be silly, Eve. As soon as you told me you were getting married, I made arrangements to hand over the money. And very glad I was to be rid of it too. You think I liked knowing that man's money was sitting in a bank account with my name on it? Nasty, tainted money. He got away with murder, you know, no matter what that court martial decided.'

This last is said in a garbled rush. Not looking at any of the Lesters. But wanting to leave them in no doubt, even so, as to her thoughts on the matter. On the man.

'So where is it then, this blood money?' Eve asks. 'Since you clearly didn't give it to me.'

Next to her, Clifford clears his throat, but Eve is focused on her mother's face, at the cheeks sucked inwards with surprise.

'Well, I gave it to your husband, of course. What use would you have for such a sum?'

'Clifford? But that can't be true.' She turns to Clifford, shock turning her voice shrill. 'Tell her she's mistaken.'

Clifford runs his fingers over his moustache, refusing to meet her eye.

'There was an *amount* that your mother kindly entrusted to me, and which I naturally invested in the business. Which, after all, provides very nicely for you, my dear. Mrs Jenkins twice a week. Luxuries like that don't come cheap.'

Eve frowns, unable to absorb what she is hearing.

'But the business is struggling. Can't we be honest about it for once? Surely you can't have put a quarter of a century's worth of funds into a failing company without even telling me?'

'It is not struggling, Eve. I don't know where you've got such a notion from.' Clifford bristles. 'I did not think it was something you needed to be bothered with. Of course, I had no idea about the origin of the money. Your mother told me only that it was a fund set up with a bequest from a wealthy relative. I decided it was probably for the best not to trouble you with it, but to invest it prudently on your behalf, which is what I have done. When you've had a chance to digest today's shocks you'll find I have acted at all times in your best interests, Eve. I have nothing to reproach myself with.'

Nothing to reproach himself with? The secrets he has kept from her, the myriad different ways he has found to shut her out of his world – the world it transpires he has funded with her money.

She feels again that prickling in her chest she knows to be a precursor to her old blind childhood rage, but this time she does not head it off, doesn't try to press it down deep inside her where it will grow denser, more compacted.

'Perhaps we should allow the three of you to talk in private,' says Bernard, half rising from the sofa and looking around at the Lesters and Sully, before falling back when they fail to follow suit.

'How could you?' Eve turns to face Clifford squarely, giving him no option but to look at her. 'Dictating every step of our lives – where we go, what we eat, how we live. Sealing me up in that mausoleum of a house, rationing everything, as if we hadn't had enough rationing to last a lifetime. And all the time it was my own money you were meting out to me, bit by grudging bit.'

Clifford draws himself upright.

'I never had you down as such a money-grabber, Eve.'

Noel, who has been sitting on the chaise longue next to his brother, gets to his feet.

'Just hold on a minute—' he starts.

But Eve cuts him off. 'It's not about money!' she shouts, her face so close to Clifford's a speck of spittle lands on his cheek. She sees his fingers twitch with the effort of not wiping it off. 'It's about respect and honesty and decency.'

'Enough, Eve.' Her mother's voice cuts through. 'You ought not to talk to your husband in this way, in front of all these people.'

Eve turns to face her mother, and it is as if all the hurts and slights of the last twenty-nine years, all the times she's hated herself for not being good enough, for not being worthy of being loved, converge here and now in a churning vortex with her at the epicentre. And there is nothing she can do except give in to it utterly.

'How dare you talk to me about what I ought and ought not to do,' she spits, shaking with rage. 'You, who left your own sister to rot in an asylum, who denied me the chance of having a mother who might actually have cared for me. Do you know what financial independence would have meant for me? I could have had a life of my own. I wouldn't have had to marry the first man who asked me.'

'Ungrateful girl! I took you in when you had nobody. I sacrificed myself for you. I gave you everything.'

'Except love.'

For a moment Eve and her mother stare at one another

across a high-ceilinged room in a seaside villa in France in front of a room full of semi-strangers, and it is as though none of it exists.

Then Eve's mother turns away, waving her hand, as if suddenly weary of it all.

'Oh. *Love*,' she says.

In that moment, that repudiation of what Eve holds most dear, Eve is released. Bonds she hadn't even been aware of are snipped open and she realizes she is free.

She will not travel back to England with Clifford and her mother. She will not return to that living death in the Sutton house.

She will search for Henrietta, that much she already knows. But beyond that, she really has no idea. She is scared, terrified in fact, but for once the fear will not stop her in her tracks; rather it is a burden she will drag along with her, like an extra weight in her suitcase – inconvenient and uncomfortable, but not insurmountable.

Guy, 30 April 1948

THE THIRD TIME I visit Henrietta, a different nurse meets me at the front door of Holke Hall.

'I'm afraid you can't come in,' she says, focusing on a point near my feet. When I refuse to leave, she disappears and comes back with a man who is the exact colour of sand. Eyelashes, eyebrows, hair, even teeth.

'I'm Dr Cranleigh,' he says, fixing me with his pale eyes. 'We've been instructed by the family not to allow more visits.'

'But I'm the only visitor she's had in years.'

My hoarse voice sounds like someone scraping a stick across a rusty bucket, signalling my sickness in a manner I find almost too humiliating to bear.

The doctor spreads out his freckled fingers before clasping them together in a gesture of regret.

'Nevertheless,' he says.

I remember now the dents on either side of Henrietta's head and what the other nurse said about Dr Cranleigh poking about with his ice pick.

'Why did you operate on her?' I ask.

'For her own peace of mind. She'd often wake up screaming in the night. It was disturbing for her and for the other women. This type of surgery uses the most modern techniques, I assure you. I studied them in America.'

The young doctor burns with scientific zeal, and I shudder.

'How can I remove her from here?'

The words are out before I even know what I am saying, and immediately panic bubbles up in my gorge at what I have just suggested.

But I needn't have worried.

'Impossible. As I'm sure you know. Only family . . .'

Outside on the stone steps, away from that smell of antiseptic and urine and fear, I gulp in the fresh air. My own unbridled relief at being free makes me feel sick with shame.

As I walk away my anger builds. This is not what I was led to believe. Henrietta is not well cared for. Nor is she so beyond reason that she does not understand where she is or who she is with. She might yet have a life. She might yet have comfort.

And if I have been lied to about this, how can I believe anything else Mary has told me? That Eve is better off not knowing the truth, that I have done enough harm, that she is happy and settled where she is.

The promises I made all those years ago no longer apply now I see how I have been misled. I have kept secrets too long and now they are killing me just as surely as this lump on my neck.

I will do the right thing now while there is still time.

Not for my own sake.

For theirs.

30

12 June 1948

IT IS AS if the world has been reborn overnight, the sky a vast sheet of blue silk, the air fresh with the scents the rain has unleashed – pine and thyme, mandarin, grapefruit and juniper – the sun a soft, warm cloth pressed to tired skin.

Eve stands at the very edge of the sea with her bare feet covered by the clear water, turned deliciously cool by the storm. The scratches on her legs are no longer so livid, and she hardly notices the pain from her wrist. To the right the coastline of Juan-les-Pins meanders in a series of small bays and rocky inlets stretching right round to Cannes, while straight ahead, the green Île Sainte-Marguerite keeps its secrets close.

She is glad Sully persuaded her to stroll down here to the little fisherman's beach near the very tip of the Cap, glad to be away from Villa La Perle where so many things have happened, so many buried truths been dragged blinking into the light.

'At least think about it,' says Sully, who is perched on the edge of a wooden boat that was once painted green and yellow but whose colours are now faded and peeled so that only flakes remain.

Sully is wearing short trousers and a white shirt unbuttoned over that brown barrel chest. His bare legs with their whorls of thick dark hair dangle over the boat's prow.

'I would change all the names and identifying details. No one would recognize themselves.'

'I would,' says Eve.

'Yes, but only you. And I'm sure you'd get a say in who played you. Elizabeth Taylor or – I know, how about that new one? Whatshername. Ava Gardner?'

'No,' says Eve. She cannot tell if Sully is serious about turning the events of the last week into a screenplay, but she wants him to be in no doubt about her thoughts on the matter.

'This is my life, Sully. Or rather, what's left of it.'

The truth is, Eve has no concept of her life at this point. Whenever she tries to grab hold of what has happened in the last few days, it slips through her fingers, elusive as that little patch of engine oil over there, floating on the surface of the sea. Her mother. Henrietta. Francis. Guy.

'And must you really leave tonight? Your mother and husband have already returned to England. No one is here to put pressure on you. And, after all, you've spent the best part of three decades unaware of Henrietta's existence; what difference will a day or two make?'

Eve bends, splashes her face with water, the cold shock of it reminding her that, despite everything, here she still is.

'I must see if I can find her. There are things I need to know.' She is trying to strike a note of breezy determination she is far from feeling. 'Anyway, at least this way I get to travel back with the Colletts, so really it's all worked out for the best.'

Sully reaches a toe into the sea and flicks water at Eve.

'Let's see. Your real mother is in the nuthouse, your real father was murdered in front of you, the man who tried to seduce you turns out to be a pro-Nazi blackmailer and your husband has embezzled all your money. How exactly is any of that for the best?'

'Not embezzled, exactly,' says Eve, but her protests have a hollow ring. Since last night she has had to re-examine all the events of her life through the lens of this new knowledge, with the result that nothing seems impossible, no motivation beyond suspicion.

Lying awake in that big bed, with the moon sharp and thin, she'd thought again about Clifford's business troubles, which seemed to predate even their wedding. Might it be possible that her mother mentioned her little nest egg *before* Clifford proposed to her? Might in fact this piece of information have been the very thing that spurred him on to declare himself? She has long wondered why her husband chose her, when there were so many women left looking for love after the losses of the war. So many more suitable women. Gain a wife to save a failing business. Perhaps it seemed like a reasonable arrangement at the time.

She and Sully begin walking back to the house.

'At least you don't have to stay with him.' Sully's voice sounds different, stripped for once of its habitual amusement. 'When the villa is sold you'll be a woman of independent means.'

'Only if he agrees to a divorce, or I drag us both through the law courts.'

Sully opens his mouth to say something, then thinks better of it.

'They really are a colossal waste of time, aren't they?' he says eventually. 'Husbands, I mean.'

It is coming to the hottest part of the day. The trees and bushes they pass on the side of the road are the lush green of parakeet feathers and pungent with oleander, jasmine, lavender, mimosa. Eve inhales deeply as if she might take it deep into her lungs and her blood and tissue, so that when she is back in England looking at the grey creep of a November afternoon sky and hearing that voice once more in her head – *Is this it? Is this all?* – she can summon from within the smells of a time when she was most fully herself and just for a moment all things seemed possible.

They are nearly back at the house when a huge black car overtakes them and then pulls up ahead. A young man in a dark suit and black sunglasses that give his face a curiously beetle-like appearance steps out from the driver's door.

'*S'il vous plaît?*'

He opens up the rear door and gestures for them to approach.

Eve and Sully exchange puzzled looks. Sully is first to the car, with Eve peering over his shoulder. At first she isn't sure what she is looking at. The car is deep and dark, the windows tinted, the back seat some distance from the front, with a heap of blankets at one end of it. As Eve's eyes become accustomed to the gloom, she is startled to see the blankets stir. A hand emerges, holding a cigarette. Then finally a pale, strong-boned face and a tangle of red hair.

'Light me up, would you, honey? Those bitches in the hospital wouldn't let me smoke.'

As more of Gloria emerges from the blankets, Eve is shocked by the change in her – the way her long fingers shake around the cigarette she holds out for Sully to light, the deep violet puddles under those beautiful eyes. The grease at the roots of that famous red hair.

'I look like something the cat spat out,' Gloria says, seeing Eve's expression.

Her voice is croaky – from where they shoved a tube down her throat to make her sick, she tells them – and it is slow and thick, as if being played on too low a speed.

She is on her way to the airport. The studio has organized a plane. They've had their fairytale wedding, and now they are prepared for her to escape back to the States before any scandal might break involving her new husband and his connections to the Nazis. Laurent himself has fled the country, she says. From the rumours going around the hospital, it's likely he wasn't only smuggling out artworks, but also the odd former SS officer fleeing to South America or North Africa.

'So how did you get away?' Eve wants to know, remembering what Sully had told her about Laurent's men stationed outside Gloria's room.

'I woke up this morning and they were gone. *Pfff!* The thing you have to remember about men like Laurent, honey, is that it's all about the hunt. Once they catch you, they lose interest. I guess if it hadn't been for this art business he might have kept ahold of me a while longer, just because he could, you know, how a cat will play with a mouse for a while before killing it. So I suppose I should thank your Monsieur Meunier.'

'Not *my* Monsieur Meunier.'

She sounds just like a child.

Now Gloria is asking both of them to come with her to the

airport. She produces a bottle of champagne from somewhere. They will get drunk, the three of them, she croaks. Then she will take more pills and sleep all the way to LA. And when she arrives the whole thing will seem like a bad dream.

'I'm afraid I have a train to catch,' Eve tells her.

Then it all has to be told again. The arrival of Clifford and her mother. The revelations that drip-drip-dripped out agonizingly slowly until they formed a wave that threatened to drown her. Guy Lester's role in ripping apart her family.

'I must find her. Do you see?' Eve finishes. 'Even if she doesn't know who I am. Even if she's quite beyond help. I must see Henrietta – my mother – at least once.'

Gloria stares up from her blanket shroud.

'Son of a bitch,' she says. 'How long was I out, exactly? Seems like the whole entire world has gone and changed while I've been in that hospital.'

It is decided that Sully will accompany Gloria to the airport. He is torn at first, not wanting to leave Eve to get her train alone, but she assures him she will be fine. Bernard and Marie will take her to the station later this afternoon, and the Colletts will meet her there. She will not be lonely.

Eve sees that he is still wavering, caught between his heart and his conscience. *Be careful*, she wants to warn him. *Harden yourself.* It's not difficult to see how the Gloria Hayes in the back of the car – vulnerable, needy, licking her wounds – might say and do things that a fully recovered Gloria would not recognize.

Eve leans into the car to give Gloria a careful embrace. Under the blankets the bones of her upper arms feel as fragile as twigs.

'This here is your time, Eve,' Gloria whispers. 'I feel it.'

Eve is already halfway out of the car before she thinks to ask Gloria what she means, but by now Sully has her unbandaged hand grasped firmly in his and is looking at her so steadily and intently, she really has no option but to return his gaze.

'Don't cry, Mrs Forrester.'

Eve smiles at his absurdity before becoming aware of the slow trickle of a tear down her cheek, the taste of salt on her lip.

'Life is short, Eve. Everyone makes mistakes. Even me. Especially me. But there's no honour in holding yourself to those mistakes. There's honour only in moving forwards, even when the easiest thing is to stay just where you are.'

He crushes her against his shirt, so she finds herself gazing at a grey smudge of typewriter ink on the pocket and inhaling the smell of cigarettes and sweat and wishing that goodbyes weren't so painful.

'What will you do, Sully? When the house is sold?'

She feels his long sigh through the cotton of his shirt.

'Go back to the States, I guess. My book is nearly done. Get divorced again. Fall in love again. I'm good at the big things. It's all the bits in between I struggle with.'

'Aren't those bits just life?'

By now they have pulled apart, and Eve sees Sully nod with a small smile.

'You could be right, Mrs Forrester,' he says, before climbing into the car beside Gloria.

The driver sounds his horn as they pull away, and Eve's last view is of Sully's safe, square hand stuck out of the window, fingers outstretched like a star, shooting away into the distance.

31

HOW STRANGE IT feels to be in Villa La Perle alone, after everything that has happened.

She wanders over to the small table in the living room and picks up the photograph of Guy Lester with his second wife, trying to summon forth the anger she surely ought to feel towards the man who, with a single careless, drunken act nearly three decades ago, laid waste to her family.

But the hatred she probes for doesn't come.

She walks outside on to the terrace, where Sully's typewriter is still set up on the table, a sheet of paper stretched tight over the roller. She reads what is written on the page.

'You should not have done that,' she said, bowing her head so that her hair hid her eyes from him.

'No. And yet I did.'

'Is it any good? The last one was panned by the critics, you know.'

Noel is standing in the open doorway, wearing a white short-sleeved undershirt that looks as if he might have slept in it. His hair is lank and unbrushed.

'From the little I've read, I'd say it was his best work. Although I may not have read any others.'

Noel smiles, but then a strange thing happens. His face seems to cave in, as though it is made of hard-packed sand that is turning to powder in the sun.

'Oh, Eve. How can I make it up to you? Everything my father took from you. Everything your family lost. I can't believe it of him. That he did this terrible thing and just walked away, without ever holding himself to account.'

'But he didn't, did he?' Eve faces him with her back to the sea, the sun filtering through the canopy of leaves overhead. 'He didn't just walk away. He must have gone to see her. Henrietta, I mean. My *real* mother. How else would he have those letters? This ring?'

She holds up her hand so he can see the green stone, flashing where it catches the light.

'You know, I read the rest of the letters last night, after you had all left. She wrote them in the asylum. After he'd died – Francis. And yet even though she's writing to a dead man, they're not the ramblings of a madwoman. They give me hope. But what I'm trying to tell you is that Guy didn't come out of it all unscathed.'

'But he wasn't who he pretended to be.' Noel sounds like a child.

'Are you sure?' Eve asks him. 'What I mean is, he clearly had relationships with women he was not married to, some of whom he didn't treat well. He made enemies – look at Robin Whelan. Look at Caroline Finch. He had flaws. Are you sure you didn't just choose not to see them? Just as you have chosen not to see how difficult you make things for your brother by stepping in all the time to fight his battles for him.'

'What in God's name are you talking about?'

Eve knows she is overstepping a boundary, but perseveres anyway.

'Paying off his debts, charging in to rescue him. Can't you see how much he needs to step out from your shadows? Yours and Guy's? Can't you let him go?'

For a moment Noel glowers at her across the terrace, then he crumbles, lowering himself into one of the wicker chairs and putting his head in his hands, so Eve can see how his hair is not black, as it appears in certain lights, but made up of a range of different browns, mostly dark but intermingled with a few lighter threads. *He is not, after all, my brother*, she thinks. And the thought brings a hot rush to her cheeks.

He says something that is muffled by his hand.

'Pardon?'

'I said, I suppose you'll be glad to leave all this behind,' he says. 'My messy, mixed-up family. Me.'

She has to look away, because his eyes are too direct.

'How long before you have to leave?' he asks.

'Bernard and Marie are coming here at six to drive me to the station.'

Noel glances at his watch.

'Good. Then we have time. There's somewhere I'd like to take you. Something I want to show you.'

'But I—'

Eve's protests die away. Why shouldn't she go? Why shouldn't she do this one last selfish thing?

They drive to Antibes in the convertible and park on the front near the harbour.

'This place was overrun with American soldiers until

recently, all billeted in that god-forsaken place,' he says, indicating the huge, forbidding-looking stone fort on a tree-covered hill to their left, its four bastions keeping watch in all directions. 'They're mostly gone now, though. Everything getting back to normal, and all of us supposed to act as if it never happened. All that destruction.'

He leads her away from the sea into the old town and she soon loses her bearings as they turn down one side street, then another, tall shuttered houses rising up steeply on both sides so that Eve feels suddenly cool, out of the reach of the sun. They are halfway down a third, or perhaps a fourth street, even narrower than the last, when Noel stops suddenly.

'Here.'

Eve looks at him, puzzled, before noticing that the building they are standing next to is not, after all, a house just like the others, but a small, sand-coloured church with a pointed gable over the wooden door and two narrow arched stained-glass windows on each side.

'It's the Chapelle Saint-Bernardin, built hundreds of years ago. Come. I want you to see.'

Noel grabs her hand in his eagerness to show her inside and her palm burns where it touches his. Inside he turns to her to witness her reaction.

'Oh, it's so beautiful.'

Eve sinks down on to one of the plain wooden pews and gazes around. The ceiling immediately above them is high and vaulted and covered in blue and gold diamonds interspersed with images of different saints, while beyond the arched wall it is deep blue and studded with gold stars. The entire end wall is a nave made up of ornate gold pillars, between which are gilded statues of saints and painted frescoes.

The paintings are greatly faded in places and there are large areas where the plaster has chipped off the walls, leaving gouged holes. But the overall effect is one of harmony, the building itself a tiny, perfect jewel.

'I used to come in here sometimes to get away from whatever was going on at home,' says Noel, sitting down in the pew in front. 'My mother's illness, and then her death. Duncan crying because he didn't want to go back to school. He was badly bullied there, you've probably guessed, though I tried to protect him from the worst of it. Diana. It's nothing to do with God or religion – it was just a safe place, you know, in a world that often didn't seem very safe. It made me feel better.'

Noel has his head bent while he is talking, as if ashamed of his own frankness. Eve fights an impulse to reach out and touch him.

She forces herself to remember that she is leaving this evening. Imagines Noel's life slotting back into its easy, untroubled groove.

In this way she hardens herself against him.

'Tell me about Anna,' she says. 'You let me believe she was dead, but that isn't true, is it?'

She recalls what Clemmie said at the wedding about something dreadful happening involving Noel's fiancée, and her hints that he was somehow to blame.

'There is nothing to say.'

Noel's face has closed up like a fist. But Eve cannot stop.

'Did you treat her badly? Is that it? After all, you are your father's son.'

As soon as the words are out, she wishes them unsaid.

'I see you have formed a very low opinion of me.'

Noel stands up abruptly as if he has suddenly remembered a more pressing claim on his time. 'We should be going. You have a train to catch.'

They make the return drive in silence, Eve gazing at the passing world without seeing it.

The car pulls up outside the house, tyres crunching on gravel.

Eve climbs out of the passenger seat, wretched in spite of the beauty all around her, the pink roses and fuchsia bougainvillea. Noel remains seated.

'I met Anna here in Antibes in 1936,' he says, his eyes fixed on the steering wheel.

'There is no need for you to explain to me—' Eve begins, but he interrupts.

'We were young, but I was infatuated with her. She was beautiful and so clever and—'

'Really, don't trouble yourself—'

'German.'

Eve falls silent.

'Anna was German. Her father was a high-ranking politician. When war became inevitable, she broke off our engagement and returned to Germany and very quickly married a German officer.'

'I'm sorry. That must have been hard for you.'

'My heart took a bruising, but it soon recovered. I was young. My feelings didn't run so terribly deep. What was harder to deal with was other people's reactions to me. I was the chap who'd almost married into the German Establishment. Everywhere I went, questions were asked, suspicions raised.'

'So you compensated by flying more missions than anyone else,' Eve says. 'To prove a point?'

'Perhaps. Anyway, I'm sure you have a lot to do.' Noel rouses himself, and brings his hand to rest on the ignition key. 'Please, let me know how you find Henrietta. You can send news through Bernard. And of course we will be in touch about the sale of the house.'

Eve feels a lump form in her throat. She cannot look at him, so concentrates her gaze on his wrist resting on the steering wheel, the silver face of his watch against his skin, the hairs turned golden by the sun. Her mother's voice sounds in her head, an overheard conversation after Eve had been banished to her room following yet another row. *Eve's trouble is she's stubborn. She will not apologize, even when she knows she's in the wrong.*

'I'm sorry,' she blurts out, at the exact moment Noel Lester switches on the engine and the car roars into life.

Noel doesn't reply.

'I said I'm sorry.'

He stares at her, unsmiling. Then he gives the curtest of nods. He swings the car into reverse and backs out of the drive on to the road, so fast Eve barely has time to register he has gone. A hole opens up under her rib cage and her heart, torn from its moorings, falls away, leaving an aching emptiness.

She moves through the gap in the trees towards the house. All of it seems suddenly to be mocking her – the whisper of palm leaves overhead, the sun warming her skin, the far-off *thuck thuck thuck* of a woodpecker drumming its beak against a tree trunk.

As she approaches the front door, she hears the sound of a car approaching.

Now Noel is here again, framed in the gap in the trees, the engine still running behind him as if he was in too much of a hurry even to turn it off.

'The thing is,' he says, shouting to be heard. 'The thing is, I find I have fallen in love with you.'

He looks so furious, as if love is a state she has forced upon him against his will.

Eve does not know how to respond. Does not know what name to give to the waves of emotion breaking over her. Knows only that it is like a switch being thrown, so that everything from which she had felt so detached just seconds ago is now a part of her. The sun on the tiles underfoot, the bees in the lavender bush, the heady smell of the blossoms on the orange tree.

She looks at Noel, and he looks at her, and neither one makes a move towards the other, but something is communicated between her eyes and his and she realizes she is smiling. He nods again, as if a matter has now been resolved, and then he turns back, disappearing from view. There is the slamming of the car door. The sound of gravel under rubber tyres. The engine roar growing fainter and fainter, until finally it is just her.

In a moment, Eve will let herself into the villa and collect her things and wait for Marie and Bernard. And at the station there will be the Colletts, so kind and so attentive of her feelings despite their own sadness, and in England she will seek out Henrietta, or whatever remains of the person Henrietta once was. And then perhaps she can begin to make sense of it all – her childhood, her marriage. Noel. Guy.

But for now, she closes her eyes and breathes it all in

again – the heat and sounds and smells of the Riviera. *Here I am*, she thinks. *This is me.* And just for this one perfect moment, the slender threads that link her to the past and to the future stretch out around her, behind and in front, like a spider's web, gossamer thin, with her at the still heart of it.

Here I am.

Guy, 15 May 1948

CAROLINE COMES TO find me resting on the terrace under the trees, while Diana is over at the other house. Since we moved most of the furniture out, Diana spends as little time as possible here, whereas I find myself more attached to the old place with each passing day.

I have spent the morning packing ahead of my return trip to England this evening. This time I will find Eve. I am determined. I won't be put off by that dreadful woman, Mary. I already know she lied to me about her sister. What else might she have lied about? And after I've told Eve everything, we can make plans together for what's to be done about Henrietta.

It's a terrible thing to say, but Caroline Finch hasn't aged well. She is one of those women who bloom early and over-emphatically, everything ripening at once like one of those blowsy pink flowers with the swollen petals, but then after just one wonderful short season it's over. What was rounded and luscious is now just fat and overblown.

Impossible now to believe there was ever anything between

us. Though sometimes I do find her looking at me in a way that makes me uncomfortable.

I'm fond of her though, and I've done my best by her. I've been loyal to her in my own way. Kept her on after the war where so many wouldn't have.

So it's a surprise to see her looking so angry. Those purple blotches bursting out on her chest like some sort of bubonic plague.

'Who is she?'

She is waving some papers in my face, her cheeks stained the colour of claret, her sizeable bosom heaving with emotion.

'I don't under—'

I stop short as I recognize the document in her hand. My will. My *new* will. The one I drew up with Bernard just days after my diagnosis.

'Why have you got that? It's private.'

'You asked me to pack up your study. It was on your desk with the rest of your things.'

'My *private* things. Give it here, Caroline.'

Anger scrapes my throat, reducing my voice to a croak. But still she doesn't hand it over, standing in the doorway to the house, everything about her quivering with suppressed feeling.

'Who is she, this Eve Forrester? Is she why your bags are packed in the hallway, why you're racing back to England even though you can hardly walk without getting out of breath?'

And now I understand. *She's read it.*

'How dare you!'

Anger boils my blood, making my heart race, in the way the specialist warned me to avoid.

But Caroline, for once, will not back down.

'I did everything for you. Cooked, cleaned, made this a home. Cared for your children. All of it for you. All those years I gave up when I could have been having children of my own. And then, after all that, I had to stand back and watch you marry someone else. But I didn't make it hard for you, did I? I didn't make a scene. And what do I get at the end of it? Two hundred and fifty pounds – while *she*, this Eve Forrester, gets a quarter of all this. For what? For being young still? For being the latest, shiniest model?'

I have never seen her like this, pumped so full of righteous indignation she might explode with it.

But my own fury is far greater.

'Go!' I try to shout, but my voice is a rusty squeak, which only enrages me more. The pain in my throat is raw, as though the tissue is being stripped away.

My heart is pounding. I feel it thudding around in my chest like a cricket ball.

Caroline Finch stares at me, anger slowly giving way to alarm.

'Are you all right?'

Her concern is worse than her outrage.

'Go!' I repeat, and turn my head so she can't see my eyes filling up, frustrated, at the noise that comes out of my mouth.

The door closes behind her. And now here I am. Heart thundering, struggling for breath.

I never made any promises. Whatever commitment there was existed only in her head. I did not lead her on. I owe her nothing.

I haven't always behaved well, but I have tried to make amends.

That's why I changed the will, why I'm going back to England to find Eve and explain, and see what can be done about it all.

I'm not a bad person. I've paid. I really have.

I will not be judged.

I will not.

I am sorry.

32

11 September 1949

'SORRY I'M LATE. They've closed off the main road because of the crowds.'

Eve breezes through the front door, which opens straight into the compact, light-filled living room. The room is empty, though there is a half-full teacup on the floor next to an open paperback book which lies face down on the terra-cotta tiles, and a dent in the cushion of the battered brown leather sofa. Just three shortish strides bring Eve to the back of the house, where the French doors are flung open into the wild jungle of back garden.

She steps outside, savouring the immediate sense of well-being that comes over her at the sight of the three modest terraces stepped down the hillside, overrun with herbs and flowers and a rampant honeysuckle, and flanked by citrus trees. It is mid-September and the sun is still warm, but without the relentlessness of high summer. She has planted mint and verbena and geraniums on the upper terrace and the air is heady with fragrance as she looks down past the bursting terraces of her little garden, across the green hillsides in front, thick with olive trees and pines, broken up here and there by the tall cypresses and the roofs of other houses, their tiles baked pink by the sun. And there, in the far distance, a shimmer on the horizon that is the Mediterranean itself.

'Errol Flynn was due any minute,' she continues, descending the three shallow stone steps to the middle terrace. 'That's what they were all there for. The crowds.' Then she hesitates. 'But perhaps you haven't heard of Errol Flynn.'

Even now, after more than a year, she still forgets.

But the frail figure reclining in the faded orange deckchair only smiles.

'Thank goodness I have you to fill me in on all the important things like film stars and fashion.'

'I don't think you should take my advice about fashion.' Eve looks down at the clothes she hurriedly pulled on this morning before driving down to the market in Cannes – a blue, short-sleeved top with cream-coloured wide-legged linen trousers, belted at the waist and short enough to reveal her feet, burnt almost black from the sun, in their open-toed sandals. The trousers are decidedly grubby, she sees now, remembering too late how she wore them to garden in the day before.

'You look beautiful. You're always beautiful. As beautiful as those flowers over there.'

A slender finger gestures towards a bush sagging with its cargo of perfect white roses.

Beautiful. The word, spoken as softly as a sigh, still catches in Eve's throat, though she hears it so often now she really ought to be used to it.

'Maybe you should have a rest. You haven't forgotten we have guests for dinner?'

The truth is, Henrietta is looking tired beneath her

huge-brimmed straw hat, though the very fact of her being outside at all is progress of sorts, Eve supposes. She still has to be careful to shield herself from direct sunlight, a result of all those years at the asylum being kept indoors, listening to the sounds of the male inmates working outside. Skin pale and thin as a fly's wings.

'I haven't forgotten.' That soft voice, faint from years of disuse. 'Oh, but remind me again who is coming. I know we have that high and mighty friend of yours.'

Eve laughs. 'Gloria Hayes is the least high and mighty person I've ever met, as I keep telling you. She's just famous, is all. And that's not the same thing.'

It will be the first time Eve has set eyes on Gloria in the flesh since their goodbye in the back of that car on the way to the airport, although of course she's seen her in magazines and in the new film that has just come out to rapturous reviews. When Eve heard Gloria was coming to Cannes for the film festival – in September this year, though there is talk of moving it to June – she'd assumed her schedule would be far too hectic to allow for social calls, but then had come the message via Bernard. *Coming to see you on the evening of the 11th whether you like it or not. Movie people are the dullest people on earth. Save me!*

This last film, written specifically as a vehicle for her by renowned novelist Stanley Sullivan, has already broken box office records, but Eve remembers how people turned on Gloria after the very public collapse of her short-lived marriage to Laurent Martin, and understands she still has a lot of ground to make up to regain her pedestal. But then maybe she's had enough of all that. Even adulation must get tiresome, Eve supposes.

Laurent himself hasn't been back to France since the

Victor Meunier incident. The last Eve heard, he had bought an island in the Caribbean and was building a luxury hotel there, and a casino. She doubts it will hold his interest for long. Though no charges have ever been brought against him, Eve imagines his return would be tempting fate.

When she'd first heard Gloria was coming to France, Eve had hoped Sully might come too. After all, he had written the film script and was as much a part of Hollywood now as Gloria herself. But no. *It would be hellish to be so close to her and yet worlds apart in all the ways that count*, he wrote in his last letter. *Who knew love would turn out to be such a burden?*

'And who else?' Eve quizzes Henrietta. 'Who else is coming?'

Eve knows she should stop this constant testing, trying to probe the depths of Henrietta's troubled mind, to measure the damage wrought by both the madness itself and the treatment of it.

'Jack Collett,' answers Henrietta obediently. 'Sweet Jack.'

Eve smiles. Jack has been in the South of France all summer, researching his thesis on the Riviera's burgeoning post-war art scene, and she already knows both of them will miss him terribly when he returns to England in a week's time for the final year of his postgraduate degree.

'And Libby,' Henrietta continues, pressing her hands together in excitement just like a child. Eve, watching, feels a sharp pang of jealousy. Oh, not of Libby. Who could ever be jealous of Libby, who remains, as ever, fiercely and incontrovertibly herself? No, she is jealous of the uncomplicatedness of the relationship that has grown between Henrietta and Libby, the joy they find in each other's company, the hundred different ways they make each other smile. Sometimes, in her less lucid moments, Henrietta imagines Libby is the daughter she lost all those years before – the younger Eve – and smothers her with kisses, and Eve has to find an excuse to leave the room.

At these times, Diana, if she is here, will catch Eve's eye and raise an eyebrow and there will pass between them a look of understanding, and Eve will feel surprised all over again that she should have found in Diana Lester so unlikely an ally. Too early yet to say 'friend'. But soon, perhaps.

Between Eve and Henrietta things are getting better all the time, but occasionally the past still gets in the way. It's hard to completely shake off that persistent alternative narrative where a mother's love overcame a widow's grief, where Eve grew up wanted, cherished, safe, rather than a daily reminder of a ripped-to-shreds heart.

She has forgiven – for the most part anyway. It was not Henrietta's fault. But forgetting will take longer.

At least the nights are better now. For the first six months after Eve finally persuaded the hospital trust to release Henrietta to her care – thanks largely to the eagerness of the newly formed National Health Service to launch itself into the mid-twentieth century and find modern solutions – Henrietta hadn't been able to sleep alone. Instead she and Eve had shared a room, with Eve often kept awake by the older woman shouting out in her sleep.

'You should be under no illusions as to what you are letting yourself in for,' the hospital trust's assistant head of psychiatric services had told her. 'There can be no cure for long-term patients like your mother. There will be night terrors. She might be taciturn, withdrawn, maybe even hostile. Are you prepared for this?'

On the whole, very little of that bleak picture has come to pass, and Henrietta now sleeps in her own room, although she still wakes up screaming from time to time. Yet life is not entirely straightforward. Eve and Henrietta are still finding their way with each other, which is why Eve's heart tugs a little when she sees Henrietta's delight at Libby's name.

But that's all right.

Baby steps.

'And who else?' she prompts now, bending to sniff a sweet basil plant on the middle terrace, not because she needs it for dinner but to hide her expression when Henrietta answers, 'Noel Lester.'

It isn't that Eve is embarrassed about her relationship with Noel. Just that she wishes to protect it. Once, when she was working for the Women's Voluntary Service, she was assigned to accompany a photographer commissioned with taking pictures of smiling recipients of donated furniture for a government campaign. He showed her around his darkroom and she was struck by the patience required to hold off from snatching the photographs out of the trays just as soon as the image started showing. Well, it's like that with her and Noel. Whatever this is, it needs to be left alone to develop.

Noel doesn't agree. 'Why won't you marry me?' he asked just a few days before, as they lay entwined together in the hammock under the pepper tree on the lowest terrace. And Eve had given her usual answer: 'Because I'm still technically married.'

Clifford is dragging his feet over the divorce, as she knew he would. He tells people she is in the South of France on account of her mother's health, which, like all good lies, contains some elements of truth.

When a new buyer for Villa La Perle was eventually found, Clifford had tried to lay claim to Eve's share of the money, but for once Eve held firm. She could not forget about the money he'd already appropriated and lost, and besides, she was well aware that Henrietta's long-term care would come at a cost. She had threatened to halt the sale of the villa by refusing to sign the papers. 'Which would leave me without funds to pay the inheritance tax and goodness knows what other duties,' she'd told Clifford. 'And by me, of course I mean you, as we are still married, after all.'

Sometimes she is astounded by the person she has become. Selling Villa La Perle, to which she had become so attached, had been heartbreaking. But with her share of the profits from the sale, Eve was able to buy this little house in the hills between Cabris and Grasse, which she loves with every fibre of her heart and soul, even if Clemmie did say on her first and only visit, 'Charming, but where's the *main* house?' Clemmie says things for effect, as Eve is discovering. The trick is not to take any of it to heart.

Besides, Clemmie and Duncan are moving soon. Back to England, away from the temptations of the Riviera's casinos – and out from the shadow of his father and brother. On the whole, Duncan has managed to steer clear of the card tables since his debts were paid off, but he knows it's only a matter of time if he stays.

What Eve doesn't tell Noel is that she has no wish to be married a second time. She loves being able to go for a walk without anyone fussing that it looks like rain and shouldn't she take an umbrella, or to cook an experimental soup of vegetables from her own little plot without worrying that it has the look and texture of mud.

'What about children?' Noel had asked her out here on the hammock.

'I was a child once,' she told him. 'Why would I inflict that fate on another poor soul?'

She meant to be frivolous, but the fact is, her childhood is a sore Eve just can't seem to make heal. The things her mother never told her. The secrets that festered like mould in the dark corners of that house in Banbury.

Only Henrietta harbours no grudges.

'How can you have forgiven her?' Eve asked only the day before, when Henrietta was on unusually expansive form.

'I did her a great wrong,' came the answer. 'Mary had a hard life, with only one thing that made her happy, and I stole it from her.'

'But she would have kept you locked up in that asylum for life.'

'Mary loved Francis so much, Eve. And passion transcends reason.'

Even so, Eve herself cannot forgive. Growing up without love creates a void inside a person that can never entirely be filled, for all you try to stuff it full of new friends and family and tender kisses from someone who tells you every day that you're their world.

Still, she is edging closer towards fulfilment, particularly since she started giving English lessons to some of the locals in Cabris. The warmth that spreads through her veins from seeing understanding dawn on a child's face, or holding a halting conversation with a former soldier who left school at fourteen, is something she never expected.

On the desk in Eve's little bedroom sits the carved wooden box that Diana gave her when Villa La Perle was sold. It's the same box that had once held the love letters Henrietta wrote to her dead husband. Inside the box is an envelope with Eve's name on it, written in blue ink in her mother, Mary's, angry, cramped script.

An explanation of sorts, she supposes.

It arrived two or three months ago, having been sent first to Bernard's office. Marie turned up at the house with it, announcing herself as ever with the frustrated roar of a car engine attempting the hill in the wrong gear.

'I did not know if I should bring this to you,' Marie told Eve, guessing correctly who it was from.

One day she will open it. Just not yet.

Eve has decided to attempt a local dish for dinner tonight – *estoficada*, a kind of fish stew that involves cooking dried cod for hours with tomatoes and olives and handfuls of fresh herbs. She busies herself around the garden picking fennel, marjoram, parsley, thyme and bay, while Henrietta lies back in her chair, her eyes closed under the outsized brim of her hat.

A beetle crawls out from the clump of freshly picked summer savory in her left hand and Eve shakes it to the ground, which is laid with old honey-coloured flagstones around which grow the last of the year's wildflowers – globe thistle, pink autumn crocuses and tiny yellow Spanish broom.

For a few moments, Eve tracks the beetle's unhurried progress across the terrace, admiring its ability to adjust to the sudden change in its fortunes, its blind faith that in spite of everything, where it is going will end up being where it wants to be.

Then she rouses herself and heads back up the stone steps and in through the house to the tiny kitchen, to make a head start on dinner before the first of her guests arrives.

Acknowledgements

A Fatal Inheritance is dedicated to Fraser Macnaught, dear friend and long-term French resident, who acted as guide, driver, translator and cutter-through of bullshit while I was carrying out research for this book, despite his being part-way through treatment for lung cancer at the time. One of my abiding memories of Fraser is sitting on the terrace of the beautiful Hotel Les Belles Rives in Cap d'Antibes with my partner, Michael – his childhood friend – watching the sun set over the Mediterranean and drinking staggeringly expensive cocktails. It was mid-May 2017, four months before Fraser died, and one of us broached the subject of his prognosis. 'Put it this way,' he said, 'we're burning the expensive candles.'

That's not a bad mantra for life, it seems to me.

Thanks to Fraser's wonderful wife Nathalie, for her help and her kindness and courage, and to her father Daniel for attempting to answer my ill-thought-out questions about trains and timetables and sunrises in Cannes.

Big thanks to Clare Griffiths and her fiancé Denis Girard for help with French language questions, and to the extended Griffiths clan (Steve, Sally, Nicole, Peter, Fabienne) for always making us feel so at home in the South of France.

French inheritance laws are hugely complex, as I found to my cost. Thank you to notaries Laurence Molière-Sambron and Richard Poulin for helping me navigate my way through them. Any mistakes that remain are entirely my own.

Gloria Hayes was an utter delight to write and I am grateful to Bill Browne and Aymee Fretwell Gandy for reading through her dialogue, checking for anything that sounded too jarring to a sensitive Southern ear.

The name Ruth Collett was given to me courtesy of the real-life Ruth Collett, who won the chance to have a character named after her as a prize at a local CLIC Sargent fundraiser auction. CLIC Sargent is a remarkable charity that supports children and young people with cancer and I couldn't have been more thrilled that Ruth won. Not just because she's been one of my son Jake's closest friends since they started primary school together, but also because the fundraiser was inspired by her selfless determination to give back to the charity that supported her through her own cancer treatment.

My doctor friends are hugely long-suffering and put up with my ridiculous questions on everything from best ways to kill off characters to ways to keep them alive. Thanks as ever to Dr Roma Cartwright and Dr Mark Hindley for being the toppest of mates.

Thanks as ever to the teams of people who make my books the best they can be and try to get them into as many readers' hands as possible. To my amazing agent Felicity Blunt, and everyone else at Curtis Brown, especially Melissa Pimentel.

Thanks also to my US agent Deborah Schneider, who works tirelessly to bring my books to America and who found such a happy home for my last book, *Dangerous Crossing*, with Atria Books, and to Sarah Cantin.

Special thanks to Transworld Publishers, who have championed my books relentlessly, particularly my unflappable editor Jane Lawson and the inimitable Alison Barrow: publicist, friend and font of all book knowledge. Thanks also to Richard Ogle, who designed this wonderful cover, and to Kate Samano, and to the sales team, who are the unsung heroes of the publishing process.

Thanks to my friends and my family (even my wayward dog), and to the book clubs, the booksellers, the book bloggers and, above all, the book lovers.

I'll be thinking of you all while I burn an expensive candle tonight.

RACHEL RHYS is the pen-name of a much-loved psychological suspense author. *A Fatal Inheritance* is her second novel under this name. Her debut *Dangerous Crossing*, a Richard and Judy Book Club pick, was published around the world. Rachel Rhys lives in North London with her family.

Keep in touch with Rachel:
www.tammycohen.co.uk
MsTamarCohen
@MsTamarCohen

A DANGEROUS CROSSING
Rachel Rhys

England, September 1939
Lily Shepherd boards a cruise liner for a new life in Australia and is immediately plunged into a world of cocktails, jazz and glamorous friends. But as the sun beats down, poisonous secrets begin to surface. Suddenly Lily finds herself trapped in a ship with nowhere to go . . .

Australia, six weeks later
As the cruise liner docks, a beautiful young woman is escorted on to dry land in handcuffs. Two passengers are dead, war is declared, and Lily Shepherd's life is changed forever.

What has she done?

'An exquisite story of love, murder, adventure and dark secrets' LISA JEWELL

'Gripping and ripe with danger' *Sunday Express*

'An utter treat . . . a glorious mix of proper old-school glamour and a plot full of class war, politics and sexual tension . . . A masterful storyteller' VERONICA HENRY